ON LINE

# Miriam
## the Medium

~

*Rochelle Jewel Shapiro*

SIMON & SCHUSTER
NEW YORK   LONDON   TORONTO   SYDNEY

SIMON & SCHUSTER
Rockefeller Center
1230 Avenue of the Americas
New York, NY 10020

SIMON & SCHUSTER and colophon are registered trademarks
of Simon & Schuster, Inc.

For information regarding special discounts for bulk purchases,
please contact Simon & Schuster Special Sales at 1-800-456-6798
or business@simonandschuster.com.

Manufactured in the United States of America

1   3   5   7   9   10   8   6   4   2

Library of Congress Cataloging-in-Publication Data
Shapiro, Rochelle Jewel.
Miriam the medium / Rochelle Jewel Shapiro.
p.   cm.
1. Psychics—Fiction.  2. Housewives—Fiction.  3. Teenage girls—Fiction.
4. Long Island (N.Y.)—Fiction.  5. Mothers and daughters—Fiction.  6. Self-actualization
(Psychology)—Fiction.  7. Family-owned enterprises—Fiction.  I. Title.
PS3619.H3563M57 2004
813'.6—dc22
2003067305

ISBN 0-7432-4478-8

*For Marlene Goodman Quinn, a great friend and healer,
and the brilliant clairvoyant, the late Vincent Ragone,
and, of course, my Bubbie, Sarah Shapiro.*

# Acknowledgments

I want to thank my former agent, Caroline Carney, for selling my novel, and my new agent, Marly Rusoff, who has put time, energy, and enthusiam into seeing it through.

A million thanks to Marysue Rucci, my awesome editor, for tapping into the prediction made by the clairvoyant, Vincent Ragone, twenty-seven years ago that I would publish a novel with Simon & Schuster, and for her inspired guidance through each draft. And I thank Tara Parsons, associate editor, for her invaluable input and kindness, and Mara Lurie, Elizabeth Hayes, and all the others at Simon & Schuster who made this book possible.

I am grateful to the poet/novelist/teacher Jill Hoffman and my dear friend, novelist/columnist/teacher, Caroline Leavitt, for their brilliant suggestions and generous support throughout my long journey with this book, and to Jennie Belle, who read an early draft and told me to "always stretch for the image."

Other readers to whom I'm grateful are Mark Wisniewski, Cuddy Murray, and Ann Saunders, who used her skills as a professional organizer to help me. Many thanks also to Lisa Dawn Saltzman, Dorrit Title, Hannah Ritter, Sylvia Davies, and the insightful, bubbly teacher, Cynthia Shor, for assisting me in fine-combing the last draft. Thanks also to my brother, Barry Shapiro, for cheering me on, and to my sister, Nannette Lieblein, for always being there for me.

To Kent Ozarow and my poetry workshop, I give thanks for making me sensitive to the sound, texture, and implication of words.

*Though it be honest, it is never good*
*To bring bad news . . .*

—William Shakespeare
*Antony and Cleopatra*

*Good news . . . had gotten more expensive.*

—Alice Hoffman
*Fortune's Daughter*

# 1

MY OFFICE WAS LIKE a secret room you'd come upon in a dream.

Every morning I climbed a rickety back staircase to the north wing of our old Tudor to my haven, where crystals hung in the windows, casting rainbows on the white walls. I dressed in white and used my real name so people would trust me. If people trusted me, I could feel it. If people trusted me, I did a better job.

In that room, I became Miriam the Phone Psychic.

At 7:30 A.M., with ten readings scheduled, I needed peace and quiet. I wrapped one of my red corkscrew curls around my finger, then pulled it down straight, to an inch above my elbow. When I let go, it rolled back up to shoulder length like a deflated party horn. I took a deep breath and, on the exhale, let out a long "Om," my hair crackling with static. My thoughts were like leaves floating past me on a pond. I let out another "Om." The details of my office began to blend together as if I were in a steambath, everything edgeless, fuzzy.

Before I could receive any message, a note slid from under my door across the white carpet. I could see my husband's letter-

1

head—MIRROR PHARMACY. My trance state was pierced. Annoyed, I stretched out my foot and swept the note to me. I had asked Rory to leave notes for me in the kitchen so I could digest them with breakfast.

> *Dear Miriam,*
>
> *I need 1,100 bucks right away. My bills are still overdue because none of the Medicaid checks came in yet. Please get out our bonds from the vault and bring them to Mirror so I can sign and cash them before the bank closes. Maybe some bagels from Best Bagels, too. Three sesame.*
>
> *Love,*
> *Rory*

Bonds and bagels? Rory's attempt at breeziness frightened me. "Om," I chanted.

The leaf-strewn pond was gone. My thoughts went through me like a dentist's drill. I couldn't let myself worry about our problems when I was working, but Rory's business reversals might make us late on our mortgage payment. Our credit cards were already maxed out. I breathed deeper.

I thought about the whiteness of my mind. My anxiety began to lose its sharpness, like a rooftop under snow. Then the phone rang, snapping me out of myself.

"Hello, Miriam?" the voice said pleasantly. "This is Ellen Minsk."

I had never met Ellen before, but now, hearing her voice, it was as if our noses were touching. I saw curly black hair, soft brown eyes that drooped at the outside edges. I imagined myself wearing an armored breastplate that grew thicker, but still I felt an ache in my heart.

"Your heart is hurting," I said. "Was there a broken engagement?" I heard her draw in her breath.

"Yes."

An image flickered. An owl. When it landed, its head swiveled 180 degrees. I knew what that meant, but I was loath to tell her. "Your fiancé wasn't right for you. He was always looking at other women, even when he was with you."

I wanted to tell her something that would fill her, but I could feel my trance fading because of soft footsteps on my stairs. I glanced at my clock. Rory and Cara should have left already. I took three more deep breaths. Information came with oxygen.

"I see a wedding cake for you."

"How soon?" Ellen asked urgently.

"Give me a moment, please," I said. Sometimes images came rapidly, with startling clarity. Other times, it was as if I had to try on a dozen pairs of eyeglasses to get a sharp picture. I took another breath and began to see something dim. Then it got brighter—a big blue number eight. I couldn't bear to tell her that she wasn't going to meet him for eight more years. I heard the loud ticking of her biological clock. And then I saw her future husband. He had a black ribbon pinned to his lapel. A widower. Next to him were his four children, all frowning. Through no fault of her own, each of his children would hate Ellen Minsk more than the next. Her lovely brown hair would go gray.

You could tell people the truth, but there were many truths. Destiny was like an underground route with branchlets, each sprouting a different life possibility. All I had to do was nudge Ellen toward one of them that would lead her to a prince, a man closer to her age, without children, a man who would be easier to live with. I had to see what would draw him to her so her new destiny could start to unfold. I breathed. Even with my eyes open, her destiny shimmered before me. A rush of hope zipped through me. I was sure I was going to be able to help Ellen.

My doorknob jiggled. The door opened, and Cara peeked in, her face taut with anxiety. "Mom," she whispered, "you done yet?"

The shimmering began to lift. The real world began to

intrude. I put my finger up to tell Cara to wait. She was silent now, but I could feel her listening intently.

I put my finger to my lips and closed my eyes. Ellen Minsk had been dressing like a sparrow. I had to get that widower off her trail. A red rose fluttered into my mind. "Get a red coat," I said. A silver bird appeared. "And go first class on your next business trip."

"I just had my eye on a red coat in Bloomies, but I thought: *red?* It reminded me of a heart, and mine was broken. I put it back on the rack, but now I'm going to go straight to Bloomies and buy it." She laughed. "Of course, a red coat. It's exactly what I need to get out of my rut. Then, who knows what can happen? Miriam, you're terrific. I feel different already."

I could see Ellen emerge, and I felt a giddiness, as if I'd had four glasses of champagne on an empty stomach.

I hung up and turned to Cara. Her long dark hair was pulled back in a butterfly clip. She wore a black Lycra V-neck with long sleeves and tight jeans. The skin under her green eyes was shiny from concealer. Even though Rory and I always told her how smart she was and urged her to relax, she studied into the night, and anything less than an A sent her into tears.

Sometimes, looking at her, I felt an eeriness, as if my own mother were looking at me. At seventeen, Cara had my mother's green eyes, glossy brunette hair, cinch belt waist, and Rockette legs, too. She was chic and slender. And like my mother, she hated my "hippie" clothes: my tunics, my long flowered dresses, my shawls. And they both hated my "wild hair." More than that, they hated my psychic gift, inherited from my *bubbe,* my father's mother, who had been a famous psychic in Russia. My mother had said it was something from the Dark Ages, that I'd end up a crazy babushka lady.

"Cara, you know you're not supposed to interrupt, not unless it's an emergency."

"It is." She pulled at her V-neck. "Dad was supposed to drive me to school, but he's fixing his car in the driveway. I have a physics test first period, and I want to get there extra early to study some more."

A high school senior, Cara was the kind of student my mother had wished I had been. I was glad she'd be accepted into a top college, but the amount of pressure she put on herself worried me. I got a flash of a test paper, Cara's name on top. A ninety-one. "You don't have to get to school early to study," I said, tapping my finger to my temple. "You're going to do very well."

She frowned. These days, she hated my predictions, even the good ones.

"The kids in my honors classes are geniuses. How can I do 'very well' when I have to study ten times harder than anybody in the class to get a decent grade?" She rolled her eyes. "God, I wish you didn't work as a psychic."

"Honey," I said quietly, "this is what I do. This is who I am. You know that."

"Couldn't you be someone else once in a while?" she asked, wrinkling her nose at me the way my mother used to do when she was alive. I couldn't help but feel a twinge of deflation, and that niggling of self-doubt, as if I were the teenager in the room.

I had tried to do other things. When I got out of college, I got a job as a promotional writer at a publishing house, but when it slipped out that I was psychic, the managing editor had me doing readings for all her friends for free. I stayed after hours, the cleaning lady vacuuming around my feet, only to be fired for low productivity. The managing editor didn't say a word in my defense. She just handed me a tissue after I burst into tears. Afterwards, former coworkers began phoning me. The phone didn't stop ringing. "See?" my father had said. "At least you made a lot of friends."

"No, Dad," I'd told him. "They're only calling to ask whether they're going to get promoted or whether their husbands will be transferred out of state." But I was used to being used for information. I didn't resent it. Not yet.

Doing readings helped unburden me. For most of my life, I'd walked around like a big antenna, picking up private hopes and future secrets from passersby, indiscriminately. I suffered from sensory overload. The opportunity to "read" my former colleagues provided a release . . . and practice. Though it would be a few years before a chance phone call inspired me to open my own phone psychic business, those early readings—and Rory's unflagging support—helped me see what I might be capable of, if given the chance.

I shook myself from the memories and got a vision of Rory next to his white Ford Taurus, wiping off his hands.

"Your father fixed the car," I told Cara. "He's ready to roll."

"Darcy will be driving Courtney and me home," she said, then ran down the stairway.

Cara and Darcy met in nursery school, a time when Cara would sit in my lap while I did readings, gazing up at me, wide-eyed. Sometimes she patted my cheek, as if to encourage me. "Mommy's stories," she'd call my readings, and listened to them as entranced as when I told her a fairy tale. Back then, Rory's business was flush, too, and he had lots of time for both of us.

I looked at his note again. I had just made ninety-five dollars in twenty minutes. I had nine more clients today, but it was only a drop in the bucket of our enormous bills. I peeked out the window. Rory, his sandy hair damp with sweat, was trying to rub a smudge from the sleeve of his pharmacy jacket. I could see how tired he looked, how worry clung to him. The previous night he had told Cara that he couldn't drive her to Vermont for the ski club in November, because that was the beginning of the flu season and his busiest time at the pharmacy. He planned to work six and a half days a week—and take half a day off on Sundays.

I watched them climb into the car and drive off. I could help other people's businesses. Why couldn't I help Rory's? I had told a man not to invest in an ice cream parlor in a shopping center in New Jersey. It was next to a supermarket that folded, and all the other stores around it folded, too. I had told a woman that she would be ruined if she got involved in a certain multilevel marketing scheme that her friend was urging her to join. Her friend ended up bankrupt.

I had tried to guide Rory—gently and directly, both. But Rory wouldn't listen to me any more than Cara would. He wanted to do it "on his own." Now, when I should be thinking of other people's lives, I was preoccupied with my own. I saw Rory's worries that he'd lose his business. I saw Cara turning from me, shamed by what I did. And I saw myself, struggling for everyone's approval. I could help strangers put their lives together, but how could I keep mine from falling apart?

I twined my fingers together. Palms facing outward, I stretched as high as I could, imagining myself reaching up to the spirit world to touch the soles of my *bubbe*'s black lace-up shoes.

I wished my family trusted my gift the way I'd trusted Bubbie's.

# 2

BEFORE I EVEN KNEW that I was a psychic, I was drawn to my *bubbe*. She lived seven blocks from us in an apartment right above my father's butcher shop in Rockaway Beach, Queens. Back then, there was usually a line of people at Bubbie's door, but I didn't know why. My mother would whisk me past them on the way to visit my father. Still, I recognized some of the people waiting in line to see Bubbie because they were also customers at my father's butcher shop. Bubbie's doorstep was only empty on Saturdays, and that was the one day my mother would take me to visit her.

When I was seven, as my mother was rushing me past the line, Mrs. Bauman, the cashier from the hardware store called out, "Miriam, what a grandmother you have! She knows the future. Last week she told me my brother-in-law was coming from Poland, and he's sleeping on my couch right now."

Behind her, Mrs. Feinstein was excited, too. "Your grandmother is going to make a salve to cure my rash," she said. Her forehead looked like it had an apple on it.

"Maybe Miriam would like to come up with me and surprise her *bubbe*," Mrs. Feinstein said to my mother.

My mother, usually friendly to Mrs. Feinstein, said coldly, "We have to be on our way," and pulled me around the corner. "Don't listen to them," my mother snapped. "Bubbie's salves and potions are quackery. Her medicines only work if people aren't really sick. And her predictions do more harm than good. It's all voodoo, I tell you."

My mother's eyes filled with fire. "Before your father left Russia, *your bubbe* warned him not to marry me. 'I see a no-good marriage for you,' Bubbie had told him. 'Stay away from the *Amerikanishers*. Especially the one with the long *shvartze* hair, green eyes, and a beauty spot on her right cheek.'" While she was talking, my mother touched her long dark hair, then pointed to her green eyes, and the mole on her cheek to show me that Bubbie had been describing her. "Bubbie was causing trouble between your father and me long before I even met him. And, your aunt Chaia, her own daughter . . ." My mother's voice trailed off. "I'm not going to say another word about her and how she ended up. It's too horrible to tell a child. Who knows what nonsense Bubbie could fill your head with? She still lives in the Dark Ages. You must never step foot in her apartment unless I'm with you."

"But I want to see what Bubbie's doing up there," I said. I wanted to be just like Bubbie. I could think of nothing more exciting than people waiting on line to see me when I grew up.

My mother's face turned white. "Don't ever say that again! If you keep it up, we'll go straight home instead of stopping in to visit your father." She waited, her brows knit. "Well, which will it be?"

"Visit Daddy." I sighed. When I turned around, there was the gold lettering on his window: SOL'S MEATS.

My father was behind the counter in his apron, with a pencil stuck behind his ear. His curly hair was the color of autumn leaves above his broad forehead and high cheekbones. His muscles were taut from hefting cow carcasses. I watched him wrap a sirloin in white waxed paper and tie it with string.

My father's cousin Max still counted off the names of my father's old girlfriends: Masha, Greesha, Bronya, Vera . . . Max counted on all his fingers nearly twice. "A real *bech-e-lor*," Max would say. But when my father was twenty-seven, he spotted my mother, nineteen, walking into a fancy barbershop, and even if he'd wanted to, he couldn't have stopped himself from following her in. He saw her sitting at the side of a barber's chair, giving a man a manicure. She had come to New York from upstate Elmira to be an actress, and she did manicures between auditions. "I want whatever that guy is getting," my father told the man at the desk. Within three weeks, my father had forgotten Bubbie's warning and asked my mother to marry him. He asked her to quit work right away. "I couldn't bear the thought of her holding another guy's hand," he said. They were married three months later. When my mother got pregnant, she stopped going to auditions. "Now the only parts I land are in the kitchen," she'd say sadly.

It was easy to see how much my father still loved my mother. His blue eyes lit up when he noticed her waiting at the door of his butcher shop. "Well, if it isn't Dorothy"—he pronounced it *Dor-o-tee*—my American Beauty Rose," he said. Unlike Bubbie, he loved that my mother had been born in this country, that she knew all the latest styles, which she sewed from *Vogue* patterns. He loved that she did the Lindy Hop, and followed recipes from *McCall's*.

Pulling off his apron, he said, "Let me wash up," and turned to the sink behind him. Then he rushed to my mother and tried to give her a kiss on the lips as he did every night. But my mother, still upset about Bubbie's influence over me, offered him her cheek instead. I thought of Mrs. Feinstein upstairs with Bubbie, and I secretly bent down and stuffed my pockets with sawdust from the floor just because I wasn't supposed to.

My father must have seen what I had done. "Putchkie," he chuckled, and lifted me up to blow a sputtering kiss into my neck. He had nicknamed me after the *pushkes*, the tin boxes on Bubbie's wall that she put coins in to give to the poor, because he said I had treasures inside me.

"It would be good to have a son to say Kaddish for me someday," he said, "but I have something better. A Putchkie to fill me with happiness." I remember, when he held me like that, feeling as if I'd swallowed two teaspoons of honey.

"Well," my mother said, "this Putchkie needs to get home to do her arithmetic."

"Bye, Daddy," I sang. All the way home, when my mother wasn't looking, I sprinkled pinches of sawdust on the sidewalk, pretending it was fairy dust. *I wish I may,* I mouthed, *I wish I might, go upstairs to my* bubbe's *tonight.* But that night, no one took me to see her, and so many nights passed that I was sure the fairies would never grant me my wish.

Two weeks later, for their twelfth anniversary, my father gave my mother a big amethyst ring with a spray of diamond chips that she'd picked out a month before. "I'll wear it forever," she'd said. She surprised him with two tickets for *The Fantasticks* and made reservations for the Russian Tea Room for dinner. "Your mother really knows how to spend my money," my father had said. I wanted a ticket, too. I felt like Schmully, the girl up the block who everyone steered clear of because they swore she'd never taken a bath.

"Putchkie should come out with us, too," my father insisted, but my mother told him, "American couples go out together and hire baby-sitters."

The day before the show the baby-sitter cancelled, and the only replacement my mother could find was Bubbie. I was thrilled my mother would have to leave me with Bubbie for a whole day and evening, but I knew better than to act too excited.

That afternoon, as we all climbed the steps to Bubbie's apartment, she appeared in the doorway, wearing her black dress with the lace at the sleeves. As always, her long white hair was braided and coiled like a crown on top of her head. She was smiling, and her pale blue eyes were crinkled. She looked so big to me, but when I reached the landing, and she pulled me to her, I was almost up to her shoulder. *"Neshomeleh,"* she called to me. That meant "darling" or "sweet soul." I could smell her lavender talc and see the white clouds she'd puffed onto her creased neck. I could smell her castile shampoo, too. "The only one that doesn't turn white hair yellow," she used to say.

Dad kissed Bubbie, and when I turned, he knelt and kissed me, too. His curls were flattened where his hat had been. He rubbed his Old Spice aftershave cheek against mine. "I'll be back when it's sandpaper," he said, then winked at me, obviously delighted that I was getting a long private visit with Bubbie. There was a spring in his step as he started down the steps.

My mother put her hand on my shoulder. "Bye," she said to Bubbie, smiling, but she didn't loosen her grip on me. I later learned Bubbie had agreed not to let her customers into the apartment today, but my mother still didn't trust her. As Bubbie went inside, my mother gave me a big kiss. Then, breathing into my face, she whispered, "I'm sure Bubbie means well, but she's a bit batty, so don't listen to anything she says."

"Okay," I said, and hurried into Bubbie's apartment, my heart drumming. Even though Bubbie's apartment had dark furniture and didn't get much sun, the rooms looked bright from her crystal lamps, white doilies, and cut glass bowls filled with hard candy.

"Look at the gifts my customers bring me this week," Bubbie said, smiling. She showed me a ship in a bottle, painted seashells, potted ferns, and a statue of Saint Francis of Assisi. I plucked the strings of the mandolin she handed me. Her closets were full of gifts, sometimes her refrigerator, too. Once my mother opened it and found a jar of jellied chicken feet and screamed.

"Can we make some sugar cookies?" I asked. I loved when she let me cut cookies out of dough with an upside-down glass.

"Sure," she said, and she led me into the kitchen. Drying herbs hung in bunches along the walls, and there were shelves of jars filled with powders and goo. For years, I thought them staples in every grandma's kitchen. "Are those what you use to make medicines?" I asked.

She looked at me slyly. "So, you know what your *bubbe* really does?"

"Only a little bit, but I want to know everything."

Her face crinkled into a smile. As she showed me how to roll out the cookie dough, there was a knock on the door.

"Mrs. Polnikov, it's Mrs. Greenhouse," a woman cried.

Bubbie frowned. "Och! I told customers not to come around today."

I wanted to see what Bubbie did with her customers. "Oh, please let her in," I begged.

Bubbie took a step toward the door, then stepped back again.

"Please, Bubbie. I want to see how you do your voodoo."

"Voodoo?" Bubbie said indignantly. "I am a healer. Voodoo is from the devil. My gift comes from God." I could see her hesitate, thinking, no doubt about the wrath of my mother. Then she sighed. "I'll let Mrs. Greenhouse in, but remember, it's our big secret."

When she opened the door, a big-bosomed woman with salt-and-pepper hair walked in. She was wearing all black and had pouches under each eye.

Bubbie showed her to the parlor, pulled up a footstool for me, and sat in the armchair with the ball-and-claw feet. Mrs. Greenhouse sat in the chair opposite and glanced at me. She shielded the side of her mouth with her hand so I wouldn't hear her, but my mother always said I could hear a feather drop.

"Do you talk to the dead?" Mrs. Greenhouse whispered to Bubbie.

"No," Bubbie said. "They talk to me."

I leaned so far forward on my stool that I nearly toppled over.

Mrs. Greenhouse took out a hankie and wiped her eyes. "I want to know if my husband blames me for not taking him to a better doctor."

"Nothing you could do," Bubbie said. "We all have our time. It is written."

"Maybe that's so," Mrs. Greenhouse said, "but I want to know if my Myron thinks I should have taken him to Mount Sinai."

Bubbie took off her silver glasses. She made her eyes dreamy. "I see a man with a gray suit."

I looked around, but I didn't see anybody besides Bubbie and Mrs. Greenhouse. Mrs. Greenhouse grew so excited, her hair fell out of its net. "Myron was buried in his gray suit!" she exclaimed.

"He is trying to tell me something," Bubbie said. She cocked her head. "He says he's with Florence."

Mrs. Greenhouse stuck out her chin. "Florence was his secretary. She was always showing up to work wearing nylon blouses with half her bosom exposed. I told Myron years ago, 'Fire her or I'll fire you.' Then I never heard another word about her. How convenient for Myron that Florence dropped dead, too."

"Och!" Bubbie said, clapping her hand to her forehead. Then her face lit up, as if she had just knocked an idea into her head. "Myron is dead for thirteen months," Bubbie said.

"How did you know?" Mrs. Greenhouse asked.

"Thirteen is written all over you. Twelve months is plenty for mourning. Your Myron is having a better time dead than you are alive. Take some of his money. Go to a *shadchen*."

"A matchmaker at my age?"

"And why not?" Bubbie asked. "I already see a fellah for you."

Mrs. Greenhouse opened her pocketbook and handed Bubbie a whole dollar. "You deserve a million," she said.

"A good healer doesn't charge a fortune," Bubbie said.

"Thank God for that," Mrs. Greenhouse laughed, "because Tillie the Matchmaker does." Then Mrs. Greenhouse put on red lipstick and rubbed some into her cheeks, too, and left the house swaying her hips like Marilyn Monroe.

After she'd gone, Bubbie told me, "People shouldn't go from

you crying. You have to know how to take *sheiss* and turn it into honey."

"Did you really see her husband, Myron?"

"Of course. The dead pop in and out like they have nothing better to do. After being shut up in a coffin, they don't want to stay put."

"How did you know what her husband looked like and what he said?" I asked. In my seven years, I had only seen a dead bird, a robin that had been squashed by a car. And once a worm I'd stepped on.

"You make your eyes look up, and a little to the right like this," she said. "But don't stare. Just look softly—then you wait and listen."

I did what she said with my eyes. I waited and listened, but I didn't see or hear anything.

She took my hand and studied my palm. "This is your lifeline. It's very long. And here's the line of your heart, and over here, the Mound of Venus for love." When she touched that spot, my heart felt as if it were swelling with love for her.

She kept looking at my hands. "I see a star-shaped crease," she said. "You don't see that very often."

"What does it mean?" I asked.

She just kept staring at my hand. Each second that passed felt like an hour. I heard her clock ticking. I heard the refrigerator hum. I smelled the orange oil she rubbed on her furniture.

She looked back at me. "Let's see what it means," she said, her voice quivering. "It might be a sign of something I've been hoping for. Let's start with your hands." She got up from her chair and held her hands above my head, and then, without touching me, she let them slowly travel down. I felt a tingling. She stopped at my shoulders. First she took one hand away, then the other. "It's the right shoulder," she said. "You must have hurt it."

"Last week I was twirling on my bed and fell off. I still have the bruise," I said, and pulled at the neckline of my sweater to show her.

"A little egg white will take care of that," she said.

She continued running her hands down my body and stopped again at my thigh. "There's something here, too," she said.

"A burn," I told her. "I tried to make cocoa by myself and spilled water from the kettle. I never told anyone, because I'm not supposed to touch the hot kettle myself."

"See, no one can hide from the gift," she said. "Now you try it on me." She lay down on the sofa.

I put my hands over her head. "What am I supposed to feel?" I asked.

"Sometimes you feel a little shock or a change in temperature in your hand. Sometimes your fingers will twitch."

I let my hands travel slowly a few inches over Bubbie's body. When I got to just below her belly, my hands stopped. "Bubbie, my hands are getting hot," I said breathlessly.

"Good for you and bad for me," she said. "It means you feel I have pain there." Her lips were tight as she smiled. She sat up and looked steadily into my eyes. "*Neshomeleh,* that was a little test. You have my gift. I could teach you how to do what I do. Then you can be *meine* official assistant."

Excitement went through me like jumping beans. "When's the next person coming?" I asked, bouncing in my chair.

"Better we eat first," Bubbie said. She hugged me to her. "Same recognizes same," she said. "When I was a little button like you, there was a healer in my shtetl named Bedya, a big woman with milky blue eyes. All the other children were scared of her, but their parents were always at her door wanting cures. I wasn't afraid, though. I never ran away like the rest of the children. One day she came up to me and told me, 'You got my powers.' She said she could tell just by the way the air shook around me. 'You come home with me,' she said. I didn't know what was going to happen, but I went with her, and she invited me to sit down and served me honey cake and a glass of sugary tea. 'When you find this out about yourself, you got to celebrate with someone who has the gift, too,' Bedya told me. *Neshomeleh,* today you and I got to celebrate together."

I helped Bubbie smooth her lace tablecloth over the kitchen table. She lit a candle and set out string bean salad on pumpernickel with honey cake and tea in her fanciest plates, but I started thinking, *Mommy isn't going to let me come back by myself again. How will I learn enough from Bubbie to be her official assistant?*

Bubbie put down her slice of pumpernickel. "Such a long face for such a happy day." Then she said, "Listen, when your mother asks what you did here, all you have to say is, 'Bubbie read the *Forward* and I listened to the radio. It was boring.' Then yawn. She'll let you come back by yourself every week."

"It's boring," I said for practice, then gave a big yawn.

"You could at least wait until you swallowed that string bean salad," Bubbie said, chuckling.

We hadn't even finished our honey cake yet when the doorbell rang again. A woman called in, "Mrs. Polnikov, it's Lydia Smolowitz. Vivi Greenhouse told me that you saw her today. You can't play favorites."

Bubbie sighed. "In this line of work, you can't have a life of your own." She got up, and I followed her to the door. A plump woman about my mother's age with carrot red hair and nose freckles stepped in. Her perfume was so strong that my eyes began to water.

"I just had to see you," the woman said.

"Well, my granddaughter is visiting, and I don't have a lot of time," Bubbie said. "We were having a little party. I didn't even touch my tea yet."

"Maybe you could just read my tea leaves," Lydia said.

I looked up at Bubbie and nodded my head.

Bubbie smiled. "Lydia, come on into the kitchen. I'll pour you some tea."

Instead of the glasses that she had used, Bubbie set out a small white teacup on a saucer and poured the tea without straining it first. The grounds went right in. I shivered at the thought of Lydia having to drink them, but Bubbie said, "Leave just enough tea to swirl the leaves in and blow so you don't burn your mouth like last time."

Lydia blew on the tea, the steam frizzing her carrot red hair, and sipped, checking the cup to make sure there was enough left after every sip. Then she picked up the cup and swirled it to the left. "One, two, three," she counted slowly. She covered the cup with the saucer and turned the nearly empty cup quickly upside down.

"The customer gets a better reading if she *mishes* it and turns it over herself," Bubbie explained to me. Then Bubbie lifted Lydia's cup, peered inside, and tilted it from side to side. "I see a shape that looks like an *A*," she said. "And the grounds are dark, so it's a man, or someone with dark hair. Hmm. I'd say here it's a dark-haired man."

Lydia's leg was jiggling under the table.

Squinting into the cup, Bubbie added, "And the *A* is near a shape that looks like a lit candle. So, somebody is burning a candle for a dark-haired man whose first or last name starts with *A*." Bubbie looked straight into Lydia's eyes. "I hope I'm not right," she said. "You been married to Sy for fifteen years."

Lydia cleared her throat and motioned her head toward me. "The child," she said, worried.

I took a pencil and one of my father's order pads out of my pocket and began to doodle so Bubbie wouldn't ask me to go in the next room, but Bubbie didn't even look at me. "Lydia, you were the one who invited yourself in, not me."

"Please go on," Lydia said. "I have to know if *A* loves me, too."

Pretending to still be doodling, I watched Bubbie put down the cup and look into Lydia's saucer. "See for yourself," Bubbie said. She pointed to a shape that looked like a triangle. "It's a fan,"

Bubbie said. "It means you better cool down. It means you'll make a big fool of yourself."

"I don't care." Lydia sighed, clasping her hands to her chest. "I need passion."

I thought about the French woman who came into Fogel's Fish Market and asked for *poisson*. Back then, I hated fish. Even when it was skinned, I could still see the scales and the jelly eyes.

"You're barking up the wrong tree," Bubbie told Lydia. "Look here," she added, pointing at a squiggle next to the fan. "This *A* of yours has a wet noodle. If you don't know what that means, come into the next room and I'll whisper it to you."

Lydia covered her face with her hands, but I could still see her blushing.

"Don't be ashamed," Bubbie said. "The reason you were drawn to a wet noodle is because, in your heart, you would never do anything to hurt Sy." Bubbie pushed away the saucer and looked into the cup again. "There's a cat in here," she said. "It means contentment. It means you'll have a long peaceful life with Sy. One that will bring you many blessings." Then she winked at Lydia. "And many licks, too."

When Lydia put her hands down, she was still blushing, but now she was laughing, too. "You're right," she said. "I knew I had to come straight to you. Thank you, thank you." She left seven dollars on the table.

Bubbie showed her out. When she came back in, she said, "Some nice tip, huh?" and tucked the money down the front of her dress. "But better than the extra money, I feel happy inside. I helped keep a family together. That's one of the best things a healer can do." She ate a forkful of honey cake. Wiping her mouth with a napkin, she said, "There's lots you have to know about doing this work. First of all, you must never talk about your customers. They got to trust you. And, no matter how bad you feel, you must not tell them your troubles. They already got enough of their own. That's why they come to you." She took another bite and chewed it slowly, then went on. "You got to remember, anger is a blindfold and a pair of ear corks for a healer. You can't get the messages and warnings you need. Sure you'll get mad, but you can't let it stick. And never use your gift to play the horses or win a jackpot. And never, ever do this work at a carnival. This work is not a show. It's something holy, like Moses seeing that burning bush, or Jacob wrestling with the angel."

I wasn't sure what she meant, but I nodded as if I did.

Bubbie ruffled my curls. "Be patient. It takes a lifetime to learn everything. Best of all, as *meine* official assistant, I'll let you do readings for a few customers. They'll get a kick out of it, especially since I'll only charge them half. But just customers from Jersey. No locals. We don't want your mother to hear about it."

I wanted to know everything, starting now. "Would you read my leaves?" I asked, holding my breath.

"My pleasure," she said.

When I let my breath out, the flame in the candle on the table began to quiver.

Bubbie took out a fresh white cup and saucer and poured the tea. I blew on it as Lydia had and then sipped down almost to the nasty leaves.

"This good?" I asked.

Bubbie nodded. I swirled the cup and counted to three as Lydia had.

"You learn fast," Bubbie said, "but I better be the one to turn the cup over or you'll burn yourself like with the cocoa."

After she turned it, I counted out loud as it drained, and then Bubbie looked into my cup. "There are three shapes that look like people. The dark shape is a man and the two lighter ones are women." She looked again. "No, wait. One shape is much smaller, so that could be a girl. They're near the handle. That means they're close to home."

"That must be me, and Mommy, and Daddy," I said, leaning closer.

She tilted the cup. "There's a shape right by them that looks like a mitten or maybe a boxing glove."

"It must be a boxing glove," I said. I thought about how my parents were always arguing about Bubbie. I looked straight at her. "Why are you mad at Mommy for being born in America? I was born here, too."

"I'm not mad," Bubbie said. "It's just hard for me to see the old ways being flushed down the toilet."

"I like your old ways," I told Bubbie.

She kissed my forehead. "You're some kiddo," she said.

"What else do my leaves say?" I asked.

"Here's an anchor," she said, pointing to some leaves in my saucer. "That means you have strength inside yourself."

"And this thing that looks like a circle?"

"It's a ring," Bubbie said. "If a ring is anywhere near an anchor, it means you'll have a good husband."

"I don't want a husband," I said.

Bubbie threw her head back and laughed. "Not yet maybe, but you will."

# 3

WHEN I WALKED into the bank to get out our last bonds, tellers were handing patrons their stamped pink slips to confirm deposits. I had the feeling that I was the only one there who had come to withdraw savings. I escaped to the vault room and signed for my safe-deposit box. The clerk showed me into a little closed cubicle where I could have privacy. I sensed women in other cubicles stashing away their rubies and diamonds until their next big bash. As I reached into my deposit box, I touched something smooth and cool. My gold heart-shaped pin! It was the first gift Rory had ever given me. I remembered when he had given it to me. It was one of those winters when drivers kept chains on their tires all season long, and shoes and carpets were spotted with rock salt. We had just come back from a movie, and we were parked in front of my parents' house in Rory's salmon-colored Plymouth, the motor running. The old heater would blow only a slant of warm air at our feet, but we sat there, hating to leave each other. And then he handed me the box, and as soon as I saw the heart centered on a piece of white cotton, I drew in a breath as warm and sweet as my *bubbe*'s sugared tea. "Do you like it?" he asked.

"I love it," I said.

"Really?" he asked.

"Really," I assured him. It was twenty-two karat. It probably hadn't cost much more than seventy-five dollars back then, but I kept it at the vault because it was priceless to me. Now, remembering how our deep, steamy kisses had fogged the Plymouth's windows, I attached the pin to my lapel with the eagerness of a young girl, and I suddenly couldn't wait to drive to his store to see him. I grabbed the envelope of bonds that had gotten thinner over recent years, and I stuffed them in my pocketbook for Rory to sign and cash in at the bank on his corner where he'd bought them, the only place they were allowed to be cashed.

As I crossed Middle Neck Road toward Best Bagels, I stopped on the double yellow line. *Maybe I shouldn't let Rory cash in these bonds,* but a red Porsche blared its horn at me, and I went on. Inside, I told the guy, "Three sesame and a quarter pound of low-fat cream cheese, please."

As he was bagging them, I heard, "*Neshomeleh,* a braided challah, too," and a warm shiver ran up my spine.

Bubbie visited me often these days, spontaneously. Each time I felt as if she had put her warm shawl around me. "They don't sell challah here," I told her.

"What don't we sell?" the bagel guy asked.

I felt my face flush. "Just thinking out loud," I said. I felt a slight pressure on my head, as if someone were tilting it down. There, in the glass case, I spotted a wire basket of rolls with challahlike braiding. Spirits weren't always good at judging earthly size. "I'll take one of those rolls, too," I told the guy.

I turned toward where I thought Bubbie was. "Don't go," I said.

"Lady, I'm not going anywhere," the bagel guy said. "You want something else?"

I shook my head, paid for the bagels and roll, and left. I always wished Bubbie would stay longer. But even though she had come for only a moment, she was to my mood what yeast is to dough.

My step felt lighter as I walked back to my blue Honda Civic. Bubbie had escaped to America without any bonds, I said to myself, so Rory, Cara, and I could live without them, too. Rory was working so hard to try to give Cara and me a good life.

On Lakeville Road traffic was bumper to bumper. The guy in front of me got out of his car and stood on the sidewalk visoring his eyes with his hand to see what was causing the delay. Other drivers stuck their heads out their windows for a report. In my mind, I saw a series of bright orange cones. *Construction,* I said to myself.

"Fucking construction!" the man yelled as he got back in his car, slamming his door, and I felt the same thrill I always did whenever I was right. I never took my gift for granted. Several cars made U-turns over the double line.

After a few minutes, traffic began inching along. When I finally got to the entrance of the Long Island Expressway, I saw what the construction was. A concrete wall was being built along the side of the road. I had seen those walls on other highways. "They're too distracting," I'd told Rory. "The shadows of spirits are dancing all over them."

"That only affects you," he'd told me. "For the rest of us, it actually cuts down on the distraction of trees and helps minimize fumes and noise for people who live nearby."

Rory kept me grounded. I touched my gold heart pin. Bubbie used to say that before a soul came into the world, he knew his whole future, but then the Angel of Forgetfulness touched his lips. "That's why you got this mark," she'd added, pointing to the indent above the bow of my lips. Whenever I thought of how Rory and I first met, Bubbie's story felt true:

I'd been looking through my college alumni newsletter and saw a circle of light around a notice about an open house party, as if someone had used a pink neon marker around it. The address was in Forest Hills. I was sure that the circle of light was a sign that something or someone would be there for me.

On the night of the party, it was sleeting. I had to take two buses to get there, crammed into a seat beside a mother with cranky kids on one bus and a bunch of teenagers sneaking smokes in the back of the other. My blue Borganza fake fur was twinkling with ice crystals. I asked half a dozen passersby for directions and was led past the courts where the tennis matches were held into a neighborhood of historic landmark brick homes. I found the house easily. The windows were dark, and I didn't hear any music, but I rang the bell three times anyway. After a few moments, the door opened. A man with a craggy face and pointy beard stood there. *He must have graduated with the Beat Generation,* I thought. "How can I help you?"

"The open house party," I explained.

He blinked at me. "It was last week."

I felt my face burn with embarrassment.

He opened the door wider. "Would you like to come in? Get out of the cold? A cup of coffee, maybe?"

He was very nice, but I was scared to go into a strange man's house with no one else there. "That's all right," I said bravely. "Sorry I bothered you."

"No bother. I'm throwing one next year, too. Check for the date."

"Bye," I said, trying to still my shivering. I made my way back toward the business district. I was so disappointed that I felt like crying. My circle of light had blown out. *Quit the self-pity,* I scolded myself. *You're not starving in Europe. No one has looted your house. Your parents are safe in their bed.* But my usual consolation didn't work. Tears blurred my vision and made my cheeks even colder. On the curb, I stumbled and twisted my ankle. *The Cossacks aren't chasing you,* I told myself as I hobbled along. *No one is setting you on fire.* My ankle began to throb and burn so much that I couldn't take another step. I started to sob in front of a late-night drugstore. A minute later, a man in a white lab jacket came out to see what was the matter. The pharmacist, I thought. I was so grateful to see someone. I saw how young he was, how handsome. His sandy hair had thick waves. His eyes were like choco-late. "What's wrong?" he asked, and I pointed at my ankle. He knelt and wrapped his fingers around it. "Pretty swollen," he said. I was freezing all over, but my skin warmed under his touch. His eyelashes were long and thick—I wanted to lick them.

"I'll carry you into the store," he offered.

"Oh, no," I said, but he lifted me up in his arms and set me down on a chair inside. My teeth were chattering. He helped me out of my wet coat and put his ski jacket on me. He was so tall that it went over me like a cocoon. He made me Sanka and wrapped my ankle in an Ace Bandage.

"I'm Miriam Polnikov," I said. My whole body was beginning to warm.

"Rory."

I loved the way his lips puckered as he said it. "Kaminsky," I filled in. Then I was scared he'd realize I had Bubbie's gift, that I was psychic. "Your name is on your pocket," I explained. "I don't think I ever knew anybody named Rory before."

"My mother wanted me to have the best opportunities in this country. To her, there was no one more all-American than a cow-boy, so she named me after Rory Calhoun. When I was still in diapers, she dressed me in chaps and a cowboy hat. And now look at me—a pharmacist. I've never even gotten on a horse."

I tried to think of something horsey to say. "I got on a horse once and got right off. I had no idea how far off the ground a horse's back was."

He nodded. "Speaking of horses, you'll be needing a ride home. I manage this store. I can close in ten minutes and drive you."

"But I live all the way in Rockaway."

"That's even more of a reason." He began to close out the reg-ister. I watched him take charge of everything: flipping light switches, closing and locking drawers. I liked it, his confidence.

"The car's up the block," he said. "It would be against the law to leave you in the pharmacy alone. I'll carry you to it."

This time I didn't argue. He wrapped his ski jacket more tightly around me and lifted me up. I put my arms around his neck, my head against his shoulder. I burrowed my face into his warmth. When we got in the car, he put on the heat, then walked back to slide the big gate across the storefront as my father had done at his butcher shop every night.

Rory smiled at me a lot as he drove me home, and when he stopped at a light, he put his arm around me. It was a good, sure hold, not like my last date, David, whose hand crept down my shoulder, inching toward my breasts. Rory was an up-front guy.

"I'd ask you out for tomorrow night," Rory said, "but I have to go to my cousin's engagement party."

In my mind, I saw an annulment paper. "His marriage won't last a year," I blurted out.

"What!" Rory said.

I bit my lip and quickly turned on the radio as a distraction, but I could see him glancing at me from the corners of his eyes.

"Duke, Duke, Duke, Duke of Earl, Duke, Duke, Duke of Earl," I sang along with Gene Chandler. Rory joined in with a tuba voice, and we started laughing.

Now, buoyed by the memory, I belted out, "Nothing can stop me now, cause I'm the Duke of—"

A guy talking on a cell phone swerved into my lane. I lay on the horn, and he swerved back, still talking on the phone. *I better pay attention to the road since nobody else is,* I warned myself, but soon I was thinking about Rory again.

The first time he came to my house, he came early in the morning, so excited to see me that when he dashed in, he smacked his forehead into my mother's hallway chandelier. A couple of the crystals fell off and shattered on the ground. "I'm so sorry, Mrs. Polnikov," Rory had said, his forehead creasing. "I'll be glad to replace them."

"Don't give it another thought," my mother said, forcing a smile. I was relieved, but then she added, "Those crystals are from Czechoslovakia. The Communists shut down the factory. Once they're broken, they can never, ever be replaced."

I wouldn't have blamed Rory if he'd turned around and left without me, but he stayed and placated my mother by getting a silver tray off a high shelf when she asked him to. My mother leaned back against the kitchen counter, smiling in spite of herself. "He's the Human Stepladder," she murmured to me.

Afterwards, he took me to breakfast at the diner for plain old hash browns and fried eggs, but I never tasted food so delicious. I didn't want breakfast to end. I didn't want him to leave. I started to say, "Well, maybe you could call me—"

Then he interrupted, "How about we go to Battery Park and then for a ferry ride to the Statue of Liberty?"

We stood at the railing, looking out over the choppy waters of the Upper New York Bay, tourists chattering around us, some in languages I'd never heard before. The spray left tiny beads on Rory's face. I couldn't resist. I reached up and touched his cheek. He turned so his lips were on my palm, and he kissed it. It was like a current through my lifeline. Then the Statue of Liberty came into full view. People around us pressed against the rail, snapping pictures, but Rory and I grew still. I thought of my father, traveling to America in steerage when he was only seventeen. "The crew expected us to stay down there," my father had told me. "We were packed in like canned kippers. The few toilets overflowed like the Atlantic in a hurricane. The dysentery, the fevers. And then, I came on deck into the bright sun and saw the Lady, and I said the *shehecheyanu* prayer."

I leaned against Rory's arm, took a deep breath, and said aloud, "Blessed are you, Lord our God, ruler of the universe, who has kept us alive, sustained us, and enabled us to reach this moment. Amen."

I looked up at Rory. His face was as impassive as a guard at Buckingham Palace, but his eyes were glazed with tears.

When the boat docked, as we climbed the steps toward the top of the statue, we stopped at a landing to look out a window. "I was never here before," I told him.

"Me neither," he said, and held me tightly to him. The top of my head only reached his shoulder. The other people climbing to the torch filed by us.

On the way home, he told me that his parents had died two years before, his mother of an aneurysm, his father of emphysema. Rory took out his wallet and showed me a picture of them standing in front of their store—KAMINSKY'S DRY CLEANERS. His father would have been as tall as Rory, but his back was bent, and his thin face was so creased that it looked as if it could use a good pressing. His mother was short and plump with a bubble of blond hair and a forced smile.

"I loved my parents, but I'd never want a life like theirs," he said. "We lived in three small rooms behind the store. It stank of carbon tetrahydrate. The doors of our kitchen cabinets were always falling off. The furniture was battered, the wallpaper peeling. My parents worked so much, they never had time to make friends or entertain or go on vacation. From the time I was eight, my father expected me to work with them, too. I hated all those white shirts hanging in plastic skins like ghosts." Rory shuddered. "I moved out as soon as I could," he went on, "and put myself through school. When they died, they left me some insurance money, but I wish they would have had that for themselves to enjoy while they were alive." His voice got garbled. "They had been in Auschwitz."

"I'm so sorry," I said.

"At least my parents got to die of natural causes," he said.

"My father always says, 'It's a blessing for a Jew to die in his own bed,'" I said. Then I told him about Bubbie's and my father's sufferings in Russia.

"It's as if we already have history together," he said, grabbing my hand and holding it to his heart. I felt as if a lost part of my own body had been returned to me.

Rory took me all the places we never got to go to as kids—to the

Empire State Building, where we rode the elevator to the top floor and looked down at the city. "Someday all this will be ours," Rory joked, and I laughed out loud. We went to the circus and fed peanuts to the elephants. At the UN, we sat in on a meeting of the General Assembly, and we chose to listen to the French translation through shared headphones because we thought it was more romantic. I liked that Rory took charge, made plans. My father had run his business, but when he was home, my mother was hard-pressed to get him out of his armchair. Rory arranged get-togethers with his buddies and their girlfriends, so we could all double date. People thought I was shy, but a good listener, and they loved my laugh—my father's hearty Russian laugh. And Rory taught me how to play tennis. I was never very good at it, but I got a kick out of his cheering if I managed to hit the ball over the net. We spent afternoons at the bird sanctuary on Cross Bay Boulevard in Queens. He didn't stand there for hours looking into binoculars or telescopes on tripods or the zoom lens of a pricey camera like other birders. Instead, he held my hand, and we walked the sandy paths between the swaying reeds. When he saw a snowy egret spread its wings and lift off, tucking in its gawky legs, Rory straightened his spine and lifted his head, as if he, too, were about to fly.

I couldn't remember being this happy since Bubbie was alive. But keeping the secret that I was psychic from Rory became a barrier between us, like a concrete wall on a highway. I knew I had to tell him. I just had to, no matter what.

For our one-month anniversary, he took me to a Greek restaurant in Astoria. The walls were mirrored. Bunches of plastic grapes hung from the ceiling. The tables against the wall were nestled in archways. "I have something I have to tell you," I said nervously.

His gaze was steady. "What?"

I looked at a couple at the next table. The man was holding the woman's hand against his heart. They looked moony-eyed. "See that couple over in the corner?" I asked.

He glanced at them. "I'd rather be looking at you," he said.

"They're going to break up," I told him. "A fight. Any minute."

He glanced back at them. The couple leaned toward each other, talking in hushed tones. "You're way off," Rory said.

All of a sudden, the woman bolted up, her chair clattering to the floor. "You lied to me!" she cried, and she grabbed her coat and left. Instead of chasing after her, the man sat there, calmly twirling his spaghetti on a fork. It was over, and he was relieved.

"He never intended to marry her like he'd promised," I told Rory.

Rory looked at me and cocked his head. "You know them?"

I shook my head. "Never saw them before."

His eyebrows rose above the frames of his glasses. "How did you know?"

"I'm psychic," I whispered.

He sat there quietly, looking at me as if I were a stranger. Examining. "Why didn't you tell me before?" he asked softly.

I was twisting my napkin. "I was afraid."

He stayed very still. This disappointment would hurt more than all the others. I hadn't dated anyone seriously enough in high school to risk telling them about my gift. But when I was a freshman in college, after dating a law student named Steve for six months, I told him I was psychic.

"Great," he said. "You can come to the track with me. You'll help me pay my tuition."

I explained that my *bubbe* had warned me never to misuse my gift like that.

"I see," he said, but he didn't. The next time we went out, he handed me a lottery card and asked me to pick the numbers. I refused to go out with him again.

I thought of Harvey, an actuary whom I'd dated a whole year before I confessed. We were in a taxi, coming home from a concert at Lincoln Center. "I love you," he murmured. I thought I loved him, too. He was courtly. He opened doors for me and took my arm when we walked. He bought me out-of-print books that had ribbon bookmarks sewn into their bindings, and he dreamed of a house in the country, a simple life, something I had thought could make me happy, too.

"I'm psychic," I announced.

Harvey snorted back a laugh. "And I'm a warlock," he said.

"No, really," I had told him, explaining that I took after my bubbe, who had been called a healer back then.

He listened, nodding. When I finished, he said, "I think you should see a shrink." He didn't open the door for me when I got out of the cab.

"Afraid of what?" Rory asked me now.

"Afraid you'll think I'm crazy."

"Crazy?" he finally said. "What's crazy? I mean, look—I admit I've never gone to a psychic, never even thought of going to one. I don't even read my horoscope in the paper. But I have a science background, and science proves crazy things all the time. If I had a gift like yours, I wouldn't settle for a regular job. I'd make my living at it."

"You would?"

"Of course. And I'd be proud. You're different from other people. Special." Then he smiled, leaned forward, and grabbed my knee under the table. "You're my live wire," he said.

I got a thrill, but I moved my knees to the side. "I wouldn't go to the track with you or to a casino and don't expect me to win the lottery for you either."

"Who asked you to?" Rory said.

I swung my knees back into his reach.

As we drove to Sanford Avenue in Flushing where he lived, he gave me deep kisses at every stoplight. My dark secret out, I felt slaphappy.

We kissed in the elevator all the way to the sixth floor of his building. His apartment was a large studio with an oversized bed. He must have noticed me staring at it. I was picturing a chorus line of girls in the bed with him. "Do you entertain a lot?" I asked nervously.

"No, I'm a restless sleeper."

Rory sat down on the bed. My legs quivered as I walked toward him. He took me in his arms and drew me down. He undressed me slowly. "I love your red curly hair," he murmured. "And your skin is like a bar of Ivory Soap." He ran his hands down me. "I love your long neck and round tush," he said, "and your short, thin eyelashes."

"Hey," I said, "eyelashes are supposed to be long and thick."

"I don't know what's supposed to be," he said. "I only know what I like. And I like that I'm a foot taller than you."

"You're the size a man is supposed to be," I said. "I like looking up to you."

As he touched me, I felt his pulse beating in his fingertips, as if he were sending Morse code to every nerve in my body. Our breathing sounded like oceans.


Afterwards, as I lay in his arms, he dozed off. I still had a curfew—1:00 A.M. If I got home even a minute later, my father was at the window, swaying with fatigue as he watched for me. It hurt me so much to see him exhausting himself at the window that I tried to be punctual.

"Rory, I have to go home," I whispered.

"We have to do something about this," he said. "Marry me." I felt myself flush with pleasure.

When I told my mother, she said, "Rory has no family and ours is small, so we'll invite most of the temple."

Instead, a month later, Rory bought me a big bouquet with pink ribbon streamers. He wore a white jacket, and I wore a white lacy granny dress, and we drove to City Hall in Jamaica, Queens.

Rory had copies of our blood work, our birth certificates, and our rings. "I forgot a witness," he said as we were about to get on line for the judge.

An old man wearing dark glasses approached us. "I'm blind,"

he said. "Instead of accepting charity, I make my living as a witness."

I felt as if Bubbie had sent him. Rory gave him fifty dollars.

After the ceremony, we went back to his apartment to celebrate with a bottle of Dom Pérignon. We stood at his window, looking out at the rows of other apartments, toasting each other and all of Flushing. Then we called my parents.

"How could you deprive me of being mother of the bride?" my mother hollered. "What was the rush? Do you have a loaf in the oven?"

"No, I'm not pregnant, Mom."

Rory took the phone from me. "Mrs. Polnikov," Rory said. "I can assure you that Miriam isn't pregnant."

She was shouting so loudly that Rory had to take the receiver from his ear. I heard her say, "What did you do, Mr. Pharmacist, give her a pelvic exam?"

"Oh, Mom," Rory said, winking at me.

She was quiet a moment. He must have disarmed her. He put the receiver between us so we could both listen. "Well, congratulations, I guess," she said.

Then my father got on. "A grandchild is great at any time," he said.


When I opened the door to Mirror, I was stunned at how Rory's money problems were showing in his business. The bright blue vinyl floor with the yellow crowns was faded to a sand color. Rory had hired a man to wax it recently, but the floor was too porous to take a shine. A few weeks ago, he'd painted the walls and ceiling overnight so he could save money. He was handy, but he'd been so exhausted that, beneath the paint, I could see where the spackling hadn't been properly sanded.

I looked toward the prescription department. Rory was on the phone, his back to me. He didn't see me come in. Fred, who had been working at Mirror Pharmacy for thirteen years, was behind the side counter. He was chubby, with big blue eyes and shiny blond hair that flopped over his forehead. A picture of his wife, Anita, and his small son, Jeb, was taped to the cash register, and he kept glancing at it, touching the edges with his fingers. Fred was waiting on a customer, so I sat down on the chair against the Peg-Board wall, opposite him.

Fred was saying to the guy, "I can't wait for my three-year-old to get big enough for Little League so I can volunteer-coach. I'm the kind who will look out for his players. I could have been in the majors if my coach hadn't put me in a game too soon after a knee injury."

The guy looked at his watch. "Sorry, Fred, I've heard this story before. And I'm running late, so I'd like my prescription."

Fred was friendly—maybe too friendly. He was famous for that story. I knew his other weakness too well: whenever Fred helped out with the paperwork, it took Rory days to fix the ensuing mess. And sometimes he got lost on deliveries and took an hour to come back. After the customer left, Fred gazed into space. I cleared my throat loudly.

"Mrs. K.," Fred said, startled. "How are you and your lovely daughter?"

"We're fine," I said. He beamed at me. Fred rarely missed an opportunity to chat, but I didn't want him to neglect his work any further, so I remained quiet.

After a moment, he said, "If you'll excuse me, I've got a big box of coupons to sort."

I looked over at Rory. He was still on the phone, so I began to straighten the insole display. Everything was out of order—cushioned insoles stuck in with the bunion pads, and pads with doughnut holes for heel spurs stuffed in with the arch supports. As I looked for the proper place for an arch support, a woman said, "It seems to be the last one in my size. Are you buying it?"

"No," I said. "I don't work here. I'm the silent partner," and it was true. When Rory first bought the pharmacy with his inheritance, it had been called Dubin's. Right before opening day, he'd said, "I've got a surprise for you." He drove me to Dubin's and pointed to the new sign on the top of his storefront. MIRROR, it said in big red letters. I looked back at him, puzzled. "It's both our names together. "*Mir* and *Ror.* You and me. A partnership."

We kissed under the sign as if it were mistletoe. When we finally went inside, Rory walked up and down the narrow aisles, pointing at the empty shelves. "I'm going to put the beauty line here and the first-aid items over there. And the walls will be all whitewashed Peg-Board," he'd said proudly. "It will give me lots of options. Over here will be my office." He showed me a matchbox of a room. Then he took me to the prescription section. He looked like a giant in there. "Aren't the counters too low for you?" I asked.

"They were built for a short pharmacist," he explained, showing me how he had to stoop. "As soon as we buy a house, I'll redo the pharmacy and the office."

With Rory's encouragement, I'd started doing readings in a café in Long Beach, and on my days off, I came and brought him lunch. Everybody was crazy about him. Customers stopped in just to say hello to him. They called him Doc.

Now I heard Rory say, "No, Mrs. Applebaum, you can't return your leftover Prilosec. It's unsanitary. . . . Of course I'm not saying your hands are dirty, but by law . . ." He held the receiver away from his ear. "Mrs. Applebaum, would you kindly lower your voice?"

Another customer came in. "Listen," the man said, "I don't have time to jaw. I came to pick up my insulin." Fred asked to see his Medicaid card.

It felt like yesterday that customers paid for their prescriptions by personal check, cash, or house charge. Then slowly, there were forms to fill out, credit card fees, additional calls to get permission to fill prescriptions. These days all Rory's money was from third-party payments—Medicaid, Medicare, union plans, HMOs. While he had to pay his bills to distributors on time, the third parties had no deadline. The more prescriptions Rory filled, the more we were in debt. The sight of the Medicaid card made me sick.

Then Rory turned and saw me. A light went into his eyes. "Mim, I'm so glad you're here!"

His sandy hair was rumpled because he hadn't had time to get a haircut. His glasses were tilted. "I brought you bagels and bonds," I said.

"Thanks," he said, wincing as he typed a label for medication. He had carpal tunnel syndrome from twisting on caps and typing. For the first time, I noticed he was developing a stoop like his father's from bending at the short counter.

The first five years Rory had the store, he'd made a lot of money. "Why don't you get the construction work done so you'll be more comfortable at work?" I'd asked.

"Mim, I'm too busy," he'd said. "You know how they print the drug prices in the Red Book? Now the drug companies are hiking up prices so fast that Red Book is coming out with monthly supplements. I have to waste hours every week searching through them. I know it doesn't sound like much, but I'm trying to invent a system out of chaos. I'm alphabetizing the names of the drugs in a Rolodex, and writing in the unit cost in pencil so I can change it with every hike."

I'd suggested computerizing the system. But Rory explained there was no pharmaceutical-specific software. He'd spent hours developing his own program. Now Rory had no time *and* no money for the renovations.

I spread cream cheese on a bagel and fed it to Rory while he was typing. "I was starving," he said. "I had no time for lunch."

I glanced over at Fred. I could see a cartoon bubble over his head with him thwacking a home run, the crowds in the stadium cheering for him. WORLD SERIES, a banner said. I had a sense that every game had been played out at Mirror. "Can't Fred help out more?"

Rory began counting out pills. They sounded like hail dropping into the plastic tray of the pill counter. "You know how it is with Fred," he said, shrugging, as he slid the pills into a vial with a metal spatula.

I knew all too well. "There's so much that you can't control about the business," I whispered. "But you should change what you can. Get rid of Fred already and hire somebody competent."

"Give the guy a break, Mim. You can't see all that he does. Besides, he has a family to support."

"So do you. You're not a charity organization."

"Mim, you don't get it. With the business in decline, I can't afford help. Who could I hire for that money? A kid would only be available after school hours. I need someone with me full-time. Fred has his faults, but he's honest."

Rory wouldn't look at me as he spoke.

I bridled. "Isn't the pharmacy half mine? A partnership? You won't even try to find someone else," I argued. "If you don't have time to interview people, I'll be glad to do it for you. I'll screen them psychically. I know I'll find somebody better for you. In the meantime, I could adjust my schedule to help out."

Now he looked at me with amusement. I knew he was thinking about my helping him when he first opened the store. I'd been so distracted by spirits that the register was always short at the end of the day and I was engaged in a constant battle with Bubbie for selling antacids instead of peppermint oil.

"I know being a clerk isn't my gift," I said. "I was just filling in. Fred's here all the time. He should have been able to get the hang of it by now."

"Honey, please—mind your own business, and let me mind mine."

I drummed my fingers on the counter. "Take a look at Fred. I bet he's still doing nothing."

But Rory didn't look. "I can't go into this now," he said.

I glared at him. "You can't cut me off like this."

"I'm busy," he said.

"Well, I'm busy, too, but I brought bagels and our savings bonds for you." I handed him the envelope.

"For *us*," he said. "We saved for them together, and now they're going to help *us* out when we need it."

His jaw was set. I had hurt his pride. "Sorry," I said, "it's the wrong place to discuss this. We'll talk tonight."

"There's nothing more to say, Mim. Discussion over."

"The discussion is always over when you want it to be," I said angrily. Without saying good-bye, I started walking out. I expected him to come after me. A million thoughts about what he could do or say came to me as I got in my car, but he didn't follow.

When I got home, I went down to throw in a load of wash. *Why doesn't Rory believe me?* I wondered. *Why doesn't he trust that I could know things? That I can see?*

When we were first dating, I'd phoned him at work only to find he'd called in sick. At his apartment, he answered the door smelling of liniment. He was wearing a sweat-soaked T-shirt and a pair of cut-off jeans. He was in so much pain, he could hardly walk. "Oh, Mim, I think I hurt my back." His eyes looked wild with panic. He staggered to the bed, his palms at the small of his back as he lay down on his stomach.

In my mind, I saw a shadow on his kidney and then a little gray rock. "Rory, we have to go to a doctor."

I drove to Booth Memorial Hospital while he groaned beside me.

"You'll be all right," I kept telling him. I saw a calendar with two days crossed out. "It's a kidney stone, and it will pass through you in two days." As soon as I said that, I was terrified that he would have something incurable.

At the hospital, the doctor X-rayed him. "The bad news is, you have a kidney stone. The good news is, it's small enough to pass through you without surgery."

When the doctor advised him to urinate into a strainer and

bring the stone to his follow-up visit, Rory and I were actually able to laugh.

But I just as quickly learned where my advice was not welcome. I stopped in to see him at the pharmacy where he worked a few days later. People were lined up, prescriptions fluttering in their hands. I knew I wouldn't get a chance to talk to him until there was a lull, but that was fine by me. I liked watching him in action, seeing how kind he was to his customers, how he'd take the time to explain to a man the possible adverse reactions of a drug and ask whether a woman's niece had recovered from the flu yet.

"Do you have good ear drops?" a man asked, holding his ear, wincing.

He was older, raspy-voiced, and as I looked at him, I saw a flash of red on his jaw and I knew, instantly, the pain wasn't caused by his ear at all. I couldn't help myself. I tapped him on the shoulder. "The trouble is, your bite is off."

"My bite?" The man frowned. He looked from me to Rory, and Rory raised a brow at me.

"These drops are excellent," Rory said firmly, and the man took out some bills.

"Honey, please," Rory had said after the man left. "I love you. I love what you do, but it can make trouble. My customers have to feel that this is scientific. They have to trust me. Listen," he added, smiling. "You do your thing and I do mine." I must have still looked hurt. "Sorry," he said. He chucked me playfully under the chin and went right back to filling prescriptions.

What I thought back then was, *I don't want my marriage to be like my parents' marriage. I don't want to look into a teacup someday and see boxing gloves.* So, I accepted his apology and vowed to myself not to use my psychic gift in the business, even if half the biz was supposed to be mine. It had worked for me while Rory was doing well, but now Mirror was swallowing Rory and all our household funds. As I rubbed bleach into the collars of his pharmacy jackets, I felt like wringing their necks.

# 4

I STAYED MAD AT Rory all week. The anger came out of me in household aggression. I reheated his dinners on broil instead of warm, washed his pharmacy jackets with my red sweater, and replaced his old down pillow with an extra-firm foam.

Cara had been eyeing me. "What's up?" she asked when she cornered me in my bedroom.

"Nothing," I told her as I threw Rory's shoes into the back of the closet.

She stared at me for a moment; then without saying another word, she turned and walked out.

On Sunday, Rory and I were in the backyard doing chores. Rory cleaned the windows while I raked. We tried not to look at each other. His cell phone rang. As he fumbled to get it, I saw Fred's face. "It's Fred," I said sharply. I didn't have to be psychic to know what he wanted. He called at least one Sunday a month to say he'd be late on Monday or wouldn't get there at all. "He's calling to either tell you he'll be late tomorrow or he won't be coming in at all," I said.

Rory glowered at me, then put down his squeegee, and answered the call. "Fred, what's doing?" he asked breezily.

*As if he didn't know,* I thought, but instead of Rory saying, "I'll see you Tuesday, then," he said, "I'll check our schedule with Miriam and call you right back." I stared at Rory.

"Mim, Fred and Anita want us to come over to their house this afternoon."

The last thing I wanted to do was go over to his house. "Aren't you with him enough all week?"

"Mim, if you only got to know Fred as a person, you'd see why I keep him on. Just last week, I was going nuts from the pressure, and Fred showed up at the back door in a Frankenstein mask."

*Fitting,* I thought, but years ago, Bubbie had told me anger stops you from picking up messages and warnings, and this week alone she had been proved right. I'd been so angry that I'd drawn complete blanks with four clients. I returned their money, but I still couldn't shake the feeling that I'd let them down. On top of that, I'd lost the heart-shaped pin Rory had given me. Now there was just a hole in my lapel. For my work and my marriage, I had to take steps to smooth things over between us. "I'm glad Fred provides some comic relief," I said, but I was raking the grass with harder strokes.

"We'll only stay a short time, Mim. The last time you saw Fred's boy, Jeb, was at his christening. He's three now. Fred's been after me for weeks. I can't keep making up excuses."

A formal visit to a church had been obligatory. I was sure if we went to Fred's house socially, it would be like jumping into quicksand, bubbling down into the muck of having Fred work for Rory until retirement, or until Rory was dead from overwork.

"I miss playing with a little kid," Rory said. "When Cara was Jeb's age, I used to put pot-holder mitts on my hands and pretend they were puppets. Remember? And I taught her birdcalls. "Coo-ooh, coo-coo," Rory called. "Now Cara's off with the debating team."

I sighed. "Okay, I'll go to Fred's."

"You won't be sorry," Rory said, but I already was. As Rory called Fred back, my rake made grooves in the grass. Bubbie had warned me of the dangers of letting anger stick, that it could block my psychic instincts, but she hadn't told me the solvent to remove it.

Rory changed out of his tattered jeans and put on khaki pants with a button-down shirt. I put on a long denim snap-front dress and a woolen poncho. We bought an apple pie and drove to Fred's house in Middle Village, Queens. It was only a half-mile from Mirror, but I'd never even driven by his house before. It was a yellow-shingled, narrow house, one of the few that hadn't been knocked down and replaced by co-op developments. The garage was so big, it could house another family.

Anita stood in the doorway, waving to us. Her auburn hair rippled down past her shoulders. She was slim and pretty in a black skirt and a pink fuzzy sweater, her smile like the "after" shot for an ad for tooth-whitener. Before she had Jeb, she used to stop in at Mirror to visit Fred and bring her famous chocolate chip cookies. I remembered how we'd laughed together when Fred did his Cookie Monster imitation. I was almost looking forward to seeing her now.

"Welcome," Anita called.

We walked up the path, Rory carrying the apple pie.

Anita opened the door, and Jeb toddled out of the house, his blond hair in a bowl-over-the-head cut, his round tummy pushing against his striped shirt. His eyes were enormous. "Oh, he's adorable," I said.

"What adorable?" Rory said. "He's a guy. Right, macho man?" Rory handed me the pie and lifted Jeb in the air. "Up we go into the wild blue yonder!" Rory sang. Jeb giggled and patted Rory's face with his hands. I remembered the feel of Cara's little hands on my cheeks.

Anita showed us into the living room. "We like things homey," she said.

The walls were painted yellow like the outside of the house, and the furniture was an easy-care plaid. But what caught my eye most was a TV as big as our stove with a PlayStation hooked to it, and shelves of video games for it.

"You know how to play these games already?" Rory asked Jeb. Jeb didn't answer.

"He doesn't talk much yet," Anita said. I worried that something might be wrong with Jeb, maybe a hearing problem. "All clear," I heard. I checked his throat for enlarged tonsils, but everything seemed fine.

"If Jeb could tell you the truth," Anita said, "he'd say those games belong to his father. Fred doesn't like anyone else even touching them unless he's around."

"Speaking of the devil, where is Fred?" Rory asked.

"He's working upstairs. Your visit is probably the only thing that would get him away from his computer. For a lot of reasons, I'm so glad you decided to come." She cupped her hand to the side of her mouth. "Fred, they're here," she called up the staircase.

"Great, send them up," Fred shouted. "I have to show them my office."

Rory, still holding on to Jeb, went up in front of me, counting each step out loud as he climbed. "Careful of the pictures," I told Rory. The staircase wall was filled with framed photos of Fred, Anita, and Jeb, surrounded by other smiling faces. I sensed beating hearts, open hands, and full pockets. *Most of their relatives are alive and very generous to them,* I thought.

Fred's office was huge. He must have taken over the master bedroom. There was a desk with a state-of-the-art computer, a color printer, and, in the middle of the room, a big table stacked high with sports magazines and papers. "Sorry. Just have to finish off the sentence," Fred said without looking up. His blond hair was mussed, as if he had been tugging his fingers through it to help his brain produce ideas.

We waited. He pecked rapidly at the keyboard with only his index fingers, but minutes passed. The sentence Fred was typing had to be a record-breaking run-on. Rory shifted from one leg to another. I didn't know where to put myself either. Only Jeb seemed comfortable with the silence.

Finally, Fred got up from his chair. "Hey, boss. Hey, Mrs. K.," he said, grinning. He held a thick manuscript out to us. "Read a few lines," he said. "You'll love it. It's a real heartbreaker."

Rory was holding Jeb, so I took it, and read out loud:

## TOUCHDOWN
### By Fredrick A. Hurlburt

Bob Smith was seventeen as he sat on the sidelines, his knee still throbbing from the wrench during the last game. He tried to get up, but it hurt so bad. "Oh, no!" he ejaculated, but his coach, Coach Reardon of Saint Francis High School in Tucka-hoe, New York, clapped him energetically on the shoulder pad.

"You can do it, Bobby boy. You have to," the coach cried convincingly.

Bob Smith's father was a cop, so Bob didn't like somebody shoving him and hollering in his face, but Coach Reardon just looked in Bob's eyes and waited.

"I'll do it, sir," Bobby said earnestly and respectfully. "For you, for the team, and for Saint Francis."

"Atta boy," Coach Reardon exclaimed happily, giving him one more clap.

I pressed my lips together to keep my expression neutral. "An autobiographical novel?" I asked.

He threw out his chest. "No, it's about me," he said. "And I like the way it sounded when you read it out loud. Could you read some more?"

It was at least five hundred pages. My wrist hurt from the weight of it. "I have a sore throat," I said.

Rory shifted Jeb to one arm, took the manuscript from me, and handed it back to Fred. "Why don't we all go downstairs and get some water?" he suggested.

I squeezed Rory's arm.

"I just wanted my boss to see my real work," Fred said.

Rory clapped him on the back like he was Coach Reardon. "Good for you," Rory said. "Every man should have a hobby."

"This is more than a hobby to me," Fred said. "Writing is my life. My book is never out of my mind."

*That explains his daydreaming at Mirror,* I thought.

Anita came into the room and took the manuscript from Fred's hands. "He reads it to me every night," she said, clutching it to her chest, her hazel eyes lighting up with pride. "The way Fred goes at his writing, I'm sure he'll make it big someday." After she set the manuscript down gently on the table, she flung her arm around Fred and leaned her head against his shoulder. "I'm behind him all the way."

When someone was going to make a literary splash, I saw stacks of books with their names on them on a table at Barnes & Noble. I didn't see that for Fred. I wished I could tell him that he should give up the writing—and Mirror Pharmacy—that he should go out and look for a better paying job. I couldn't help but feel sorry for Anita, who kept expecting her husband to be a big success as a writer.

"Let's have something to eat now," Anita said.

The appliances in the kitchen were the avocado color my mother's were before she remodeled. There was a plaque hanging next to the window:

> No matter where I serve my guests
> It seems they like my kitchen best.

"I hope you don't mind," Anita said as she set out a tuna and potato chip casserole and a bowl of canned peas and carrots. "We're very informal."

"This is perfection," I said, and to me it was.

At our first Great Neck dinner party at Hattie Corrigan's— Hattie, with her Texas-size diamond and her blond hair permed like a sculpture—I had been unnerved by her cloth napkins that were pleated to stand up like fans in the crystal stemware. I was afraid I'd scratch the gold rims of her china as I cut my beef Wellington. During dinner, Kirk Corrigan opened the bottle of wine I'd brought. It cost me twenty dollars and change, a lot of money nineteen years ago. Kirk took the first pour. When he tasted it, he wrinkled his nose. "Too woody," he said.

"We'll use it for cooking," Hattie added.

Rory kept Jeb on his lap while he ate.

"You should relax and enjoy your meal," Anita told Rory. "I'll take him."

"No," Rory said, tucking a napkin under Jeb's chin. "This feels like old times. I didn't have one clean pair of pants until Cara was too old to sit on my lap."

"Once Cara put her lamb chop in Rory's shirt pocket," I said, laughing.

Fred looked at me. "Rory told me your father was from Russia," he said. "We get a lot of Russian customers. I bought a Russian-English dictionary so I can talk to them. Not talk, really, but point out words and have them point out answers. I'm trying to become more fluent to make them comfortable. I've learned how to count to twenty and to say, *pahzhahlslah,* that's 'please,' *spahssee-bah,* 'thank you,' *Kahk vi seabya chavstuete?* is 'how do you feel?' and the one I use most, *shokreeh pohprahvlahtehs,* 'get well soon.'"

"It's nice of you to make the effort," I said, warming toward him. My father only spoke Yiddish, but he'd often told me that whenever an American even tried to understand him, his heart sang. The thought of my father's face lighting up in gratitude made me heady.

After dinner, I offered to help Anita clean up. "The best help would be if you played with Jeb while Rory and I played a game on the PlayStation," Fred said.

I looked at the dirty pots and dishes.

"Fred's right," Anita insisted. "Just enjoy Jeb."

I held my hand out, and Jeb took it, and we went into the living room, while Rory and Fred parked themselves in front of the giant TV screen. They whooped it up like boys, while Jeb sat in my lap, calm and silent as Buddha. His hair had the honeyed scent of Johnson's Baby Shampoo. I felt suddenly choked up. *"Farklempt,"* Bubbie would say. I remembered how much I'd wanted a baby before Cara was born, but I couldn't get pregnant. I wished I'd had a "loaf in the oven" as my mother had suspected when Rory and I eloped. Every day, I took my basal temperature as my gynecologist had suggested. I followed Bubbie's remedies, too. I sprinkled blood drained from a koshered cow in my backyard. I made a silk pouch and crushed eggshells in it, then sewed it to the belt of my old cotton bathrobe, and wore the pouch tied to my stomach. I bathed in buttermilk and put sprigs of jewelweed in my bra right at the cleavage, but nothing worked. I felt like calling up to the ethers: "Bubbie, will I ever have a baby?" but I knew that if the answer were no, I'd upset Bubbie as badly as myself. I had to find a disinterested psychic.

*Free Soul,* a New Age newspaper that I advertised in, had arrived in my mailbox that very morning. Besides my ad, there were three whole pages of psychics looking for business. Right away, I eliminated all the male psychics. I was afraid if I told a man how much I wanted to be pregnant, he'd offer to impregnate me. One ad was by a woman named Via. The headline said, READINGS VIA SCENT. I read the body of the ad. You could either go to her house to be sniffed in person, or send her unwashed underwear. Another woman, Aliyana, claimed her psychic information was beamed to her by aliens. I chose Isabel, a phone psychic. "In business over forty years," her ad had said. She would be wise.

*"Hola,"* Isabel had said. As soon as I heard her voice, I felt an instant connection, as if she were Bubbie, only Spanish. She told me we could do the reading right away, that she'd trust me to send her a money order. She said, "You are a person who can be trusted."

"Why can't I get pregnant?" I immediately asked her.

"You are pregnant," she said.

"I am?" I started to laugh and cry. "I really am?" Even as I wept with happiness, an image of Isabel began to form in my mind. "Is your hair in pink foam curlers?" I asked.

Isabel laughed. "You see me?"

"You're wearing a flowered housecoat."

"I do readings over the phone, so I don't have to bother getting dressed."

"Do you wear glasses with little rhinestones on the frames?"

*"Escúchame,* I didn't call you for a reading. You called me. Remember?"

"I'm a psychic, too," I told her.

"Everyone who calls here spends an hour telling me how psychic they are, but you, *querida,* hold the stars in your hands."

"Oh, that's what my Bubbie saw in my palm—a star." I had tears in my throat.

"I can already see that your little girl will be a beauty," Isabel said. "When she's born, look to see if she has the caul over her head, the hooded membrane. That's one of the signs of our gift. *Buena suerta.* Good luck if she does have the gift, and good luck if she doesn't."

I didn't know what she meant. I was so excited to tell Rory the good news that I didn't ask.

"Mim, this is great!" Rory whooped. "I hope the baby will have your eyes. And your gift."

"Oh, Rory," I'd told him, "knowing other people's future is no bed of roses."

My attention was caught by the ruckus Fred and Rory were making. "Pushover," I heard Fred say, laughing, knocking his shoulder into Rory's.

"So, you won a game," Rory said, laughing just as hard. "Don't think you're so hot," he added as if he and Fred were siblings and Rory was enjoying his childhood for the first time. "If I had these games at home to practice on, you wouldn't have won."

"Whether you had these games or not wouldn't have mattered," Fred boasted. "I'm on a winning streak, I tell you."

I thought about how even though Fred had a modest house and income, he was full of enthusiasm for his life, whereas Rory and I were dragging through our weeks. I suddenly realized I was jealous of Fred and Anita. What was the secret of their happiness? I touched Jeb's soft hair. Maybe I had been wrong about Fred.

I closed my eyes and tried to imagine Rory and Fred at the pharmacy ten years from now. I wanted to see if Fred would still be employed there. Instead, I got a vision of Fred dressed up as a Santa Claus with a sack slung over his shoulder. Fred really was like Santa Claus with his hearty laugh, trying to help all those Russians with his dictionary.

During our drive back to Great Neck, Rory asked, "So, what do you think of Fred now?"

"He has a good side," I admitted. "I can see why you like him."

Rory rubbed my arm and smiled. He whistled as he drove home.

# 5

ON THE MORNING OF the fourteenth anniversary of my mother's death, I sat in Cara's room, in the rocking chair where my mother used to hold her. I folded my arms around myself and rocked back and forth. "When somebody dies," Bubbie had said, "you got to cover all mirrors in the house for the seven days of Shiva. After that, when you take the sheets off, if you're looking for the person's spirit, the mirror is a good place to look."

All morning I wandered the house, my eyes darting at mirrors and reflective surfaces, hoping for a glimpse of my mother wearing her Persian lamb coat with the padded shoulders and her big-brimmed hat with a bird of paradise on the front. She had never gotten to be an actress, but she dressed like one every day. She smoked the Gauloises her cousin introduced her to after serving in France in World War II. She dabbed Evening in Paris cologne on her neck and wrists. For fourteen years, I'd waited for that scent to signal her presence.

Now I sniffed the air, but instead of Evening in Paris, I smelled my father's Old Spice. I looked out of the right corners of my eyes. My father was standing in Cara's doorway, wearing his dark blue zip-up jacket and his gray hat as if he had just come home from work. I stood very still. He took off his hat, smiled at me.

"Daddy, where's Mom?" I asked out loud, but he faded off.

I thought of all the spirits who had contacted me. George Washington had once walked up to me in my bathroom, his cheeks hollowed, holding his wooden false teeth in his hand. "Go to the dentist," he'd told me. When I went, I learned of an infection on the roots of my right molar. Alice B. Toklas had once sat in a spindle-backed chair in my kitchen and offered me a hash brownie. She had wanted me to relax. Sometimes the former owner of my house, Mr. Tegman, walked around and around my rooms. He had Alzheimer's disease and he kept calling me Hilda. Emily Dickinson wrote a poem at my desk, though the page was blank when I looked at it. Even animals had visited. The spirit of Chouchou, my client Cynthia's beloved standard poodle, showed up in my living room, barking at me, but I never figured out why. All these spirits, but my own mother's spirit had never darkened my door.

And why, I thought, should my mother appear to me? Not only had she tried to squelch my gift all her life, but at her life's end, my gift hadn't done her a lick of good. I hadn't even realized she was sick. It was Rory who had said, "Mim, I'm worried. Your mom is getting too thin."

"Oh, you know how vain Mom is," I told him. "Always dieting. Black coffee for breakfast and lunch, salad and a can of tuna for dinner. Besides, my father's only been dead less than a year. She's still in shock."

Rory shook his head. "I'm telling you, Mim, you better take her to the doctor."

It took me weeks to talk her into an appointment. She sat in Dr. Zucker's waiting room, knitting a sweater for Cara, her index finger with the wool wrapped around it wagging at me. The only time her lips moved was when she counted stitches. After her examination, Dr. Zucker let me come into the consultation room. His brow was creased. "I hope it's nothing, but I'm sending your mother for further tests to make sure."

"I thought I would be famous before I died," was all my mother said.

She moved in with us, and I took her for her chemo treatments, held her hand when she couldn't hold food down. "Cancer is the best diet going," she said. At the dinner table each night, she said, "The only thing that really helps me is looking at *my* Cara."

I tied a bright silk scarf over her bald head that made her green eyes appear even more lustrous. "You look as beautiful as ever," I told her.

But when she looked at herself in the mirror, she moaned, "Oh, my God. I look like a babushka lady!"

Within a month, she lay dying. I slept in a lounge chair next to her bed, watching over her. I longed for her to tell me that I was a good daughter, that she loved me. I wanted to ask my mother, "Ma, do you blame me for not seeing what was happening to you sooner?"

One night, she grabbed my arm and pulled me toward her. My eyes filled. I thought the moment of her telling me that she was proud of me had come. "Being a psychic is slob work," she whispered hoarsely. "It can make you crazy, and you get paid in chicken feet." They were her last words to me. By morning, she was dead.

Now, I went up to my office. I looked in the small mirror I kept on my shelf, searching for a wisp of my mother, but I only saw my own face. When the phone rang, I knew it was a scheduled call from a new client, Laura Pierce. "Hello?" I said. I heard Laura breathing, but she didn't answer. "Hello?" I repeated.

"I'm sorry," she finally said. "I've never had a reading before. I feel like a fool."

People often said this, as if contacting a psychic lowered their

IQ by twenty points. I was glad for the pause—I hadn't been able to get any psychic information on her in advance. When she had first phoned for the appointment, she had cupped the receiver, whispered so low, I couldn't get any vibrations.

"I . . . I want to know about someone," she said now.

I saw darkness, a tombstone. She wanted me to contact someone who had died. I closed my eyes. I shook inside from nerves. I always had NCT—new client tremens—but this was worse. It tripled when I was expected to be a medium—to contact loved ones who had died and report their messages back to the living. It was a far cry from reading a client directly—when I was able to see jumpy clips of the past, present, and future like a film reel.

I glanced at the clock. Three minutes had passed. I could feel my client's impatience. Then her disappointment. Clients didn't expect these pauses. I heard her breathe.

Then I saw a vision. A woman walking on the shoulder of a black tarry road. I felt a flood of relief at the information, but then I saw a truck speeding around a curve, and my heart sank. A small dashboard-type Madonna appeared. Probably the woman on the road had been Laura's mother, but sometimes strangers' spirits showed up by mistake.

"Did your mother have blond hair?" I asked.

"How do you know that? Do you see her? Where is she?"

"She was in an accident," I said. "A truck hit her." I tried to keep my voice steady, but it was hard. I had heard the thud of impact.

Laura began to cry. "I saw it all. The car broke down. My mother went for help. I could have gone. I was eighteen, but she insisted I stay in the car with the door locked."

"It wasn't your fault," I said softly. "I would have wanted my daughter to stay in the car, too."

"I know, I know," she sobbed. "I have two daughters myself now, and they are always complaining that I overprotect them. But what's killing me is even though I keep pictures of my mother all around me, all I can remember is her walking down the road and that truck coming."

Sometimes, as a medium, images were so emotionally potent it was as if I were channeling the client's grief, anxiety, even their hope. I had to swallow hard before I could speak.

Now I had a vision of Laura's mother in a kitchen. There were children wearing paper hats at a table set with party favors. She set a birthday cake on the table. "Is your birthday soon?" I asked my client.

"Today."

"Good. Birthdays and anniversaries are a great day for making contact," I said, not mentioning I'd spent years trying on my own birthday without luck. "I see your mother is in the kitchen and she's signaling to me to wish you a happy birthday." I zoomed in on her apron. "She's wearing an apron with a butterfly on it."

"That's hers. I still have it." I heard her relief. As I waited for her to compose herself, the image of her mother faded, then was gone. Before she hung up, Laura said, "Miriam, thank you so much. Knowing my mother is all right and that she's around me makes me feel as if my lungs can take in more air. I feel such a peace."

After Laura said good-bye, I could still see the glow around her. I sat with my head in my hands and rubbed my temples.

The contact made me yearn for my own mother. I had to get some message, some sign. I had hated my mother smoking, but now I even yearned to see her purse her lips around the end of her long black cigarette holder, then light her Gauloise with her green marbleized combination lighter. As a child, I was fascinated that a lighter could have a pencil at the other end of it. I wished my mother were still alive so I could see her doodle my squiggle-haired portrait with it. I wish I could see her kneel at her rose-bushes again to mulch them with coffee grounds. I wished her Singer sewing machine were humming in her bedroom instead of silent in our basement, that I could watch her delicate hands guiding the fabric, the front sole of her high-heeled shoe on the drive pedal. The last thing she had sewn at that machine was a blue frilly dress for Cara's third birthday, but she never did get to finish it.

Tears rolled down my face. Whenever I cried, my mother used to say, "Honeybunch, don't cry or you'll lose your dimple."

I wanted to hear her say it now. I felt my psychic energy flowing through me with great force.

I lit my blue serenity candle, put on my "Om" CD, and sat back down in my swivel chair. Closing my eyes again, I chanted along. I tapped my forehead at my third eye and tried to coax my mother's spirit to come to me by remembering when she thought I was a good girl, when I had pleased her. "Mom," I said, "remember when I bought you those black stockings when no one else was wearing them yet because I thought they would last longer? And you loved them because they were sexy and you wore them even though the neighbors were gawking and pointing."

I waited. My mother didn't appear.

I thought about her Evening in Paris. Her Helena Rubenstein lipstick. The beauty spot she penciled on her cheek.

I waited for her for an hour. It was almost as if I'd convinced myself that we had a date. Just when I was about to give up, I felt a prickly sensation that spread over the whole right side of my head and shoulder, too. "Mom?" I said. I looked out of the corner of my eye, hoping that I'd see her. Instead, I saw my next-door neighbor, Iris Gruber, peering at me through her second-story bedroom window, her German shepherd, Baron, next to her, his paws on the sill.

I remembered my mother's advice when Rory and I were moving to Great Neck. "Now that you're moving to a classy neighborhood," she commented, "if you tell people that you even *think* you're psychic, they'll worry that you'll know they bought their little Dior number in Filene's or that they pilfer from dollar stores or they pee in the country club pool. They won't want a thing to do with you, so bite your tongue."

Shortly after we'd moved into our house, Iris and Dick Gruber had rung our doorbell to introduce themselves. They were both wearing gold-framed designer eyeglasses and beige slacks, and I could have sworn they both colored their hair with Clairol Ash Brown, but they had nice smiles. Iris held out something long and covered with foil. "It's my special jelly roll," she explained. "I bake it for all the new neighbors."

"Come right in and have some with us," Rory said.

"Oh, sorry, we're going to play golf now," she said.

"Besides, it's too high in cholesterol for us," Dick added.

After they left, Rory and I devoured the entire jelly roll. I was on a sugar high. Then I scrubbed clean the scalloped board on which she'd presented it.

The next day, I rang Iris's doorbell. "Thank you," I said, returning the fancy board. "It was delicious."

She took the jelly roll board and ran her hand along it. "It's ruined," she said. "What did you do to it?"

"I washed it with Brillo."

Her eyes narrowed. "You're just supposed to rinse it," she said, her voice high pitched. "Didn't you know that?"

Tears actually sprang to my eyes. I tried to think of some way of getting back into her good graces. There was a mezuzah on the doorpost. "I'm not much of a *balehbosteh*," I said. It was a Yiddish word for a knowledgeable housewife.

Instead of smiling, she said, "What are you, then?"

"I'm a psychic," I blurted out. I didn't know where it came from; I'd promised myself that I'd heed my mother's warnings.

Iris blinked at me. "You're a what?"

The air between us crackled. Feeling as if I were facing down my mother, I drew myself up. "I'm a psychic," I said in a stronger voice.

"That's what I thought you said," Iris answered, shaking her head. "The last thing I need is to live next to a psychic. I hope you haven't mentioned this to anyone else." Without waiting for me to answer, she closed the door firmly.

I trudged back to my house. *You don't have to be friends with your neighbors,* I tried to assure myself. Maybe when Iris thought about it, she'd calm down. Maybe she'd even come over and apologize. And in any case, my clients always came around to the back door. Iris probably wouldn't even see them.

Two days later, when a client came into my office, I saw her aura waver like a candle in the wind. It made me nervous; I couldn't concentrate. I waited a few moments, but still nothing came. "Okay, what happened?" I finally asked.

"The woman next door was spying on me through her window," my client said. "I didn't think anything of it until she came out of her house to watch me walk up your driveway. I feel as if her eyes are still on my back," she added, shivering.

I was unsettled, but I figured that this was a one-time-only event. But it happened more and more. I tried to get some privacy by letting the hedges between our houses grow. In response, Iris ordered her gardener to cut them down to nubs. When we complained, Dick's lawyer informed us the hedges were on the Gruber's property line. Rory and I would have had to give up a foot of our driveway to grow our own bushes. Clients who continued coming waited in their cars until the exact moment of their appointment because I had no waiting room and no one to let them in while I was doing the previous reading. If Iris saw anyone waiting outside for me, she phoned the police to tell them there was a suspicious character in a car idling near her driveway. When the police stopped responding, she'd sic Baron on my clients' cars. Though he was more bark than bite, some clients stopped coming; others came in shaking; but try as she might, Iris couldn't scare them all off.

But one day, I was mulching the flowers on the side of the house when I felt prickles on my back. I turned my head, and Iris was looking down at me through her gold-framed glasses, her hands on her narrow hips.

"I've had enough of this!" she screamed. "Anyone who goes to a psychic is crazy. You're bringing a steady stream of lunatics to this block. I'm going to all the neighbors to start a petition to run you out of this town."

This was my worst nightmare. All of Great Neck would know. Cara wasn't born yet, so I didn't have to worry about her going into hiding. But Rory, already in disgrace on the block for leaving his dilapidated car out "on display" in the driveway and for mowing the lawn himself instead of hiring a gardener, would be branded with a scarlet *P* for being the husband of a psychic.

"But Iris . . . ," I said to her retreating figure, and then I heard her door slam.

Slowly, I got up, dusted the dirt off my hands, went inside, and lay on my bed to recover. When I closed my eyes, I got an image of Isabel, the phone psychic, in her bathrobe and pink curlers. Suddenly, a pink lightbulb lit up in my head. I didn't have to have clients come to the house—I could be a phone psychic like Isabel. My problems would all be solved.

# 6

"MOM, I'M HOME," Cara shouted upstairs. "The Key Club was cancelled."

The Key Club was supposed to provide ushers and the concession stand workers at school plays. "Kids don't need ushers," Cara had complained last week. "They sit wherever they want. All we do is copy posters . . . like they've never heard of color Xerox."

But ever driven, Cara took on as many extracurricular activities as possible for her college applications. Including the Key Club.

Lately my efforts to engage Cara had met with stony silence. I found that the older she got, the more she'd push me away. I couldn't tell if it was general adolescence or something worse. Before she went off to college, I wanted as much time with her as possible. No way did I want her to ever question my love for her.

Downstairs, Cara and her two best friends, Darcy and Courtney, were in the hallway, throwing down their backpacks. "Oh, Mrs. Kaminsky," Darcy said, flipping back her long blond hair. I noticed the new streaks she'd put in and how she looked more and more like her mother, Barbara Traubman. In stark contrast, the ends of Courtney's brown hair were bright red, and her turquoise contacts made her look like an alien. Her mother had been a *Vogue* model. "Hey," Courtney greeted me. When they had turned sixteen, Courtney had gotten a nose job, and Darcy had gotten her underchin liposuctioned. Only Cara didn't have a weekly manicure and pedicure. Now the three girls wore black shirts as if they were mourning their girlhood.

"How's the consulting going?" Darcy asked me. Cara shot me a look and then looked down at if she were examining her shoes.

"Fine," I said brightly. All Cara's friends thought that I was a "personal consultant." Still, Cara rarely brought them to our house, and they never bothered to ask me what "personal consultant" meant. "My mom just likes to talk," Cara said to them once. I let it go.

"Come on," Cara said now. "Let's go to the den." She began shooing them away from me as she always did. Not only did she not want them to find out about me; she didn't want me to find anything out about them either.

"My mom sends her regards," Darcy said. Barbara Traubman was a speech therapist in the Great Neck schools. She used her position to learn and spread gossip about the students, the staff, and all their families. If Barbara hadn't found out I was psychic by now, Cara's secret was safe.

"My best to her, too," I said.

Courtney and Darcy were smiling, but I couldn't help notice how dim their auras were and how much sadness they were bearing. Suddenly, to the right of Darcy, I saw an image of her crying, "I'm so fat," as she looked into the mirror. The vision blinked on and off, meaning that this happened every day. I got another image that made me gasp—a toilet plunger! Darcy was purging herself! And above Courtney's head hovered a wedding ring split in half. She was terrified that her parents would get a divorce. *DTs,* Cara called it, divorce trauma.

I felt helpless about their big problems, but I wished I could give the girls some comfort by telling them, come June, I saw Courtney in her prom dress on the arm of Justin Portnoy, the captain of the football team. And I would have loved to tell Darcy that she was going to be the homecoming queen. But if I did, I knew Cara would never forgive me.

"I'll fix you girls a snack," was all I said, retreating to the kitchen.

I took the soy pizza out of the freezer. I could hear Cara laughing from the other room. All these years, she still had the same hiccupy laugh she'd had as a baby. I sighed and turned on the oven. Then I suddenly became aware of Courtney's aura, red-tipped like her hair, but with panic. Poor girl, to be living with the stress of impending divorce. I overheard Cara say, "Courtney, remember you have Darcy and me. You won't be alone. We'll always stand by you."

Every so often I saw the woman Cara would become, and I was proud of her compassion. I tried not to dwell on the fact that she just didn't have any compassion for *me* right now.

When Cara was six, she'd asked me, "Mommy, how do you know things about people if they don't tell you?"

"Plain old intuition," I'd said, trying to downplay it. "Everyone has it."

"Do I?"

"Of course you do, sweetie."

Cara brushed the ends of one of her long pigtails across her chin. "But how did you know that the lady on the phone this morning had an earache in her right ear?"

I hesitated. I'd waited for this moment, worried how to handle it. I never thought it would come so soon—but Cara was perceptive. I found myself panicked. *What if she goes around telling people? Will I be run out of town by Iris Gruber?*

"I have ways," I finally said, fluffing her quilt.

"Like what?" she asked.

I sat down on her bed and sighed. "Like I see colored lights around people that show me how they're feeling." I picked up her sixty-four-color Crayola box and pulled out the pink, red, yellow, blue, green, and violet. "If you know what those colors stand for, even before someone says, 'Hi, Cara,' you can tell a lot about them, what they're feeling or even what they might do."

"So, what do the colors stand for?" she asked.

"Well, for instance, Bubbie said that pink stands for love and blue for sadness."

"Besides crayons, what else did Bubbie say?"

I looked at my daughter, who was genuinely curious, innocent. I knew I had to tell her the truth. "Bubbie said that there are always shadows of people passing by who used to live on earth, and they tell you things, too," I told Cara. "But this has to be our little secret."

"Our secret?" she said, delighted. "Just you and me?"

"That's right."

"I won't tell anyone," she promised, and locked her lips and threw away the key. She had kept that promise, and today there was no chance she'd renege.

I checked on the pizza. I felt as if warming rays were coming from my own body. Cara stepped into the kitchen, frowning.

She opened the oven, sniffed, and took the pizza out with a potholder.

"Darcy doesn't think she has a good figure," I said quietly. "Maybe you could give her a compliment."

She narrowed her eyes. "You think you know my best friends better than I do," she snapped. "Well, you don't."

The withering look she gave me was so similar to the looks my mother used to give me, I got goose bumps. "Okay," I said. "Okay."

She sniffed at the pizza again. "Soy?" she said. "Don't we have any normal stuff?" She pulled out a six-pack of Diet Cokes, then went back to her friends.

I hunted through the cabinets, found some chips and salsa, and brought them to the den. The girls were sprawled on the floor on the couch pillows, mesmerized by a soap opera. "That guy playing the singer is hot," Courtney said. "He looks like Ricky Martin."

"I heard Ricky Martin wears butt pads," Darcy said.

Cara leaned to the right, then left, knocking her shoulders against theirs. "Shut up," she said, laughing. "I want to hear what he's going to tell Selina."

I put the bowl of chips down on the coffee table and gingerly sat on the edge of Rory's lounge chair. The girls swiveled their necks and glanced at me, then turned right back to the TV. I was glad they didn't seem to mind my being there. I drank in their youthful exuberance. The singer told Selina, "I never met a girl like you. You're different. Like no one I ever met before." I stifled a yawn, but the girls were so rapt that they didn't even chew their chips. A commercial came on. A gadget turned an onion into a rose. Then a woman wearing a turban appeared on the screen. *Olivia's Psychic Hotline.* She wore beads and false eyelashes and one gold earring. She waved her hands over a crystal ball and said in a voice that went up and down like a trombone slide, "I know your future. I can see—"

"Let's see what's on channel five," Cara said, and grabbed the remote.

"No, leave it," Darcy insisted. "I love this junk."

"Me too," Courtney agreed. "What a joke! You know she's going to rip you off."

"They should call it the Psycho Hotline," Darcy said.

I watched Cara's aura wane, like a flickering candle.

"We give accurate information with a personal touch," Olivia claimed. "Try us and see. Call for your free question." A 900 number appeared at the bottom of the screen. "Only one question to a family. And no one under eighteen."

"Let's call her," Darcy yelled, knotting her blond hair back from her face.

"She won't give *you* a reading," Courtney said. "You sound like you're three."

Darcy, forgetting I was in the room, flipped her middle finger.

Courtney thrust the phone at Cara. "You do it. It's your house."

I wanted to stop them for Cara's sake, but I knew that anything I said would only make Cara resent me even more.

"I can't call," Cara gasped. "I'm having an asthma attack."

"I didn't know you have asthma," Courtney said. "I'll call the psychic. My voice is very sophisticated." She picked up the receiver and put the phone on speaker so they could all listen. I sat there, trying to be invisible. After several minutes of being on hold, a woman said, "Hello, I'm Sybil."

"I'm calling for the free question," Courtney said, then blew her bright red-tipped bangs off her forehead. "What college will I go to?"

"I see a big school," Sybil said. "It has a lot of green around it."

"But what's the name of the school?"

"Let me see," Sybil said. There was a long pause. "Your free minutes are up. If you'd like to continue, it's two dollars and fifty cents per minute."

"Forget that!" Courtney said, and hung up.

Darcy screeched with laughter, but Cara's face blazed.

"What a scam!" Courtney said.

I sucked in my breath, unintentionally loudly.

Cara glared at me over her shoulder. "You know, Mom, you don't have to stay here and baby-sit us anymore."

I stood in the kitchen, putting away dishes. For half an hour, I could still hear them talking. When the house was silent, I ventured back into the den.

"I couldn't help noticing how embarrassed you were," I said to Cara.

"Yeah, well look what kind of skeevy people promote themselves as psychics."

I looked at her long silky hair, her heart-shaped face. Bubbie would have said Cara was *shain vi di zibben velten,* beautiful as the seven worlds. "Oh, I wish you had known Bubbie," I said. "She was a great healer."

Cara let out her breath and rolled her eyes. "Ma, let's not go back to the Dark Ages, okay?"

That phrase brought a chill. "Dark Ages" was something my mother had said about Bubbie. Cara was only three when my mother had died. *Is my mother speaking through her?* I was shaken, but I said, "Did you know that major universities like Princeton and Duke have parapsychology departments these days?"

"Yeah, like Sybil the Psychic is a Yalie, and Olivia with the turban went to Radcliffe."

I watched Cara stalk from the room. The slam of her bedroom door reverberated through the house, making me feel so disheartened that I didn't know what to do with myself. I heard my office phone ring. Grateful for the distraction, I dashed up the stairs and answered it.

"Hello, this is Phyllis Kanner," a woman said in a fake breathy voice. "I've seen your ad for years. I guess it's finally time for me to book a reading. What's your time frame?" she asked. She had a high-voltage energy, the type I'd felt from CEOs. I wanted her to think I was busy. "Hmm, I'm booked for the next two months. Oh, wait," I said. "Yesterday I had a cancellation. If you'd like, I could do it now."

"Would I ever!"

As I took down her charge account number, I began to see her in my mind. "Is your hair blond, shoulder length, combed over to one side with little fringy bangs?"

"Yes. How did you do that?"

"If I get an immediate image, it's a good sign. I know I'll be able to read you."

Her features began to fill in one by one. I got a quick image of her putting in contacts. "You wear contacts," I said. Then I saw Chiclets. "And your front teeth are capped."

She gasped. "Do you have a video phone?"

I laughed. "No, then you'd see me, too."

"What else do you see about me?" she asked, delighted.

"You have freckles on your nose."

"But I've covered them with makeup."

"The psychic sees all," I said jokingly, but she didn't laugh. I could feel her concentrate, her aura becoming more intense as if someone had turned up her wattage.

"I'm seeing a four alongside an eight. Are you forty-eight?"

"You'll never get that out of me. Not my weight either."

As soon as she said "weight," I saw a shovel against a starry sky. She was a night eater. She was so easy to read, it was as if she had a slide show in her head that she was projecting to me. "Last night you licked the cream fillings out of a box of Oreos," I reported.

"I never expected such minutia," she said.

A limp noodle appeared in my mind, followed by a bottle of Gold's horseradish. "You're married to a much older man," I said, "and he's very bitter." Next I saw a long surge protector with room for ten plugs. She had had many affairs. "I'm glad you have so many outlets," I said discreetly.

"Let's not talk about my marriage anymore," she snapped. "Do you have a take on my career?"

I saw flashes of her talking on the phone. The same image kept coming up over and over. "You talk on the phone all the time. Are you a phone psychic, too?" I joked.

"I am on the phone all the time, but to promote New Age talent. I can help you get your name out there, too. I can get your face on every magazine. I can get you on radio. On TV."

As she waited for my response in silence, I could hear her nervous system firing off like caps in a toy gun. "No, thanks," I said. "That would be my worst nightmare."

She laughed. "Honey, people are lining up, begging me to work for them."

"I'll think about it," I lied.

Then she asked me about three psychics who were my

competition. I told her that they were very successful and would continue to be so. I asked her if she represented Olivia's Hotline.

"I'd never take on Olivia's Hotline!" she said. "I only represent the truly gifted. Do you know how lucky you are to have your gift? *Very* lucky. Now back to me. What do you see for my future?"

"I see you getting a bunch of even more successful clients."

"I have to make you one of them. What will it take to make you sign with me?"

I thought of Cara, disgraced in front of her friends. "I value my privacy," I said.

"Well, I guess a psychic can't tell what's good for her own future. Give me your address. I'll send you my business card should you have a change of heart."

I gave her my P.O. box.

"Oh, for heaven's sake," she said. "I'm not a killer. My clients adore me. They trust me with their children, their homes, and their darkest secrets, for God's sake. You can tell me where you live."

I felt myself wavering. *Don't do it,* I told myself, but I gave her my home address anyway.

After she had written it down, she said, "Think about it. You don't have to answer right now. Just imagine yourself with oodles of money, and you'll call me. I know it."

I found myself itching to get off the phone. Her voice was so breathy that I felt as if a giant vacuum cleaner were sucking me in.

Immediately I was upset about Cara again. I wondered if she ever remembered that when she was seven, just the age I had been when Bubbie began mentoring me, she'd declared, "I want to learn how to know what people think and what will happen to them. I want to have a special room and when I'm big, I want people to call me to ask for advice."

I'd swallowed hard. Cara hadn't been born with the caul, the membrane of afterbirth covering her head that Isabel had told me was a sign of another psychic coming into the world. And Cara's eyes were a deep brown. Though Isabel never mentioned it explicitly, Bubbie and I both had pale, nearly translucent blue eyes that I'd always thought were symbols of our gift. When I didn't find the star-shaped crease in Cara's palm, the twinge of sadness that she probably didn't have my gift was accompanied by a sort of relief.

"Cara, I'm so happy that you're normal," I'd said. "Do you know how beautiful that is? You're great the way you are. You're the lucky one. When people find out I'm psychic, they won't talk to me about anything else. It makes it so hard to have friends." She'd nodded like she understood. But the next day, I came home and found her leafing through a New Age catalog addressed to me. *Tools of the Psychic* it was called.

She looked up at me, her eyes shiny with excitement. "I want a Magic Eight Ball," she'd said, "and a set of those fortune-telling cards, and a Ouija board, and a book that shows you how to read palms."

I was shocked at how much thought she'd already put into it. I knew that those parlor games and kids' tricks wouldn't help, but she was so hopeful, so revved up, I couldn't tell her no. "Well," I said slowly, "if you really want those things, save up your allowance, and I'll order them for you."

"Okay," she said, "but I don't want to wait"—she counted on her fingers—"thirty-seven weeks. Give me some chores to do."

I'd seen her this determined before. At four, when she wanted her first Barbie—a doll I didn't approve of—she not only picked up her socks and toys from her floor for two weeks, but she also dusted all the living room furniture she could reach and even tried to rake the whole yard. Now I figured she'd work herself to the bone to get the psychic paraphernalia. "I'll order them, and you can pay me back whenever you can." I sighed.

With dread, I ordered from the catalog.

When her friends visited, she stashed everything in the back of her closet. Otherwise, they were out all the time. But she never asked for my help.

One afternoon, I found her sitting at her desk, her hands poised on the stylus of the Ouija board. "Will I be invited to Andrea's birthday?" I heard her ask as she steered it toward YES. "Yes!" she cheered. Andrea had already told her that she'd be getting an invitation.

Next, she turned her attention to the tarot deck. The directions in the manual were so complicated, I could see she was getting upset.

"You know," I suggested gently, "you can just pull three cards to see what the day will bring."

The first card she picked showed a dejected figure walking away from eight cups on the ground. Dashed hopes, I thought. The way Cara grimaced, I could tell that she knew the meaning, too. "I'll pick another card," she said. It was the Tower—lightning, fire, smoke, people jumping out windows. Her hand shook.

"Let's put the cards away for now," I said.

"I'll start over," she insisted. "My question is, What will Mommy and Daddy give me for my birthday?"

Instead of picking cards at random, she went through the deck and chose the three that she wanted, cheating the way my mother used to at solitaire.

"Here's the Wheel of Fortune, so we're driving somewhere," Cara said. "And it's next to the Star, so that means we're going to a Broadway show. And right here is the Sun. 'The sun will come out tomorrow,'" she sang. "That means we're going to see *Annie*."

My legs felt as if they were going to buckle. Just yesterday, when she was at school, I'd ordered tickets for *Annie* by TeleCharge. There was no way she could have known. I called Rory. "Oh, God, I was wrong. Cara really is psychic." My throat filled with tears as I told him about her tarot reading.

"Mim, last night she was egging me on about her birthday surprise, and I told her it rhymed with *fanny*. Cara's just enjoying herself." He laughed. "Let her be."

When she was almost nine, Cara stopped asking the questions

whose answers she already knew and became frustrated that none of her predictions came to pass.

"Teach me how to be psychic," she pleaded.

On the one hand, I didn't think my teaching her would yield any better results. On the other hand, I was too scared if it did produce results, the gift would take over her whole life as it had mine. But Cara wouldn't let go; she spoke to me of nothing else.

What kind of future would she have if she did succeed in being like me? In high school, I was humiliated in an Improvisation class. I said to Alex, a scene partner with whom my character was supposed to be in love, "I'm glad Colleen dumped you last night. Now you know how I feel."

His jaw dropped, and his face got all red. "Hey, how do you know about that?"

No one could have been more surprised than me—I was just improvising. A few more incidents like that, and no one wanted to do skits with me anymore. They started calling me Voodoo Girl. I dropped out.

Being psychic even interfered with my getting good grades. I was sitting in bed reading *Death Comes to the Archbishop* for English, and Bubbie appeared to me. "Read Sholem Aleichem instead," she insisted, so I did. My English teacher called my mother and me in for a meeting. "Miriam's smart," he said. "She just follows the beat of her own drum."

My mother glared at me. "I should drum up the money to send myself to college instead of you," she'd snapped.

One rainy day, Cara wore me down. I lit a candle in the kitchen and placed a chair for her in front of it as Bubbie had once done for me. "Stare at the glow around the flame," I said. "We're training ourselves to see auras." There was no stopping now. I watched Cara stare at the flame, light pooling on her face as if she were a figure in a Georges de La Tour painting. "Now stare over here," I coaxed, placing my finger at a point just above me and to the right of my head. "Soon you'll begin to see the light around me."

Cara concentrated very hard. She stared and licked her lips. Finally, she burst into tears. "I can't see it," she sobbed.

I stroked her hair, trying frantically to think of how to solve the situation. "I know," I said brightly. "Bubbie taught me that sometimes it's easier to make things disappear than appear. Once, when I was visiting her, she held up the board we used to roll out cookie dough on together and told me to stare at it and chant the Yiddish word for water: *'Vasser, vasser, vasser.'* She told me it would make the board ripple like water and that after a while, I wouldn't see it at all. I said *vasser* so many times that my throat got dry as dust, but finally that board rippled and then all the edges were gone and soon it disappeared altogether. Maybe we should start that way."

"Yeah, let's," Cara said, her voice high with hope.

I picked up my cutting board and held it out in front of Cara. "Stare at it and say, *'Vasser, vasser, vasser.'*"

But Cara, not having grown up with Yiddish, said, *"Wasser, wasser, wasser."* She stared for a full ten minutes, her voice getting hoarse. Then she turned to me, tears streaming down her face, her bottom lip quivering. "There's no ripple," she cried.

"Bubbie said it all takes patience and practice," I told her. "We'll practice again."

But Cara never wanted my help again. For a month, whenever I needed my cutting board, I had to fetch it from her room, which was the only reason I knew she was practicing.

Finally, late one afternoon, Cara slammed the board on the kitchen counter. "I can't make this stupid thing disappear!" She was trembling with fury.

"Then stop," I said. "It's a silly, idiotic trick. It doesn't mean anything. Who cares if the cutting board turns to water or not? How will that help the world?" I saw her soften, wanting to believe me. There was a cloud over her heart chakra, and I would have done anything to dispel it.

For two whole years, Cara didn't speak about psychic lessons.

But when she was eleven, she saw a flyer on a bulletin board in a supermarket:

## THE PSYCHIC CHILD

YOUR CHILD CAN BE TAUGHT
TO DEVELOP HIS PSYCHIC SKILLS
WITHIN HOURS

- Sharpen natural intuition
- Increase test scores

Once again she set her heart on learning. I saw that intense determination reappear on her face. How could it hurt if she went? I asked myself. I didn't really believe the classes could give someone a gift, but maybe it would make Cara feel better.

For two days, Cara hummed around the house. My cutting board disappeared into her room again and I heard her happily chanting, *"Vasser, vasser, vasser."* The phone rang. "It's Daddy, isn't it?" she said. I didn't have the heart to tell her that it was the dry cleaners asking when Rory was going to pick up his suit.

The first day of class, as we drove through Lynbrook, I noticed the teacher's block had nearly identical houses. Hers was distinguished by the zodiac banner hanging from a flagpole. She opened the door wearing a long earring and a dashiki.

"I'm Star," she said. We shook hands. "Please make the check out to Sandra Kornbluth."

She led us down a flight of steps into a finished basement. I followed and sat on an old couch. The basement was paneled with knotty pine. I felt as if thousands of brown eyes were staring at me. There were seven other kids besides Cara, but all much younger. The chairs looked as if they were from a kindergarten. I sat on a long leatherette couch with all the other mothers in a row.

Cara had dressed up for the class. Her hair was French braided, and she wore platform shoes and lip gloss. She kept her chair apart from the others. I thought perhaps she'd be too embarrassed to stay in a class with such little kids. But she was determined.

"We are going to use music to get ourselves into a very relaxed state that opens our minds," Star said in a singsong voice. She took a pitch pipe out of her pocket and played *do.* "Now I want you to sing the note 'do' with me," she instructed.

Cara tried to throw herself into it. She lifted her head and chanted loudly, "Do, do, do."

A freckle-faced boy shouted out—"Doo-doo!"—and the rest of the little ones burst into giggles.

"Well, I see you've had enough chanting," Star said. "Now I want you to close your eyes and imagine the color of your bedroom at home." Her voice became hypnotic. "Now picture your bed. Picture yourself getting into your bed. Feel your head on the soft pillow. If you have any cuddly animals, picture yourself hugging them as you go off to sleep."

The other kids were squirming, but Cara gave me one long look and a thumbs-up, then scrunched her eyes tightly shut.

"Now slowly open your eyes," Star said. She handed each of them a set of cards in primary colors. Then she held up a little red ball. "I've hidden a red ball just like this one in one of the mugs on that shelf," she said, pointing to them. I want each of you to close your eyes, imagine the red ball, and ask yourself which mug it's in—the red one, the blue one, the green one, or the yellow one. It should only take a moment to get your answer. As soon as you see the color of the mug in your mind, open your eyes, put that same color card on the top of your pile and don't show it to anyone else."

"Huh?" a little girl said.

Star demonstrated what she meant three more times before the children understood. "Now close your eyes again," she said. "Picture the red ball. Picture me putting the ball inside one of the mugs. See in your mind the color of the mug."

*Blue,* I thought, trying to beam it into Cara's mind.

A boy with a cowlick yawned. "I want to go home," he whined.

His mother shook her head at him. Star went on, unfazed. "Okay, open your eyes. Choose the card with the same color as the mug." She waited. Then she said, "Hold up your cards." Most of them held up the blue cards. Cara held up the green one.

Star picked up the green mug and turned it over. Nothing fell out. She turned over the blue mug. The red ball bounced out. A boy ran to catch it.

"Don't feel bad," Star said to Cara. "It was just your first try."

Being singled out only made it worse. Cara's cheeks flamed.

In the car, going home, she said, "Next class, wait in the car for me. I think you make me nervous."

When the second class was over, the other kids ran to their mothers, yelling "I'm psychic," but Cara's face was again grim.

Star put her arm around Cara. "Sometimes there's a calling," Star said in her most condescending tone, "and not everyone is called, but I'm sure you have other talents."

"Not everyone has the calling," I said in a polite voice, "but it's apparent to me that you'd better get to the doctor with your ulcer."

Star clutched the neckline of her dashiki. "Excuse me?" she said.

Holding my head high, I said, "I know what I know." As we drove away, I felt proud of myself for standing up to her until I saw Cara slumped next to me, her head hanging down.

"Don't let her upset you," I said. "She's just a housewife in a dashiki."

"How come you didn't say that right away?" Cara demanded.

I didn't know what to say. I'd thought she'd see it for herself or just tire of the class.

"So, you didn't know right off that Star wasn't any good?" Cara said.

I said nothing. I saw Cara refueling herself, perking herself up. "Maybe psychics are just guessers," she said.

I looked at her, the tiny glimmers of hope springing from her head. I would have done anything not to have her suffer. I put my hand on her shoulder. "Maybe you're right," I said.

When we got home, she opened the pantry door and took out a big black leaf-and-lawn bag. Then she went upstairs. I heard her opening drawers and banging them shut. An hour later, when I dragged that bag out to the curb with the rest of the garbage, the 8 Ball fell out. I read the words that had floated up. DEFINITELY NOT, it said.

"I'm going to find my own talent," Cara announced that evening at dinner. "Something real. I only believe in what can be counted and proved, in what everyone can see."

"Good for you, honey," I said.

"That's my girl," Rory chimed in, ruffling her hair.

From that moment on, Cara had nothing but disdain for psychics. She never listened to my stories about Bubbie anymore, and when I told her anything I'd found out psychically, she'd put her nose up in the air and say, "Says who?"

That's when she began to study hard, when she enrolled in all honors classes, when she joined every club and team.

"I've got to get into a top college so I can do something important in my life," she'd insisted. She'd had the Peterson's guide since freshman year. She highlighted passages. She'd sent away for brochures to the Ivy League schools herself and collected their banners. Her heart was set on Cornell.

"They have like a zillion courses to choose from," she'd said, "and I could ski a lot, too." By the time she was a sophomore, she wrote to the president of Cornell to ask if she could have an informational interview, and got it. She was always studying, even at the dinner table. She was probably going to get into a good college, but she no longer sang in the shower. She no longer belted out the song lyrics from the inserts in her CDs. Instead of singing for her own pleasure, she insisted I take her to a musical appreciation institute in Syosset to be tested and ranked on her singing. She no longer doodled in her notebooks, on napkins, or if nothing else was available, on the backs of her hands. Now she spent hours trying to copy reproductions of old masters. She'd end up in tears. Her wastepaper basket was always full. Though she joined the basketball, hockey, and lacrosse teams, she got depressed whenever she was benched. I could see the faint traces of Rory's worry line already etching into her young forehead.

The other night, I'd been finishing up a reading with a client, Rebecca, who had been trying to get me to psychically stalk her old boyfriend. "What's his new girlfriend's name?" she'd demanded.

I got a vision of a beach and then a big letter *Y* drawn into the sand. *Sandy,* I thought, but I wasn't going to tell Rebecca that. She'd already phoned every woman who worked in her boyfriend's office and accused them of stealing him away from her. "I don't have that information," I said.

"I'm psychic, too," she seethed. "I know you know her name. Well, if you won't tell me her name, at least answer this: Is Todd humping her right now?"

Just then I heard jingling up my office staircase. Cara was wearing her ankle bracelet with the bells she'd bought at a street fair. Worried that she'd burst in, I felt myself stiffen. This was a very delicate reading. Todd had taken out an order of protection against Rebecca when she'd climbed his fire escape to spy on him. I had to convince Rebecca that she must stop thinking about Todd and, for her, there was only one way to go about it. Then I sensed Cara's hand on the doorknob. "Not now," I called out to her.

"You mean Todd isn't humping this other woman now, but he will be in like an hour?" Rebecca gasped.

I blurted out what I should have led up to cautiously and gently: "Rebecca, you have to go to a psychiatrist and get medication so you can get your mind off Todd."

"So, are you trying to tell me I'm crazy?" Rebecca had shrieked, and hung up.

I sat there, stunned. It was 9:42 P.M. I'd worked straight through dinner. I sensed Cara still behind my door. I opened it. "Cara, I worked so late," I said. "I'm sorry. What did you want to tell me?"

"Nothing," she said sharply, and jingled back down the stairs.

I tried to phone Rebecca back to soothe her, but she didn't answer. Sighing, I went downstairs and found Cara conjugating verbs in the den. *"Je fais, tu fais, il fait, nous faisons, vous faites, ils font."*

She'd probably wanted me to help her study, but now she'd shut me out.

An hour later, at 11:00 P.M., Rory came home from work. I went over for my hello kiss.

*"Je serais, tu serais, il serait, nous serions, vous seriez, ils seraient,"* Cara was droning.

"Hi, Cara," he called to her. "How was your day?"

"Can't you see I'm concentrating?" she said angrily. *"Je sois, tu sois, il soit, nous soyons, vous soyez, ils soient."*

He joined her in the den. "Maybe you're working too hard," he said.

She put a bookmark in her *501 French Verbs.* "You're a fine one to talk," Cara told him. "You're always working, and Mom is always in her office with the door closed. I hardly even have parents."

I felt as if I'd been slapped. Rory's eyes watered.

"Cara, we'll figure it all out," Rory said. "We'll all have lots of time together. We're just a little pressed now."

*"Now?"* Cara said, managing to get in the last word by storming up to her room.

# 7

CARA STOPPED COMING up to my office, and I began to miss her interruptions. Every time I heard a creak on the floor, I'd sit up straighter, expectant. Every time I heard her footsteps on the stairs, my heart lightened, but then the steps would veer away, and I'd find myself folding inward again. She stopped wangling rides to school with me in the mornings. Instead, she dashed out the door to catch the bus with her dark hair still dripping. She left me notes instead of telling me where she was going after school and what time she'd be home from the library or a sports meet or a friend's house.

"Honey," I'd said to her that morning, "how long is this going to go on?"

"Nothing's going on," she said, sliding past me, her eyes down.

Now, at midnight, I lay in bed sleepless, trying to think of a way to get through to her. I was just thinking I could strap our bikes to the back of my Honda and we could drive to Flushing Meadow Park to ride around the old World's Fair grounds when I heard a noise in her room. I didn't have to be psychic to know she was laying out outfits on the bed and floor, anguishing over which she'd wear the next day. She'd made a code inventory calendar of all her clothes which she ticked off daily so she wouldn't wear the same outfit too often. She was methodical, like my mom, but Cara was driven by peer pressure, too. All her friends came from so much wealth. Besides having Christian Dior saddlebags hanging off their backs, they wore Chloë or Dolce & Gabbana jeans, and took myriad private lessons. Darcy, enrolled in swimming and gymnastics since she was walking, would unsurprisingly receive the athlete of the year award. And Courtney, who'd been given a tiny violin and a class in the Suzuki method when she was two and a half, was now playing the flute. Her mother drove her to Manhattan three times a week to study with a teacher who played in the Philharmonic. They were all in honor classes, all overachievers.

Every holiday, while her friends, already familiar with Europe, were touring the Third World, hiring Sherpas to carry their twelve-piece matching sets of luggage through the Nepalese mountains, Cara had to stay in Great Neck. Sometimes I found her leafing through travel brochures her friends had left for her "in case she changed her mind." Once I found her asleep at the computer and blinking on her screen was THE ALLURE OF PARIS.

"We live in New York, one of the greatest tourist spots in the world," I would tell her. "Let's go to Central Park or the MoMA." She'd just shake her head. "We can eat at the Hard Rock Cafe," I'd add, but she'd just slump in front of the TV or look longingly at exotic places in Rory's stack of *National Geographics*.

Cara, Rory, and I used to have so much fun together for hardly any cost. We'd spend weekends putting together huge puzzles on the kitchen table and then eat at rickety snack tables for weeks until we had the heart to dismantle them. On summer nights, we'd walk through Kings Point Park and listen to the chorus of crickets and birds. Maybe, I thought, if Rory had more time with us, Cara would feel better about herself again. But with our economic pressures, Rory would be spending more time at Mirror instead of less, and I wanted her to feel better right now. I got up and went to her door. A slant of light from under it lit the dark hallway. "Cara," I called softly.

She opened the door, surrounded by her outfits behind her on the bed and on the floor. She looked frazzled and upset, her hairbrush in her hand. Big dark circles were under her eyes, and her skin was sallow. "Are you all right, honey?" I asked.

She shrugged, then looked away from me. "I'm fine. I just have a knot in my hair."

I looked at my daughter and could tell that there were more knots inside of her than in her hair. "Let me try," I said. "I can get the knot out."

She hesitated, then plunked herself down on the chair in front of her vanity mirror and handed me her brush.

Gently, I tugged at the knot, pulling it carefully apart, strand by strand. Her shiny brown hair was thick, but the brush glided down from her crown to the ends at the middle of her back. I ran the brush through it over and over, her hair caressing my hand as much as my hand caressed her hair. Her shoulders relaxed, and then she sighed deeply. I could feel waves of peace go through her. In her hair, I could see strands of Rory's sandy color and glimmers of my red. "You used to sit on a phone book when your grandmother brushed your hair," I said, blinking away the tears that were starting to well up in my eyes.

"I kind of remember," Cara said. Our eyes met in the mirror. "I'm sorry, Mom. I don't believe in what you do, but I know you'd never cheat people like that Olivia on TV."

I kept brushing.


I fell easily into sleep that night. When I opened my eyes at 7:00 A.M., Rory's empty side of the bed made me anxious. He'd taken to leaving for Mirror at 4:30 A.M. The pharmacy didn't open until nine, but he needed those extra hours to do paperwork. I sighed. Maybe he'd collect this month's third-party payments after all, but in my mind, I saw turned-out pockets, one of my symbols for debt, and I knew that no matter how many hours he sat there trying to collect what was due him, we'd never catch up.

Our elm tree groaned. The tree surgeon had explained that the elm had a callus in its fork that rubbed together to produce that sound. It would be $250 to shave the callus down. I felt pasted to the bed by discouragement. Then I noticed a stain on the ceiling in the corner of my bedroom. It was shaped like a kidney, and looked fresh. The roof was leaking; a disaster, considering our stucco facade. Expensive emergencies always seemed to happen when you had no money. And I knew that when workmen crossed the line from Little Neck to Great Neck, their prices went up by a third. I had to get back to my office.

Cara was in the bathroom, taking one of her long showers that made mold bloom on the tiles and steamed the wallpaper off the walls. I knocked on the door. "Lunch in the fridge," I called.

"I left my application to Cornell on my dresser," she hollered. "Sign on the bottom line right after me."

"It's only November. Isn't it early to apply?"

"Dr. Zannikos wants to keep them on file in the guidance office," she said.

Without knowing why, I felt vaguely uneasy, and I wanted to wait for her to come out of the shower. But then it hit me how much tuition to Cornell would cost, and I went straight to my office. I needed money so badly that I stared at the phone and rubbed my palms together. "Get me a winner," I said as if I were at the track.

Within minutes, I got my wish. The phone rang. "Hello. My name is Kim. I need a reading right now." She sent out strong psychic vibrations. Her voice was honey. I could already tell a lot about her. First thing I saw was her hair. It was black and down to her waist, and she was shapely, with almond eyes. Pictures were coming into my mind rapidly. I scribbled notes—men, wedding rings. "I am seeing so many men around you," I said. "They are all interested in you. Some of those men are married," I warned.

"Most are," she explained. "I do erotic massage."

Then I saw the massage parlor. Naked men lying on tables. I saw one man who had genitals like a small clove of garlic. Another had a dimpled whale belly with clumps of hair. These were the men she was supposed to jerk off. They called it the Happy Ending. Kim wore white gloves. I saw lights around her. Acting ability.

"You could be an actress," I said.

"Really?"

"Of course," I said. I thought of the pleasure she had to feign with those paunchy men. "You already are an actress," I said.

As the reading went on, I found out she was working long hours to support a man who claimed he was flying all over the country to promote himself as a sports agent. I saw a map of the United States with a woman standing in each state, calling his name, some of them with babies in their arms. "There are other women," I said, but Kim wouldn't believe me.

"He says he never met anyone like me," she insisted.

I sighed. I had heard that line so often that I wondered if there was a school of dark arts that taught it to two-timers. "You don't trust him all that much or you wouldn't be calling me," I said. "I'm like a private third eye."

"I trust Dennis with my life," she said. "He'll be with me always. I'm so hot for him."

I squirmed. Bubbie had said our work was supposed to be holy. *Think of Kim as the burning bush,* I told myself, but the joke fell flat. It was so disturbing to hear her self-destructiveness, that while she continued to obsess about him I studied my appointment book. That week, I'd done thirteen readings so far, and it was only Wednesday—$95 × 13 = $1,235. I had six more readings scheduled, and there was always the possibility that there would be more. If this kept up, I could make well over three thousand dollars for the week.

"Dennis wants all his friends to get to know me personally," Kim was saying. "He brings them to my apartment for free massages."

I added up my advertising costs: $395 a month for the quarter-page ad in *Soaring Spirit,* $215 a month for a tiny ad in *Light Years,* and the guy who designed my new Web page for $250 had charged me an extra $200 for hookups to mall sites. Total—$1,060 for the month. All things considered, I was still going to rake in a small fortune. Then I remembered that, just like last month, I was going to have to cover the five-thousand-dollar mortgage on Mirror this month until Rory got his money from Medicaid. I added it all up and was dismayed. My earnings were barely enough to cover Rory's expenses.

In August, when all the shrinks were away, I'd earned six thousand dollars in one week. But then Rory had decided to take a course in fitting people with braces and trusses and other mobility aids. "Think how it will build the business," he'd said excitedly. Surgical supplies weren't returnable, so he got stuck with four motorized wheelchairs that he was still paying off. I was like Kim, supporting an unreliable man.

"Dennis says he doesn't want any men in my apartment when he isn't there," Kim said.

I thought about Anita backing Fred in writing that horrible novel, and I felt a tug of sympathy for her again. At least she and Fred had all those relatives in their wall of photos pitching in with their big hearts, full pockets, and open hands. My father used to sneak to the closet and slip a twenty into my pocket whenever Rory and I visited while my mother packed us off with an onion brisket or a tray of tomato surprise. The surprise was that there was egg salad inside the tomato. But the Grim Reaper had taken all our family support. Teary-eyed, I went back to my calculations. The refrigerator where Rory kept medications had gone on the fritz. Repair—$128. The medications inside that were spoiled—$500 or more.

"Dennis is even jealous of my elderly superintendent," Kim said.

I stopped my calculations and concentrated on her. I noticed her aura change as she spoke about Dennis. "Whenever you say Dennis's name," I told her, "your aura gets smaller. Your energy pours out of you and into him. You've got to take your power back. Listen, right now, close your eyes and chant the word *power* with me.

"Huh?" she said.

"Power, power, power," I chanted, and she joined in. I had to get my power back, too. "Your aura is getting huge," I said. It looked as if someone had sprayed purple neon paint all around her. "You are coming back to the powerful woman you were meant to be," I said. "Keep up this chant at least a few minutes every day, and you'll be ready for an audition."

"The only part I want is Dennis's wife."

The purple around her became a washout. "As soon as you said his name, your power fizzled out."

"Dennis *is* my power," she insisted.

She was like a train heading for a brick wall, but there seemed to be no way for me to pull the brake. She didn't trust me. I saw a blue cap and gown. "Are you a college grad?" I asked.

"Yes."

I was shocked. "Why would a college graduate be in your line of work?"

"Did you go to college?" she asked me.

"Yes."

"Then why are you a phone psychic?"

My mother would have gloated.

After I got off the phone, I followed my own advice. "Power, power, power," I chanted. The last time I'd felt powerful was the delicious moment in Miss McNamee's third-grade class when, just as she was about to whack me with her pointer for day-dreaming during the lesson on rainfall in Brazil, her dead mother appeared to me. And when I repeated what the mother had said out loud—"Josie, I should never have made you get rid of that baby"—Miss McNamee turned her back to the class, and her shoulders shook. I knew she was crying, and the room went silent. I was drunk with my own power. Jo Ellen Wastler, who always hoarded chocolate, offered me two squares of her Nestlé Crunch. "You can have my O'Henry when you're done with that," she said. Everyone wanted to be my friend.

That afternoon, my mother was waiting at the entrance of the schoolyard for me. She looked like a magazine mom in a beautiful yellow dress she'd sewn on her Singer. She wished I would wear fancy dresses every day as she did, but I hated retying the bows in the back every hour.

"Mommy!" I called, waving madly.

As she blew me a kiss, Miss McNamee marched toward her. My mother's brows shot up. I watched them talking and then watched Miss McNamee walk away, her face like a drawstring purse.

"Mommy!" I called, running over to her.

In front of the whole schoolyard, my mother grabbed my wrist and dragged me home the fourteen blocks along Rockaway Beach Boulevard, her high heels clip-clopping. As soon as we got in, without saying a word, she slapped my face. "You must learn to bite your tongue," she said.

Even now I felt hot-faced with fresh shame. I got up from my desk and decided to call it a morning.


Usually, when I stepped outside, my worries flapped away like a flock of blackbirds, but even though the leaves were turning gold and the air smelled like wild mushrooms and pine, today my burdens still sat on my shoulders. I thought about the clients I'd read over the last week. The doctor who thought aliens had put an implant in his ear, a guy who thought he was being haunted by his mother-in-law's dead parrot, a man who hadn't had sex in eleven years, a woman who believed she had had sex with a demon. I was becoming a tabloid psychic, and no matter how much I earned at it, my profits were swallowed by Rory's losses.

The sky was as cloudy as my mood. As I walked up Welwyn Road, I tried to think of all the atoms in my body growing brighter. My wattage felt low.

When I got to the post office, I pulled open the heavy door. The interior walls were dark paneled, scratched, and scarred. The counters had no pens, and their broken chains reminded me of lost souls. The gloom went right through me.

I opened my P.O. box. Most of my clients paid me by credit card, but some wanted to send money orders. I no longer accepted checks because they bounced. I had been expecting three money orders, but only one envelope was in the box. Better than nothing, I told myself. I opened it. There was a letter inside, a photo, and a self-addressed envelope, but no money order. I looked at the photo. It was a close-up of a huge pregnant belly, the navel sticking out like an elf's tongue.

*Dear Miriam,*

 *You did a reading for me a year and a half ago and told me that I would be having a baby. I'm over forty and pregnant. I have to know if it's going to be healthy. Please get right back to me with your answer.*

*Love,*
*Rayanne*

A psychic sonogram? I wrote on the back of a registered letter form:

*Dear Rayanne,*
   *I wish you the best. Please consult your doctor in this matter.*
                                                              *Fondly,*
                                                              *Miriam*

I stuck a stamp on it, dropped it into the out-of-town box, then glanced at the people in line to mail packages. Their auras didn't merge. They had tight boundaries around them like plots in a cemetery. Lonely, I thought. I had to admit that even with all the spirits around me, with a husband and a daughter, and all my clients, I was lonely, too. Life was lonely with a husband consumed by work, a daughter full of shame, and clients as disembodied spirits on the phone. It was lonely without my parents and Rory's. Great Neck was lonely with its castles and manicured lawns and dogs named Baron.

As I walked along Welwyn Road, a young blond woman wearing skinny-heeled Manolo Blahniks and carrying a Fendi bag came toward me. Despite our differences—my hair was natural, my bag was tapestry that I'd bought for twenty dollars at a street fair, and I was wearing Birkenstocks with socks—I made it a point to give her a big smile so the world would be a less lonely place for both of us. She looked me up and down dismissively.

Up the block, the meter maid was writing out tickets. There were a couple of vacant parking spots, but the Mercedes, the Lincoln Navigators, and the Porsches were double-parked anyway.

When I reached the next corner, another blond woman dashed out of Paradise Salon, her hands up as if she had just been robbed. "Help!" she called to me. I rushed to her. Then she held a quarter out to me in her outstretched palm. For a moment, I was insulted. "Would you put this in my meter?" she asked frantically. "I just got my nails done." Her nails were long and red and they curled under. I put the quarter in. "Thank you," she said grimly.

*I should be grateful someone actually spoke to me in this town,* I thought. In Rockaway, women in housedresses and men in shirt-sleeves had sat in front of their houses on stoops, beach chairs, or milk crates, shooting the breeze with passersby. I'd wanted to stay in Rockaway, but Rory had argued, "We lived in Queens all our lives. It's time to move to the North Shore." That very weekend, as we drove on the LIE to look for houses, at the first exit past Queens I said, "Stop! I don't want to be far away from where Bubbie lived. I don't belong with fancy people. Don't take me any farther."

I walked home over the small bridge that divided one side of the Village of Thomaston from the other. I was so alone that if it weren't for the cars whizzing on Grace Avenue, I would have thought I was the only person on the planet.

When I was a child, Bubbie had been the one person who made me feel like I belonged. I was eight and a half years old the day she died, and I was right beside her as she lay in her four-poster bed, her white hair loose. Even with the castile shampoo, her hair had yellowed after all. Her whole face had yellowed, too. Her cheeks looked like cliffs. My father stood on the other side of the bed, swaying, his lips moving like they did in shul. Tears streamed down his face.

"Bubbie has the Big C," my mother whispered. "She has a tumor in her womb." It sounded like a rhyme. It sounded as if it wouldn't hurt at all. "It's here," my mother said, placing her hand low on her own belly. I remembered the day Bubbie had taught me how to read body energy and how hot my hand had gotten when I passed it below Bubbie's belly. "Bubbie's dying," my mother said softly.

"Bubbie, you can do something," I'd cried. "Use your potions. I'll bring you anything you need. Leaves or bark or seaweed. Anything. Please!"

Bubbie raised her skeleton hands as if to say, *What can I do?*

I was desperate. I remembered her giving a wheezing man a bag of garlic cloves to tie around his neck and eucalyptus leaves to breathe in. I ran into the kitchen and found them. Then I remembered Bubbie had told a woman that senna leaves could cure anything. I took a handful of them from a jar marked SENNA. I ran back to Bubbie's room. She couldn't lift her head, so I set the bag of cloves on her neck. I held the eucalyptus leaves to her nose. Bubbie was hardly breathing. There was no time to boil water. I sprinkled the senna leaves all over her bed. "Don't die, Bubbie," I pleaded. I bent close to her and whispered. "I need you to finish teaching me all your cures. You promised I could be your official assistant. I want to stay with you always. Don't leave me. I'm your *neshomeleh*," I cried. "I need to learn everything you know."

Bubbie touched my arm. Her hand was ice. Her lips moved. She was speaking quieter than a whisper. I put my ear to her mouth. "Trust," was all I could hear.

"Trust who?" I had cried. "Trust what?"

But she was silent, and I no longer felt her breath on my ear.

Now I was the one who wasn't breathing. My legs were like wood. I stood at the curb, my eyes glazing with tears. All the windows of the houses across the street looked blank, as if no one had ever lived there. A nurse pushing an old man in a wheelchair looked right through me.

I remembered feeling this invisible to my family after Bubbie had died. A year later, my father was still sighing, "Mama!" and crying like a baby.

"Bubbie could have had a hysterectomy like every other woman," my mother shouted at him. "But no, she had to be her own doctor and give herself idiotic herbs, castor oil packs, and mustard plasters."

My father banged his fist on the table. The dishes jumped in fright. "Dorothy, have some respect," he hollered. "Mama knew things that the doctors will never know. She must have known that they would cut her up for nothing. She must have known it was her time. She was eighty-six. For God's sake, let Mama rest in peace."

"You're still taking her side over mine," my mother spat back at him.

They didn't even notice I was in the room, listening. There had been no one on my side except Bubbie. I went out to our second-story porch right off my room and climbed over the rail. Standing on a tiny ledge, hanging on with my arms behind me, I leaned forward like one of those wooden figures on the front of ships. I looked down over Eightieth Street. I said good-bye to the world. I said good-bye to Herby, the grown man who lived with his mother. His parrot was on his shoulder. I said good-bye to the Cat Man, who scaled fish at Fogel's Fish Market and to the million yowling cats that followed him. I said good-bye to Joel, who was swinging his skinny polio legs by leaning on the silver crutches that made bracelets on his arms. I couldn't bear to be alone in the world with Bubbie's gift. I thought about how easy it would be to let go of the railing and go twirling down like the little nose caps on the maple trees. Then I heard whispering.

"Och, *neshomeleh,* och."

It was Bubbie's voice. I clung to the railing, trembling, sweating, and breathing in the salty breakers of air, then climbed back. Once my two feet were on the porch, I looked up at the sky, waiting, listening. I smelled the lavender talc Bubbie used to puff on her neck. It was as if Bubbie were in the air all around me. I felt her love in the warmth seeping back into my skin, in the shine on the pointy-edged leaves of the holly tree.

"You're *not* going to tell me you're holding this parking spot for someone, are you?" a man snarled at me from his black Mercedes, interrupting my reverie.

I blinked at him, surprised that he could see me. "No, I'm not," I said, and continued walking.

When I got back to Grace Court, I passed the houses of the newly divorced. There were the Changs, the Millsteins, the De Salvos, and I suspected that the Corrigans would be joining them soon. A few months ago, Rory had told me that he'd seen Kirk Corrigan driving his Ferrari on the Long Island Expressway with his arm around another woman. We'd been to the Corrigans' for a dinner party years ago. Afterwards, I'd run into Hattie on the checkout line of Waldbaum's. As she finger-combed her wing-tipped blond hair, she said, "I never asked you what club you belonged to."

I thought she was asking me what my interests were. I didn't belong to any clubs, but my mother, when she was a girl in Elmira, had won a 4-H Club blue ribbon at a state fair for raising a perfect rabbit. "The Four-H Club," I said.

Hattie laughed. "Too bad you were so quiet at my party," she said. "You're a riot."

I thought she was warming to me. I felt my smile becoming genuine.

"And your husband was so shy, too, that I barely got to know him," she added. "What does he do?"

"Rory owns Mirror Pharmacy," I said proudly.

"I've never heard of it. Where is it?"

"Springfield Boulevard in Queens."

"No wonder I don't know it," she said, her nose in the air. "I never go to Queens." She waved. "Got to run. I'm busy, busy, busy."

And what if she'd known I was a psychic?

Even my father had urged me to be secretive. "In Russia, someone finds out a Jew has two chickens, next thing, the Jew doesn't even have an egg. They take the whole coop, too." I thought about how my possessions were safe in Great Neck. It was just my pride that was up for grabs.

Then I was ashamed of the small pleasure I'd felt at the thought of Hattie getting divorced. If I'd had some salt, I'd have thrown it over my shoulder. Divorce could happen to anyone. Great Neck had a 60 percent divorce rate. It wasn't that couples were any unhappier in Great Neck than elsewhere on Long Island. It was just that Great Neckers could afford to split up and still live in style. And anyone who got divorced tried to move here to be with more divorcees. It was like the Second-Chance Club. I hoped I wouldn't ever join it.

Later that afternoon, I was nestled in the warmth coming through the den's bay window, reading *The Autobiography of a Yogi* when I felt prickles on the back of my scalp and neck. *There's a spirit behind me,* I thought. "Who's there?" I asked. There was no answer. Slowly, I turned and looked behind me. Iris Gruber and Baron were staring at me from the plot of grass edging the curb in front of my house. I was furious. *Why is she always spying on me? And now she's training her dog to do it, too.* I got up and stared right back at them. Neither of them flinched. I began to feel intimidated. I couldn't hold my gaze steady any longer. I closed the curtains.

An hour later, when I opened the door for Cara, my eyes darted around for Iris and Baron.

"What are you looking for?" Cara asked.

"To see if Iris Gruber and Baron are in front of our house again."

"Mom, what's the difference?" Cara said as she came in. "Iris always carries a poop scoop."

I didn't want to tell her that Iris was spying on me. Like my mother, Cara would only blame me for attracting that kind of attention to myself by being a psychic. "You're right," I said, and then I noticed that she was wearing a corduroy jacket that wasn't hers. It was pricey—a DKNY, but the collar was frayed and the elbows were worn. "Where's your new denim jacket?" I demanded.

"I left it in my locker."

I looked straight into her eyes and saw Darcy wearing Cara's jacket. It was unmistakable. It had the cookie-cutter *C* that Cara had drawn on the right lapel with a fabric marker. I saw Darcy admiring herself in the mirror, running her hands down the sleeves. I knew she'd never give it back. "Darcy's wearing your jacket," I said.

"Stop spying on me!" Cara shouted, but she licked her lips nervously.

"Cara, a spy watches someone for a malicious purpose. I'm your mother. I want the best for you."

She humphed.

Then I noticed her face looked flushed. "Are you feeling okay?" I asked.

"My head hurts, and my throat is scratchy."

I suspected she was getting sick from how worn she'd looked last night as I brushed her hair. I put my lips to her forehead. "Oh, you've got a fever."

"I don't have time to be sick," she said. "I've got a French exam tomorrow and an oral report due on Socrates. In honors classes, if you miss even a day, you have to go for after-school help to catch up."

I touched her neck. "Your glands are swollen, too. Go up and put on your pajamas. I'll get out the Iodex." That was the black salve that Bubbie used to rub on swollen glands and then wrap with a warm flannel.

"Oh, no," Cara cried. "I hate Bubbie's remedies."

"Go upstairs and put on your pajamas," I ordered.

After she went up to her room, I went into the kitchen and heated up a cup of apple cider vinegar in the microwave, crushed a garlic clove into it, and brought it up to her with the Iodex and the flannel.

She sat up in bed. I handed her the cup of vinegar and crushed garlic. She took a small swallow, grimaced, stuck out her tongue, and shook her head. "No way am I going to drink any more of this!"

"The cider vinegar kills germs and the garlic clears the sinuses," I said, but she set the glass down on her night table and pressed her lips together.

I handed her the Iodex. Her top lip curled in disgust. Just the fear of missing school wouldn't get her cooperation. "Rub it on your glands or you'll be too sick to go to Darcy's party on Saturday."

"Oh, I'm not going to miss a limo to the city and an orchestra seat for *Lion King*," she said, already rubbing the Iodex in. She wrapped the flannel around her neck and I pinned it; then she lay down again, shivering under her covers.

"You should be glad that your mother is a psychic. Look how I can watch over you and protect you. If you're ever in trouble, all you have to do is chant 'Om,' and I'd hear you in a flash. I'd come right to you."

"I hate that word *om*. I'd never say that."

"Then say, 'Och!' That's what Bubbie used to say whenever she had troubles." I handed her the rest of the apple cider vinegar and crushed garlic brew.

"Och!" Cara said, rolling her eyes. "Och!"

# 8

SOME DAYS LATER, I forced myself to sit by the phone when I didn't have appointments. I figured a prospective client would be more likely to book a reading if he got me live than if he were greeted by my voice mail.

The phone rang. *Staying home paid off,* I thought.

"Can you find my raincoat?" a man asked. "It's a beige London Fog in size forty-two."

"No, I'm the wrong kind of psychic for that," I explained, disappointed. "There are psychics who specialize in finding lost articles, but I'm not one of them."

"Could you give me the number of one?" he asked.

"Hold on," I said. I'd just seen an ad for a psychic finder on the back page of *The Celestial Times.* I checked my desk, my wastepaper basket. "Sorry," I said. "I can't find the number."

"You sure are the wrong kind of psychic for me," he said, and got off the phone without thanking me.

The phone rang again. Before I could say hello, a woman asked hesitantly, "Are you the psychic?"

"Yes."

"I want to make sure all your information comes from the light of Christ," she said gravely.

*"Vo den?"* I asked, meaning "Where else?" in Yiddish.

"Is Voden another name for Jesus?" she asked.

"No, I'm Jewish," I explained, and she hung up. I sat there with my head in my hands.

The phone rang again. "H-hello," a woman said, frightened. I knew who it was. Orthodox Arlene. She'd called a million times for readings, but could never bring herself to go through with them. Even though the Old Testament was full of visionaries and dreamers like Joseph and Isaiah, Arlene's rabbi forbade his congregation to speak to a fortune-teller, especially a necromancer, one who tells the future through communicating with the dead.

"Arlene," I said, "don't book a reading. You shouldn't do anything that's going to give you more stress." *Or me,* I thought.

"All right," she said angrily, but I knew she'd call back in a few months. She always did.

I had never discussed my work with a rabbi, but Bubbie had told me what she and Bedya and the other babushka ladies in her shtetl believed. "You may be too little to understand now," Bubbie had said, "but when the body dies, the soul divides into three parts. One part goes up to the heavens. The next hangs around during the week of shiva, visiting everyone he loved, and sometimes everyone he hated, too, and then flies up to the heavens to blend like egg whites into the part that went up right away. The third part of the soul, the *ruach,* can fly up and come back whenever it wants."

*Ruachs* were the only parts of the soul I could ever contact. I wondered if there was one holy place in the heavens where all the first and second parts congregated. A big shul in the sky, maybe, with no Yom Kippur pledges of money necessary. Probably it would be nonsectarian like Temple Isaiah over on Stoner Avenue that became a Korean church on Sundays. If that were so, maybe I could have told the Christian woman that my information came from the Church of All Souls.

I took a long breath, and as I did, I smelled the scent of lavender. "Bubbie?" I asked.

*"Ver den?"* she answered, and as soon as she said, "Who else?" I knew she'd been listening all along. I felt my cheeks get hot.

I looked all around. "Bubbie, where are you?"

Then I saw a blur to my right. As if a defroster had been turned on a fogged windshield, Bubbie's face began to emerge. "You should tell every one of them, *'Gai kuken ahfen yam!'"*

"I can't tell them to go shit in the ocean, Bubbie. You said never do this work for the gelt, but Rory and I need money. You don't understand. Your expenses were low. In Russia, you lived in a house with a straw roof and grew your own food and milked your own cows. When you came here, you lived over your son's store. Things are different these days."

*"A shanda!"* she said, and then the fog covered her face again.

*A sin?* I asked myself. Whose sin? The rude people who phoned me? My sin for needing money? *A shanda* the amount I have to charge to survive? Or worse, *a shanda* that I'd told my Bubbie who always watched over me that she didn't understand my life? The fog began to dissipate. "Oh, Bubbie, I'm sorry," I said. "Come back," but when she was gone, she was gone.

I sat staring at the place where she'd been. I remembered the reverence that Bubbie's customers, even those who had just come to inquire, had given her. Sometimes, entering her parlor, they almost bowed.

When the phone rang, I had to force myself to answer it. It was Cara, calling from the phone booth at school. "There's a game today at three thirty," she said. "Will you come? The coach said he's going to play me." Last year she'd sat on the bench the entire season.

"Fantastic!" I said. She had been pushing me away so much lately, that I was thrilled to be asked. "Of course I'll be there. First row."

"Gotta go, Calculus, see you," she said happily.

• • •

When I got to her school, a security guard motioned for me to park in the side lot. A heavyset woman with brown permed hair came out the building, then waved at me as she rushed toward the lower parking lot. It took me a few moments to realize that it was Nancy Curson who worked in the attendance office. Her daughter had been in Cara's Brownie troop, which had met in my basement after the Girls Scout House in Baker Hill was torn down. That was nine years ago. Since Cara had grown up and away from me, whatever thin thread had stitched me to the community had snapped.

The bell rang. Students came out, yelling, pushing. The underclassmen headed for the buses. Most of the seniors had cars parked in the lower lot. Mercedes, Porsches, even a DeLorian that opened like a silver bird lifting one wing. Cara was lucky we could afford her sneakers.

I had fifteen minutes before the game started. I decided to take a walk. I got out of the car and opened my parasol. It was another nod to Bubbie, who always said a woman shouldn't be sun-dried like a raisin. I never thought I'd do the same, but when I started doing readings for a living, I not only became more psychically sensitive, but my skin began to burn and peel even with sunscreen. When Cara was little, she made me buy her a Holly Hobbie umbrella and opened it whenever she walked with me. She looked so cute, strangers used to ask to take our picture. Now, whenever I opened my parasol, Cara said, "Mom, can't you walk on the other side of the street?"

"It's not raining," a boy called out, then drove off.

I ignored him and walked through the lower parking lot to get to the track.

I fast-walked on the track, swinging my free arm for exercise. Ahead of me, I saw cloudy letters in the sky. *"Gai, gai."* Go, go. It was what my father had always said to hurry me.

Why was he hurrying me now? I remembered the day, a Tuesday, when Cara was a year old, and I left her with my mother and drove to town. Driving on the Cross Island, I had headed for my father's butcher shop. I parked the car. It was eerie. I could see the window in the apartment above the store where Bubbie used to live. I almost expected to see her watching for me. I went inside his store. No one was behind the counter. I thought my father must be either getting something from the freezer or in the back room, cutting off a side of beef with a cleaver. I was excited to see him. I felt like bending down, scooping a handful of sawdust and putting it in my pocket as I had done when I was a kid.

"Dad?" I called out. "Daddy?"

In the back room, my father was on the floor, lying on his back in the sawdust. There was blood on his apron. For a moment, I thought he had been shot.

"Daddy, Daddy!" I cried. I fell to my knees and kissed his broad forehead. It was cold.

Why hadn't Bubbie or some other spirit hurried me before the heart attack killed him? I thought now. Was I doomed to get only psychic postscripts? I gripped the handle of the parasol so hard that my fingers hurt.

I looked at my watch. It was almost game time. I put my parasol back in the car and went inside the doors leading to the gym and sat on the first tier of the bleachers. The other parents all seemed to know each other—they were like another team among themselves. Then Courtney, who had given up basketball for fencing, waved to me from the top of the bleachers, and Darcy's mother smiled and I felt like part of the team, too.

It was toss-up time. Darcy was on her tiptoes facing an opponent. Cara's brow was furrowed. Her tongue peeked out the corner of her mouth. The ref threw the ball in the air. Darcy leaped up, managed to tap it to Cara. Cara dribbled it down the court. There was a thunderous sound from their sneakers on the wood. I felt the vibrations. One of the mothers leaped to her feet, shouting, "Go! Go! Go!" as if she were translating for my father. Then a girl in orange shorts elbowed Cara in the stomach and grabbed the ball. Cara buckled over. The ref blew the whistle.

"Oh," I cried involuntarily.

"Foul!" he yelled.

Cara was given back the ball. She held it toward her face, her lips moving as if she were praying. She began to sweat, and so did I.

I felt a tingling sensation on my right arm. Then I saw, out of the corner of my eye, that my father was sitting next to me on the bench. He had his apron on. He pointed to his nose. He was trying to tell me something. *Daddy, what is it?* I thought. He pointed to the court. I looked straight ahead. I saw a quick prescient image, like a video on fast forward. Number seven on the other team threw the ball into number three's face on our team. Number three cried out and cupped her nose with her hands. Blood leaked down her wrists, the front of her shirt. *What do I do?* I wondered. I didn't want to reveal myself and embarrass Cara, but if I didn't, number three would get badly hurt. I froze for a moment; then I ran onto the court. The coach blew the whistle. The girls stopped playing and stared at me. Cara was like a statue. All the color left her aura.

"Number three's nose," I shouted.

The girls nudged each other and giggled. Cara covered her face with her hands. The coach came over to me. "Mrs. Kaminsky," he said.

"There's going to be an accident," I explained. The girls' giggling and whispering started up like a wave. "Cara's mom," I heard. "That's Cara's Mom." "Cara," they whispered to her, but she didn't answer.

The coach took my arm. "Ma'am, if you will just sit down," he said gently, but his grip was iron. I couldn't stay there and helplessly watch the girl get hurt. I looked up. Now the people in the bleachers were all watching me. Darcy's mother was watching me, too. I looked over at Cara, who was the only person in the whole gym whose eyes weren't on me, who instead was looking at the floor as if she were searching for a hole to fall through. I went into the hallway to compose myself. The game suddenly began again. I heard noise and commotion, but I couldn't go back to watch it. Not now. I got in my Honda. Life made no sense. The sun was blazing down on my roof. I felt as if I were locked in a steam cabinet. I was so distraught that I didn't think of opening a window.

How would I explain to Cara what had just happened? Would she believe that my father was there, too? It wasn't my fault that I was like a stylus on a Ouija board. I was only trying to help. When the ambulance wailed toward me, I wasn't surprised. I watched the ambulance pull up to the gym door, watched them bring out the girl, blood pouring from her nose. I was afraid someone would remember that I'd predicted this. Maybe they would be caught up in the surprise of all that blood. My jaw hurt from clenching my teeth.

Ninety minutes later, Cara got in the car. I didn't say anything, but waited for her to speak.

"Alicia Gordon did get her nose messed up," she said. "Everyone was staring at me."

"At your next game, I promise I'll keep my mouth shut, no matter what."

"No, don't come to any more games," she said quietly.

I tried to speak gently. "My father warned me that there would be an accident." I looked at her. "It's hard to be a mother and a psychic. You know me. I put my foot in it."

"You sure did," she said, eyes flashing. "Everybody was talking about what you did. Brenda Johnson—five on my team—said, 'Is your mother one of those white witches?' And worse, after the ambulance left, Darcy and Courtney cornered me. 'What's with your mother?' Courtney said. 'She totally freaked me out.' And worse, Darcy actually said, 'She's not a psychic, is she?'"

I gripped the wheel so hard that my fingers hurt. "What did you tell them?"

"I told them you were going through menopause," Cara said.

I almost laughed, but then I saw her cheek, streaked with tears—and my insides turned to water. All I could say was, "I'm so sorry, Cara," but the silence filled the car like hot steam, making it hard to breathe. I put the radio on Cara's favorite station and suggested we stop for some frozen yogurt. Anything to clear the air to make her feel better; but she turned her face from me.

When we got home, I asked if she wanted something to eat. She shook her head and slowly went upstairs, and I heard her door shut with a click, which hurt far more than if she'd slammed it. I stood there, heart pounding. I phoned Rory.

"Mirror Pharmacy," he said. In the background, someone was shouting, "In Russia you do not need a prescription for penicillin."

"But here you do, Mr. Bentslovik," Rory said.

"Then I go to Brighton Beach and buy penicillin right off the street," he insisted.

"Rory," I said.

"Oh, sorry, Mim. Listen, I can't find my cell phone. Would you look around for it?"

"Okay, but I have something to tell you."

"What is it?"

I told him about the basketball game as fast as I could.

"Oh, shit, my computer just went down," he said as if he hadn't heard a word. "I gotta run. I'll call you back, Mim."

I placed the receiver in its cradle and tried not to cry. I tried to remember back to when I wasn't desperate for money and my readings were a solace to me, but at this moment, I couldn't.

My house suddenly seemed too enormous for me to find his cell phone. Normally, I'd dial his number and listen for his phone to ring, but last night, when we were about to make love, I'd asked him to turn it off. In the bedroom, I looked everywhere, but I couldn't find it. I shut my eyes and pictured a blueprint of our house, and waited for a room to light up, but nothing happened. I had told that guy with the lost raincoat the truth. I wasn't any good at locating objects psychically. I took a step forward, and my toe bumped into something that was half under the bed. I looked down. It was Rory's cell phone. I turned it on, and it started beeping. He had a message. Maybe it was urgent. I listened to his voice mail. "Message one, Monday, eight forty-five P.M.," the robotic voice said.

"Boss, this is Fred. I forgot to mention this afternoon that old Mrs. Scarletti claimed I didn't deliver her order, but I did. She just forgot."

I was glad Rory hadn't listened to that call. He would have gotten himself all upset, and it would have ruined our time alone together. Why couldn't Fred handle business during business hours? Mrs. Scarletti must have already chewed Rory's ear off by now. I put the phone down and decided I'd better just take care of my own business.

As I approached the landing, my office phone rang. I dashed upstairs and answered it. All I heard was heavy breathing, which I confused as my own. "Hello? Hello?" I said, but the person breathed louder. Prank call. I closed my eyes and tried to see the wacko at the other end of the line. "You have brown hair, thick glasses, and a scar on your upper lip," I said. He stopped breathing. "And you live in the basement of your mother's house in Ozone Park." He gasped and hung up.

As I straightened the papers on my desk, I sensed a stirring in the air. There was a scribble of light near the window, like an artist's gesture drawing. And then, I clearly saw my father again. He was sitting at our old white enamel kitchen table. He licked his thumb and counted out ghost money from a big wad of cash as if he were preparing his nightly bank deposit. As he counted, the piles of cash were disappearing.

I got frightened. "Daddy," I said, "what does this mean?" and then he disappeared, too.

• • •

The next night, Rory sat across from me at the dinner table, wriggling in his chair like a kid who was forced to stay in after school. I had insisted that he come home early for a family meal. In my urgency, I had completely forgotten that Cara had a late-night concert for All County Chorus in Amityville. "At least you and I can be together," I said lamely.

I could hear Rory thinking, *My luck, Medicaid will pull a surprise audit. I have to get everything together. I have to meet with my accountant. I'll have to stay up three nights straight to make a dent.*

I reached for his hand. "You used to love being a pharmacist, remember?"

"Yeah."

"Customers brought you Irish soda bread, baklava, bottles of sake, fried chicken and pots of collard greens."

He nodded. "Now I don't get a chance to breathe. I'm so overwhelmed. I resent it if a customer so much as says hello. I try to duck them so I can get my paperwork done. And when they tell me their troubles, I don't even feel sorry anymore. And they're so damn belligerent these days. I wouldn't dare perform even the simplest first aid on anyone. They are always threatening to sue over nothing. You should hear them carry on because I won't commit fraud. They want me to bill their HMO for an antibiotic and give them some herb like echinacea for free instead."

"What good is all this chasing down money when we're always in debt anyway?" I said. "As soon as Cara graduates, let's sell the house and the business. We could move to the country and grow our own food. You could work for a pharmacy in a small town. I could go back to a tearoom, not have to pay giant advertising bills, and have reasonable hours."

Rory let go of my hand and pushed away his plate. "I can't," he said. "I used my parents' insurance money as a down payment on the business, and the business was what bought this house. That money was my parents' blood."

I felt tingling in my shoulders and neck. I concentrated on what Rory was saying, but then I saw a cloudy light over his shoulder. The light shaped itself into two figures that, little by little, became brighter and clearer. I smelled dry-cleaning chemicals. It was Rory's parents. His father was holding a wire hanger. His mother held a small iron, the kind used for collars. It was as if they were still running their business. My heart quickened. "Rory, your parents are here. Right behind you."

He started to turn.

"Don't look at them directly or they'll disappear," I warned.

He kept his eyes on me. His face was a mixture of yearning, surprise, and exhaustion. His parents were whispering to each other. "For what did I suffer?" his mother said. "Our boy, he works as hard as we did."

"But it's all worth it," Rory's father said. "His own business, and look, a big house on Long Island, yet."

"But they're poor," his mother said. "Look at my boy's face. He's always worried."

"We worked way harder than he does, and what did we have? Bubkes. At least they've got something to show for it."

"You're right," Rory's mother told her husband. Rory had told me that his mother always ended up taking her husband's side.

"I think your parents want you to give up the house and business because you work too hard," I lied.

"My father would never say that," Rory said, glowering at me. "I think you're just trying to get your own way."

I felt heat flush to my face. Rory got up and went behind his chair and whirled his arms around as if to prove there was nothing there. He was putting his hands right through them. Their images began to mix together like the light batter of angel food cake. I held my breath. I was afraid he would turn to a pillar of salt, but all that happened was that he got angrier.

"I leave a pile of work to come home and be with my family and what do I get? A séance. Did I ask for this?"

"No," I said softly. He had never wanted me to do this for him. But I hadn't been trying. It had just happened.

We sat in silence. I remembered how guilty I'd felt when my father put his bare feet up on the hassock at night, and I saw his corns, calluses, and swollen ankles from standing on his feet all day to support my mother and me. It was only after I met Rory that I started to let go of the guilt and let myself live more fully. Both of us had. On our honeymoon, I would have been content to drive to Niagara Falls, but instead we flew to Jamaica. We snorkled, holding hands under the water, gliding by iridescent fish, thin as dimes that skirted the pink-tinged coral reefs. The first time I saw a seahorse up close, so tiny and perfect, swimming with its head high as if it were its own jockey, all I could think was that I was as surprised by it as I was by love. I turned to Rory and kissed him, right then and there, mask to mask, our mouths clumsy. We climbed the rocks to stand under the waterfalls.

"This is too good to be true," Rory had said. He looked astonished, as if he distrusted happiness.

"It's all true," I told him. "Every moment of it."

Behind the cascading curtain, we kissed some more. When we stepped out into the sunlight again, Rory pointed up to the wild parakeets flapping in the air. We stood there watching their wings of pale blue, lime green, bright yellow, white.

"It's like a bouquet flying by in a Chagall painting," Rory had said.

Those nights, instead of staying in our hotel with the other tourists, we went to small dark bars filled with calypso music so loud you could feel the beat pulsing up from the floor. Rory sang softly in my ear: "Back to back, belly to belly. We won't stop until the cemetery." But we had stopped. Our lives had become as circumscribed as a ball tethered to a pole while all around us neighbors were calling Ollie's Airport Service to fly off somewhere almost as soon as they unpacked from their last vacation. Now Rory drummed his fingers on the table.

"I'm sorry I brought up your parents," I said, even though they were the ones who'd brought themselves to me. "But if I see things for you psychically and I don't tell you, how can we really be close?"

"We've made it up until now, haven't we?"

I got a vision of a night sky and an ocean silvered by a low-hanging moon. *Romance,* I thought, and then two ships appeared, but they were sailing away from each other.

# 9

I WAS SO WIPED out from brooding over the lack of close-ness in my marriage that I had to begin my morning meditation in bed instead of in my office. "Om, om," I chanted, my blanket becoming like a wave rolling with my breath, my sand-swirled ceiling, the leafy pond for my thoughts. "Om."

Cara's CD player began blasting.

"Honey, turn it down," I called, but it was too loud for her to hear me. I started to drag myself out of bed when I remembered reading recently that psychic powers could be beefed up by lis-tening to two things simultaneously that came from different directions. It made sense. I had to be able to hear whispered mes-sages from spirits as I was listening to a client. I rolled over and put on Rory's clock radio, and the news came on.

"Rats in New York City," the commentator was saying. "Walk-ing God like a dog," the singer wailed. I tried hard to hear both simultaneously. "What ya say?" "Giuliani?" "Funk blast embez-zlement from union Lewinsky." "Yo, yo." I couldn't do it. I was getting a headache. I turned off the news and knocked on Cara's door.

She opened it, still in her striped Gap nightgown, the phone receiver cocked between her head and neck. "Hey, Darcy," she said. "I know, I know."

"How can you listen to the blasting rap music and Darcy at the same time?" I asked.

"I just can," she said.

*If the article were true,* I thought, *there should be a whole generation of psychics.* I was glad I hadn't wasted any more time with the exercise. "Turn it down, honey," I told Cara.

"Okay, Mom," she said, and in the same breath, "Darcy, are you kidding?"

I got dressed and went up to my office, appreciating the silence. Then the phone rang.

"I just read your ad in *Soaring Spirit,*" a woman shouted. "I can't get over you psychics. Don't you know you're supposed to have a line that says, "'For Entertainment Purposes Only'? It's required by law."

"No, I didn't know that," I said. "Thank you for telling me."

"I'm calling the cops," she said. "All you psychics ought to be thrown in jail."

The phone rang again. Since I felt that I was on a bad streak, I debated about answering it, but then I thought, *Some people are directed to call me by a higher power. I can't let those people down.* "Hello," I said.

It was a man who wanted a reading in exchange for massaging my feet. "I'm a reflexologist," he said, "and if you want, I'll paint your toenails afterwards."

I hung up, grabbed my jacket and my parasol, and went outside. Across the street, Hattie Corrigan's gardener was sprinkling lime on her lawn. Bundles of newspapers were stacked at the curb along with plastic bins of empty cans. I glanced at the Grubers' house and noticed a circular Amish hex sign with red tulips. A blue eight-pointed star was hanging on the side of their house that faced ours. Was Iris worried that I'd put a hex on her, or was she trying to put one on me? Iris, like most people, probably didn't know that those hex signs really meant good luck, but I felt a chill down my vertebrae. "Pooh, pooh, pooh," I said as my *bubbe* had taught me to ward off evil.

I continued walking and came to the wooden sign with the *Thomaston, Inc. 1931* in ornate script. Lively fall flowers surrounded the sign. The only ones that would last the whole winter were the squat green cabbage plants with their veiny mauve centers. I felt dislocated, the way Bubbie must have felt when she first came to America. "You walk everywhere and you don't see one cow," she'd told me. In the distance, the roar of leaf blowers sounded like a border war.

I walked all the way to Northern Boulevard. I picked up a fried egg on a bagel with ketchup from a deli near the new medical buildings, then crossed East Shore Road and headed for the park in Manhasset. I didn't know its name. Cara used to call it Duck Doody Park. The name still fit. Stepping gingerly, I walked along the path by the weeping willows that doubled themselves in the pond. The ducks and geese made V-wakes in the murky water. I looked at the heart shape of two swans bill to bill.

I thought of how Rory and I used to be like that. Now he was stuck at Mirror Pharmacy, filling out an unending pile of payment forms like a woodcutter condemned to cut wood until something broke the spell, and I was shut up in my office, doing a job that was becoming thankless. When I threw the rest of my bagel and eggs to the ducks, they came at me in a gaggle, beaks opening and closing, throats hissing.

"I don't have any more food," I said, but they came closer, chasing me, nipping me, running me out of the park. I imagined the Great Neckers would approve.

I hurried home. In the living room, I felt something like a spiderweb brush against my cheek. I jumped back. I saw a gauzy film and then slowly, it shaped itself into a spirit. An ancient Chinese man with a brown stain on his right cheek, like a leaf. He wore a blue silk robe and a cap that looked like a yarmulke. I didn't want spirits from other people's families traipsing through my house; they should confine themselves to my office.

"Shoo!" I shouted, but the spirit kept motioning me toward my office. I went upstairs. The phone rang. It was Kim, the erotic masseuse.

"I was calling you all morning," she said crossly.

"Oh, that's why the ghost of one of your ancestors was in my living room. An ancient man in a robe. He had a leaf on his right cheek."

"*Eee!*" she cried. "That's my grandfather. What did he say?"

In a blink, he appeared in my office, standing near the wicker chair. He began talking to me in Chinese. It sounded like "Oh, boy, oy." I shrugged to show him that I didn't understand.

He nodded, then opened his robe. He was naked and hairless. His skin was melting candle wax except for his tiny red penis. Right in front of me, he grabbed it.

I turned away. He sprang into the path of my vision. His robe was closed now. He was pointing at the phone.

*It's a charade,* I thought. He was acting out that he knew how his granddaughter earned her living. "Your grandfather doesn't want you to work in the massage parlor," I told Kim.

"What does he say about Dennis and me?" she asked.

Her grandfather passed the side of his palm against the middle of his neck.

"Continuing with Dennis would be as bad as slitting your throat," I told her.

"But last night I read my cards," Kim said. "Ten of Cups came up for me and Dennis. Happy marriage, happy marriage."

Her grandfather shook his head.

"Kim," I said, "even if you don't trust me, believe your grandfather when he says there isn't going to be a marriage for you with this man."

"Another psychic told me that Dennis and I were together in

a past life. I was his sister and I murdered him and that is why he hurts me now."

I clapped my hand to my forehead. It was a common mistake to use a past life as an excuse to ruin this one. "You have to get rid of this guy." Her grandfather nodded. "Your grandfather agrees with me."

"It's my karma to love Dennis," she insisted. "You might not be picking up Dennis's true vibrations. You tell me what Dennis looks like, and then I will believe you."

I got an image of a man with dark wavy hair and blue eyes, but I was afraid if I was wrong, I'd discredit myself, and then Kim wouldn't get any help. "Tell me Dennis's last name," I said. "Then I'll be sure."

"You kidding me? If I tell you, you will look him up and try to get him for yourself."

I looked at her grandfather and shrugged, hoping he'd confirm Dennis's description. Sometimes spirits carried family albums with them, or wanted posters, or instantly developed a strip of small pictures like those in the old Woolworth's photo booths. But Kim's grandfather looked tired. He sat down in the chair. Suddenly, he separated his palms while touching his fingertips together as a symbol to show me something.

I took a guess. "There's trouble under your family's roof," I said to Kim.

"Yesterday my father called from Beijing to confess that he is seeing another woman."

I saw a procession of women around her father. They were topless. *He frequents the same kind of places that Kim works in,* I said to myself. It felt to me almost like incest. "Why is he speaking about divorce now?" I asked as diplomatically as I could.

"He says he has fallen in love. I understand. I love Dennis."

"Remember your power chant?" I asked. "Would you like to try it again?"

"No. I want you to tell me about Dennis."

"Your father is the root of your problem," I said.

"I hate my father. I only want to talk about love."

"Love and hate are the same energy," I told her. Her hate for her father was magnetizing her toward Dennis.

"Don't try to mix me up," Kim said.

I was afraid her grandfather was disappointed with my efforts. I wondered what would happen to Kim now. I tried to see if she would get rid of Dennis, if she would go for an audition and land a part, but it was all too new. It took time for things to change on a deep level.

"I'm sorry," I mouthed to her grandfather.

Then I heard two Chinese syllables. I repeated them. "Ping, ping."

Kim sucked in her breath. "That's what my grandfather called me. My nursery name was Ciu Ping. I loved my grandfather." Then she began to cry. "I went away from all he taught me, and look what happened. I'm so so sorry."

Our time was up, but I'd never leave a client in that shape. "It's all right," I said. "There are always ways to make amends."

"What does my grandfather want me to do?" she asked anxiously.

If Kim rekindled her connection with her grandfather's loving spirit, she'd remember what real love was. It might save her. I watched his spirit intently, waiting for instructions.

Her grandfather began moving his lips, nodding slightly to a rhythm. A vision of a pagoda rose from the top of his head. "He wants you to go back to the temple," I said. "He wants you to pray and chant." Then it was as if her grandfather had projected a slide onto the screen of my mind. I told Kim what I was seeing. "He wants you to make an altar to him in your living room. And he wants you to light incense."

"Tell him I will," she said, but her grandfather had already faded out.

I eased Kim off the phone, hung up, and I went down to the kitchen. Cooking was the best way to banish ghosts. I got out three pounds of raw chopped meat and put them in a bowl with an egg, breadcrumbs, spices, and a few sprinkles of water. I grated raw onions until I was crying, but as I was shaping the meatballs with my wet hands, I felt as if I were doing Kim's job at the massage parlor. I began thinking about sex. The Orthodox didn't have sex on Friday nights, but Rory and I were Reformed. A lot of my married clients had stopped having sex practically after their honeymoon. I was lucky. Rory and I were still at it, but we were so rushed these days. When Cara was little, weekend nights, after we put her to bed, Rory and I used to give each other massages. We made slow, tantric love that we'd learned from a tape. Afterwards, we took long showers together, soaping each other. He shampooed my hair. We were love drunk. "Too good to be true," he used to murmur. Monday mornings, after he left for work, I pulled up the sheet on his side of the bed, brought it to my face, and breathed him in. I couldn't let him go. Now, with him working so hard, he was too tired, and Cara was either up all night studying or out somewhere where we would have to pick her up.

I sighed. The phone rang. It was Rory. It was as if my thoughts had summoned him. "I love you," I said.

"Love you, too. What's for dinner?"

"Meatballs," she said.

"For *shabbes?*" he asked.

"Meatballs and challah," I said.

When Cara got home from school, I barely recognized her. She had a red star painted on her cheek, and her hair was in a hundred braids knotted with beads. She took a breath, drew herself up, and smiled at me. The star rose nearer her eye. She shook her head slightly so the beads in her hair knocked together and jingled.

Relax, I told myself. She's the right age for fads. I remembered wearing white lipstick and sprinkling silver glitter in my hair. "You look cute," I said.

Then she took off Darcy's old jacket, and my mouth dropped open. Under it, she was wearing a tight red lace blouse. You could see her bra right through it. "And where did you get that blouse?"

She fingered the buttons proudly. "The thrift shop at Saint Paul's. Isn't it great?"

"They sell something like that in a church?"

"Mom, it's for charity."

Maybe I was wrong, I thought. I saw a lot of teenagers dressed like this. "Trashy chic," they called it. A lot of grown women dressed like that, too. Maybe it wasn't such a big deal. I didn't want to fight with Cara over everything. I became tongue-tied. I needed a second opinion. I needed Bubbie, but was she still mad at me for putting money first? *Bubbie,* I silently called.

Then I smelled lavender, and I heard Bubbie whisper, "*Vay,* dressed like a *kurveh,* and for charity no less. A girl in our family should go to school like that!"

I looked into Cara's face. "You didn't wear that in school, did you?" I demanded.

Cara averted her eyes. "Yeah."

"Och!" Bubbie said, and her scent evaporated.

It was all too much for me, too. "You went to school like that, and the dean didn't call me?"

She shrugged. "For what?"

"Don't ever wear anything like that to school again!"

Cara rolled her eyes, but she put the jacket back on and held it tightly around herself. She looked up at me. "For your information, I kept the jacket on all day."

"Well, keep the jacket on all night, too," I said. "It's *shabbes,* and your father is coming home for dinner."

Rory got home before sundown. The dining room table was set with my mother's embroidered tablecloth and Bubbie's brass candlesticks. Cara's hair was still multibraided, and the star was still on her cheek, but she'd changed out of that red shirt and wore a blue sweater from my closet. I put a cloth napkin over my head and lit the candles. As I waved my hands over them and recited the prayer, I felt Bubbie's presence and saw her hands floating over mine, and hoped that someday when I was gone, Cara would feel my hands over hers as she lit candles.

When Cara was six and we were in Maine, she'd missed lighting the *shabbes* candles so much that we had to stop in a Christmas shop and buy two red candles set in green cut-glass holders and light them back in our motel. I remembered how sweet and sure her voice was when she sang the haftorah on the *bima* at her bat mitzvah. We used to go to temple every Friday night, but Rory was so tired these days that his snoring disturbed the service, so we celebrated at home. Rory said the *barucha* over the challah, gave us each a slice, and then did the prayer over the wine. He put his hands on the crown of Cara's braided hair and blessed her. Then he kissed the star on her cheek.

As I served the meatballs with *kasha varnishkes* instead of spaghetti, I thought, *This is just what Cara needs—a quiet spiritual evening at home.* But Cara's brow was furrowed, and she picked at her food.

"A penny for your thoughts," Rory said to her.

"Courtney's parents are in marriage counseling." Cara sighed.

I put down my fork. I knew better than to bring up the split wedding ring I'd seen over Courtney's head. In Great Neck, there were marriage counselors on practically every corner. Divorce lawyers, too. "I don't know whether I'm sorry to hear that or glad to hear that," I said.

"Lisa Cohen's and Suzie Lincoln's parents are in marriage counseling, too. But Darcy's mother said that Suzanne Berk's mother already had one foot out of the marriage." Cara was twisting her napkin.

"This is what I get for offering a penny for thoughts on *shabbes*," Rory said.

"Raj Patel, whose grades are good enough for Harvard, will probably have to work his way through a state school," Cara continued. "Raj's parents are more loaded than Courtney's, but they're splitting and remarrying, and neither wants to pay his tuition." She began to speak faster, her voice getting shrill. "He might have to go live with his married sister in San Diego and go to a commuting school there. Even if we kids study as hard as anything, we still don't have any security. Parents can just decide to divorce and leave you out on a limb. You're better off being an orphan. At least you know where you stand and the state provides for you."

Rory put his palms on the table. I thought he was going to get up, but he stayed in his seat. "Couldn't we talk about something positive for once?" he asked. "Would it be too much to ask for a pleasant evening together?"

"Whatever," she said, pouting.

I knew how serious this was, how kids were affected by divorce and how the harmful effects continued even when they were adults. Deliberately, I reached for Rory's hand and squeezed it. Cara noticed, and her whole body relaxed, and soon a smile played over her lips.

"On Wednesday," Cara said, "we had a test on *Crime and Punishment* and Larry Somes wrote a bunch of crib notes on his palm with pen. He finished early, and was worried someone would see, so he sat there with his hand on the side of his face like this." She put her elbow on the table and propped her head up with her hand. "He was sweating, and when the bell rang, and he put his hand down, the blue smeary answers were backwards on his face. He gave himself away like Raskolnikov. Busted!"

We all started to laugh. Cara's face lit up. She told us more funny stories about kids at school, and Rory told some about his customers. I was glad to keep quiet. Besides, I loved watching Rory being a dad. When he wasn't overtired or overwhelmed, he had a real knack for it. For the first time in months, my heart felt full.

• • •

Our *shabbes* dinner with Cara ended so well that she seemed eager for more family time. On Sunday at noon, she asked us to pick her up from a sleepover at Darcy's so the three of us could go to Nathan's for hot dogs and then to a movie at Roosevelt Field.

I usually tried to avoid Darcy's mother, Barbara. But when we drove up to their house, Barbara was in her driveway, her blond permed hair blending in with the sheepskin collar of her short leather jacket. "Oh, no," I said to Rory. "We'll be here for an hour."

We struck up a conversation. I tried to concentrate on what Rory and Barbara said, but I felt a prickly feeling on my back, a disturbance in the field behind me. In a moment, I heard the sound of hell opening its gates with a terrible roar. "What's that?" I shouted, and turned to see a boy on a motorcycle come tearing up the street. He wore jeans tighter than flesh, a black leather jacket looped with chains, and a leather collar studded with metal. His head was shaved, except for a topknot flapping like a yellow flag, and when he took the turn, the motorcycle leaned into the road, angled so close, he almost skidded. We all gasped as if we were watching a horror film.

When he was out of sight and the noise died down, Barbara said, "That's Lance Stark. Whenever he tears down this block, he usually has a tootsie clinging to him, a different one every time. He lives in Kings Point with his mother, Pepper. Between you and me," she said, lowering her voice, "they're filthy rich and she's a lush."

She always prefaced her remarks with "Between you and me" as if that permitted her to break a professional confidence.

"He looks too old for high school," Rory said.

"He was left back at least once," Barbara whispered, "and it's no wonder. He can't keep his mind on schoolwork. Last semester, he was kicked out of Buckner Academy. Even in kindergarten he was famous for dragging little girls into the coat closet."

Rory shook his head. "The kid has big problems."

"You're right," Barbara said gravely, but her eyes were sparkling. Cara had accused me of being a spy, but I got the clearest image of Barbara stealing into a doorway marked STUDENT RECORDS. I saw her reading students' files with that same sparkle in her eyes, and she was licking her lips, savoring every dirty secret to spread around town in her perfect speech. My stomach turned. Maybe being fed all Barbara's gossip was what made Darcy purge. I bet Barbara was so involved with everyone else's kids that she didn't even know what her own daughter was doing. I looked at my watch, hoping she'd think we were in a hurry, but she went right on.

"Lance is probably on his way to getting kicked out of our school, too," Barbara said. "Just last month he was suspended for showing his tattoo in class. An arrow on his stomach pointing down. And I heard that last year, a junior named Chrissie Slovak tried to commit suicide because of him."

Just then, Cara stepped toward us from the doorway, staring off in the direction of the motorcycle, her mouth open. I got a psychic flash of her whole body fading out, as if it were being erased. "Cara!" I called.

She came out of her trance. "Hi," she said to me. She hugged Darcy, then thanked Barbara, and got into the car as if nothing out of the ordinary had happened.

# 10

FROM THE MOMENT I heard Cara's footsteps coming down to breakfast, I got a funny feeling, as if I should know something that I didn't.

"Morning," she said sleepily. She was wearing a big blue bandana low on her forehead, a black turtleneck, and tight jeans.

I felt like saying, "I can see the outline of your thong panties," but I swallowed that remark. "I made some oatmeal for us," I said.

She wrinkled her nose. "It's been years since I liked that."

"Want some coffee?" I asked.

She perked up, as if I were finally catching on and treating her like an adult. "Yeah, sure. Thanks."

I poured her a cup. She took a few sips. "There's so much I didn't get a chance to tell you the other night," she said, her words rushing out. "Monday morning we had to be evacuated from school by the police. It stank so badly that they thought there had been a murder. Turned out Beth Prensky had left her dissection chicken in the locker over the weekend." Cara held her nose and waved her other hand in the air. She went on for ten minutes, describing what everyone had said and done. I was so delighted with her cheerful company that I was afraid to move.

"Mom, I've begun having lunch in the cafeteria in the office building on the corner of Lakeville and Northern," she finally blurted. "I know you don't like me to leave school grounds, but nobody can stay in school all *day*. You can't even go to the bathroom. There's so much cigarette smoke, you practically need a gas mask to breathe. And you know what grosses me out the most?"

I shook my head.

"Kids wad up toilet paper, wet it, and throw it up on the ceiling. It sticks there and dribbles down on you."

Her heart was opening to me again. I leaned forward.

Then the phone rang, and she sprang to answer it. "It's for me," she said. "Oh, hi, Darcy," she added, loudly. Still talking, she went out the kitchen door, closed it, and went halfway down the basement steps, straining the long phone cord. I tried not to listen, but I heard her whisper "Lance." My coffee suddenly tasted as if I'd lightened it with sour milk. It couldn't be the Lance from the motorcycle, I thought. He certainly wouldn't travel in the same circles as she did.

When she sat down at the table again, I asked, "You know that boy Lance Stark?"

Her eyes looked dreamy. Her wrist faltered, and some coffee sloshed over the rim of her cup. "Everyone knows him," she said, but she wouldn't meet my eye.

I leaned forward, waiting to hear more. Instead of finishing her story, she eyed the department store ads in *Newsday*. "Why are you staring at me?" she demanded.

"Oh, sorry, I didn't know I was."

"Well, you are." She picked up her backpack. "Courtney is dropping us off at Darcy's after chorus. I'll be home at six thirty."

"Okay," I said, but I felt uneasy. It sounded like a lie.

In my mother's file box of favorite magazine recipes, I looked up "Muffins, oatmeal," and made three batches to salvage the wasted breakfast.

Afterwards, I went up to my office and waited for the phone to ring.

"This is Vincent Guardelli," a man said in a voice rich with gravel. "You got some time?"

My nerves were too frayed to just jump into a reading with a new client. "You have to book in advance," I said.

"With my life, I never know what's going down from one minute to the next. It's either now or never."

Again I thought of all our debt. "All right," I said. I told him the cost of the reading.

"No problemo," he said. As I took down his name and credit card number, I thought, *This is the kind of client I need.* But then my mind went blank. *Vincent Guardelli,* I repeated to myself. It sounded familiar, like someone I should know, someone famous. Sometimes famous people called me and used an alias. They even had credit cards under assumed names. I took deep breaths. I felt my pulse slow. In my mind, I saw Vincent. A burly guy in his late fifties with thick black hair, handsome in his own way. Then my mind and pulse began to race. I remembered an article in *People* magazine I'd read in my dentist's office. Vincent Guardelli was the famous stand-up comedian, Vince Guardel. Vincent Edward Guardel. I had seen him on TV.

"You still there?" he asked.

"Yes, I'm just warming up." What had that article said? Vince Guardel had been married five times. Each time to a progressively younger woman. And he had been close friends with Sinatra. Now I had something to go on. I began audaciously. "'Strangers in the night,'" I sang. "'Two lonely people, we were strangers in the night.'"

"Huh?" he said.

"Weren't you friends with Frank Sinatra?" I asked.

"Nah. I never had any use for the guy."

He wouldn't admit he knew Sinatra. I told him about his five young wives.

"I just have one old ex-wife."

I didn't know what to say.

Then I heard him sigh. "Vince is blue," he said.

For a moment, I got even more confused. Then I realized he was talking about himself in the third person. But his voice had given me something to go on. I was back on track. A woman came to mind. "I see a woman. She's thirtyish. Yellow haired, pretty."

"That's the broad that's killing me."

I saw a hypodermic needle, a test strip, and a bottle of whiskey. He was diabetic, an overeater, and a tippler. "She isn't what's killing you. You don't take care of your health."

"Nah. It's aggravation that will do Vince in. It's worse than a Magnum."

As soon as he mentioned a gun, I got frightened. Vince wasn't Vince Guardel, the comic. He was a gangster. I got a vision of a man at the bottom of the East River wearing cement shoes.

"Today I buy this broad a diamond tennis bracelet, a lynx coat, and a Rolex. I don't say boo about it. Then it's like, what did you give me? And she goes bananas if I want to see her every night. Says she has her own life. Women's lib crap."

I twisted the phone cord tightly around my finger.

"Last night," he went on, "I wanted to see her, and she claimed she had plans with a girlfriend. So what do you think? Is she doing a lesbian thing with this so-called friend of hers?"

I could tell that, to him, if a woman didn't do exactly what he wanted, she was either a bitch or a lesbian. "No," I said. I was angry with him, but I kept my voice calm. "She had a prior commitment, and she honored it."

"Mind if I have a cigar?" he asked as if we were beside each other in a car.

"Fine," I said.

He stopped to light up. "I spent the whole weekend by myself.

That's not right, no matter how you cut it. Not right. I send her five thousand smackers a month for her co-op, I buy clothes for her kids, wine her and dine her. She thinks she's something because she went to college."

He was spoiling for a fight, and it would be with me if I didn't play my cards right. I stayed silent, let him rant. I felt like a geisha to an abusive man.

"My last love couldn't get enough of me," he said.

I saw her hands in his pockets. It was only Vince's money that she couldn't get enough of.

"Say if I was to go out with you," he said, "would you spend the whole weekend with me?"

"I'm married."

"So?"

"I never fraternize with clients."

"Fraternize," he said, laughing. "How old are you?"

"Sixty-seven," I lied.

"You're no sixty-seven. I'd give you thirty-five, forty tops."

"Let's get back to you," I said firmly.

"Yeah, back to me. So last week, when she agreed to see me, I take this broad to the Plaza for the whole weekend. I rent an extra room for her two girls. I do everything I can to be a stand-up guy. Then I'm taking her out, and she puts on a pair of pants with socks. I tell her, 'You can't wear that. That's what I'm wearing. Put on a pair of stockings and a dress,' and she has a fit. She's telling me that I'm too controlling. Controlling! I just want to go out with a broad, not with a guy."

As he ranted, I remembered my mother putting on her stockings and straightening her seams. She had told me that during World War II, when stockings were as rare as hen's teeth, she'd drawn seams on the backs of her bare legs with eyebrow pencil. She wore high heels every day. When it rained, she put thin rubber boots over them and in winter, the boots had a trim of Persian lamb. "Women wear pants these days," I told Vince. "Maybe this woman is too young for you. Maybe you should try someone a little older."

"Vince with a battle-ax? Forget about it! After all I've done for her, she says if I don't stop pushing her, she might not ever see me anymore. Who does she think she is?"

"A girlfriend," I said. "A girlfriend is allowed to change her mind."

He sighed again. "If we break up, could I send her little girl a present? One girl, the oldest, is a bitch in training. But the little one calls me Uncle Vince."

"If you aren't seeing her mother anymore," I said, "it wouldn't be right to send a gift to the child. Especially not to one girl and not the other."

"Then I'm not sending nothing to no one." I heard him draw on his cigar. "You're nice to talk to," he said. "I own the most successful bar and steak house in New York. You must have heard of it? Guardelli's on Fifty-third and Madison."

"Of course I know Guardelli's," I lied.

"Why don't you come down sometime?" he said. "Ask for me. I'll give you a meal like you've never had before. The best wines."

"I don't fraternize with clients," I repeated.

This time he didn't laugh. "Listen, I know how to treat a woman. She spends a weekend with me, I send her to Elizabeth Arden. I tell the manager there, 'This is Vince Guardelli. I'm sending a lady friend over. See that she gets everything you got to offer from head to toe.'"

Sounded good to me. I barely had time to shave my legs.

"And you know all I really want out of this?" he said. "A little love. That's all."

"You're going about it in the wrong way. You make the woman feel bought."

"So, should I cut off this broad's rent check?"

I thought of the woman out on the street with her two little girls in tow. "Not yet," I advised.

"You're talking out of both sides of your mouth," he said. "You're like the rest of them. Like her. She wants a meal ticket and wants her freedom, too."

I was beginning to get frightened for the woman. What if she crossed him? Would she end up rubbed out? "I don't see her in your life long term," I said nervously.

"Come to Guardelli's for lunch today. I'll send a car for you."

"No, thanks," I said.

"Yeah, I forgot. You don't fornicate with the clients."

"Our time is up," I said curtly.

When I got off the phone, I shivered and stuck out my tongue. I went upstairs and took a hot shower. As the silvery water beat against my skin, I said to myself, *I bet Bubbie never had to deal with a client making a pass at her.*

Suddenly, the water got way too hot. I quickly turned it off. When I stepped out of the shower, there was Bubbie, putting on lipstick in front of the mirror. "So, you think no men were interested in your *bubbe?*" She blotted her lips on a tissue. "I had to keep a brass andiron in my parlor just in case any of them got funny ideas. I chased Moitel the knife sharpener all the way down the stairs with it."

"You never told me that," I said.

"You were a kid then. There's lots of things I didn't tell you. You remember the marriage I saved between Lydia and Sy? Sy came a week later and said he was in love with me. And there's more. Much more," she teased, very pleased with herself as she faded out. Her face with its pink smile lingered in the mirror.

When Cara came home, she didn't speak, but I had a sense of her excitement, as if she were trying to hold something inside.

"How was your day, honey?" I asked as I set out our salad and chicken cutlets.

Suddenly, she pulled off her bandana. She had dyed her

brown hair a shoe-polish black. "You dyed your hair!" I said. I stopped eating.

"It was so boring before," she said, staring down at a clump of it in her hand, as if she couldn't believe what she'd done either.

Her hair looked like a black broom. "Your hair wasn't boring. It was gorgeous."

"To you, maybe. But . . ."

I saw radiance around her, as shiny as her hair used to be. Then she took a breath and said, "My boyfriend loves my hair this way."

I got prickles up my spine. I hoped her boyfriend wasn't Lance Stark. "Who is the lucky guy?"

She stuck out her chin. "Lance Stark," she said, her green eyes defiant.

I sucked my breath in so hard, it sounded like a gasp.

"You didn't know?" Cara asked, and I shook my head. "You didn't know it psychically?"

"I didn't know," I said quietly, and then the corners of her lips turned up in a smile.

I should have known from the moment he rode by on his motorcycle and I saw the way she gazed after him, but I guess I didn't want to believe it. I got a sudden image of the hallway at school. The water fountain. The phone booth. I saw Lance strutting down the hall. A girl rushing over to him, draping herself around him. Thank God it wasn't Cara. The girl took his hand and put it on her ass. I dropped my fork. "I don't know why you have to go looking for trouble."

"I didn't look for him, Mom. Lance came to me, and he's not trouble. I left my history notebook in the cafeteria, and he tracked me down to give it to me."

She was gushing. I had to measure my words. One slip and she'd shut herself off from me, but I was so nervous that I blurted out, "His tattoo speaks volumes. He's too fast for you." It was such a passé expression that I hoped Cara wouldn't even know what it meant.

"People say a lot about him that isn't true," Cara said. "Kids do all kinds of things to their bodies, but that doesn't show who they really are."

I thought about the terrible things Barbara Traubman had told Rory and me about Lance. "Did you know that he hurt another girl so badly that she tried to commit suicide?"

"He didn't, Mom. He wasn't even seeing Chrissie. It was a rumor. People blame Lance for everything."

There was a small whirling light to the right of Cara. I felt my eyes circling to follow its orbit. The light grew larger and stilled. I sensed a spirit. "That boy is a no-goodnik," my father's voice said, and then tuned out.

"So you're dating Lance?" I asked, trying to sound casual.

"You don't have to date to be in love. Nobody dates anymore. That's not what love is about." Her fingers were curled down on her palm as she checked the glitter polish on her nails.

"So, how do you know him?" I asked. "Is he in any of your classes?"

"Everybody knows Lance. You know what, Mom? He said he's never met anyone like me before. You don't really know him and neither does anybody else. Not the way I do. You should see him with me. He's so polite. Every period when the bell rings, he's waiting at my classroom door. He carries my backpack, holds doors open for me. If kids bump into me, he makes them stop and tell me they're sorry. He doesn't argue over grades, trying to get two points more, like the boys in my honors classes. He never talks about school at all. It's such a relief. And, Mom, he named his motorcycle after me—*Cara Mia*."

*Mamma mia,* I thought.

"He's even writing a poem about me," she added.

"Those are things he's doing for himself," I said.

"You don't know how smart he is. He can make up rap songs off the top of his head about loneliness. And he says that I inspire him. That I have a talent for love."

As she spoke of him, Cara lit up, but I felt as if a terrible darkness were swallowing me.

"If you only knew how hard he has it at home," she said. "His parents split up. He doesn't want to live with his mother, and his Dad lives in a girlfriend's apartment where there isn't enough room for Lance. Lance's grandmother lives in Great Neck, but she's too old and doesn't understand him. I'm the only one he can really talk to. He tells me about everything, and I tell him everything, too. Anyway, Mom, it's my life." Her chin jutted forward.

I knew from having tried to talk my clients out of terrible romances that it only made them more defensive, more loyal to the rotten guy and more angry at me. I had lost clients that way. I didn't want to lose my own daughter. "Yes, it's your life," I agreed.

She cocked her head, as if she was surprised that I wasn't arguing with her. She began to relax back into her chair, but then her lips compressed, and her brow furrowed. "Listen, Mom, you aren't going to go around acting as if you can spy on me, are you?"

She had all her bases covered. "Acting as if" implied that my gift wasn't real and "spying" was her way of making me feel guilty for it. Bubbie had told me that anger was both a blindfold and ear corks. I had told Cara how I really felt about Lance. I wasn't afraid of confrontation, but arguing with her over my gift would just throw a smoke screen over the matter at hand. I hoped what I'd said about Lance would plant a seed of doubt in her brain. I stilled myself, forced the corners of my mouth up into a smile, and said calmly. "Of course you can count on me to respect your privacy."

"Okay, good," she said, the worry line disappearing from her forehead. "And please don't mention this to Daddy."

"All right," I said. "It's just between us—girl talk."

She stood, walked off, and started up the stairs. Then she leaned back so she could see me through the doorway. "Mom," she said, smiling and sighing, "you know how you go into a trance? Well, now I know what it's like to be in one, too."

# 11

IN BETWEEN WORRYING about Cara, I felt compelled to use my psychic powers to help Rory with his business, even though, like Cara, he was dead set against it. If I found out things that could help him, I could drop hints, ask leading questions. "Sometimes you got to do things sideways," Bubbie used to say.

I was in bed with my notebook propped against my knees, drawing a picture of the front of Mirror. I tried to get it as detailed as possible. I even left off a piece of the O that had blackened on Rory's sign, but I didn't get any psychic clues. I turned the page and began drawing a floor plan. After it was finished, I found that I had drawn a dark hole right in the center. I stared at it, wondering what it could be.

"What are you up to?" Rory asked as he got into bed.

"Oh, just doodling," I said. Quickly, I closed my notebook and tucked it guiltily under the covers.

Rory yawned. It sounded like the drawbridge of a castle being let down from creaky hinges. Then the lights were out, and both of us fell asleep.

In a dream, I heard a bang and saw a red flash, my symbol for gunfire. I woke up trembling. I was getting a warning. Rory had been robbed four times. Once he was almost killed because he had so little cash in the store. It hit me that the black hole I'd drawn in this plan had been a bullet hole!

The phone rang. Even before I picked it up, I knew it was Rory's alarm company. "This is ADT Alarms," a man said. "Your store alarm went off three minutes ago." I hated to wake Rory, but no one could enter a pharmacy without a licensed pharmacist.

I shook Rory's shoulder and told him. He groaned and pulled his pants and shirt on.

I grabbed his arm. "Don't go in to investigate alone," I said. "Call the police."

He pulled away. "The police give out fines after three false alarms, and I've already had three this year. That's why when the store isn't open I have the alarm company ring me direct. Besides, if I wait for the police, it'll take twice as long."

"Please," I said, "I'm sure someone's in your store. I see movement." I held on to his arm for dear life. "Either promise me or I'm not letting go."

"All right," he said as he left.

I got under the covers and tossed around. I tried to see what was going on psychically, but I was trying too hard and nothing would come. I got up and paced the house. I straightened the pictures on the wall and the disarray on the coffee table. There were three field guides for bird watching that Rory hadn't touched in years. A local *Pennysaver* was rumpled in his armchair. I noticed he had circled an ad for the Tennis Bubble. He no longer had time for tennis either, and with his carpal tunnel syndrome, he would have to wear a brace to get a good grip on the racket. What if there was no time left for Rory to do everything he had been putting off? It was all so sad. I left his things where they were and went back up to bed to stare at the ceiling, trying to will him safely home.

An hour and a half later, I heard Rory's car. Before I even saw him, I felt a wave of heat. I knew he was furious. I sat up in bed. He came upstairs, his bloodshot eyes crazed.

"Well, instead of checking out the store myself, I called the police like you insisted," he said loudly. "They went into the store with guns drawn and what did they find? A mouse had eaten through the alarm wire. The police slapped a hundred-dollar fine on me and asked me if I wanted them to arrest the mouse."

I felt sick. I wrapped my arms tightly around my nightgown. My "bullet hole" was actually a mouse hole.

"It's so late," Rory said. "I might as well have stayed at the pharmacy instead of driving home. Miriam, you're a great psychic, but you can't do a thing for my business. Think of it as the 'separation of church and state.' Think of it as my constitutional right in this marriage to not have you reviewing every move I make at Mirror."

My throat tightened. "Yes, I hear you," I finally said.

Rory got into bed, his back to me. I could see how angry he still was, and worse, I could feel it, like chilly waves lapping against the shore. I pulled the covers over my head as if I could hide from myself.

When I woke up, he was already gone. I felt the house moving about me, a living thing. I tried to fix on Rory, but couldn't concentrate. *Is he still mad at me? What is he doing right now?* I finally called him, but he was busy. "I'll call you later," he said. "Oh, and take the car in for an inspection. I'll be home at ten. Take care."

I hung up. He hadn't said he loved me.

All afternoon, I fumbled through my readings. When I went to heat up a piece of pie, I saw the crown of my father's brown felt hat reflected in the window of the microwave. I wanted to turn around to look at him, but I stayed very still so I wouldn't waste a moment of his presence.

"Tell my granddaughter that if she gives up this *oysvurf*, a prince I'll send her."

"Thanks, Daddy," I said, but he was gone.

I felt my heart squeeze. Kim might let me deliver a message from her dead grandfather, but Cara never would. *It's not so bad,* I told myself. *At least my father still knows what's going on in our lives.*

Cara's Five-Star notebook that she used for her French journal was open on the chair. Mme Bernschwager checked the journals every Wednesday. Today was Wednesday and the double pages had no writing on them at all, just hearts pierced by arrows. I thought of Lance and the arrow pointing down. I turned the page. "I love L," Cara wrote. How could she have forgotten the journal? She used to care too much about school, used to study so hard, I swore I picked up some of the facts by osmosis. Now I was lucky to pick up anything, and when I did, it had Lance in it. All the comfort my father's appearance had given me left me like air from a popped balloon.

Cara came home so late she missed dinner. I'd been prepared to talk to her about her new irresponsibility. "The basketball coach kept us way after practice," she explained, averting her eyes.

The thought that she might be lying was so painful that I couldn't ask any more questions.


The next morning, she taped a note on my door:

> *We have a basketball game in Manhasset. I'm going to Darcy's afterwards for dinner. I'll be home at 7:30.*
>
> *Cara*


I peeled the note off. A fleck of paint came off with the tape. She hadn't asked permission to eat at Darcy's, and she hadn't even written "Dear Mom" or "Love, Cara." *This is as bad as Rory not saying "I love you" to me on the phone.* I knew I was sensitive, but these were our family rituals.

In the bathroom, I splashed cold water on my face as if I could shock myself into some calm. *Better,* I thought. My mother used to tell me, "Smile and the world will feel lighter, even if you don't feel like smiling." I smiled at myself in the mirror, but all I saw was that the medicine chest was coming loose from the wall. Everything in our house was breaking down.

*Work,* I told myself. *I can work.* I did four readings—a woman who wanted to know why her husband insisted on having their Irish setter sleep between them; a man who wanted me to describe the dress his sister would be wearing to a party so he could show up in the same one; an eighty-nine-year-old woman who asked if, in her next life, she was going to sleep with Mel Gibson; and a girl, Cara's age, who wanted to know if she'd be with her boyfriend long enough to make it worth tattooing his name on her right butt cheek. I was too depressed to cook dinner. Instead, I drove to Gino's to get a pizza. I carried the box out to the parking lot behind Sam Goody's and spotted Cara's basket-ball coach, Mr. Cuddy. I knew he might still be mad at me for interrupting the game, but I could apologize, couldn't I? And then he could tell me what a good player Cara had become. I felt my pride flickering from just seeing him. I put the pizza box on the top of my car. "Coach," I called. He walked toward my car, his hair gelled back, his hands in his chino pockets, the silver whistle flopping on the chain around his neck. "I'm sorry I interrupted that first game."

"And I'm sorry Cara quit the team," he said.

I blinked. "What?"

"She quit."

"I thought she was playing right now," I told him.

"She quit two weeks ago."

I felt myself freeze.

"Are you all right?" Mr. Cuddy asked.

"Migraine," I said apologetically, turning my head as if he could read my shame. I hurried to the car and once inside, I couldn't seem to catch my breath. Cara wasn't tied to the house as I had been by my father's strict curfews. I didn't talk over her the way my mother had talked over me. My mother used to wave away my excuses with a flick of her wrist and say, "I already know the whole story from beginning to end," as if *she* were the psychic. *Is lying to me what Cara needs to do to find her own identity?* Was she trying to get Rory's attention? Or did she have a secret life? I thought about my having told her over the years that my gift was "our little secret." Was the pattern of secrecy that I began coming back to haunt me?

The coach was still watching me. I felt his eyes as I turned on the ignition, as I drove slowly past him. I gripped the wheel, but I couldn't keep my hands from shaking. And even once I was inside our house, I couldn't do more than sit in the living room and close my eyes and wait.

Seven thirty came and went, and Cara wasn't home. I resettled on the couch, putting a throw pillow in the small of my back, and closed my eyes. I saw Lance, his shaved head, his bleached topknot, the arrow pointing downward. He was standing in a room. Details began to fill in: a black light, a big TUPAC LIVES poster, bottles of liquor, probably from his mother's stash, and a double mattress on the floor. And then I saw my daughter standing there on colt legs, her eyes flying about the room, then settling on him like a tiny jeweled beetle caught in a web. He began to unbutton her blouse.

"I . . . I don't think I'm ready for this," Cara said.

"Cara mia, I'll make you ready," he said.

I jumped up and opened my eyes. *This can't be happening,* I told myself. *It's just a projection of my fears.*

At eight thirty, I phoned Darcy, hoping Cara would be there. I was relieved when she, rather than Barbara, answered. "Cara isn't home yet, and I thought she might be at your house," I said. "Is she there?"

Darcy hedged. Then she whispered, "Don't worry, Mrs. Kaminsky. Cara just left. She'll be home soon."

I heard a scuffle and muffled voices, as if Darcy were covering the receiver with her hand, but I could hear her pleading with her mother, "But Cara will kill me. I promised I'd say she was here."

Suddenly, Barbara was talking to me. "Listen, Miriam—"

"No, no," I heard Darcy crying in the background.

"Shut your mouth, Darcy," Barbara said. "We could get sued for giving a minor an alibi." Then she said, "Sorry, Miriam, Cara hasn't been here at all today, and I have no idea where she is. Shall I call around for you?" Barbara asked, her voice rich with interest.

"No, thanks," I said breezily. "As a matter of fact, I think I hear Cara right now."

After I got off the phone, I paced the house furiously. More lies. Cara had lied to me. *Lied.* The word felt like a sharp stone on my tongue.

Ten minutes later, the key turned in the lock of our front door. It was Cara. Her hair was tousled; her lips swollen from what must have been hours of kissing.

I couldn't contain myself. "Cara, I know you weren't at a basketball game, because you quit the team, and I know you weren't at Darcy's. Stop lying. Where were you?"

"What is this?" she said. "The Inquisition?"

I stared her down. "I'm giving you the chance to come clean."

"I was at Lance's," she said quietly.

"What were you doing there?"

"Listening to CDs."

"Who else was there?"

"His mom."

*His mother the lush,* I thought. "But you told me you were going to basketball and then Darcy's."

"Look, I'm all right. I can take care of myself."

"You lied," I said.

"You lie, too!" she snapped. "To your stupid clients."

"Maybe you don't believe in my work, but how do I lie to you?" I asked, shocked.

"You act like it's real," she spat. "All that mumbo jumbo. Like you really know what's going to happen!"

"I know that you and that boy are headed for trouble!"

"Well, I know my future, too. Better than you do! And I know my future's Lance!" She turned around and stormed up to her room. I heard her door slam.

By the time I heard Rory's wheels spit the driveway gravel that night, I knew he was already worked up about something. The entry light shone on the plastic bag he was carrying. He handed me the bag of pharmacy jackets that needed to be laundered.

I tattled on Cara without stopping for a breath.

"That hoodlum on the motorcycle!" Rory said. "Only a few minutes ago, he was zipping along beside me on Lakeville, then, without signaling, he cut in front of me onto Northern. I almost ended up on the divide!" I saw a vein in his temple throb. "I yelled out the window to that hood, 'Hey, buddy, watch where you're going,' and he gave me the finger. This is the boy our Cara likes?"

"Yes," I said. "Lance Stark."

"Son of a bitch," he muttered. We could hear her Ween CD blasting from her room. "I'm too upset to talk to her now," Rory said, and slumped onto the couch, his head in his hands. "That boy is just the tip of the iceberg. Medicaid changed their forms and I need new software to process them. Plus, the new software isn't compatible with my hardware. I have to get a whole new computer. And we're not talking a little PC. The system I'll need runs about thirty thousand dollars. Medicaid has no mercy. I'll have to take out another loan."

I saw what was in his mind: a foreclosure notice on our house,

Cara and me standing at the curb next to stray cats that were lying on our couches and armchairs.

He dropped his hands from his face, straightened his back, and drew himself up. "I'll talk to her now," he said.

I heard him knocking at her door. "Cara, it's Dad. Open the door."

I made myself busy so I wouldn't snoop. But as I pinched back the dead leaves from our spider plant, I saw Cara and Rory in my mind. I knew Cara was sitting on her bed and Rory in the rocking chair. He was leaning forward, his elbows at his knees. He looked in control. I blinked away the vision. I didn't want to interfere, even psychically. I had to sing "The Star-Spangled Banner" in my head to jam their conversation. By the time I reached "The rocket's red glare," Cara was screaming, "I hate my life! I can't live like this!" As I ran to the steps, Rory was coming down.

"Relax," he told me. "It won't help if you get hysterical, too. She's just blowing off steam. She didn't like that I told her I didn't want her seeing Lance anymore and that you'd be picking her up after school until we can trust her. By the way, is that okay with you?"

"I can't take it anymore!" Cara was shouting.

"She's just doing a Sarah Bernhardt," Rory said.

In my mind, I saw three letters: SOS. "I'm worried about her, Rory."

"She'll be fine," he said, putting his arms around me. I blinked away the SOS and leaned into him, feeling his strength. Yet I knew that no matter what punishment Rory and I meted out, what surveillance I maintained, Cara and Lance would find a way to have clandestine meetings.


When I woke up the next morning, I smelled dampness and followed the scent downstairs. Now the wall in the den was leaking. I couldn't put off repairs any longer. I called several roofers for estimates. I gave them Rory's pharmacy number. If they were too expensive, Rory would veto it, but at least I wouldn't have to go back and forth between them, haggling.

In the afternoon, I drove slowly over the speed bumps on the long road leading to Cara's high school. The wooded area was lush: beeches, pines, and patches of kudzu. Canada geese were flying over the playing field. The track team coach was running along the road, his team following like goslings.

Cara was waiting in the parking lot, eyeing all the other seniors who were headed for the student lot, either to drive their own car home, or, if they hadn't turned seventeen yet, catch a ride with a friend. When she spotted my Honda, she hunched and pulled her fleece jacket over her head as criminals do when they're being dragged past reporters. She opened the door, threw her backpack into the car, then slid in, keeping her face turned away from me. She was furious at being picked up after school like a baby. I could hear her thinking: *This is America. My parents can't tell me who I can and who I can't see.*

"Hello," I said.

"Hi," she said coolly, her jaw set.

"You don't have to like it," I said, "but Dad and I won't have you sneaking around."

She shrugged. "You mean if I had announced I was going over to Lance's house, you would have let me?"

"Of course not," I said. I stopped myself from saying anything else. I couldn't lose my temper. I had to stay calm to protect her from Lance, from herself. Psychic or not, I was just like any other mother in this pickle. In Cara's eyes, I was passé, housebound, and unworldly. How could I, her mother, possibly know what real love was? How could I stop her before she got hurt? I could've cried, but I held myself together. "Cara, at least promise me you'll never get on that motorcycle. It's suicide."

"Okay already," she said. "I promise."

I didn't know how long she'd be able to keep that promise. As if this weren't a big enough problem, when I stepped in, I saw the whole den ceiling was dripping. "Bubbie, now do you see why I need gelt?" I cried out in exasperation. I didn't think she was there. I didn't smell lavender.

"So, you expect me to feel sorry for you?" she said.

I was startled. The mildew must have overpowered her lavender. I turned to where her voice was coming from. There she was, standing on the coffee table, lifting her skirt up daintily over her ankles in case the water got higher.

"This *vasser* is nothing," Bubbie said. "The floods your father had at his butcher shop were so high, he had to put on fishing boots up to his thighs. He divided the canned goods with washed-off labels between your mother and me. For weeks, we never knew if we were opening brown gravy or canned peaches."

"I remember," I said.

"And in Berdichev, I had to wade through a bitter cold river at night with the Cossack dogs barking behind me. *Neshomeleh,* you got to be brave. There's always a reason to do what's wrong. Even if it's hard, you got to do the right thing. You got to be a healer first and not worry about the gelt, no matter what."

"I'll try," I told her. "Bubbie, what I really need to know is how can I keep Cara away from Lance?"

But Bubbie had had enough of our earthly air. She began to float upward, paddling her arms and kicking her legs. "A little saltpeter in her food," Bubbie said, and disappeared.

I laughed and then sighed. I knew she was just joking, but Bubbie knew a lot of cures for lovesickness that she'd never had time to teach me. I needed to know them now. I blamed my mother. A fresh hit of resentment rose up inside me. All my mother's efforts went into trying to stamp out my gift. I remembered the nights she poured cold water on my face because I had talked in my sleep. She did pencil rubbings on my blotter, then read the impression of what I'd written in the mirror, spying on me. She steamed open letters I wrote to a pen pal in England. When I read a book, she waved her hands between my eyes and the page to make sure I was really reading. Every time I so much as daydreamed, she poked me.

If my father hadn't interceded, I probably wouldn't have gotten to see Bubbie at all. "You can't keep a child away from her *bubbe*," I'd heard him say one night from their bedroom. "There ought to be a law against it."

"Oh, so now I'm married to a lawyer," my mother had said. "Well, there should be a law against your mother filling our child's head with garbage that gets her into trouble."

"Dorothy," my father shot back, "you either bring Putchkie to my mother tomorrow morning or I'll take her myself. Mama has lost so many, she can't lose Putchkie, too."

This softened my mother's heart. "All right," she said. "But I'm staying right there with Miriam, and you tell your mother not to say one word about her *bubbe meisehs* or we're leaving."

After that, I never saw Bubbie alone again. With my mother there, all we could talk about were recipes and avocado plants. Once, when my mother left the room to go to the bathroom, I pointed to the mound on my palm right near my thumb, the one Bubbie had told me was for love. I wanted Bubbie to know how I felt about her, that I remembered all the things she'd taught me, and that I wanted to learn more.

*Plink, plink.* The water was dripping into my pots as fast as the tears rolling down my face. I couldn't stand the sound anymore. I went up to my room, closed the door, sat down in the upholstered corner chair, and put my legs up on the footrest. I lay my head back and had almost drifted into sleep when I heard Cara singing a love song in her sweet soprano about someone filling her senses like a mountain in springtime or a walk in the rain. I found myself wishing that she were yearning for someone who deserved that song.

I thought about what my family would have done if they'd

ever found out I was seeing a boy like Lance. "Lance in the Pants," my mother would have called him, and I would have burned with shame. My father would have looked so pained—his bottom lip puffed as he grit his teeth—that no crush on anyone could have let me do that to him. On top of that, even the thought of disappointing my *bubbe*'s spirit would have put out any fire I felt for a bad boy. But for better or worse, I didn't have my mother's acid tongue, and though Rory's suffering was great, it wasn't enough to inspire that kind of obedience in Cara.

That night, all alone, dumping the pots of water into the sink, splashing the counter and my shoes, I tried to find the right words to convince Cara not to see Lance. But the ones that would be sure to set her against me always raced to the forefront. "He's unworthy of you. Psychically, I see him with another girl on his motorcycle," I would tell her. I dried the heavy enamel pot, bent, and put it inside the cabinet. "He's just using you like he's used the others. You'll end up pregnant or diseased or both." Cara's music floated in. I was too exhausted right now to talk to her anyway. *Morning,* I told myself. Everything looked better in the morning.

But in the morning I was running late. The alarm hadn't gone off, and by the time I woke up, Cara was almost out the door. "Only ten more months until college," I said brightly. I wanted her to remember that she had a future so she wouldn't blow it on Lance.

"Who cares?" she said.

I stood still. "Don't you remember that you said you wanted to get into a good college so you could find out what you want to do in life?"

She shrugged. I could hear her thinking: *What I want to do in life is be with Lance.*

College had been the most important thing in the world to her until Lance. How could she have changed so fast?

She stepped out the door, then stepped back in. "Hey, why is Dad's car in the driveway?" she asked.

He had gone to the bank to apply for another loan. The parking and traffic were so bad that he knew it would be quicker if he walked. "He had some errands in town," I said.

"Oh," she said. "Got to run," and she dashed off.

Up in my office, I sat down in my wicker chair and imagined a calendar page for September. In the thirty numbered squares, I looked for images or signs of her departure for college—suitcases or her unpacking in a room that would be her dorm, but the calendar remained thirty empty rooms with no Cara in them. *Cara isn't really going to throw away her college education on Lance,* I assured myself. But I remembered the time my client, Colette Menkoff's son, Marcus, a physics major at Duke, became so smitten with a cashier at Blimpie's that he became a Hare Krishna, like her. Colette had sobbed, "Marcus calls himself Daubs Dilip now. What kind of a name is that for a Jewish boy?" Edwina Jackson had worked three jobs to send her daughter, Luelle, to an all-girls boarding school in Vermont instead of going to Evander Child in the Bronx, but somehow Luelle hooked up with a guy on the lam for armed robbery. After he was arrested again, Luelle married him anyway. "I do," she said, pressing her lips against the glass barrier that separated them.

I heard Rory on the steps. "Busy?" he called.

"No," I said, opening my eyes as he stepped into the room. For a moment, I was startled. His hair was freshly cut, and his glasses were off. He was wearing his navy suit with the silk striped tie, the matching pocket hankie, and his diamond clip tiepin, and gold cufflinks. I wasn't used to seeing him in a suit except for the high holy days. His pupils were swallowing his irises. I could tell he wanted me. It was almost desperate. He had just asked the bank for another loan. I felt desperate, too. I stood up, and he pressed me against the wall and kissed me hard. His breathing was like a souped-up engine. We broke apart to undress. My clothes slipped off easily, but I had to help him with his cufflinks and tiepin and the tight button at his collar. We rolled on the floor, naked, locked together. As Rory was entering me, I got a flash of Fred inside an OTB. "Twenty on Tea Biscuit," Fred said. I tried to shut Fred out, to concentrate on the tom-toms of my pleasure. I bit Rory's shoulder and shut my eyes, but there was Fred again. I breathed deeply, as if I could breathe in the excitement, leaving no room for worrying about Fred. Then, suddenly, I wasn't thinking of Fred. I was in synch with Rory's movements. Slick with sweat, Rory was thrusting himself inside me. I was so excited that my thighs were trembling, but all of a sudden, I became distracted. Something was pulling my attention away, and then Rory's cell phone rang. He groaned.

"Don't look at it," I pleaded, but he reached for the cell phone anyway.

I lay on the floor, my arm flung over my eyes. I heard Rory go to my desk and dial my phone. "What?" Rory shouted. "Towed? Fred, Fred, calm down. Wait. I'll be right over." Rory hung up, shaking his head. "The delivery van's been towed."

"Separation of church and state or not," I said, "I have to tell you that I got a vision of Fred, clear as day. He stopped off at an OTB to place a bet and probably parked at a hydrant. Believe me," I said. "I can even tell you the name of the horse."

"I don't want to hear about it," Rory said as he hopped into his pants. "What about the armed robber who turned out to be a mouse?"

"What about all the great work I've done with clients?" I said. "What about when I knew that you had a kidney stone?"

But Rory was on his way out the door.

# 12

Rory came home early to take Cara and me out to dinner to help her get her mind off Lance. It was a nice gesture, but I was still angry with him for not believing me about Fred. "I went down to OTB today to corroborate my psychic flash," I told Rory. "Tea Biscuit had come in first, nine-to-one odds. Fred must have raked in a bundle. Maybe you should hire him to place bets for you on his work time instead of being your clerk."

"Will you stop!" Rory said.

"No, I won't. You and Cara go to dinner without me."

When Cara came downstairs, Rory asked, "Would you like to go to Millie's?" Millie's was a chichi restaurant on Middle Neck Road.

"Sure," she said. "Who would pass up a dinner at Millie's?" She pulled at the front of the tattered sweatshirt she lounged around in. "I better change," she said.

Rory took off his pharmacy jacket and put on faded jeans and a denim shirt as if he were Lance's age. I noticed an embroidered blue polo pony over his pocket, and I was surprised because Rory never cared about designer clothes. I would have asked him why he'd spent money on a Ralph Lauren shirt when we were so strapped, but the horse reminded me of Tea Biscuit, and my mind went racing off to Fred at OTB again.

Cara came downstairs wearing the peach sweater set I'd bought her that she'd sworn she wouldn't be caught dead in, and a respectable gray skirt. Her scalp was so dark from touching up her dye job that you couldn't see her middle part. "Ready," she said.

Gallantly, Rory held out his arm, and she took it. She reached up and kissed him. "Daddy," she said the way she had when she was a little girl. Then she looked at me. I was still wearing my white yoga outfit, and I was barefoot. "Mom, aren't you coming?"

My jaw was tight. My pulse was tap-dancing on my temples, but I forced myself to smile. "No," I said. I couldn't say one more thing or I was sure she'd hear the anger in my voice.

She narrowed her eyes at me and then looked at Rory.

"Coming?" he asked her, avoiding my eyes.

"Okay," she finally said, and followed him out the door.

I went to the window. Seeing them walk down the path together, I remembered my father taking me to Sunday lunch at Central Deli when I was a teenager. Even if we had to wait an hour, we'd hold out for our favorite corner booth. "Your mother," he'd say, "she thinks if she feeds me just lettuce, I'll live forever," then he'd take a big bite of his fatty pastrami sandwich. He'd lean forward and ask, "So, how's by you?"

When I told him about my last tiff with Mom, the girls from Belle Harbor who called me "weirdo," and my trigonometry teacher, Mr. Siddeons, who hollered at me for looking up at the ceiling when I had to answer a question, my father's kind smile took all the hurt away.

It was a far cry from lunch with my mother. Every so often, she would put on her silk jungle-print sheath and a feathery hat and take me to Le Bonheur in Hewlett. She'd order us both a salade Niçoise and herself a glass of sherry. Her green eyes sparkled as she looked at me, as if she momentarily forgot about stamping out my gift and just let herself enjoy having a daughter. After coffee, she'd light up a Gauloise and tell me stories about when she first came to New York and worked as a manicurist. "My boss told me that at his barber school, they practiced on drunks from the Bowery," she once said, exhaling in languorous drifts. "A guy at the door checked their heads for lice before they were allowed in. When the drunks were in the chair, if you turned your head for a second, they drank the hair tonic. It was about ninety proof," she added, laughing. As she tamped out her cigarette, she'd confide, "Your father thinks if I don't smoke, I'll live forever."

I wished my mother hadn't smoked and my father hadn't eaten so much fatty foods. Batting back tears, I went to the basement to do a wash. Rory and Cara were famous for leaving pens in their pockets. I'd see the blips and squibs the ink made on their pockets, like messages I could never scrub free. I lay their pants and shirts on top of the washing machine and frisked them as if I were a cop. There was a piece of paper folded into a skinny strip in the pocket of Cara's jeans. I got chills, a premonition. I unfolded the strip. The handwriting was like rows of spears.

*Baby,*

*It's deep between us. I was never so gone about a girl. Already we're blood. You're my air. Without you, I'd die. I remember what you said, that you'd do anything for me, go anywhere with me, be anything for me. I keep telling myself that over and over, convincing myself that it's true.*

*Love you to death,*
*Lance*

I felt as if someone had slammed me against a wall. *I keep telling myself that over and over,* he wrote. Why was he convincing himself? The laundry room was warm and muggy, but I rubbed at my arms as if I were freezing. *Without you, I'd die.* I shook it off like a bad dream. Kid talk, that's all it was. Flirting with death like Romeo and Juliet without really knowing what it meant. "I hate my life!" Cara had shouted. "I can't stand anymore!"

I blinked away a vision of Juliet, dead. *No, Rory was right,* I told myself. I was being melodramatic. Cara was just throwing one long tantrum. When she was a child and threw a tantrum, Rory used to calmly tell her, "You're really a reasonable girl at heart," and she quieted down immediately. If I couldn't talk sense into her, maybe he could. He could be her calm in this storm.

When Cara found out that she didn't have my gift, she drifted toward Rory. She wanted to help out at Mirror on Fridays and on weekend mornings. He was delighted to involve her, delighted with her interest. "Cara is a crackerjack with the computerized cash register and with figuring out clever ways of displaying merchandise," he'd told me, and she piped up, "Today, I handed out lollipops to the mothers of sick children. And I even told a woman who was coughing which syrup to buy."

"Good for you," I'd said, and I was truly thrilled for her. "When I tried to help your dad at Mirror, a woman came in for depilatory wax for the dark hair on her upper lip. By mistake, I sold her black mustache dye. She came back furious." Cara laughed. It became her favorite story.

She wore a name tag Rory had made up—CARA KAMINSKY, PHARMACY ASSISTANT. It made me smile every time I saw it. It reminded me of Bubbie offering to make me her official assistant. Cara was so proud that she sometimes wore the name tag to school. Then, when she was nearing twelve, a good-looking boy began coming into Mirror to buy packs of gum. I watched them smile shyly at each other. Often I hung around to browse the shelves and visit with Rory. I noticed that when the boy wasn't there, Cara kept glancing at the door, hoping he'd come in. Once, he finally got up the courage to say, "Do you live around here?" There was a sparkle in the air around them.

"No," Cara said, batting her lashes. "I live—"

Just then, Mrs. Anderson plunked her wing-tipped Maxi pads on the counter. "Menopause will be a thrill compared to all this bleeding," Mrs. Anderson moaned. Cara looked up at the ceiling as if she wished she were anywhere but the pharmacy. The boy hung back, waiting, but when Mrs. Anderson finally left, the sparkle was no longer in the air. The boy paid for his gum and left.

Cara took off her name tag and slapped it on the counter. "This isn't for me," she said.

Rory studied her. "Are you embarrassed, honey? You shouldn't be. The human body is a miraculous thing and—"

"No, I'm not embarrassed," she interrupted. She looked around the store. "I just don't want to be around douches and enemas all day."

Being Rory's assistant had gotten her through a bad patch, but she never went back to work at Mirror again.

I had to wonder if Rory could get her through this Lance phase.


As soon as I heard Rory's car in the driveway, I opened the door and watched him come up the walk alone. "What happened?" I asked.

"On the way home, I told her that a guy like Lance couldn't possibly love her. I just meant he didn't see how truly wonderful she was, how special. I told her guys her age had raging hormones. Was that so bad?"

Cara must have thought he was trying to give her a lesson on the birds and bees. "No, I guess it wasn't so bad." I sighed.

"But all I did was make Cara angrier and angrier. She told me I was disgusting and got out at a light."

"Where is she?"

He shrugged. "She headed toward the station. Maybe she was

going there to call that hoodlum from the pay phones. Or maybe she was going to get a taxi at the cab stand." He hung his head. "I blew it." He was exhausted, defeated. He went upstairs and got right into bed. I put on his Lands' End jacket and sat on the front steps waiting for Cara. Iris Gruber was at her window. She narrowed her eyes at me, then pulled down the shade. Finally, Cara appeared up the block. As soon as she approached, I walked toward her. "Dad isn't waiting to have another big talk with me, is he?" she asked. She stopped as if she wasn't going to take another step toward home.

"No, he went to sleep."

"Good. He is the world's most embarrassing person. And he just doesn't get anything."

"He loves you," I said.

"Love," she said, and her eyes were suddenly dreamy again and I knew she wasn't thinking of her father's safe, encompassing love. She was thinking of love that rode on a motorcycle, love that didn't wear a helmet, love that didn't obey any rules but his own, and it made me terrified.

Inside the house, I wanted to talk to her more about Lance, but her aura was jagged. It was clear anything I said would lead to another fight, and this time, I'd be the one who didn't "get anything."

Upstairs, Rory had fallen asleep facedown, arms out, in his clothes. I suddenly felt sorry for him. I untied his boots and worked them off his feet and slipped into bed beside him.

The next morning, from the corner of my eyes, I saw my father standing near my bedroom window. He was leaning toward me, his blue eyes intense, as if he wanted to tell me something, but his lips were still.

"Daddy," I whispered.

"Ma," Cara suddenly said, entering the room, "I can't wear

this." She was wearing a white blouse and pantyhose, and holding up a navy skirt with a fallen hem.

My father looked at me anxiously and disappeared. I covered my face with my hands.

"You okay?" Cara asked.

"You never know how long you'll have with your father," I warned.

Cara dropped the skirt. "Is something wrong with Daddy?" she asked with a start.

"No, honey. I was thinking of my own father."

She touched me on the shoulder. "I'm sorry," she said. She hesitated, then picked her skirt off the floor. "I have to wear this to chorus, and half the hem is down. Can you do it up again?"

I sighed. Every time I did a hem, it fell down. "Your grandmother was the needlewoman," I said. "Me? In junior high, I had to edge a cloth napkin for Home Economics, and I somehow ended up sewing it to the lap of my dress."

I thought of how strong my mother's hems were and the stitches so tiny they were almost invisible.

"I'll be late!" Cara said, nervously bouncing on the balls of her feet.

"Put the skirt on," I told her. "I'll tape the hem up for now. Tomorrow I'll bring it to the woman at the dry cleaners."

After the hem was taped up and Cara left, I did three readings in a row and sat there wondering why my father had appeared to me. Did he have something to tell me?

There was a glow to the right of my desk. "Daddy," I said happily, thinking he was back to finish our visit. Instead, the superintendent from the building where Rory and I used to live appeared. He was wearing his overalls and his utility belt hooked with tools. His mouth was in an O shape, as if he was as surprised to find himself in my office as I was surprised to see him. Then he scooted off as he did when he was alive.

He had always been ducking me. The whole year we lived in

that building, three outlets didn't work and the radiators knocked, hissed, and leaked. But now it was a comfort that he had dropped into my office. It helped me remember that sometimes spirits came with nothing in mind but a "how do you do?" Maybe Dad had, too.

My phone rang. It was Phyllis Kanner. "Have you thought more about signing with me?" she asked.

"I'm afraid the answer is no and no," I said.

"Well, I never accept no for an answer," she said.

I had to smile at her chutzpah.

"Are you a medium as well?" she asked.

"Yes."

"I want to contact my uncle Jake. Let's book another reading."

As long as she was a paying customer, how could I refuse? She booked an hour appointment.

"We'll devote the whole reading to my uncle Jake," she said.

Spirits didn't necessarily take up a whole reading. They rarely delivered long soliloquies like Hamlet's father's ghost. What I heard was more clipped and high pitched, like a scratched 45 rpm of Alvin and the Chipmunks. "I'll try," I said.

After I got off the phone, I remembered my mother saying, "If you talk to dead people, death will be drawn to you like flies." Shuddering, I wondered if it was merely a coincidence that both Rory's and my parents were dead, or whether spending so much time contacting the dead was making everyone I loved drop like flies. I suddenly got frightened for Rory and Cara, and gripped the armrests of my chair.


Two days later, the UPS guy handed me a long box that looked like it could hold a dozen roses. I opened it on the dining room table. There was a welter of pink sparkle tissue paper inside. When I pulled the tissue paper apart, I shrieked. It was a prosthetic arm. There was a note on a letterhead: PHYLLIS KANNER, MANAGER OF NEW AGE TALENT.

*Dear Miriam,*

*This is Uncle Jake's arm. When I call for my reading, it should help you make contact with him if you hold his hand.*

*Sincerely,*
*Phyllis*

It gave me the willies. I put the arm back in the box and brought it up to my office closet.

The day of Phyllis's phone appointment, I was so nervous that I didn't eat. I put on my "Om" CD and chanted along with it for an hour, but I was still worried. Sometimes spirits were séance-shy. What if Uncle Jake's spirit didn't show up? Once, as I was trying to contact a client's father who had been in the navy, a pirate showed up. "Avaunt, me hearty," he said, and ordered us all to walk the plank.

As I waited for Phyllis to call, I forced myself to get Uncle Jake's arm out of the closet. I had to close my eyes to make myself touch it. I ran my hands over it. The plastic was cool. I moved the elbow, then each finger. Nothing came to mind. I picked up the arm and put it against my forehead, making sure that it touched my third eye. My mind was still a blank. I put the arm back in the box. I knew why this was happening: I had a bad feeling about Phyllis and her ulterior motives. She didn't seem sincere in her need for a psychic. Even though I had told her I didn't want a talent agent, she seemed to be persistent in auditioning me.

The phone rang. "Phyllis here," she said. "Has Uncle Jake told you anything yet?"

"Your uncle's lips are sealed," I said. "He probably didn't believe in psychics."

"You're wrong. He used to go to a tea-leaf reader. He was the one who got me interested in psychics in the first place."

I felt flustered but tried to keep talking. My mouth was dry with anxiety. "Uncle Jake had trouble with his salivary glands," I said.

"They were fine. He could eat a whole pumpernickel without even a drop of water."

I was squirming. "I see an old man," I said. "He's indistinct. Looks like he's in a big snowstorm."

"There, you're right. My uncle Jake made eiderdown quilts and pillows. The air in his shop was always full of floating feathers. Oh, I shouldn't have told you that," she said.

I felt encouraged. I had a pulsing sensation in the area of my third eye. I felt it protrude like a zoom lens. The feather storm died down. Uncle Jake put his thumb up. "Thanks for the pickles," he said. I repeated it.

"I'm impressed," Phyllis said. "Uncle Jake spent his last years in Boca Raton. Whenever I visited, I brought him a case of pickles from Essex Street. Uncle Jake, if you could only tell me how, I'd mail your Essex Street pickles to heaven."

"You don't need to," I said. "Spirits eat whatever they want, anytime they want, without putting on a pound or any other bad consequence. I can't tell you how many times I've seen my dead father having a plate of forbidden schmaltz herring and not even having to follow it up with Mylanta. I don't think spirits can actually taste their food, but the memory of the taste is just as delicious."

"*Shtupping,* too," Uncle Jake said.

I repeated that to Phyllis.

"What?" she said. In spite of herself, she laughed.

"Having intercourse," I told her.

"I know," she said. "Uncle Jake was quite the ladies' man. The older he got, the younger the wife. I am just shocked he said this in front of you."

"Phyllis," Uncle Jake is saying, "you're a chip off the old block." I thought of our last reading. I thought of Phyllis's old and bitter husband. "I think Uncle Jake is telling me that you're going to be like him in the future."

"Really?" Phyllis said, laughing. "Well, I'm glad to know that."

I saw a cartoon of a penis festooned like a maypole. "A younger man is heading your way," I told her.

"I feel like I've won the lottery," she said, laughing some more. "Miriam, I've seen the greatest psychics in the world perform, and I've never heard anything like your readings. You must let me represent you."

I thought about all the strategies I'd used to keep my psychic powers private. I began working on the phone instead of in person, staying distant from acquaintances so that they wouldn't discover my gift, and starting that secrecy pattern with Cara. And when I was still a child, Bubbie had told me that this work was holy, that it wasn't a show. "Never do it at carnivals," she'd said. "No thanks," I said to Phyllis.

"What would it take to change your mind?"

"A lobotomy," I said.

Quarter past eleven, and I could barely keep my eyes open, but I forced myself to stay awake for Rory. As soon as he came into the bedroom, I saw the image of a raven over his head.

"Something bad happened at Mirror," I said.

"You're always trying to read my mind," he snapped. "Can't I have any privacy?" He sat on the bed, untying his shoes. He stopped, and then turned to me, sighing. "Okay," he said quietly. "Something terrible happened at Mirror."

"What?" I asked, my heart pounding.

"Well, you know, I bought a whole new special computer with the thirty-thousand-dollar loan so I could run Medicaid's new software. Now the software doesn't work. The software company didn't know the Medicaid laws, and all the claim submissions are being returned unpaid. I can't get the software company to correct the problem or refund my money, and I'm married to them." He said the word *married* as if he had just bitten into a rotten egg.

"But, Rory, we're already hanging on by a thread," I said angrily. "Didn't you check the software company out before you gave them our money?"

"I'm their first client in New York. They wrote the program for Arkansas, but we New Yorkers are in trouble." Then he rambled about the competition, the chain stores, how the Rite Aids and the Genoveses and all the rest were aligning themselves, waiting. "They're selling *tsatskehs*—beach balls, wind-up turtles, so they can sell the drugs below cost." His voice was getting louder. "As soon as they put the little guys like me out, they'll jack up their prices, scalp the government. You'll see."

"Rory, you're raving like my father used to about the hikes in beef. Cut it out."

"I come home over my head in trouble, and you won't even listen," he said.

Rory didn't really understand how I listened with my psyche, how I could hear even many of his unspoken thoughts. I touched his hand. "I'm listening now," I said.

He took my hand in his and kissed it. "Mim, I want so much for us, for Cara. I'm tired of just trying to hang on during disasters." He squeezed my hand harder and leaned down, burying his face in my shoulder.

"We don't need to be rich to be happy," I said. "We just need to be out of debt."

"That's why I want to push forward," he said, lifting his head. "I want to print up a catalog and send it all over Queens. I could go mail order. I've already priced it out. It'll be about eighteen thousand altogether, mailing included."

He sounded like his old self as he said it, confident, secure. Maybe it was right. Maybe the mailing would save his business, but I felt as if I'd been punched. "Eighteen thousand dollars. Where are we going to get that much money?"

"I don't need the whole thing right away," he said. "Just one third down. We could cash in an IRA account."

"That IRA account is our pension. We could end up living off food stamps."

"But if I send out that catalog, we won't have to worry about the present or the future anymore."

Rory used to be full of great ideas for his business, and Mirror had flourished. But once his business reversals began eleven years ago, he grew so panicked that he developed the opposite of the Midas touch. I thought about the surgical supplies that were still sitting unsold in his shop, the mailing list he had bought last year for four thousand dollars that never brought in one new customer. And I remembered his circulars blowing in the March wind, stuck in trees, snaking along the gutters. "I hate to say this, Rory, but for the last eleven years, all our money has gone into your business, and we've hardly seen anything back."

His expression grew dark. "That really hurts, Mim. You know how hard I work."

"I do know," I said. In snowstorms, Rory shoveled his way into the store, and used a cigarette lighter to defrost the lock so he could open the security gate.

"I love this curve," I said, and stroked his cheek. I saw his face soften. His mouth moved. "I like this curve, too," I said, and then he slowly reached for me.

Later, lying in bed, his body heavy against mine, I felt as if I were on a beach, a blanket over me, my body both gritty and slick. I felt the sun beating down, opening each pore. I could hear the ocean, like rashers of bacon frying on a grill. We stayed like this, lazing. I didn't think I could ever survive without Rory's arms around me. It made me feel safe. It was like a charm.

Just then, he murmured into my ear, "You think you can up the number of readings you do?"

# 13

"MA, THERE'S A MAN in my window!" Cara screamed.

I raced up the steps to find Cara in bed with the covers pulled up to her chin. Through the glass, a man was shouting back at her, "I'm from Tip Top's."

"Shush, honey," I said to her. "He's fixing our roof."

"Nice to tell me now," Cara said.

"I didn't know myself that they were coming today." I stepped to the window. "You should have phoned before you started," I shouted, but the man's work boots were already disappearing from the top windowpane.

"This is a loony bin," Cara said.

"At least it will be a dry one," I said, and pulled her shades down as I had always asked *her* to do before she went to sleep.

Cara got up. She was wearing a long black T-shirt that I didn't recognize.

"Is that a Halloween shirt?" I asked.

"No. Smashing Pumpkins is a rock group."

I knew it was Lance's—it smelled of cigarettes and a dusky cologne.

"You'd better give it to me to wash," I said. I wanted to boil and bleach until it was a pale, shrunken tatter.

"No thanks, Mom," she said, smiling. "I like it this way." She ran her hands down her sides as I imagined Lance had.

Sighing, I climbed to my office. The roofers were scrabbling along the roof, tossing old shingles into the garden.

The phone rang. "'El-lo," a man said. "Am I speaking to the psychic?"

"Yes."

"Aaah. I am so pleased," he said in singsong. I could barely understand him, but he was so cheery that I knew why he was calling.

"You called to sell me an ad."

He giggled. "Oh, you are a clever, clever psychic. Yes, indeed. I represent the most widely distributed Hindu newspaper in New York."

"I'm sorry. I don't have any money."

He hung up quickly.

I slumped on the desk, my head in my hands. No one had prepared me for being broke. My father had had a cash business. And my mother had had a cash business, too—skimming from the household budget.

"This is where I keep my *pechel*," she'd told me, delighted, as she took down one of her hatboxes. It was the only Yiddish word she approved of. Inside her tall, black-feathered gendarme hat with the rhinestone clip, she opened the bunched tissue paper to reveal a wad of cash like the one Bubbie had sewn into her own hem when she was escaping her shtetl.

"Rory and I will always trust each other, and we'll share whatever we have," I said somberly.

"Well, some people have to learn the hard way," my mother had said as she put her stash back into the feathered hat and closed the closet door.

The phone rang again. "Do you rid a house of bad spirits?" a woman asked in a hush-hush tone.

I was so panicky about getting the money for the roofers that I was willing to try anything. "Yes," I said.

"I chose you from the psychic ads because, from your number, I could tell you live in Great Neck, too. What do you charge to come to the house?"

I hesitated, then tripled my fee.

"That's reasonable," she said, and I wished I had gone higher. The roofers were bumping their ladders against the eaves. There were footsteps overhead.

"What's that noise?" she asked.

"It's the roofers."

"You have poltergeists," she insisted. "You want to bring them here and give me more trouble?" She hung up. I got up, stretched my arms out to the side, and spread my legs. Then I jumped up and down, clapping my hands over my head as I brought my legs together. I did twenty jumping jacks, but I still couldn't calm myself.

I knew at times like this it was best to leave the house to clear my thoughts. At every stoplight during my drive to the post office, I recited an affirmation I'd read in a book: "The Universe brings all the right people to you at the perfect time for your highest good." I needed the miracle of money. But when I opened my P.O. box, there were no checks, only junk mail. I was about to toss it all out when I noticed one envelope that said in purple script, *From the World's Most Accurate Psychic—Lucinda Bright.* I tore the envelope open.

*Dear Miriam,*

- *I know, Miriam, when (and how much) money you have been hoping will fall into your lap.*
- *I can predict, Miriam, when a certain relationship you've been agonizing over will change for the better.*

- *I will tell you the precise moment, Miriam, when your chronically tough luck will go from bad to good.*
- *Miriam, I will reveal to you the secrets for attracting good fortune in your life.*

*MIRIAM, IN ORDER TO DO ALL THESE THINGS (AND MORE) FOR YOU, I MUST HEAR FROM YOU WITHIN THE NEXT 8 DAYS.*

I read on. She mentioned my name at least a dozen more times. I felt hypnotized. On the back, there was a form to fill out and return. Her reading was twenty dollars. I imagined all those checks, money orders, and envelopes of cash going out to *The World's Most Accurate Psychic*. Maybe this was the nudge the Universe needed to bring the right people to me. I decided I would prepare a mailing list. But mine would be more modest. I'd just head mine with *Miriam the Psychic*.

When I got home, I spent the afternoon going through my cookie tin of letters from clients. I found Desiree's letter. Her husband had gotten another woman pregnant. He had wanted Desiree to let this woman and the baby move in with them, and he said Desiree could take care of the baby. Reading the letter brought back the case in detail. I remembered the frustration of these self-destructive souls coming to me. Desiree was starving herself, and she'd let her husband have his way. I knew that no matter what I said, she wouldn't make it.

There was the letter from a widower whose wife had committed suicide by swallowing her month's worth of Haldol in two hours. He had refused to put her in a hospital for round-the-clock supervision as the doctor had advised. Now he wanted to channel her to apologize.

Another letter was from a woman with tricholomania. Whenever she was nervous, she pulled out her hair—and couldn't stop. She had tried everything, and there was no cure. I told her to shave her head and wear long earrings. After that, for days, I wanted to pull my own hair out. I had to fight to keep my hands in my lap. It was as if I were a sponge in a deep lake of their stories.

"The Universe brings all the right people . . . for my highest good," I repeated, but it didn't seem true at all. I remembered while Rory and I were having sex that he had urged me to make more money. Never mind my clients. I was beginning to doubt whether the Universe really had sent me the good husband Bubbie had predicted in my tea leaves.

The doorbell rang. I came downstairs and looked out the diamond-shaped window. It was a deliveryman. I saw a florist's truck at the curb. I opened the door. "Flowers," the delivery guy said, as if I wouldn't notice that he was holding a huge beribboned bouquet of irises, white roses, spotted lilies, ferns, and sprays of baby's breath in a glass vase. I signed for them and brought them into the kitchen. A rosebud tenderly brushed my cheek. My eyes felt dewy. It had been seven years since Rory had apologized like this. I picked up the phone.

"Thank you," I said.

"For what?"

"For the flowers. They're so romantic, but they must have cost a fortune. You shouldn't have."

"I didn't."

"What?" I cradled the phone to my neck and opened the small envelope taped to the ferns. The note said,

> *Thanks a million,*
> *Love, Vince*

"Oh," I said, "they're from a client."

"And I suppose with a romantic bouquet the client's name isn't Alice, is it?"

"No, it's Vince. A real stand-up guy."

"And how does this Vince, this really stand-up guy, know our home address?"

"I don't know. I'll have to ask him."

"What's his number?" Rory demanded. "I'll ask him myself."

"I'll handle this," I told him. "Separation of church and state, remember? If it's going to be enforced for your business, it's going to be in mine, too."

"Well, you remember to tell this guy that you have a husband. And remember to tell him that your husband is six feet four."

I felt like telling Rory that Vince had a retinue of hit men, but as Bubbie had advised, I never violated my clients' confidentiality. Besides, I wasn't even sure if that was true.

"Maybe I'll be home earlier tonight," Rory said.

"Oh?" I said, stifling a laugh. I was beginning to like Vince after all.

Not ten minutes later, my office phone rang. "Hi, doll," Vince said. "Did you get my flowers?"

"I did. Thank you, but you shouldn't have sent them."

"Can't you use a little appreciation?"

He didn't know the half of it. But I said, "A regular thank-you is sufficient. My husband doesn't like me receiving flowers from other men."

"Eh, I bet your husband could use a run for his money. Every guy married more than five minutes needs that."

All Rory was doing these days was running for his money. "No, my husband certainly doesn't need that," I said. "And by the way, how did you get my home address?"

"I have my ways," he said. "You can find the dead. I can find the living. Anyway, I need another reading."

My shoulders stiffened. I rolled them to relax. "When are you available?" I asked.

"How about now? You just put it on my charge for however much you want."

I saw dollar signs. He was trying to buy me the way he always tried to buy love. "The regular fee is fine," I told him.

"I got to talk to you about that broad again," he said. "I never had so much trouble getting over a woman. Love 'Em and Leave 'Em, they used to call me."

The number fourteen came into my mind. Then I saw a wedding cake. "You were married fourteen years," I said. "That must have been a love you couldn't easily leave."

"Heh, heh," Vince laughed. "You got a real feel for numbers. I should take you to Vegas with me sometime."

I remained silent.

"Cat got your sense of humor?" he asked.

"If you stop making insinuating remarks, you'll hear my humor." I heard the prissy spinster tone I used whenever a client was making a pass at me.

"What do you want me to say?" he asked sadly. "That I'm a chump? Okay, I admit it. The broad I was telling you about . . . I met her in an art gallery out in Arizona. She was showing her paintings there. She wasn't one of those hippie types. I hate hippies. She was done up, you know. I took one look at her and bought every painting in the show. Now here I am in my living room, her so-called art all over my walls. Who the hell else would have bought her paintings but a chump?"

I could see the paintings. They were big, mostly white abstracts, and textured like large-curd cottage cheese with a smattering of golden raisins. "If you really want to forget her, sell her paintings; give them away if you have to."

"Nobody in their right mind will take them off my hands. I'll have to throw them out."

"It's worth it. It will give you tremendous relief. I think you're already starting to get over her. Your aura has brightened up in just the few minutes we've been talking."

"You think so?"

"I know it."

"Nice to hear," he said. "Excuse me," he added, and I heard him light up a cigar and take a draw of it. "Maybe I was just sticking with the broad because she already knows my body, if you know what I mean." He whispered, "I put on a few pounds this year."

I had a vision of him with his belly rolled over his belt. "Your weight wouldn't spoil your chances with a woman, but it could ruin your health."

"I should give up cigars, heh?"

"And rich food, too."

"I'd rather give up broads," he said.

"I'm afraid you'll be giving up both if you don't cut down."

"Well, Vince has to cut this short," he said. "I have to get over to the restaurant. If a boss isn't on top of his workers every minute, I don't have to tell you what goes down."

I thought of Rory with Fred. "No," I said, "you don't."

As soon as I hung up, the phone rang again. It was Phyllis Kanner. "Have you been thinking about my offer?" she asked.

*Will she never give up?* "Phyllis, I'm so glad you enjoyed your readings, but no is no."

"I'll call you again soon," she said.

*My luck she would,* I thought.

A half hour later, a woman called for an appointment. When I asked her for her credit card number, she was surprised. "You charge my card right away?" she asked.

"Yes. A reading is a commitment."

"But what if I change my mind?"

"There's a twenty-four-hour cancellation policy," I explained.

Within ten minutes, I'd received two more calls for readings. I was thrilled. *Business is picking up,* I thought smugly. I certainly don't need Phyllis Kanner.

# 14

I WAS IN MY office the next day, straightening the top of my desk, and came across some snippets of paper with notes I'd scribbled about various clients during readings. "Mary Cutler—infected belly button stud," one said. "Morrie Rose—tinnitus," another said. "Joy Kent—long-standing affair with brother-in-law." "Harriet Chaikin—father's ghost still wears toupee." I couldn't remember the clients these notes described. As I brushed my hand over the desk, sweeping them into the wastebasket, I felt as if I were piling them into a mass grave.

In an hour, I'd have the first of the three readings I'd booked yesterday. The phone rang. *More business. Phyllis should see me now,* I thought, picking up the phone.

"I booked a reading yesterday and I'm calling to cancel and you have to refund my charge because I'm canceling within twenty-three hours," the woman said.

"Would you like to reschedule?" I asked.

"No," she said. "I changed my mind."

I felt a little shaken. Punctually, an hour apart, the two other women who had booked readings also called to cancel at the twenty-third hour. After the last one, I got suspicious. If any else called to ask about my cancellation policy, I'd refused to book them. Now I had three empty hours before Vince would call.

By the time Vince called, I was panicky about money. I picked up the phone the instant it rang.

"It's Vince Time again," Vince said in his gravelly voice. There was a bustling in the background. He was calling me during lunch at his restaurant. "Listen up," he said. "I've done enough of this phone baloney. How about a face-to-face reading? I'll come out there any time you say."

Before I began working on the phone, an elderly client, Sam, had come to my office for a reading. In the middle, he'd gotten up and kissed me hard on the mouth. I could feel his false teeth slipping down his gums. Before I could pry him off me, Rory walked in. "What's going on here?" he shouted, whereupon Sam had an angina attack. It was Rory who put the lozenge of digitalis under Sam's tongue.

"I don't do readings in my home," I told Vince.

"You mean you don't let anybody in? Not even a broad?"

I remembered Noreen, who had jumped out at me from my rhododendron bush. "I don't let any clients come to my home," I repeated.

"Then come to my place," he said.

"Vince!"

"I know. No fornicating with clients," he said slyly.

"*Fraternizing*, you mean. But ditto for both."

"Can't blame a guy for trying. That's what we're put on the earth for. But I mean it. If you can pick up all this over the phone, it blows me away to think what you could do in person."

"It's just as good over the phone," I said. "Maybe even better. I'm not distracted."

"Okay, I'm propositioning you, but not how you think. Least

not yet." He laughed again. "This is what I'm offering. A thousand smackers, cash. You come to my office. It's right in the back of my restaurant."

What if he sticks his hand up my dress? I worried. "Hand up dress," I wrote on a scrap of paper.

As if reading my mind, he said, "The maître d' will hear you if you scream. And I'll send a car for you. But when you get here, don't let on about your being a psychic. I don't need my help knowing I need help. Got it?"

I thought about how much Rory and I needed that money. *I'm a big girl,* I thought. *I can handle myself. A thousand dollars. And I would remain anonymous.* "Got it," I said. "When did you have in mind?"

"Sooner the better. I know that Long Island traffic. I had an affair at the Garden City Hotel once."

Even though I could see him thrashing around the bed with a busty woman, I was so hard up for money that I felt like going to his restaurant right away. But I wasn't used to doing readings in person anymore, and I wasn't used to doing them out of my own environment. "A week from now at eleven A.M.," I said.

"I'll try to hold out," Vince said. "And by the way, I'll send my car for you. You gotta get picked up by nine thirty, tops, to get here in time."

"I can take the train," I said.

"Sure you can, but why the hell should you when I've got a limo?"

Again I saw dollar signs. And lipstick. *This guy is rolling in dough and women,* I thought. "I'll accept the lift," I said.

After I got off the phone, I had the sense that I'd lost something, but I didn't care to think what.

As I drove to the high school to pick up Cara, I felt as if Vince's thousand dollars were already snug in my pocket. I imagined myself going back to do a reading for him every week. Why not a few times a week? "Let's go shopping," I'd say to Cara when she got in the car. But when I got there, Darcy was waiting beside her.

"Hi, Mrs. Kaminsky," Darcy said. Her hair was smooth and shiny as a sheet of yellow glass. "Mind if I come over?"

I still was annoyed with Darcy for lying to me about Cara being at her house. "Fine with me as long as your mother knows where you are," I said pointedly.

"Oh, my mother knows," Darcy said, and she got in the car, sighing. "My mother knows everything."

Cara's brows came together. She let out a breath that sounded like "tuh." "Every mother *thinks* she knows everything," she said, "but she doesn't."

The truth was that I couldn't know everything about Cara. Not only did my love for her sometimes block my psychic ability, but psychic ability wasn't a light switch that turned on and off so easily. Being close to someone fogged the messages. Meanwhile, in seven days, I'd be meeting with a mobster. Cara didn't know everything about me either. We were more alike than she'd ever believe, I said to myself, ruefully. I felt my face flush with shame. If Cara ever found out what I was up to with Vince, I'd lose all credibility with her. She'd never listen to me about anything again. It was probably her worst fear—and my mother's, too.

I stopped at the Korean grocery, bought the girls a bag of chocolate Mallomars and myself a bulb of garlic, a bunch of basil, parsley leaves, and pine nuts. When we got home, the girls went up to Cara's room with the cookies.

Alone, I plucked the basil leaves for the pesto sauce into my Cuisinart and threw in the rest of the ingredients, adding a handful of cherry tomatoes for color and pressed the lever. I must have had Vince on my mind, because the sauce reminded me of blood on a lawn, a drive-by shooting.

• • •

When Rory got home, he scowled at the vase of flowers on the table in the foyer. Then he handed me a small package in Mirror gift wrap. It was a travel-size Arpège that I knew had been sitting in his locked glass cabinet almost since he'd opened the store. But with our finances, the gesture made my heart flutter. "Thanks," I said, and we kissed.

I served Darcy and Cara their dinners in the den, and Rory and I ate at the dining room table with candlelight.

"You really outdid yourself," Rory said as he took a second helping. "A meal like this makes me feel as if my pockets are as full as my stomach."

"They may be soon," I said, and I told him about going to Guardelli's to give Vince a reading.

"No way," Rory said, leaning forward, searching my eyes. "Unless you can do it on a Sunday, and I can come with you. That guy has designs on you."

I was starting to feel extremely grateful for Vince. "Sundays are out of the question," I said, even though I hadn't even asked. "I'm well aware that Vince is attracted to me, but it's part of my job to know how to handle that."

"Right, I saw how you handled it when that old guy kissed you in your office."

"He caught me by surprise," I said. "Remember that floozy who came behind the counter at Mirror, and wanted you to examine teethmarks on her breast so you could suggest an ointment?" I demanded. "You managed to give her the ointment without the exam."

"That's different," he said. "Of course I wouldn't look at a customer's breast."

"Well, you'll have to trust me, too. This is a great opportunity. Vince is paying me five hundred dollars."

I was shocked that I'd halved the amount. I'd always been

totally honest with Rory in money matters, and now, like my mother, I was planning my own *pechel*. I realized I didn't want all my money disappearing into his business and immediately felt as if I'd crossed some kind of line, that I was inching toward dividing assets, toward divorce.

Worse was when I reached over and squeezed Rory's hand. "You can trust me," I said.

I was used to buying things for Cara that we didn't have the money for, but I couldn't bring myself to use our credit card to buy myself something to wear for Vince's reading. I searched my closets. I found a long Victorian dress, but it was too low cut. There was a black dress with full sleeves that looked too witchy.

I came across my mother's navy suit. "Don't bury me in it," she'd said, jokingly, before she died. "God will know I copied it from a Chanel."

Copy or not, I wanted to wear my mother's suit. I thought it might make her beam angelic light on me to protect me.

I tried it on. The wire hanger had stretched one shoulder of the jacket. The way it poked out, it looked as if my mother's spirit had grabbed hold of it to try to keep me from going to Vince's. I put the suit back in its zippered bag. For once, I was glad her spirit wasn't around, glad she couldn't see me now. Not to mention Bubbie, who I imagined was keeping hidden for a reason.

As Rory and I were getting ready for bed, he said, "I want you to know I'm still totally against you going to this Vince," and continued to button his pajama top.

"There's a lot of things I'm totally against in your business, too," I said. "Are you willing to discuss them?"

He cocked his wrist and put his palm up. "Absolutely not." I bristled, but when I climbed into bed, he began kissing me all over. Vince was right. Rory did need a run for his money.

I started to worry. I loved Rory, but I knew from my clients that if you put yourself in compromising situations, the unheard of could happen. One of my clients, who had been happily married to a real hunk, contacted her junior high school boyfriend over the Internet out of curiosity. They decided to meet for coffee to talk over old times. The boyfriend had aged badly. He scratched at his psoriasis and informed her that he couldn't have milk in his coffee because of his spastic colon, but after they drained their cups, they ended up at the Marriott, and she eventually left her husband and three daughters with broken hearts.

In my continuing search for something long and sensible to wear, I went down to the big cedar closet in our basement. When I entered it and felt around for the light chain, boxes avalanched from the top shelf. When I finally turned on the light, I saw how packed the racks were with clothes from "the year of our Lord," as my mother would have said. I didn't have time to do anything about the chaos. Though I'd had a week to prepare for the reading, I still hadn't found anything to wear to it. I had to stay focused. I found a long-sleeved white blouse that would have had an air of innocence if it weren't so filmy. I wanted something with a full skirt. My mother had made me self-conscious about my behind. "For God's sakes, wear a panty girdle," she'd told me, though Rory thought it was one of my greatest assets. I dug farther into the closet and came up with a pale blue apron dress with a white corded belt that looked like a drapery pull. I put it all on.

Cara came downstairs. She gasped. "You look like a refugee from Woodstock."

I remembered Vince saying that he couldn't stand hippie types.

"Perfect," I said.

• • •

Vince Day. My doorbell rang at 9:30 A.M. on the dot. I looked out my diamond-shaped window and saw a thug's face. Eyes like apple pits, a nose like a pepper-studded sausage. "You Miriam?" he asked.

I opened the door partway. Keeping the toe of my shoe against it in case he tried to push his way in, I nodded.

"I'm Rocko. Vince said to pick you up."

I felt him eyeing me up and down. I had on pale pink lipstick and two smudges of sheer blush. Half my hair was twisted into a bun on top like Bubbie's and the rest curled to my shoulders. He shrugged. He didn't know what to make of me.

At the curb, there was a white stretch limo. I put a white wool wrap over my outfit and skulked out of my house, praying that none of my neighbors would see me. The street was eerily quiet. Suddenly, Baron began barking like crazy, and Iris peered through her vertical blinds.

Rocko opened the back door for me. The limo's interior was midnight blue. I could have conducted a séance in there.

"Vince said you can have yourself anything you want," Rocko told me. He pressed a button, and a cabinet door slid to the left. It was a full bar. Inside the refrigerator was soda, ice, champagne, a plate of grapes, Brie, and truffles. I imagined being one of those psychics who was flown across the world to do readings for sheiks and pashas.

On the TV affixed to the cabinet, a bony woman in leotards was on the floor, her back arched into a Cobra position. "Breathe," she instructed.

I breathed and kept breathing, the entire ride to the city. I got an image of Rory in the basement of Mirror, kicking a big empty box of Depends. "This is Vince's head," I heard him say. It was like when we first met and other guys asked me to dance. I had to smile. Then I glimpsed my father sitting on the leather seat across from me, tsk-tsking. "This is the way to treat a husband?" he said, and the smile slid from my face. As the limo got closer to the city, I got down to business. I tried to prepare myself for the reading by getting images. All that came was the smell of Vince's cigar, his strong cologne. By the time Rocko stopped at Madison and Fifty-third, I was nauseated. GUARDELLI'S, the big striped awning said. Rocko came around and opened the door for me. I emerged like a celebrity.

"You Miriam?" the maître d' asked.

My throat was so tight I could only nod.

"Follow me," he said, and he led me inside. The restaurant hadn't yet opened. There were red velvet puffy chairs and white tablecloths with short-stemmed roses in small crystal vases. The chandeliers hung down like starry stalactites, and the walls were flocked red paper. The help was bustling around in preparation. When they saw me, they poked each other and whispered behind their hands. The maître d' smirked.

"I'll take you to Vince," he said, leering.

As I followed him, I had a sense of myself as part of a long procession of women who had been marched through the restaurant and offered up to the big Guardelli. My cheeks were aflame.

The maître d' knocked on a big oak door. "Boss, the dame is here."

"Show her in," Vince said. When the door opened, I smelled cigar smoke. Vince got up from his huge desk. He was about five feet nine inches and hefty, but looked impressive in his gray suit with its silky sheen. His dark eyes shone like mica. His black hair was thick, slightly silver at the temples. He looked sophisticated, continental, and more attractive than I'd hoped. I felt stupid in my blue apron dress with the drapery pull.

"Take a load off," Vince said, gesturing toward the red velvet chair, his diamond pinkie ring flashing.

I sat down. He pulled his buttery black leather armchair out from behind his desk, and sat across from me. His eyes were appraising. I began to squirm.

"The broad I was telling you about," he finally said, "I've quit with her for good, but it feels like she took big scoops out of my heart." He puffed on his cigar. "Vince's empty," he said through the smoke.

His hurt, I could see, was deep. It wasn't just about this girl-friend. I had to find out how to help him. I took three deep breaths. A small light appeared to his right, and slowly, it began to take the form of a man in a white apron. He looked like Vince. He held up his thumb. It was badly misshapen, flattened and pur-ple. Then I felt the kind of cold I used to feel when I went near my father's freezer cases.

"Was your father a butcher?" I asked, my voice nearly break-ing from missing my own dad.

"Yeah," Vince said, his eyes wide.

"He injured his thumb, didn't he?"

"It got flattened in the door of his freezer case."

"He's here," I said. "He's trying to tell you something. 'Gin,' he said."

I thought about how some boozers never gave up, but Vince said, "Pops loved Ginny. She was my wife. She took care of him after he got the stroke. He probably wants me to go back with her. But you know Vince. He has an eye for the babes."

Vince's father jacked his damaged thumb up. "You're right. Your father does want you to go back to Ginny."

"Pops was a loyal guy. He should get a medal for staying with my mother all those years." The corners of his mouth were trem-bling. "Is my mother around?" he asked.

I rolled my eyes up and took more breaths. No other spirit appeared. "She might be, but she's not coming through."

"Figures," Vince said. "She was never around. She lived for bingo and the church."

I felt for Vince. I thought of how I yearned for my mother's spirit to be around me, to protect me, and how she probably thought that if she revealed herself to me, it would only encourage me in my babushka lady ways.

Vince cleared his throat.

What came to me was, *Oh, my God, I might be alone with a gangster right now.* Instead of Tony's mother, two ghostly figures appeared. One pointed his hand like a gun at his own temple. The other grabbed his own throat and let his tongue hang out of his mouth. *They must be acting out their own executions,* I thought. I didn't know whether I was seeing the visual fallout of my own assumptions or whether any of this had really happened. My heart knocked against my chest. I didn't want to mention any of this to Vince. I might get to know too much. Then I'd be a witness to his crimes. I could end up hung and quartered like a side of beef.

"You're a woman I could never lay a hand on," he suddenly said. "You're like the statue of the Virgin Mary that was in my mother's front hall."

A mother had saved me after all. "Always think of me like that," I said firmly, and the spirits disappeared.

As if to get his mind off his real losses, Vince began droning on again about how much money he'd spent on this "broad," and reevaluating whether or not she was a lesbian. "What should I do now?" he asked.

"Open yourself to real love," I said. "You have pink light floating over your heart. It's just a glimmer now, but you can make it light up your whole world. Just take three deep breaths," I told him.

As he inhaled, I noticed the buttons on his jacket straining to stay in the buttonholes. On the second breath, he coughed. By the third, his body sank more deeply into the leather chair.

"Picture your heart-light getting bigger and bigger," I intoned. "Now imagine it surrounding you, then radiating all through the room, warning everyone in your path. Now out onto the street, into the world. It will draw you to your true love."

He opened his eyes, leaned toward me, and crossed his hands over his heart as if Cupid had just shot him with an arrow.

"I'm the statue in your mother's hallway," I said. "Remember?"

"You're no statue," he breathed.

I got up from the chair. "Our time is definitely up," I said.

He stood up, took a huge wad of cash from his pocket and peeled off ten hundred-dollar bills, put the money in my hand, and closed his hands around my fist. His thick brows came together above eyes that were smoky with lust. "Stay," he pleaded.

If I had to scream, who would hear me besides Vince's hired help? My heart was beating so loudly I was sure he could hear it. "Will you call the limo or shall I?" I said firmly, pulling my hand from his.

"Rocko's waiting at the curb for you." Vince sighed. He shrugged. "Next time."

There wasn't going to be a next time. I stuck the money in the pocket of my Virgin Mary dress and slowly backed out the door. Rocko was on the sidewalk, leaning against the limo. When he spotted me, he opened the door.

# 15

When I finally got home, through the den window, I saw Cara and Darcy poring over magazines. I sneaked up to my bedroom, changed out of my apron dress, and came downstairs.

"Mom," Cara called, hurrying in from the den. "More flowers came for you while you were out," she whispered, pointing at the coffee table.

Pink roses. I knew they were from Vince. It was an even bigger bouquet than he'd sent last time.

Cara narrowed her eyes at me. "What's this all about?"

"A grateful client keeps sending them," I said. I was so upset I began to sneeze violently. "I must be allergic."

"Well, tell the guy who's sending them to just *stop,*" she hissed, looking over her shoulder to make sure Darcy wasn't listening.

"I did, but he sent them anyway," I whispered. "Do me a favor? If anyone tries to deliver flowers for me, don't accept them."

"Oh, gross," she said, and walked off, muttering and shaking her head.

I checked my phone messages. There were none from Rory.

If the situation had been reversed, I would have been calling him every minute. I picked up the phone anyway.

"So," he said, "how did you make out with your stand-up guy?"

Cara didn't deserve the embarrassment of thinking her mother had a guy chasing her, but Rory sure deserved to have a run for his Miriam.

"I really helped him open his heart," I said.

"I don't want you to go back there," Rory said. "I have a much better idea. I heard a psychic on the radio this morning. She wasn't nearly as good as you are. You could get on a show like that. The money will start rolling in, and you wouldn't have to go to shady places to collect it."

I sensed bubbles of excitement dancing in his aura.

"What are you talking about?" I asked. "Cara would flip if I went public."

"Mim, all I'm asking you to do is consider it, okay?"

"You must be joking," I said, but he didn't laugh. I was so insulted that I felt a heat spreading over me from my head to the pit of my stomach. How could Rory not know how risky it would be to become more visible? He had seen, firsthand, what happened when people found out what I did. A few years ago, Tiffany, a client, had talked me into accepting an invitation for Rory and me to go to her wedding because she'd been so grateful that I'd told her, "Join Outdoor Singles. Your future husband is waiting to meet you there." Jeff had fallen in love with her on their first hike.

"I'll come to your wedding if you promise not to tell anyone I'm a psychic," I told her. She'd promised, but during the toasts, she raised her glass, and announced, "This wedding wouldn't have come about without my psychic, Miriam," and shone a spotlight on me. Immediately, people crowded me, grilling me about stocks and the amounts of their next tax assessments.

"Get my coat," I told Rory, and I retreated into the ladies' room. While I was sitting on the toilet, a tall woman peered over the top of the stall. "Where can *I* find a husband?" she demanded. Then I heard a man's voice. "Hey, this is the line for the psychic," he'd said, "and I was here first."

There was a man in the ladies' room! I figured a group like this was the best-case scenario. Just as easily, I could have been shunned or ridiculed, run out of the event. I couldn't go public again. Bubbie had told me that my gift was holy, not a show. I hung up on Rory. All he thought about these days was ways to make more money. Then I heard Cara and Darcy talking in the den:

"When you go to college, you have to have a dart board," Darcy said. Her older sister went to Brandeis. I felt my hopes rise that Darcy would revive Cara's interest in going away to college.

"I don't play darts." Cara sighed.

"I know you don't. You get one for your room so guys will hang out there. A good dart board runs fifty bucks."

College boys with darts sounded much safer than Lance.

"The mattresses at college are like morgue slabs," Darcy went on. "We'll have to buy one of those foam egg-crate mattress covers. And instead of a regular blanket and a pillow, what you get is a whole set. A down comforter with a pillow sham and a dust ruffle and you can even get coordinating curtains. And we need those pillows with armrests. They call them *husbands* because they support you."

I could already hear the *ca-chings* of the cash registers in every department store on the North Shore. We were going to need an absolute fortune to send Cara away to college, and if she didn't go, we'd need a fortune in psychotherapy for her *and* for me.

The phone rang. "Hi, this is Phyllis Kanner." She was more persistent than a Jehovah's Witness. "I'm not going to give up until you sign with me. It's ridiculous for you to be locked in a room doing reading after reading like a piece worker in a sweatshop. You have a great gift. It's cash-in time."

"Thank you, but I'm not interested."

"I'll call you when I have a bite," she said as if she hadn't heard me.

After I hung up, I put my head in my hands and sat there, too discouraged to move. And then I felt a prickly sensation, as if Iris Gruber were watching me. I looked up. My father was in the doorway, wearing baggy dark slacks and his yellow nylon short-sleeved shirt with the plastic pocket protector.

"Putchkie, you think you got *tsores?* What you got is not so bad," he said, and glided out the door.

"Thanks, Dad," I called after him. I always needed him to remind me that Rory and my troubles weren't as big as I thought. At least we never had to sell matches in the freezing cold like my father had when he was only a little boy. We weren't gnawing on our last crust of black bread or smelling the stink of the smoke rising from our burnt village.

*Everything's relative,* I thought. But that night, when Rory walked through the door, he put his hand against the wall as if he was having trouble holding himself up.

"What's wrong?" I asked, alarmed.

He blew out his breath and shook his head. He reached into his pocket and handed me a letter. It was from the Department of Water Commission. It said that he owed them fifteen thousand dollars.

"You use that much water?" I gasped.

"No. For the past month, I've phoned them, faxed them, hired a temporary pharmacist twice so I could go down in person to straighten it out, but I still keep getting bills. They get higher all the time from the fines. I feel as if I'm drowning. How much more can I take?"

I suddenly noticed how much weight he'd lost. His cheeks were hollow, and there were dark shadows around his eyes. I thought of how my father had dreamed of a condo in Florida every time he had to go into his freezer case. He hadn't lived long enough to buy it. My heart squeezed into a fist at the thought of losing Rory.

I took Rory's arm as if he were an invalid and sat him at the kitchen table. I set a bowl of beef and barley soup in front of him, but he seemed too tired to pick up the spoon. He looked at the wall and then at me.

"I'm not being a medium now," I said, "but I'm sure your parents wouldn't have wanted you to live in misery. We're still young. We have options. We could live more simply in the country."

Rory put his palms flat on the table and leaned toward me. "If I get out now, I'll get nothing for the business. My parents' sacrifices will have been for nothing. What else am I qualified to do? The thought of living in the country is sweet, but the chain stores are out there, too. I'd end up at some CVS or Genovese, standing on my feet all day with kids fresh out of pharmacy school, working for beans." I saw the desperation in his eyes; then he looked away like a guilty child. "Our only hope is if you go on the radio, get out there."

I thought about Phyllis Kanner begging me to sign with her. I looked at Rory's face and felt a wrench in my heart. "Okay . . . ," I said shakily. "I'll try, but this is going to be a mess for Cara."

"It'll be a worse mess for her if we go broke," he said quietly.

"I'm not going to mention this to Cara unless it's a real possibility," I said. "So let's keep it between us."


The very next morning, I called Phyllis Kanner. "Hello, this is Miriam the Psychic."

"I knew you'd come to your senses," she said eagerly.

"I'm just making an inquiry."

"I live right over in Great Neck Estates. Why don't I just come by and talk to you in person?"

I felt like telling her to come right over, but I wanted Rory around to hear what Phyllis had to say.

"How about tomorrow night at seven?" I asked. Cara would be at Junior Temple Club.

"Marvy," she said, and I sighed.

• • •

"Miriam!" Phyllis said the following night when I answered the door in my white tunic. During our first reading, I had thought she was forty-eight, but now, seeing the gray film in her aura, I sensed she was in her mid-fifties. No one else would have known. Her face was tight and shiny from plastic surgery. She was plump in a white coat, her hand at her throat to show off her four-karat diamond. A big camera hung from a strap around her neck.

"Please come in," I said.

I could hear her appraising my possessions as she looked around. It was as if she were casing the joint: *Oak ice chest, $750. Stiffel floor lamp, $200 or so.*

"Love seats, nine hundred fifty at Bloomingdale's warehouse," I said wryly. "Won't you sit down?"

Her gray eyes twinkled. "You really are something," she said, laughing. Then she stepped back and looked me up and down. "Hmm," she said. "A pair of heels would give you some height. I'll take some preliminary head shots."

"But I don't even know if I'll sign with you yet."

"This is just so I can decide on your look," she explained. "If you sign, I'll have a professional photograph you, of course. But this way I have a photo on file in case something comes up." Then she lifted her camera and studied me through the lens.

"Should I smile?" I asked.

"Just be natural," she said, but I felt my face tighten up as she stared at me through the viewfinder.

Twisting her mouth to the side, she said, "Well, I guess with those pale eyes and that wild hair, we can capitalize on a sort of ethereal look." She snapped a dozen pictures. "Yes, ethereal," she said. "A background of a starry sky would help, too." She let her camera hang down on its strap and cocked her head at me. "Maybe you could use some darker foundation on the sides of your nose to make it look a little less wide."

I squirmed.

"Oh, my dear," Phyllis trilled, "I didn't mean to upset you. It's just that my mind starts clicking away, and sometimes I forget my social graces." I thought I saw a glint of pleasure in her eyes, but she tucked in her bottom lip as if she were really upset. When she sat down on the love seat, she noticed Cara's picture on the coffee table. "And who is this beauty?" she asked.

"My daughter, Cara," I said proudly.

"Is she psychic, too?"

"Not at all," I said happily, and then I had a twinge of guilt at what Cara might think of my going public. I thought about how shamed Cara had been by the TV psychic, her humiliation at the basketball game when I shouted out that Alicia's nose would be broken, and the twinge of guilt became a terrible pang.

"Too bad," Phyllis said. "I could have double-billed you—a mother and daughter act. The audience would have loved it. I could have gotten her on the cover of *Vogue*."

"One psychic in the family is enough of a challenge," I said. "And I want to use a stage name so my family and I can have some anonymity."

"Of course," she said. "And Miriam Kaminsky doesn't grab me anyway. How about Simone Savant?"

"Who? I need something closer to my own name. Maybe we can just use Miriam," I suggested. "No last name. I've always done that. A lot of other psychics do that, too." I told her about Isabel.

"Miriam it is," Phyllis said.

Then I heard Rory's Taurus pull into the driveway. As he was unlocking the door, I said, "My husband, Rory."

Rory had on a pale blue shirt and striped tie and his good black coat as if he were the one who had to make an impression.

Phyllis rose from the love seat. "A pleasure," she said, and she shook his hand, her eyes gleaming. "Now I see where your daughter gets her looks."

I felt as if a chicken bone had stuck in my throat.

"Your wife could be a gold mine if she'd agree to sign with me," Phyllis went on, leaning toward him. "You have no idea of the market out there."

"I know," Rory said. "I was the one who encouraged her to work at it in the first place."

"Really?" Phyllis said, cocking her head. "And what do you do?"

"I'm a pharmacist. I own my own business. Mirror Pharmacy on Springfield Boulevard in Queens."

"And how are you standing up against the chains?" she asked.

Rory began his diatribe against chains. I had heard this so many times that I went off to the kitchen to get the coffee and the chocolate babka. When I got back, Rory was saying, "Thanks for listening. Phew. I feel better already."

I set the cake and coffee down on the table a little too hard. This meeting was about *my* business, not his. "Is there any charge for me to be your client?" I asked.

"Usually, but I'm so eager to have you with me that I'll make an exception. I won't charge you until we get you on *Oprah*. You'll only get eight hundred dollars this time," she said, "but the next gig I get you will bring at least six months of your present earnings. Once you hit the big time, I get twenty percent." She took the contract out of her bag and handed it to me. "It's so straight up that you won't even need a lawyer. Sign on the dotted line, and we can begin."

I was surprised at how quiet Rory was. He seemed to be in a trance. Usually, he got involved in deals. Now, he was deferring to me. *A true separation of church and state,* I thought. I liked this. It was a chance for me to become a real businesswoman. "I don't want to get locked into a contract," I told her.

"Well, I can't very well put you in the limelight and let someone else snap you up, can I?"

Rory finally came out of his trance. "Let me see it," he said. He barely read it. "Clear as a bell. It's all just as she says." He kept nodding his head as if telling me, "Say yes, yes, yes." It got my back up.

"Leave the contract with me," I told Phyllis. "I'll look it over. But I'm not promising anything."

"No, but I'm promising you something," she said with delight. "Success like you never dreamed of. You're the psychic. Don't tell me you don't see it in your own future, too?"

I was so overwhelmed that my mind was cloudy. I could hardly see what was right before my eyes, let alone my future. "I have to think about this further," I said.

After we watched her climb into her Lexus, I noticed Rory was glowing. He looked so exuberant, so boyish, I actually tousled his hair.

"She's good," he said. "You ought to sign, Mim. It's amazing the way this opportunity came to you. It's as if it's for your highest good."

I felt as if I were being pulled apart on a rack.

"Rory," I said, "do me a favor. Don't use my affirmations against me."

In the morning, the phone rang. My neck muscles were so knotted that I could barely lift the receiver.

"Hi," Phyllis said. "Have you made a decision yet?"

The screws on the rack were tightening. I was weighing everything—Cara's feelings, our giant expenses, what would happen to our lives if Great Neck found out I was a psychic. And if I did become successful, Rory's business might gobble up even more money, and then I'd feel twice as resentful. "I haven't quite decided yet," I said.

"So tell me, what did your husband think about our meeting?"

"He's leaving it up to me," I said. I didn't want her to know how much he was pressuring me to do it. I didn't want to give her an edge.

# 16

I reread Cara's cut slips from the attendance office over and over. Yes, they really were informing me that Cara had skipped out of eighth period on Monday and Tuesday. She had never done anything like that before. Stuck to the back of the slip was a yellow Post-it:

*Dear Miriam,*

*Don't worry. It's just senioritis. By the way, my daughter still has the wishing well she made in your basement during Brownies.*

*Fondly,*
*Nancy Curson*

Nancy was kind to try to soften the blow, but senioritis or not, I had to put a stop to Cara's cutting. I had an ally at the attendance office now, but I still felt an urgency to drive over to the high school to make sure Cara hadn't cut today, too.

I arrived in the middle of seventh period. Walking up the steps to the entrance, I could see into the student parking lot. There was a couple sitting on a motorcycle, face-to-face, a *Kama Sutra*–like position. They were practically having sex and in front of the whole school, no less. In my day, young people did those things under the boardwalk.

I stared at the couple again, and then their bodies shifted and I suddenly noticed the girl had a jacket like Cara's, and the boy's head was partly shaved, with a yellow topknot like Lance's. Then the girl stretched and sighed, and my heart plummeted to my shoes. "Cara!" I shouted. When I reached them, I felt inexplicably embarrassed, more than anything. "You promised not to go on the motorcycle," I said breathlessly.

Cara flinched, startled. "What are you doing here, Mom?" She smoothed her shirt, patted down her hair.

"I received a few invitations in the mail," I snapped, and held up the cut slips.

She looked at me, wide-eyed, for a moment, then slowly, still holding Lance's hand, she swung her legs down and got off the bike. "Mom, Lance," she said, by way of introduction.

"Hey," Lance said, his yellow topknot flopping to one side. He had a cocky smirk on his face.

I'd had enough of him. I nodded without looking at him directly, but still I could see lightning bolts of energy zigzagging from his hand into Cara's, filling her whole body with a kind of negative power. "I was on the motorcycle, Mom, but it wasn't moving," she said. "We were just sitting on it. It might as well have been a park bench."

"Don't worry," Lance piped up. "Even if Cara rides with me, she'll be okay. I've done one twenty without a scrape," he added proudly.

My heart knocked in my throat. He had to know that he was scaring me. Cara had such a gratified expression on her face that if I hadn't still felt the deep psychic sting of my own mother's slap on my cheek, I might have slapped her. "Let's go," I said to her. "We have to talk. In private."

She huffed, then gave Lance a long look, pink haze drifting between them. Finally, she followed me.

I could feel his gaze, like tentacles reaching after her. "You'd better get back to class right now," I said when we were out of Lance's earshot.

"Mme Bernschwager's absent today, and the substitute got sick, too. My class was shuffled into a stupid study hall with a dorky dean. I didn't even have anything with me to study."

"Since when do you make your own rules?"

Cara looked back at Lance, then shrugged and tossed her head. "I thought of it as using my own judgment."

These days she had an answer for everything. "No more cutting under any circumstances," I said. "And to be carrying on with that boy anywhere, but especially on school grounds, is very poor judgment."

"The only thing we were carrying on was a conversation," she said.

I thought of how his legs had wrapped around her thighs, and how she'd been running her hands down his back. "I'll walk you to study hall," I said.

She looked alarmed. "Mom, don't worry. I'll get there on my own."

I accompanied her to the glass door and held it open for her until I saw her go up the stairs, the pink haze trailing.

"There's only one thing left to do about this," Rory said, reading the two cut slips.

"What?" I asked.

"If we can't talk sense into our daughter, we'll have to try to talk some sense into that boy. I have to lay down the rules to him. I'll have him come here this Sunday afternoon at one."

"Okay," I said, expecting Cara to protest, call him old-fashioned. I could picture her sneer. But how could I tell Rory not to try?

Rory went to the foot of the steps. "Cara, come down," he called. "Your mother and I have to talk to you."

As she padded down the steps barefoot, I could hear her thinking: *Here they go again.* "I know," she said, tightening her terry robe around her, her eyes green pools of defiance. "I'm so grounded that I have to stay home until I'm like eighty, right?"

Rory clenched his jaw. "Wrong," he said. "We want to meet Lance. We'd like you to invite him to our house at one on Sunday. There's a few things I'd like to discuss with him."

To my surprise, she bounced on her toes and said, "Yes!" her face breaking into a big smile. "Once you get to know Lance, you'll love him. He has an awesome sense of humor."

"Tell Lance to leave his motorcycle home and put on some decent clothes," Rory said. "A tie, maybe."

"I don't know if Lance will go that far," Cara said, but she was still smiling. "I'll call him right now to tell him."

As soon as we were alone, Rory and I looked at each other, alarmed. "I can't believe I'm letting that maniac into our home," he said.

"I can't either."

He was quiet for a few moments. Then he touched his chin. "Maybe we can tell Cara that we thought better of it, that we changed our minds."

"Can we do that?"

"Of course we can. We're the parents."

"Maybe she hasn't even called him yet," I said.

"That would be a break," Rory said. We hesitated, then took each other's hands, and started toward the steps, but Cara appeared in the doorway. She looked as if a light had been turned off inside her.

"Lance said he doesn't 'do' parents," she announced.

"Well, Cara," Rory said, "how can we believe he has honorable intentions toward you if he won't meet us?"

"He does, Daddy. It's just that he has 'trust issues.'"

The last client who told me he had "trust issues" had booked his reading with a stolen credit card.

"He should do it for *you,* Cara. That's the point," Rory said. "You tell him he's never stepping foot in this house. And I better not hear any more stories about you missing classes because of him or anybody else, young lady."

Cara turned on her heel and left the room.

Rory looked to me. "Maybe it's better this way," he said. "Lance has just solidified our position."

I couldn't see anything but a deep fog. I hoped Rory hadn't pushed Cara further into Lance's arms.


In the morning, a woman called. "I'd like to book a reading," she said. "When are you available?"

I looked at my calendar. "This Friday morning," I said agreeably.

"No, that's when I go for my hair and nails," she said.

"Is this Wednesday evening better for you?" I asked.

"Sometimes we go to the club on Wednesday nights," she said.

"Tell me all the hours you're free," I said, "and I'll see if I can accommodate you."

She told me when her therapist appointment was, when her physical trainer came, and when she went to her allergist and her dermatologist. "It's unusual for me to be up before noon," she said, and chattered on about her insomnia and all the treatments she'd had for it.

Fifteen minutes had passed, and she was no closer to booking an appointment. "I'm sorry, but I can't stay on the phone any longer."

"I'm ready to book," she said. "But what if I change my mind? Do you have a cancellation policy?"

It occurred to me that she might be the fourth of the twenty-three-hour cancellation crew. "You know what?" I said. "I'm not getting any psychic information about you. You'd be better off calling another psychic."

"But you were highly recommended," she argued.

"Ask for another recommendation," I said, and got off the phone.

The phone rang again. I thought it was her again, calling to waste my time, but I answered on the last ring before my voice mail went on.

It was Phyllis. "I've got a real coup," she said, breathless. "*The Rita Cypriot Show.* Nationwide. It's big time staring you right in the face."

Big time suddenly seemed better than wasting time with the cancellers and the chatterers. "TV?" I said. "I had only considered radio."

"If you don't snap this up," Phyllis said, "I'll have to call one of my other psychics. I swear, no matter how hot a psychic you are, if you turn this down, I can't afford to put any more time into you."

I hemmed and hawed. Then I heard something slam in my mind. It was either the door of opportunity or the lid of my coffin. I looked to my left to see what the future held. I saw a skyscraper. At least it wasn't a cemetery. Maybe it was a good sign. Then I thought of Cara, the ordeal my going on TV would be for her.

"You're a very foolish woman if you don't jump at this opportunity."

The word *jump* worried me. I saw myself leaping out of the skyscraper. I blinked it away. Now I saw Cara jumping.

"I'm getting impatient," she said.

I covered my eyes with my hand. "But I don't want to be seen."

"This is either your launching pad or the end of the line."

That's what I was afraid of. "Okay." I sighed. "I'll sign your contract and put it in the mail."

"This is the luckiest day of your life," she said.

After we got off the phone, I sat back in my chair, my hands behind my head, looking out the window. Maybe it was the luckiest day of my life, I thought. Who knew? Bubbie had said a psychic couldn't tell her own future.

"But *neshomeleh,* I can tell yours," I heard. I shifted my eyes to the right, and there was Bubbie, wearing her silver brooch in the middle of her lace collar, tortoiseshell combs in the sides of her hair.

"Bubbie, you look so pretty today," I said, but her eyes flashed.

"In this work, you aren't supposed to go for the gelt. And you're never supposed to do it for show. You go on TV, I can't help you no more," she said.

I thought of the mess Rory and I were in. "Bubbie, you told me that one of the greatest things a healer can do is save a family. That's what I'm trying to do with my own. We need the money to send Cara to college. And I can't keep letting Rory go downhill. I have to save him. Sometimes you have to put the living before the dead."

"So, you *fenagle* what I taught you so you can do what you want and flush the old ways down the toilet?" she snapped. "Well, if you go on that show, you won't see your Bubbie around no more."

I could feel myself on the edge of panic.

"Bubbie, you can't stay mad at me. Remember? Anger is a blindfold and a pair of ear corks."

Bubbie pressed her lips together and narrowed her eyes. The only times I'd ever seen her this angry was when a client was ungrateful or when my mother tried to keep us apart.

"You can love a person, but not love what they are doing," she said.

Bubbie got paler until all I could see was the small rainbow reflecting from the crystal onto the white wall. *She'll be back,* I told myself, though I was shaking. Whatever I chose to do, I was still her *neshomeleh.* I had to believe her spirit would never leave me.

I phoned Rory at his store. I could hear the whirring of his printer running in the background, spewing out form after form, itemizing what his customers owed him that someone at Medicaid, Medicare, or the other third-party payment plans would end up misplacing.

"Did you ever hear of *The Rita Cypriot Show?*" I asked him.

"Sure. My customers talk about it. Why do you want to know?"

"I'm signing with Phyllis. I'm going to be on that show."

"Mim, that's great. It's great for both of us." There was so much excitement in his voice it brought to mind kernels bursting into popcorn. "People say Rita Cypriot really knows how to put her guests at ease, get the most out of them."

I could feel myself softening under Rory's encouragement. Rita was going to ask all the right questions and lead me to success. I felt my breathing get regular again.

Fifteen minutes later, Phyllis called me back. "It's not a done deal yet," she said. "Tomorrow morning at nine, the production assistant, Janice Whitman, is going to phone you for a reading to make sure you're the real thing."

"Okay," I said. I knew the test could always provide a way for me to opt out.

That night, I tossed and turned until the bedding was a tangle. I needed Rory's comfort. I rubbed the back of his neck. "Rory," I sang softly in his ear. He stirred, and I pressed my body against his back, but he refused to wake up.

I went downstairs, poured myself a shot of Dewar's, and began sipping. I felt like a sugar cookie dunked in tea. As soon as my body hit the couch, I fell asleep.

Later, I felt movement around me. My eyes fluttered open. Rory was leaning over me. He kissed my forehead. "I'm leaving for work," he said. "I should have been the one to sleep down here. I was so tired I could have slept anywhere. I know you'll knock that production assistant's socks off," he said. I looked at the wall clock. It was 4:30 A.M. I wished he had let me sleep.

Before I knew it, someone was shaking my shoulder. I opened my eyes. It was Cara. The sun was up and streaming through the windows.

"You and Dad didn't have a fight, did you?" she asked. I could hear her thinking: *First the Changs got divorced, the Hassams, and the Goldsmiths, now my mom and dad.*

"No. I just couldn't sleep," I said. I trudged into the kitchen to eat breakfast with her, but I couldn't even take a sip of tea. I hoped she wouldn't notice. Any intrusion from Cara might cloud my mind today. After I showered and dressed, I went straight upstairs to my office. I got out a pen and a piece of paper to write down whatever popped into my mind. "Om," I sang out frantically. "Om," I tried to imagine what the production assistant looked like. She had brown hair. No, it was red. Or was it black? I was afraid that my psychic powers had utterly failed me. When she called, I'd have nothing to say. I'd feel her scorn pour over my head like Drano.

The phone rang. My hand trembled as I picked up the receiver. "Hello," I said.

"Hi, this is Janice Whitman, the production assistant for the Fox show. It's audition time. Tell me about myself."

I tried desperately to get some detail to impress her, something in her office. But everything was dark like the parts of an old mirror where the silvering was worn off. I was silent. "You are punctual and efficient," I said nervously. Then I heard a buzzing in my ear. "And you have a problem with your ear?" I asked hopefully.

"No, but my daughter does. In fact, now you got me worried. I want to phone the baby-sitter. I'll call you back in a few minutes," she said.

*Phew,* I said to myself. As soon as she got off the phone, images began to come to me. I could see her vaguely boxed in a room with papers piled high on her desk. On her wall, there were tacked-up memos, a picture of her daughter, and a photo of a man painting at an easel. I wrote down "Artist." I got images of her whole family. She had a sister. I saw the image of a sword in the production assistant's heart. "Sibling rivalry," I wrote.

When she phoned back, I read her what I'd written down.

"Oh, my God," she squealed. "How did you know?"

"It's my job to know," I said smugly. Then a new image came to me. A high-heeled shoe kicking over a pile of money. "Are you footing most of the bills in your family?" I asked.

She sighed. "My husband's gallery just closed. He's looking for another."

I got a future flash of the paintings stacked all over their loft apartment. They weren't selling. He was a bad artist. "He hasn't had much luck with his paintings," I said. "I see loads of unsold canvases."

"Every word Phyllis told me about you is true," she said. "You are the real thing. I have a ton of work to get to. Before we hang up, I'd like to ask you one question. Will my marriage work out?"

I could hear her fear. It was like the sizzle you heard if you stuck a fork in a toaster. Then I saw a hand removing a wedding ring. "Invest in yourself," I cautioned her. I saw a TV screen coming from her mind. She was hosting her own show. "I know you want to have your own show someday. Make your own dreams come true."

"So then you're saying my marriage won't work out?"

"That's unclear at this time," I hedged. "But I do see you having a great chance of success if you keep the focus on you."

"I appreciate that. I'm astonished. You really are the real thing. I'll make arrangements for you to be on the show. We'll tape it Tuesday, January twelfth, and I'll get back to you on when we'll air it."

We said our good-byes, and as soon as I hung up, I worried about Cara. I would have to figure out how to tell her.

• • •

As soon as Rory got home, I ran to him. "I passed the audition," I said.

"Great," he said, and squeezed me against him.

I started to tremble. "Rory, I'm so nervous. Will you take the day off on January twelfth to come to the studio with me?"

He wrapped his arms around me, but I could feel his tension.

"I'd love to, honey. More than anything, but the pharmacist who used to fill in for me got a full-time job, and I don't have anyone else trained. And I just can't close for a day. People count on me to fill their prescriptions."

I understood, but couldn't stop tears from filling my eyes. "I feel very alone, Rory."

"You could ask Phyllis Kanner to go with you," he said. "I bet that's part of her job."

"She makes me even more nervous. I want *you* to be with me, Rory."

He held me tight. "This show will enable me to ease up so we can be together more. We'll take a family vacation. That's the whole point, Mim, for me to have the time to be there for you and Cara."

For a moment I felt bolstered, and then the thought of having to tell Cara made my heart sink again.


The Saturday afternoon before the show was to be taped, I knew I had to come clean with Cara. She was lying on her side on her bed looking through *Seventeen,* her head propped up with her hand. She was wearing Lance's rock band shirt again. "Cara, I'm going to be on TV," I said brightly.

"Oh? What for?" she asked without even closing the magazine. In her circles, this wasn't uncommon. Darcy's mom had been on TV complaining about the lice epidemic in Great Neck. Courtney's mom, who used to be a model, still appeared in an ad for Playtex bras.

I took a deep breath. "For my gift," I said. "For my psychic gift."

She closed *Seventeen*. Without a word, she walked to her dresser, yanked her junk drawer out, and angrily turned it upside down. Marbles, tampons, sunglasses, pens, date books, barrettes, and Pez dispensers scattered on the carpet. "You can't!" she cried. "My life will be over. Why are you doing this to me?"

I went to hug her, but she crossed her arms over her chest.

I dropped my hands. "Dad and I need the money," I said quietly. "It will help me build my business so Dad can expand his. Kids your age won't be watching."

"They better not," she said. "They just better not." She bent and began scooping up handfuls of things back into the drawer. Without looking at me, she said, "When is it going to be on?"

My mouth felt dry. "All I know is they're taping it this Tuesday."

She got up to put the drawer back in her dresser. She was so angry that she forced it in at the wrong angle.

"Let me do it," I offered.

"You've done enough already," she said bitterly. "I just want to be left alone."

"Okay," I said. With as much dignity as I could muster, I walked downstairs, sat on the landing, and tried to figure out how to ease the situation. I needed Bubbie.

"Bubbie?" She didn't answer. *She'll come around,* I thought, if I wait long enough. Fifteen minutes passed and I got *zitsfleish,* so restless that I couldn't sit there another second. I just had to be near Cara. I went back up to her room, but she had hung a DO NOT DISTURB sign on her doorknob.

As the day progressed, so did my panic about going on TV, especially without Bubbie's support. When Rory got home, I said, "I've got to practice on you for the show."

Rory pulled at his collar. "I don't think that's such a good idea," he said.

I knew Rory didn't like when I did psychic things to him, but I didn't have time for his objections. I handed him a *National Geographic*. "I'll go upstairs," I told him. "You pick a picture and concentrate hard on it. In fifteen minutes, I'm coming down to describe the picture to you."

"But, Mim, I'm starving."

"Do it!" I said frantically.

He shook his head at my frenzy. "Okay."

I went upstairs and set a timer. I sat in one of the bedroom chairs and closed my eyes. "Om, om," I chanted. I tried to picture Rory at the round oak table in the kitchen staring at the open magazine. I put myself into the scene and looked over his shoulder. The page was blank. "Om, om." I changed my tactic, imagining myself as Rory. I imagined myself looking through his brown eyes at the picture. I concentrated. I saw the color red. The timer dinged. I came downstairs.

"I didn't get much," I said. "I just saw a lot of red."

He held up a big black-and-white photo of an Amish man hoeing a field.

"Oh, no," I cried. "I was all wrong." Then I noticed that Rory had red on his lips. For a moment, I wondered if it was lipstick. Then I saw his empty plate. He had eaten the spaghetti and meatballs. He'd been looking at what he was eating. "You didn't concentrate on the picture the way I asked you to!"

"Mim, I looked, but I told you I was starving."

"I feel as if I can't count on you for anything!" I shouted.

"That's not true, Mim. I've seen your gift. You don't need to do these stupid tests. You're a genius in your work."

He kissed me, putting his tongue in my mouth. I pulled away for a moment. "Good sauce," he said.


The day before I had to go to the TV studio, I was so anxious that I had to get out of the house. I put on my coat and opened the front door. Baron was panting on my doormat, his tongue hanging out to the side, with Iris next to him, reading a postcard. Her ash brown hair had been streaked blond and stood on end as if she'd put her wet finger into an electrical outlet.

"Can I help you?" I asked.

She startled and looked at me, goggle-eyed. The pearl neck chain hanging from the arms of her glasses shivered.

"I . . . uh . . . the mailman put this in my box, but it's addressed to you," she explained.

I had a vision of her rifling through my mail. I forced myself to smile. "Thank you," I said.

Iris turned and high-tailed it up the street with Baron. I looked at the picture on the postcard. A night sky with a big star, captioned: A STAR IS BORN. I turned it over and read:

*Dear Miriam,*

*Just to confirm. Looking forward to meeting you at the taping of* The Rita Cypriot Show *on Tuesday, January 12, at 11:00 A.M. Be here by 9:00 A.M., the latest. It will be aired on Thursday, January 21, at 8:00 P.M. Thanks for your great reading.*

*xoxo*

*Janice Whitman*

In a minute, I was panting like Baron. I crept back into the house to calm down.

# 17

THE MORNING OF THE show, I woke up forty-five minutes before the alarm was due to go off. There was a note on my
pillow: "Knock them dead. Love, Rory."

I forced myself out of the covers and took a shower. I
smoothed gel through my hair and then wound individual curls
around my finger. The mirror was still steamy, but I didn't bother
wiping it. I snagged two pairs of pantyhose before I got one on
intact. I had finally bought myself a black Ann Taylor suit. No
turban or gypsy clothes for me. I wanted to look respectable.
After the show, I figured I could always wear the suit to a funeral.

I heard Cara's alarm, then her padding in for her shower. I
waited twenty minutes for the Niagara of water to stop. Then I
microwaved some blueberry muffins and a cup of Ovaltine, put
it on her Peter Rabbit plate, and brought it up as a peace offering.

"Come in." She sighed. She was sitting on the floor in a
turquoise push-up bra and matching thong panties, a blue foam
toe separator between her toes as she painted her toenails.

I set the tray down on her dresser. "Won't your toenails get
messed up when you put your boots on?"

"It's three-minute drying polish from Maybelline," she said, not looking at me.

"I know how much you're against my going on the show," I said, "but I need you to wish me luck anyway."

She looked at me hard, considering. Again, I felt as if it were my mother's harsh expression across those delicate features. A shudder went through me. Cara shook her head. "I can't," she said. "I just can't."

On the 7:26 express train bound for Penn Station, I made sure to have a seat facing west. I was confused enough without riding backwards, too. A poster for an HBO show in front of me said, A LESSON IN DYING. The fluorescent light above me was twitching. If these were omens, they weren't good.

I wished I were anyone else on the train. The woman reading the *Times,* her attaché case at her feet, the woman taking her small daughter to an audition, reviewing her lines en route, or even the very old man who was talking at the top of his lungs on a cell phone, describing his constipation.

"Tickets, please," the conductor said. I rifled through my handbag, my pockets. I couldn't find it. I had to buy another ticket at a higher price.

For a half hour I sat, staring out at the passing scenery, dreading whatever was ahead.

"Penn Station will be the next and final stop on this train."

The train rumbled into a dark tunnel. I saw myself in the window. My hair was even curlier than usual and listed to one side. I took an Afro pick out of my bag and tried to even it out.

When the train belched to a stop, I became part of the crowd heading up the narrow steps. I felt anonymous, ordinary, a little less nervous. As soon as my feet were on the black-and-white speckled tile of the station floor, I remembered that I was headed for my TV ordeal. Everything I saw became startling. All those lit-up concession signs; people intently watching the station names light up on the big overhead monitor, knowing that once their train track was posted, they only had a few minutes to run to it.

I took the escalator up and waited on the long taxi-stand line. When I was finally at the head of the line, I reached for the door handle of the cab and saw a passenger already inside—a man in a business suit with tortoise-framed glasses and gray hair. I waited for him to pay his fare and get out.

The cab driver honked. "The cab's empty," someone on the line behind me shouted.

"There's someone in there," I explained.

The driver was Chinese. "No passenger," he said.

I still stood there.

"You crazy, lady? Get in."

As I climbed in, I could see Seventh Avenue right through the businessman. And he didn't look at me. He just kept checking his watch.

"I saw a reflection," I told the guy.

"Oh, I see," he said. He kept glancing at me in the rearview mirror as if I needed supervision.

"Sixth Avenue and Fifty-fourth," I said.

As he drove on, I chanted, "Om, om," to myself. But I couldn't concentrate. I wanted the ghost to pay half the taxi fare.

We pulled up to a big building with mirrored windows, each holding a piece of sky. Inside, the black marble floors and dark walls made it feel like a crypt. To the left and right there were elevators, but I went straight ahead to the security desk. "I'm Miriam Kaminsky," I said. "Rita Cypriot is expecting me."

"You'll be wanting the reception area," he said, pointing to the far right. At the next desk, the man phoned Janice for me. "The production assistant will be down for you in a moment," he said.

The knot in my stomach was twisting tighter. My throat was parched. I didn't know how I was going to speak at all, let alone be on a TV show.

A young woman was walking toward me. She had on a blue suit. "Janice?" I asked.

"Miriam?" she said.

We laughed and shook hands. I couldn't believe how tiny she was. I had been so scared of her that I'd imagined she was close to six feet. Her light brown hair was stiff and puffed, and she wore thick makeup. "Pleased to meet you," I said, extending my hand.

She narrowed her eyes at me for a moment and then forced herself to smile as she took my hand. After I did a reading, the subject either latched onto me, wanting to know more and more, or acted cool toward me, as if he didn't know who I was. I had a sense that Janice resented that I knew her secrets. I felt like a prostitute who bumps into a john the next day. She dropped my hand quickly as if she were afraid of further connection.

"Oh, it's lovely to see you," she lied. "The elevators are crazy-full here. We'll take the steps down to the green room."

We went down a flight. Reflections were bouncing off the shiny dark walls. I hoped that Bubbie would reconsider. She wasn't here, but at the landing, I saw my father's face, and he wasn't smiling.

The green room wasn't green at all. It was a small room with beige-flecked wallpaper, a brown rug, a couch, and two striped chairs. A big TV was set into the wall. It was running a tape of the show I was supposed to go on. The host, Rita Cypriot, was an intense woman with piercing dark eyes and black hair. She leaned toward her guests conspiratorially. She had a nice smile.

There were three telephones in the green room and a small fridge. On the coffee table were a few newspapers, clippings of the show, a basket of muffins, croissants, and doughnuts, with packets of butter and jam, and a tray of small sandwiches under a tent of clear plastic. "Please help yourself to anything you'd like," Janice said.

"Thank you," I said, my stomach curdling.

"Rita makes a point of never speaking to her guests before a show. She says it takes all the adventure out."

*Far be it from me to deprive Rita Cypriot of adventure,* I thought. My legs felt weak as I sat down on the couch.

"Thanks to you," Janice said, "I'm making an appearance on the show to give you a testimonial. After all, I was the one who had a reading with you."

"Thank you," I said.

"Makeup time," Janice said. "Penny will take good care of you."

She opened a door off the green room. The room was small and dark except for a rectangle of bright lights framing a big mirror in front of a beauty parlor chair. "Hi," Penny said. She looked like a ghost in black leggings. I could barely see myself in the round mirror.

"Rita never had a psychic on her show before," Penny said, seating me in her chair. "Everybody goes to psychics now. I'm learning to read the cards. Maybe she'll put me on her show."

"Maybe," I said, thinking, *Everybody thinks they can do my job.*

She took time matching foundation to my skin before applying it to my face. My face began to burn. I thought it was with shame, but it began to itch, too. "The makeup," I said. "It's too strong. Like acid."

"It's hypoallergic," she insisted.

"Get it off," I cried.

She wiped it off with baby wipes. I felt little bumps where the itching was. "Please may I have a glass of water?" I always carried Benadryl in case a bee stung me. I swallowed one now.

"What am I supposed to do with you?" Penny asked. "You can't go on like that."

"I have makeup with me," I said. I went through my bag and handed her what I had.

"It'll fade out under the lights," she complained as she dabbed at me, covering the red splotches. "You're going to look like a ghost compared to the other guests."

"Other guests?"

"There are two other people. The ones you're going to do readings for on the show and Janice, of course, who you already know. Rita had them come early so you wouldn't see them." She clapped her hand to her big mouth. "I wasn't supposed to breathe a word."

I went to work at once trying to picture them. "A man and a woman," I guessed.

"My lips are sealed," she said.

I looked in the mirror. Cara had said that she could pick me out of a crowd from miles away just from my curls. I thought of a disguise. "Do you have a rubber band?" I asked.

"Somewhere," Penny said, and looked through a drawer. "Here you go."

In my purse, I carried a metal brush I'd once bought in a pet shop. It was the only one that could go through my hair. I took it out and brushed my hair back tightly, securing it with the rubber band.

"I don't do hair," Penny said, but she wound my frizzy pony-tail into a neat bun and stuck in some pins.

Janice stuck her head back in. "We're wanted in the studio," she said. Little sparks of excitement were flying from her teased hair. She showed me into the darkened studio. There were two men. Already I had been wrong. Janice sat next to them, and I took the seat next to Rita Cypriot. I felt as if I was sitting in the electric chair, waiting for the executioner to pull the switch. Everything was dark except for hot lights pouring down on us.

"Hold tight," was all Rita said. The floor manager came to the edge of the stage, put up four fingers and said, out loud, "Four." Then it was three—two—and one.

Rita flashed her brilliant smile into the camera. "And now, our special guest, Miriam the Medium."

I had always thought of myself as plain old Miriam the Psychic, but I decided to keep my mouth shut.

"I won't introduce our other guests," Rita Cypriot went on.

"We'll let Miriam introduce them through her readings. She knows nothing about these two men. She has not seen them before this moment, but Janice Whitman, our production assistant, had a personal reading with Miriam over the telephone. Tell us your experience, Janice."

I sat up taller in my chair, smiling, expecting praise to rain down on me.

"The first thing Miriam told me was that I was very punctual," Janice snorted. "Well, of course. I had called her right on time. And she made some remarks about my family, but almost nothing she said about them was true. She said my husband was a painter when he's a photographer."

I was taken aback. "I'm sure I saw canvases," I blurted out.

"He projects his photographs onto canvases that are coated with photo emulsion, but he never paints. And you never mentioned our central family issue. We're trying to adopt another child."

"But I knew that your daughter had an ear infection."

"That wasn't news. I had already called the doctor. Adoption was at the top of my mind. You should have known that right off."

I was stunned and worried that it showed.

"Maybe I'm not being fair to Miriam," Janice said.

I relaxed a little.

"A photographer is a kind of artist. But," she continued, "there's a madman in my neighborhood who rushes up to me and tells me my future. You don't have to give him any clues. You don't have to say one word to him. It just spills from him spontaneously. And everything he said has come true—that I would have a daughter, even that I would appear on this show. And here I am." She pointed to herself dramatically.

I was outraged. Why was she doing this to me? I had a vision of a split wedding ring. Then nothing. Was she blaming me for her lousy marriage? If she was so impressed with the madman, why hadn't she put him on the show? "Now wait a minute," I said, but Rita held up one hand.

"Thank you, Janice, for your candor," Rita said, grinning hugely. "We can always count on you for that. Let's go to our first gentleman," her hand indicating the stone-faced man to her right. He was tall, with thick glasses. "Miriam, can you tell us his name?"

Janice and Rita crossed their legs in the same direction and smiled spitefully. I tried to muster as much dignity as I could. "I don't work that way," I said. "I'm not good with names. Sometimes when I'm supposed to introduce my own husband, I forget his name."

"Some men are forgettable, aren't they?" Janice said. The studio audience tittered.

I was hurt for Rory. My throat tightened.

"Why don't we get back to the readings?" Rita asked. "What can you tell us about our guest?"

I saw a mirror image of him, except with a smile. "He's one of twins. Am I right?"

His expression didn't change.

"Our guests have been instructed not to give you any information until after you've done the reading," Rita said.

"That's impossible," I said. "My readings are interactive. When people close themselves off from me, it blocks my psychic flow. There are even studies that show that disbelievers get poorer results with a psychic."

"Well, do the best you can," Rita said.

I felt the heat of the lights again. I saw globular afterimages. Some of them looked like glass. The stone-faced man wasn't the blue-collar type, but I couldn't second-guess myself. "He's a glazier," I said. "He puts glass in frames."

I saw the corners of his mouth twitch as if he wanted to laugh at my mistake. I was wrong. I listened hard, hoping some spirit would take pity on me, but all I heard was my own heart beating.

"I can't read everyone," I explained. "Sometimes I turn clients away. Certainly this man would be one of them. But I bet I could do a great job with his twin brother. Let me give you my card to pass on to him," I said.

He didn't even take the card I offered him. In the monitor, I saw the veins standing up on my forehead. I could hear my blood pulsing through them.

"Well, no cigar for you here," Rita said. "Let's move on to our next guest."

The other man was thin and chinless. His head was like the wooden egg that Bubbie used to darn socks. I chanted "Om" in my mind and, at last, I saw the scales of justice. "You're a lawyer," I said.

He didn't respond. I couldn't tell if I was right. I saw a quick image like an artist's scribble, a gesture drawing of him taking a ring off his finger. "And you're divorced," I added. I saw a FOR SALE sign stuck in a suburban front lawn. My Realtor symbol. "You're selling your house."

Once again he didn't respond. My third eye had been opened, but then it snapped shut.

"If you have nothing further to say, the guests will tell you whether you were correct on the things you came up with," Rita said to me.

"Not only am I not a twin, but I'm an only child," the first guest said.

"Tell us what you do for a living," Rita said.

"I'm an optometrist."

"Well, I knew it involved glass," I sputtered.

The optometrist rolled his eyes at me, and the others laughed.

"And you?" Rita asked the darning egg man.

"I just bought a co-op," he said. "I never owned a house to sell."

I had come close, but I didn't have a chance to defend myself.

"I'm a lawyer and I'm divorced," he admitted quietly.

Rita slid right over my correct answers. "Did you catch the story on our program last night about the psychic in Connecticut who swindled elderly widows out of their life savings by claiming that she could bring their husbands back from the dead?"

"I've had several clients who were swindled by psychics," the lawyer said. "I represented a woman who claimed her psychic had advised her to murder her husband."

I was not even included in the conversation, but once the attention was off me, I began to see a filmy shape behind Rita. It started to take form. I was so grateful for the vision that I blurted out, "Rita, there's a man standing behind you. He's in uniform." His hand went to his right shoulder. "I think he was wounded in the right shoulder. He's telling me . . ." I listened hard. "He's telling me that he's your father."

Rita's lips began to tremble. The cameraman at my left fiddled with the camera and pointed it right at Rita. The whole set took on a kind of quiet that I couldn't help but love. I watched Rita's face. "Rita, I see you at six years old. I see your pigtails, the gap between your front teeth." Everyone in the studio was staring at her in wonder.

"Your father just called you Snuggles," I said gently. "He told me to tell you that he's sorry he never got to say good-bye," and first one tear, and then two began to slide down Rita's face.

"I miss my father more each day," she said.

The stage manager held up his hand, and the show was over.

Janice caught me in the hallway. "You were great," she said.

"And you were awful to me," I told her.

"I'm so sorry," she said. "Our show is known for dramatic tension. I was just trying to beef it up before you won them over."

I watched to see if she was sincere. There was something clouded in her voice, and I knew I couldn't trust her.

"Anyway," she said, "just to remind you, we're airing the show Thursday, January twenty-first. Eight P.M. We're calling it 'Psychics—A Ruse or Reality?' Hope you enjoy the show," she said breezily.

I felt a chill, but maybe it was excitement. I remembered with glee the tears trickling down Rita's face.

When I came home, both Rory and Cara were waiting for me—one as expectant as a puppy, the other like a prisoner waiting for the guillotine. I told them the show would be aired next Thursday night at eight.

Later, when I passed Cara's door, I heard her on the phone. "Darcy, let's go to the movies next Thursday night at eight," she said. "I'll call Courtney, too. So what if it's a school night? It'll be cool."

She should invite Barbara, Darcy's big-mouthed mother, too, I thought. Maybe she should invite the whole town.

# 18

Thursday night, before the show went on, Rory, Cara, and I sat in the den. Darcy and Courtney hadn't been allowed to go to the movies on a school night after all. Cara, on the floor facing the TV with her legs crossed, drinking a Coke, and Rory poured some wine. Lifting his glass, he looked at Cara pointedly. "This is going to be a great moment for your mother and for us."

"The only reason I'm watching it," Cara said, "is to assess the damage."

"Thanks for the vote of confidence," I said jokingly. I wasn't going to let her upset me any more than I already was.

Rory sat next to me on the couch instead of his La-Z-Boy. He picked up the remote control and switched on the TV. It was a few minutes early. "Let's do a countdown," he said, looking at his watch. "Ten."

Forks of lightning passed through my nerve endings.

"My life is over," Cara said.

"Nine," Rory said.

My stomach flip-flopped.

"Eight."

"Cut it out, Rory," I said.

"I won't be able to show my face anywhere," Cara moaned.

"I requested that they not use my full name," I reminded Cara.

"Well, duh," Cara said. "You showed your full face. People will recognize it."

"I doubt it," I said, remembering my tightly pulled-back hair and my allergic reaction to the makeup. "I bet no one will recognize me, not even you."

"I'd better not," Cara said.

"Showtime!" Rory called out. He turned up the sound and threw his arm around me for a fast hug.

*"The Rita Cypriot Show,"* the announcer said as the title came on in red letters on a blue screen. Then there was a shot of Rita's head. "Is there such a thing as psychic power?" Rita asked with verve and amazingly white teeth. "Or is it just a ruse?" she added confidentially. "Our special guest is a self-proclaimed psychic."

"Self-proclaimed?" I repeated, but it was true. I had never gotten a degree in parapsychology, but a degree didn't make you psychic. The best psychics were usually people like Edgar Cayce with only a grammar school education or like my *bubbe* who had had no formal education at all.

"I'll proclaim you," Rory said, putting his arm around me.

A close-up of me came on. My hair was slicked down like wet feathers. My face was as pale as if it were rice-powdered. Penny, the makeup artist, had been right. I did look like a ghost.

"That's you?" Cara said astonished. "That's really you?"

"I told you that you have nothing to worry about."

Cara was leaning forward, as intent on the screen as a pilot guiding a plane in a sudden blizzard.

"Miriam Kaminsky, the psychic from Great Neck," the announcer boomed. I gasped. "They must have dubbed that in. No one had said that while I was on the show."

"I'm ruined!" Cara said, throwing her body onto the carpet.

"Calm down," Rory said. "It's an honor to be on *The Rita Cypriot Show.* Your mom's famous. Everybody will want to be your friend now."

"That's not the way I want to make friends," she cried. "Besides—you're wrong. Everyone will call me a freak."

"Quiet," Rory said. "Let's hear the show."

Janice began talking about her neighborhood madman. "He gave me a better reading than Miriam," she said. Not one word of her diatribe had been dubbed out.

The next segment was my not being able to read the two men. Each moment of it, I felt as if someone were turning up the thermostat higher and higher. I began to sweat. Cara shot me a killer look.

"I was a nervous wreck," I said. "But be patient. The good part is about to start. I saw Rita's dead father. I made Rita cry."

The lawyer was telling about the psychic who had advised his client to murder her husband, but I knew after that was the part when I saw Rita's dead father. I waited.

"Time for a station break," Rita said.

"It's coming, it's coming," I said. "Right after the station break. You'll see."

The station break was over. The guests had left, and I wasn't there either. A new guest was sitting next to Rita. "This man has spent his entire career disproving psychics," Rita said, "and the result is this book." She held it up. The cameraman zoomed in on the title—*Bring On the Nuts: The Wacky Things People Believe.* The screen split. There I was, on the left, looking worse than I ever dreamed possible, with a rerun of all my bloopers. They had cut out my triumph. I could barely take air into my lungs. Rory looked as if the wind had been knocked out of him, too.

Cara shrieked, "I hate you! As if it wasn't bad enough that you're a psychic! Now it's out in public that you're a fraud. I'm never going to school again."

"Listen, young lady," Rory said. "Josh Minderson's dad

embezzled funds from his company, and Josh went back to school. Dawn Lamont's mom was running a call girl ring, and Dawn's still in school, too."

"Those are the kind of people you're grouping me with?" I shouted.

"I'm just making a point," Rory said.

"How could you do this to me?" Cara hollered.

I looked at Cara again, who was so upset she was shaking. "I wish you weren't my mother!" she shrieked.

"Don't you dare talk to me like that!" I shouted. "Get up to your room. Now!"

After she stomped upstairs, I burst into tears.

"Don't take it so hard," Rory said, handing me his hankie. "I'm sure hardly anyone was watching. *Friends* was on."

"You must think you're comforting me, don't you? Well, I have news for you. You should have been the one who told Cara to shut her mouth, not me. She needs to see that I have somebody behind me."

"Don't take this out on me!" Rory said.

"You were the one who pushed me into this show," I reminded him. "You and your money problems."

"I've had enough!" he shouted. "Did I ever give you a list of everything I've done for you?"

As we bickered, the author on the TV said, "There's no such thing as a true psychic," and Cara screamed from upstairs, "I'm going to kill myself!"

That night, I was so furious with Rory that he chose to sleep on the couch in the basement, while I lay in bed, alone, helplessly listening to Cara sobbing.

The next day, when my personal phone rang, I had the desperate wish that it would be someone from the station calling to apologize, calling to say that next week they would put on the segment about me seeing Rita's father's ghost. I hurried to the kitchen to answer it. "Hello?" I said.

"Miriam, it's Dick Gruber," he said in a friendly tone. "Iris and I saw that show you were on. I have to thank you. Since you moved in, Iris had been making herself nuts, worried that you had some special powers. She thought you were psychically spying on her. Now maybe I can convince her to relax." Then he said, *"Beep, beep, beep."*

"Excuse me?" I said.

"I'm jamming you so you can't pick up my vibes," he said, and burst into uproarious laughter.

When I got off the phone, I was so hopping mad that I called Phyllis Kanner. "This is Miriam," I said. "Well, I guess you saw what happened to me on the show."

"It wasn't so bad," she said.

"You threw me to the wolves. I was discredited, and they cut out—"

Phyllis interrupted me. "Look, any publicity is still publicity. You'll see. You're a great psychic. You were just nervous. I'll book you to do readings for small groups so you can get your confidence back. Then we'll be on our way to international fame. I'll keep my eyes and ears open for the next thing."

"There won't be a next thing," I said.

"Oh, I'm sure there will," she said nastily. "You have a contract with me for two years. Airtight. Read it." Her call waiting beeped. "I have someone on another line. I'll get back to you as soon as I have a chance. Bye."

Though I'd planned to stay in bed all day, I couldn't sleep. I was angry at Rita Cypriot, at Janice Whitman, and especially at Phyllis Kanner. I paced the house for hours, then finally, slumped down into the love seat, my head in my hands. "Bubbie," I called, "I need your help. I need you to comfort me now. I need you to visit," but Bubbie didn't come.

When I was ten years old, I had sat in my bedroom on my

rocking chair, holding a black-and-white photo of my *bubbe,* hoping for her to appear. Bubbie had been dead a year then, and I missed her more every day. I rolled my eyes up to the right as she'd taught me. Instead of Bubbie, Fern Link showed up. I gasped. Fern had been in my fourth-grade class, then drowned over the summer. We'd had a big fight the last week of school because she told the teacher I'd thrown her lunch away. Fern's spirit looked mad at me.

"You should be glad I threw your sandwich away," I told her spirit, my voice trembling. "The egg salad smelled like farts." I got up from my rocking chair and began backing away.

Fern took a step toward me.

I began to cry. "I'm sorry I called you doody head," I said.

I turned to run out of the room. My mother had been standing in the doorway, listening. Fern disappeared, but my mother strode toward me, her mouth a grim line. I thought she was going to slap me, but she grabbed my coat from my closet and handed it to me. We went downstairs and got into our black Mercury. "I'm going to do what I never wanted to do," she muttered as we drove away. I remembered her telling me that when she was a child, she'd found a stray kitten and brought it home. Her mother had gotten mad and drove out to the farmlands and left the kitten there. I was suddenly afraid my mother was going to leave me in the woods.

After a very long time, my mother said, "Here we are."

Ahead were big yellow-gray buildings surrounded by a tall fence with circles of barbed wire on top. There were bars on the windows.

I stiffened. "You're going to put me in jail?"

"You'll see," she said.

"Is it an orphanage?" I cried.

She stopped the car at a booth. A man in a uniform was inside. He waved us through.

"Take me home," I cried, but she kept driving forward. Finally, she parked the car near the entrance and marched me inside the building. It was smoky, and the air smelled of pee. I peeked into the lobby. It was a sick-looking green. The couches had springs popping out.

I grasped the hem of my mother's topper. We went up in the elevator to the twelfth floor. The doors opened. I heard shrieks, crazy laughter like hyena calls at the zoo. I pressed my back against the wall of the elevator, but my mother grabbed my arm and yanked me out.

She stopped at a desk surrounded by nurses, and I realized that it was a kind of hospital. As we walked down the corridor, I saw grown people lying in cribs. A woman blinked at me as if she knew who I was, and I tried to hide my face in my mother's coat. My mother grabbed my hair. "Look!" she commanded. "You take a good long look, and see what's in store for you if you keep on this way."

"I want to go home," I cried.

"This is what they do with people who won't mind their own business and keep their mouths shut," my mother said.

"Mommy, I promise," I said, but she kept going, on and on down the long hall. There, in a back room, next to a bed with rails, stood a skinny woman in a gray robe with curly hair cut short as a man's.

"Chaia," my mother said, gently, "it's good to see you. This is Miriam." Then my mother said to me, "Meet your aunt Chaia. She's Dad's younger sister."

I could barely breathe. She had pale blue eyes turned up at the corners like Bubbie's. How could this be Dad's younger sister? I'd thought. Her hair was mostly gray, and she had deep creases on her cheeks.

"Say hello to your aunt Chaia," Mom prompted.

"H-h-hello," I said.

Aunt Chaia stepped forward. She reached out, patted my hair, then touched her short curls. She studied my eyes. Her mouth opened. "Is that me?" she asked.

"No, Chaia, it's your niece. Your brother Sol's daughter."

She stared some more, then began yelling, "No, no," and flailing her arms around. I stood there frozen. Aunt Chaia got louder and louder. Her wrist knocked against the crib rail. It must have hurt her, but she still kept flailing her arms.

"Nurse!" my mother called.

A nurse rushed in with three big men who hurled themselves at Aunt Chaia. For such a thin woman, she fought back powerfully. They grabbed her hands, lifted her up, wrestled her down into the bed, and tied her to the rail with white cloth.

"We don't want her to hurt herself again," the nurse explained.

My mother took my hand and walked so fast I stumbled. The whole way down in the elevator she didn't say a thing. When we left the building, my mother, half-running, took a shortcut across the wet grass, her high heels sinking in. As soon as she got into the car, she said, "Your aunt Chaia heard voices and saw things like you do. It was what Bubbie taught her that made her like this. Who knows what screws are loose in the head until you start fiddling with them?" She glared at me. "Poor Chaia couldn't stop telling people what she knew about them and their relatives in their graves. She screamed it in the streets. Your father and Bubbie claimed Chaia was just telling the truth, but she couldn't control herself. People threw stones at her. She's been locked up since she's twenty-two. It's a curse, not a gift. People will want to stone you for it. *Chaia* means 'life.' But look at her. She might as well be dead. Bite your tongue so I won't ever have to put you in a place like that. I couldn't bear it."

I could barely hear my mother through my own sobs. "Mommy, I'm sorry," I cried back then. "I'll never do it again."

Now as I got up from the love seat I was shaking. Tears and sweat stung my eyes. My mother had been right. People did want to stone me. My hands flew to my chest. I felt the blows from the Grubers, the guy with the darning-egg-shaped head from *The Rita Cypriot Show*, the nasty optometrist, the author who persecuted psychics, and the home viewers made up of people I didn't know. I even felt the stones from Rory and Cara.

Bubbie must feel as if I threw a stone at her by going on TV. If only I'd stayed in my office where no one knew me instead of going on that show. "Never, ever do this work at a carnival," Bubbie had warned me.

"Oh, Bubbie, I'm so sorry," I cried out. I rolled my eyes up and to the right and waited. "Bubbie, Bubbie, where are you?"

# 19

THE NEXT DAY, Iris Gruber phoned. "You've certainly broken new ground in lawn ornamentation," she said nastily.

"What do you mean?" I asked.

"Look out your front door and you'll see," she said.

I was afraid someone had burned a cross on my front lawn. I went downstairs, put the chain on my door, and opened it a crack. There was a huge heart-shaped wreath covering all the grass. I wouldn't even be able to get it through my door. *Vince,* I thought.

"Congrats, doll face," the card said. "We'll get together again real soon. Celebrities turn me on."

I began tearing at the wreath with my hands, plucking the roses, the baby's breath. I plucked it down to its Styrofoam base and jumped on it until it broke into gritty hail. I didn't care who saw, though no cars passed by. When I was finished, I was sweaty and exhausted, but it felt better. I got some Hefty trash bags and a rake and cleaned it up as best I could. Then I went inside and lay down for a nap. The house settled with a creak. I was spooked. I thought about all the people who had phoned me with gripes against psychics or weirdos who had gotten my number mixed up with phone sex. I thought of Vince and his goon. I didn't want to be alone, unprotected. We didn't have an alarm system. I decided to go to RadioShack and see if I could buy something that would scare off intruders. I skulked downstairs and scanned the driveway before getting into the car.

There were so many electrical gadgets lighting up and beeping at RadioShack that it was like a jamming center for my psychic vibrations. I bought a battery-powered alarm to put on my key chain, but I couldn't calm down. My palms were sweating on the wheel as I drove to pick up Cara from school.

When I pulled up, there was a crowd of kids around her. I saw a boy with YIPES shaved into the back of his head. I rolled down my window and heard him say to Cara, "Tell me my future." He was jeering. I saw Courtney and Darcy scowling at her.

"We were supposed to be best friends," Darcy said. "Remember the basketball game when I asked you if your mother was psychic?"

"What else haven't you told us?" Courtney said. "How can we trust you anymore?"

The Yipes boy noticed me and strode toward my car. He sprawled himself over the hood, his face so close to my windshield that his breath made a cloud. "Yo, Mama Psychic," he said. "Whazzup for me?"

"I see that you're going to get off the hood of the car because deep down, you're really a gentleman."

He burst out laughing and stayed on top of my hood. Then the other kids noticed me in my blue Honda. A few of them stood back, pointing at me, elbowing each other. A few others began to come close, too. Cara got into the car. "Go!" she ordered me, but the Yipes boy was still on the hood. Then I realized that Yipes was Clarence, a little boy who we used to drive home from Community Nursery School. He peed in his pants once and wet our backseat. To spare him, I had pretended I hadn't noticed. Now I yelled, *"Pisherke!"*

"Mom!" Cara shouted at me, but my remark had worked. Clarence slid off as quickly as if I'd burned him. I felt relieved. But when I got on the service road, I saw Cara, her head down, her cheeks flushed with shame. I took my hand off the wheel and reached over to touch her shoulder. She shook my hand off.

"You don't have a gift," she said. "A gift brings good things. You have a curse, and you've messed up my life with it."

I wondered if my mother heard Cara and felt vindicated?

"Don't pick me up at school anymore. You just make things worse."

"I'm so sorry, Cara," I said. "This was the last thing I wanted to happen. I really wanted to make life better for you, to give you everything you were missing."

"Yeah, yeah," Cara said. "A lot of good that does me." She began to cry softly.

I worried if my mother and Bubbie had teamed up for once to get back at me for having gone on that show. Then I pulled myself together. *Stop driving yourself nuts,* I told myself. *If Mom and Bubbie wanted to teach me a lesson, they'd never do it in a way that hurt Cara.* Still, the feeling of being cursed clung to me all the way home like the smell of camphor from a sweater stored in mothballs.

When we got back, Cara shut herself up in her room. I stayed outside her door, listening to pages rustling. I heard her music briefly, and then quiet, which meant she had her headphones on.

The phone rang. It was Rory. "My mother was right," I cried. "My gift is a curse."

"What curse?" he asked. "Mirror hasn't had such a good day in years. Fred told everyone in the neighborhood that it was you on TV. Now people are coming in, asking about you, and leaving their prescriptions for me to fill. One way or another, we're making out."

*Now Fred is a PR man?* "Well, I'm glad you're happy," I said, "but Cara is miserable."

"After you do a few more shows, it will all settle down. The money will start rolling in for both of us, and people will get used to the idea. There are lots of famous people in Great Neck. Alan King lives right over in Kings Point, and nobody bats an eye about it."

"Rory, I'm never going to do another show!"

"But you signed a contract."

"Let Phyllis sue. I don't care. I only care about Cara."

"You think I don't?" Rory said.

"Of course you do," I said.

"We'll talk more tonight," he said, and got off the phone.

I couldn't understand why Rory would want his wife to be publicly humiliated for any amount of money. Why wasn't he on the phone with lawyers, trying to get me out of that contract?

I went back to Cara's door and leaned my head against it. No matter how at odds we all were now, I assured myself, we were still a family. Rory used to carry baby Cara around in the middle of the night, patting her back when she was crying. Every time he turned, I saw her little face over his shoulder. I wished he could soothe her now. I listened as the music blared. She had taken off the headphones. Nirvana was singing "Territorial Pissings." I knocked. "I'm going out to get some fried chicken for dinner," I called.

"Whatever," she said. I could hear the vitriol in her voice.

I put on my jacket and went to the front door, but then I was afraid to open it. What if my old client, Noreen, had seen me on TV and was once again lurking in my rhododendron bushes, waiting to jump out at me? I breathed deeply, opened my door, and got in the car. At Poultry Mart, the line was long. I felt like one of the chickens turning on the barbecue spit. I bought mashed potatoes, broccoli rabe, and two pounds of drumsticks. On the way back, I stopped to buy a lottery ticket at Fredrick's, the luncheonette across from the parking lot. All the while, I looked over my shoulder suspiciously at every shadow. I got in my car, locked all the doors, and kept the windows shut.

At home, I carried the foil bag of chicken upstairs. From the hallway, I heard Cara say, "It's not wrong if we love each other, is it?" I almost dropped the chicken as I hurried to her door. It was partway open. She was on the phone, her back to me, swaying as if she were slow-dancing with Lance.

"I don't know," she said. "I guess I'm just scared to do it."

My heart froze. I opened the foil to tempt Cara with the aroma. Ever since she was two, she loved Poultry Mart's fried drumsticks. "Dinner's on," I called.

"I'm not hungry," she called over her shoulder.

"It's your favorite," I said.

"I'm on the phone," she said, covering the receiver.

I sighed. As long as Cara was in *her own home* talking on the phone about how scared she was to "do it," I figured she was theoretically still safe. "Okay, then, we'll all eat together when Dad gets in," I said, and I put the chicken in the fridge.

Rory came in at eleven thirty and went straight to bed. Cara had brought her dinner to her room. I slipped into bed beside Rory and he stirred. I could hear his brain activity—a whirring sound, like a tornado heading for me. I felt a knot in my gut. I wasn't sure I wanted to ask him, "a penny for your thoughts."

"I've been thinking about the contract with Phyllis Kanner," he said. "If she still wants to be your agent, that's a very good sign. We have to be open to any opportunity that's presented."

"I'm returning that affirmation book to the library before it does any more damage," I said.

"Think about it, Mim. We could both expand and incorporate. You could be . . . say . . . vice president of my corporation, and I could be the VP of yours."

It was a complete reversal of everything Rory had ever stood for. My head was spinning. "But I thought you wanted to keep what we do separate. Like church and state, remember?"

Rory shook his head. "That was before. And I was wrong."

"Where did all this stuff come from?" I squinted at Rory, trying to see his aura. There was a lot of stringy yellow in it, almost like hairs. It was like finding a blond hair on the shoulder of his suit. I was getting, as Cara would say, "freaked out."

Rory shifted, taking his arms from behind his head. Then he looked at me. "I need your help now, Mim. What do you want me to do? Beg? Can't I be trusted?"

I thought of how, on our honeymoon, we'd gone river-rafting and the raft tipped in the rapids. I'd fallen in, and Rory had jumped in after me and saved me without a thought for himself.

Rory sat up in bed. "We have to make more money or I'm finished." His whole face trembled. I kissed his worried brow, but he turned over and put his head under the pillow. It was as if his psychic vibrations had a force field around them, keeping me out. Then I was the one sitting up in bed, the night crowding around me like a throng of taunting spirits.

But I awoke more determined than ever not to accept any more offers from Phyllis Kanner. I would find other ways to make more money. I made flyers with my phone number on the bottom that people could tear off and thumbtacked them to the bulletin boards of every health food store in the area, including the Health Nuts in Little Neck. As soon as I got home, my office phone rang.

"Hello," a woman said, "are you the psychic on the bulletin board in Health Nuts?" She was the first of five who called to book an appointment. I could make money without a profit-gobbling new ad or a costly mailing. Who knew it was so easy?

I had so many clients that I didn't leave my office until after ten. When I came downstairs, Rory was on the phone, his hands cupped to the receiver.

"Oh, I've got to go," he said, and hung up without even a good-bye. Fred was probably defending himself against the complaints of customers who hadn't received the prescriptions he was supposed to deliver. A shot of anger ripped through me, but Rory looked so hangdog that I wanted to tell him my good news to cheer him up. "I have a bunch of new clients," I said. His expression didn't change. I figured he was going to tell me about a new blow to the business. I'd been through this so many times—my larger profits leading to his bigger losses, that I shouldn't have been surprised, but my legs felt so weak that I had to sit down on the bed next to him. "So, what happened this time?" I said, an edge of sarcasm in my voice.

"Nothing." He sighed.

I remembered a client who was so furious with her husband for having gone into debt. To avoid telling her that he was in the red again, he went to a loan shark. When he couldn't pay up, they murdered him. I nuzzled my face against Rory's shoulder. We hadn't made love for three weeks. I expected him to press me down on the bed, put his mouth to mine, cup my breasts with his hands, but he sat, rigid.

"I'm just overwhelmed, Mim. I can't."

I let out a long breath. "Remember the long walks we used to take?" I said, as if telling a soothing bedtime story to a child. "The time we found an abandoned shopping cart, and you pushed me through the back streets of Rockaway? And the time we went to the beach right before a hurricane and the wind lifted me off the sand, and you grabbed my arms, and we were hysterically laughing?"

He dragged his hand over his face. "That feels like lifetimes ago," he said.

"That's the way it will be again once things ease up," I promised, but he didn't answer; he was so drained. His chest hardly rose when he breathed. Still, I couldn't help feeling rejected. We had never gone this long without having sex. I lay down and curled myself up in a fetal position. I felt itchy, wired. I fluffed and refluffed my pillow. I lay on my stomach, then my side. I pushed my hair off my neck, the covers off my shoulders. Finally, I fell asleep.

Later, I had the sense that someone was watching me. When I opened my eyes, Rory was standing at the side of the bed, staring at me. "Rory?"

"Just getting up to go to the bathroom," he said, and in a blink, he was out of sight.

I half dozed for a while and woke again. Rory still wasn't in bed. I could hear the creaking of the living room floorboards. Something wasn't right. I tried to pick up on what was bothering him. I closed my eyes. All I saw was a colorless blank, as if someone had pulled a shade on my third eye.

# 20

SNOW WAS FALLING ON Great Neck. I wore clip-front rubber boots, a thick sweater under a down parka, and a wool scarf. I was bundled up like a kid. Snow always reminded me of my father, pulling me on a sled through the streets, but today I could only think of the coldness between Rory and me.

On my way into town, Dick Gruber yelled out his front door, "You have to be crazy to go out in this weather!"

"It's fine," I said, and he closed the door. The Grubers skied in the Alps, but wouldn't set foot on a snowy sidewalk. Across the street, kids had built a snowman and tied a Gucci sweater around his neck. I walked into town and stopped at Bruce's, a combination bakery and restaurant, for lunch. There were Barbie doll cakes with ruffled icing dresses and fruit pies that had art deco designs. The aromas of the sweets mixed with the pungent onion ryes and warm pumpernickels. For a snowy day, the line was long. Everyone was there with such energy and purpose—to buy something or meet someone—that I felt aimless.

At the counter, two women were arguing over who should be waited on first. One man was complaining that his son's name was spelled in pink on his birthday cake. I could hear the young guy waiting on him thinking, *Then why the fuck did they name the kid Leslie?*

As I waited, I spotted Darcy's mother, Barbara, at a table near the window. She was with a friend. I waved and forced myself to smile.

After ten minutes, a waitress showed me to a corner table and handed me the voluminous menu. "I already know what I'll have," I told her. "Tuna on toasted rye."

The waitress strode off, her rubber soles thwacking. As I popped a miniature prune Danish in my mouth from the complimentary basket, I felt as if mosquitoes were buzzing around my head. Barbara was probably telling her friend all about my failed TV appearance. I turned toward Barbara for a moment. The friend's back was to me, so she was using her compact mirror to spy. Then I heard Barbara ask her waiter to wrap up the remainder of her club sandwich. I tried to appear too busy to chat. I read my place mat as if it were the most interesting thing in the world. When the waitress set my sandwich down in front of me, it was a half a foot high. I opened my mouth wide and took a bite.

"Miriam," I heard Barbara say, and then she was standing at my table.

"Hi," I said, with the tuna behind my clenched teeth.

"So?" Barbara said. She was watching me as if waiting for me to tell her something. There was an odd glitter in her eyes, like a snake biding its time before it struck.

"Gary and I were at the Rainbow Room for our anniversary last Wednesday night," she finally said, "and there was Rory with a blond woman. We waved to him." She paused, waiting. "With a blonde," she emphasized.

All of a sudden, those blond hairs that I'd seen in his aura came back to me. I pushed the tuna to the right side of my mouth with my tongue. "Last Wednesday night? Are you sure?"

She wrinkled her forehead in a mock display of concern. I

knew she went for chemical peels to smooth out her forehead lines. She'd never crinkle it unless she really had the goods on someone. "We were going to go over and say hello, but you know—" Her voice trailed off.

I tried to remember. One night last week, maybe Wednesday, Rory had called me from Mirror and said he'd had a report to write out for Medicaid. He'd said if he didn't get it done in time, he might face an audit. He said he might be there all night. "Don't wait up for me," he'd said. I sat up worrying about how I could help him—and he'd been at the Rainbow Room with a blonde!

I wasn't going to give Barbara any satisfaction. "Oh, that was his syringe buyer," I said.

"Well, I'm glad I didn't stop at his table, then," Barbara said as she casually worked her fingers into her leather gloves. "It being business and all." Then she smiled. "No matter where you go, you find fellow Great Neckers. We really get around."

"Sure do," I said. I tried to swallow my tuna. It stuck in my throat. I began to cough.

"Look at this," Barbara said. "I'm always telling my kids, 'Don't talk with your mouth full,' and now I've made you choke. I'll phone you soon. Let's get together," and she took off with her friend and her bagged club sandwich.

My thoughts raced. *Rory at the Rainbow Room?* I had never even been there. I had heard about its revolving floor, the breathtaking view. Had he been there without me? And more important, who was he with? I closed my eyes. I saw only white again. I felt sick to my stomach. "Check please," I said. Before the waitress had even written it, I put money on the table and left.

Outside, I kept going over what Barbara had said. She must have mistaken Rory for someone else, I decided. Women were always gawking at him, but he never encouraged them. He wasn't the type. Once, a woman who looked like Sophia Loren had come in for a diaphragm and asked him to show her how to put it in. "The directions are in the package," he'd said, but she kept hanging around, chirping how she needed his personal touch. When he finally got rid of her, he called me at home, laughing over it. "I can't leave you alone anywhere," I'd told him, laughing, too.

*No.* I told myself, *Barbara was wrong.* I had failed on the TV show, but not in my marriage. I walked along, my heart colder than the weather. When I got home, as I bent to put my wet boots on the mat, I saw a book of matches. For a moment, I was worried Cara had started to smoke. I picked it up and looked at the cover. RAINBOW ROOM. I stood up so fast, my head felt light. *Slow down,* I told myself. *There has to be another explanation.* Sometimes drug reps took Rory out. But the reps only took him to diners. I began to worry that Rory had never spent any of his late nights at Mirror, that he'd been in another woman's arms all along. I resisted the impulse to call him right away and demand an explanation. I wouldn't be able to see his expression, and worse, he might have the time to think up a great alibi.

I closed my eyes and took a few deep breaths. I saw the same whiteness I'd seen before, but slowly it began to take on shadow and form. The image was dim, but I could see Rory dancing with a blonde in his arms. I could only see her back. How had I missed that he'd been out dancing? Now that Barbara had seen him, it would be the talk of Great Neck. I could imagine her hissing about it—of course he'd leave me after I'd proclaimed myself so miserably on television. I had to know who the other woman was.

Once again, I summoned up the image. I saw the woman's blond hair, her spangly blue dress with spaghetti straps, her fleshy back. I waited until the floor turned so I could see her face, but then the image popped and blackened like a worn-out bulb. I tried to think of the blondes I knew. Almost every woman in Great Neck was blond.

Bubbie would have the answer. "Bubbie?" I called, and

waited. There wasn't a sound, a scent, a glimmer. I was shocked that she still was holding that TV show against me. Hadn't I paid heavily enough for my error? I took a few deep breaths and waited for the scent of lavender, for a glimpse of her braided hair, for one Yiddish word to reach my ears, but I was still on my own.

It was up to me to decide on a strategy. I thought about my options. I could search Rory's dresser drawers, his closet. I could have him followed. I'd never thought about doing these things before, but meeting Barbara had given me a warrant for it. My limbs felt leaden. I tried to stir myself into action, but all I could do was sit on my bed and worry.

That night, Cara was in the den, MTV blasting. Through the racket, I could still hear her thinking about Lance. *His mouth curls up more on one side than the other when he smiles.* Sigh. *His eyes go right through me.* Another sigh. For once I was glad her mind was busy with Lance and her music was blaring. I didn't want her to hear anything that might be said when Rory got home.

I looked out the glass storm door. Under the streetlights, the snowbanks looked like fallen clouds. Sidewalks were shoveled into paths as narrow as tightropes. Our driveway was a greenish-gray from the Kitty Litter that Rory had strewn over it for traction. He claimed it melted ice better than kosher salt. The plow had come through that morning, but fresh blankets of snow had settled on the road.

Finally, I spotted Rory's white Taurus, snow falling off in chunks from its roof and hood. He pulled up close to the curb and got out. I threw on my jacket and ran outside in my house slippers. "Rory," I called.

He startled at seeing me in my slippers in the snow. "Hi," he said. His smile seemed forced. "I'd better clear the front walk before coming in," he said, and opened the trunk to get out his shovel.

I wasn't going to give him a chance to pull himself together before I confronted him. I walked right up to him and stared into his eyes, which jiggled as if he couldn't bear to look straight at me.

"What?" he said, digging into a mound of snow at the entrance of the driveway.

I didn't want to see what I saw, but there was no getting around it. His aura was spiky like the graph of a guilty man's lie detector test. "Who was the blonde Barbara Traubman saw you dancing with at the Rainbow Room?" I demanded, flashing the book of matches.

He tossed a shovelful of snow onto the white lawn and dug into another mound. He couldn't look me in the eyes. "Oh, that," he said, and bit his lip.

"Who was she?"

He blew out his breath. "Phyllis Kanner."

*Phyllis?* My knees felt as if they might buckle. Phyllis, whom Rory had been so eager for me to sign a contract with? Phyllis, whom he'd assured me had come into my life for my highest good? I'd seen the proliferating outlets she'd plugged into, my symbol for her many affairs, and it had been me who had told her, "A younger man is coming your way." Who knew that the younger man was going to be *my* husband? I felt as if I were leaving my body. "How long has this been going on?" I demanded.

"You're way off track," Rory said. "Let's go in and discuss this." He tried to take my arm, but I yanked it away.

How could Rory have done this to me? To Cara? What would Cara do if she found out? I shivered and dug my slippers into the snow. "I'm not moving until I've found out just how much of an idiot I've been." The toes of my slippers darkened.

Rory stuck the shovel straight down in a snowbank and let go of the handle. "You're not the idiot," he said. "I am. I should have seen her intentions. She first came to Mirror to enlist me to help her sign you."

"How did she know where you worked?" I asked.

"During her first phone reading with you, you gave her our address."

"Just so she could send her business card," I said.

"Well, once she knew we were local, she asked around and someone told her I owned Mirror. She drove to the store and told me she had a great business opportunity to discuss with me, and we could do it over dinner. I asked her what it was about and she said, 'Your wife's career.' And I said, 'I can't get involved,' but she insisted it was crucial and I wouldn't regret it, so I had dinner with her at La Baraka."

"You went to that French restaurant in Little Neck with her, too?" I shrieked.

"Just to find out about the opportunity," Rory said. "All we talked about was you, Mim."

I could feel my pulse vibrating in my wrists and throat. "You mean you knew her *before* she came to our house with the contract and pretended you were meeting her for the first time?"

His face went red. I could sense his blood pressure skyrocketing. He just nodded.

"And of course, you had to go dancing with her, too," I said.

"That was after the TV show," he said. "She wanted you to stay in your contract. She told me that one strike didn't matter, that she could still build your career."

"You took her to the Rainbow Room?"

"It was on her expense account," Rory answered in a low voice. "And *she* asked *me* to dance. What was I supposed to do, say no? I was only there because I was desperate for a way out of our financial mess. I thought I had let you and Cara down. I couldn't live with myself!"

"So, to solve that you fucked Phyllis?"

"What?" Rory said, so astonished that his head jerked back. "What did you say to me?"

"Fuck Phyllis, fuck Phyllis!" I began to scream.

"Calm down," he said. "Cara will hear you," but I knew Cara was listening to her music.

The snowplow came back up our street. The Grubers' side door slapped open to let Baron in, and it took an awfully long time to close. Mrs. Hasaam, who paper-trained her toy poodle so it wouldn't have to leave the house, was trying to coax the dog out into the snow to get a closer view of us. Rory and I were on stage, but I didn't care what anyone thought.

"Fuck Phyllis, fuck Phyllis!" I continued to shout.

Rory grabbed my arm. "What's the matter with you?" he hollered. "Don't you trust me? Phyllis came with one idea, then got another. As soon as she stopped talking about your contract and began talking about her and me, I told her, 'No way!' I told her, 'I love my wife.' I only met with Phyllis because you and I have money worries. I shouldn't have done it behind your back, but I was afraid you'd say no. I was desperate. Don't you know me well enough to know that I'd never have sex with anyone but you, Mim?"

"No, I don't. I don't know you at all. You told me you were going to be at the pharmacy all night writing a report for Medic-aid so you wouldn't get an audit. You lied, Rory. What other lies have you told me that I don't know about?"

"Listen, I'm sorry. I had to see what Phyllis had in mind," he said. "I didn't want you to miss the opportunity of a lifetime."

"An opportunity for you, not me. You were trying to run my business. You steamrolled me into signing with Phyllis, but when I saw Fred at OTB, you pulled your 'separation of church and state.' We were supposed to be partners. MirRor. Mirror. You and me!"

He stuck out his chin. "When you *saw* Fred in an OTB! Come on, Mim."

"Don't you remember our one-month anniversary in that Greek restaurant when I first admitted I was psychic, and you called me your live wire? You said, 'If I had a gift like yours, I'd never waste it on a regular job.' You and Bubbie were the only ones who encouraged me, and now you're acting as if I'm crazy. If you don't believe I saw Fred at OTB, you really don't believe in me."

I bent down, grabbed a clump of snow, and threw it in his face.

He blinked at me, in shock. "I did the wrong thing, Mim," he said, wiping his face with his sleeve. "I wish I could take it back. But nothing happened between Phyllis and me. You have to believe me."

I thought about the past three weeks, how I'd cuddled up next to him in bed, but he'd been too tired or too distracted to make love. I remembered how he used to love to run his tongue up my neck, how he kissed my eyelids.

"You fucked her!" I said.

He yanked the shovel out of the snowbank and threw it down. "No, I didn't, but maybe I should have," he said angrily. "At least she was sympathetic toward me."

"Sympathetic?" I shouted.

"Yeah, Phyllis said I was quite a guy."

"Has Phyllis lived with you for twenty-one years?" I shouted. "Has she gone with you to visit your parents' graves? Was she the one who gave birth to your only child? Did she risk everything, including her *bubbe,* to go on a TV show so that your business wouldn't fold? You really are quite a guy to go running around behind my back!" I spat out.

Rory pulled at his face. "Mim, I was out of line to say that. I'm sorry for lying. But you're accusing me of something I didn't do."

He reached out to me again, but I stepped back. His left brow was quivering, a sign he might cry. "Just remember Cara," he said.

"What are you worried about? That she'll hear you were out on the town with another woman?"

I turned and walked ahead of him toward the house. Cara met us at the door. "Hey, where were you guys?" she asked.

I couldn't pretend everything was fine. "Better not come close," I said. "I think I've got the flu."

"Yeah," she said. "Your eyes look all puffy. Why'd you go out with slippers in the snow?"

"It's one of Bubbie's cures," I said, and escaped to my bedroom. I started flinging Rory's clothes out of the closet. The tangled mess looked to me like my marriage. I spotted the Ralph Lauren polo pony shirt that Rory had probably bought to impress Phyllis. I cut off its arms, and then I cut off the pony and threw the whole mess in the garbage. I felt a burning sob rising in my throat.

There was a knock at the door. "Mom, you all right in there?"

"Fine. I just need some sleep."

"Why is Daddy making up the couch in the basement?"

"I don't want him to catch whatever I have."

"Oh," she said.

I got in bed, exhausted, and cried myself to sleep.

I stayed in bed the whole next day. I didn't work. I didn't cook. I just lay there, seeing Phyllis in Rory's arms, whirling on the rotating dance floor. Now I could see her face, her eyes big, her tongue licking her lips. She looked at Rory as if he were a box of Godiva chocolates. I thought of how manipulated I'd been by Phyllis and Rory. Suddenly, I was sure it was Phyllis who had told four of her friends to book readings with me and cancel within twenty-three hours. She'd wanted to unsettle me so I'd sign with her.

When Cara came home from school, she brought me up Campbell's chicken noodle soup on a tray with a stack of saltines. It was something she would have done as a child. I choked back my tears. "Oh, honey, thank you," I said.

She touched my forehead. "You don't have a fever."

"It must be all your TLC. I'll probably be up and around tomorrow."

But the next day, I cancelled all my readings and stayed in bed again. I had to keep rubbing my eyes to get rid of images of Rory naked in a bed on top of Phyllis Kanner, his butt going up and down.

How could I know whether these images were true or whether they emerged from my fears? Once, when Cara was at summer camp, I got a vision of her tumbling from a height. I phoned the camp to see if anything had happened. It turned out she was in gymnastics, curling her body over the high parallel bar when the director, who fancied himself a comedian, announced from his office over the loudspeaker, "Cara Kaminsky, your mother is worried about you." She was so embarrassed, she nearly fell. She wouldn't answer my letters for an entire week. But no matter what I told myself, the terrible images of Rory and Phyllis kept flashing. I began to suspect that he'd known Phyllis for years, that he was the one who suggested that she call me in the first place.

One day slipped into another. When Rory got home, he would come to the bedroom door, and call in, "Mim?" and I'd answer, "Let me be." I'd hear him telling Cara, "Your mother just needs lots of rest now."

After four days of bedrest where I hardly got up except to use the toilet, I heard Cara say to Rory in the hallway, "How come you didn't bring any medicine home for Mom?"

"It's viral," he said. "It has to run its course."

"So is most stuff," she said. "But you always bring home cough drops or VapoRub or something. Dad, what's going on? You and Mom have been acting weird lately."

"Except for Mom's little bug, everything is fine," Rory said too loudly. Then, as if to drive home his point, he whistled as he went downstairs. I wondered how he could have enough energy to fake happiness.

Seven days later, I got up at 2:00 A.M. and went downstairs to make myself a cup of Yoga calming tea. Outside, the wind made the limbs of the elm groan as they swayed. I looked out through the small panes of the French doors leading to the tiny porch. I saw a figure. I stayed very still. I thought it was a spirit, but then I recognized the striped pajamas, the thick messy hair. Rory was out there in the cold, leaning against the brick wall, his hands rubbing at his face.

I opened the French doors. I could hear little loaves of snow escaping the metal snow-catchers and falling from the roof. "It's not going to help anything for you to get sick," I said.

"I should have been the one sending you flowers instead of that Vince," he said, reaching for me.

"Don't!" I said.

"Mim," he said, his arms still out to me.

I thought of his hands on Phyllis's fleshy back. "I can't bear for you to touch me," I said.

"What are you going to do?" he asked, slowly dropping his arms to his sides.

"I don't know," I said, and it was true. "I can't even think about the future now." As soon as I said that, I felt as if I'd turned on a light in a dark corridor in my mind and found thoughts that had been hiding there for a long time. I suddenly knew that I didn't want to be asked a single question about the future—by anyone. I was tired of having to wait until the client gasped with astonishment or rebuked me. I was tired of having clients demand that I tell them what their mothers' nicknames were when I had already told them what she'd said to them when they were five and what she was wearing at her funeral. And all for nothing. Where was my Rainbow Room?

"I'm through, Rory. I don't want to work as a psychic any-more."

He was silent for a moment. "We can still be together, can't we?" he asked quietly.

I wanted to say no. Until I knew for sure he hadn't slept with Phyllis, until I could trust him again, I wanted to pack up and leave. I breathed in deeply. "I don't really know yet," I said, and turned away.

The next morning, while I was still in bed, Phyllis called. "Hi," she said brightly. "I've been calling your office like crazy. I thought you might have gone away."

I thought of the time I walked in and Rory was whispering on the phone before he hung up. He'd been talking to Phyllis, not Fred! He must not have spoken to her since our fight or Phyllis wouldn't be phoning me now. "No," I said, "I've been right here in *my* home, looking into my crystal ball."

"Well, I'm so glad you're there." I could feel sparks of lust jumping off her skin. It probably had been too long for her since she'd been in Rory's arms. "I've got some strong leads for you," she said.

I couldn't believe the gall of this woman. "I had a lead of my own," I said. "I saw you trying to seduce my husband in the Rainbow Room in your backless blue number with the sequined edging."

"What are you talking about?"

"Phyllis," I said, "you can't hide from Miriam the Psychic." I sensed her squirming. I didn't know whether it was from the realization that she'd lost me as a client or because she was losing her link to Rory.

"I want nothing further to do with you," I said. "I'm tearing up our contract, and if I hear from any lawyers, your husband will hear from me."

There was a long pause. "Okay," she sputtered, "but you better send back my uncle Jake's arm."

"The arm is in the mail," I lied, and hung up. I stood up and took Phyllis's contract from my files. Then I got Uncle Jake's arm out of my closet. I wanted to get rid of the arm just as much as the contract. I wanted Phyllis out of my life forever. I tore up the contract and stuck it in the florist box that the arm had come in, retaped the top, and rewrapped it all in brown paper.

A half hour later, I was at the post office, handing Uncle Jake's arm to the clerk. I thought about how Phyllis had touched that box, and I flicked my hands in the air to clear away any of her energy. I walked briskly away from the post office. On the corner of Bond Street, on the curb that was slanted to make it wheelchair accessible, I fell. All this anger was as dangerous to me as Bubbie had warned. I forced myself to walk slowly up Grace Avenue, stopping to look at the pocketbooks and costume jewelry in the window of Moon River Beauty Salon.

At the Garden Shopping Center, kids were bursting out of Tiger Shulmann's in their karate gear. Women poured out of the North Shore Fitness Center next door wearing beige Lycra body suits.

I put a quarter into a slot to release one of the chained-up Waldbaum's shopping carts and headed into the supermarket. Inside, I passed the pyramids of fruits, the bakery, and deli counters, the wheels of Gouda. At the fish counter, I suddenly heard, "Mirror, mirror, on the wall." It was my father's voice! But he wasn't talking about Snow White. He was trying to get a message to me. "Mirror, mirror, on the wall," he repeated. *The pharmacy,* I thought. My father wanted me to go there.

I abandoned my shopping cart, rushed back to my car, drove up the Horace Harding service road, and turned onto Springfield Boulevard. I parked up the block from the pharmacy, put on dark glasses, and slouched down in my seat like an undercover detective. My stomach was queasy with fear. I had no idea why my father had told me to come here. I was scared of what I might see.

Mirror's window was plastered with specials. Rory was practically giving away Mylanta and Preparation H. I saw old Mrs. Felcher leave the store, holding the arm of her seventy-year-old son, Ernest, who still called her Mommy. In front of the all-night Egyptian luncheonette next to Mirror, the Egyptian men hugged each other. Rory had told me that when he got to Mirror in the wee hours of the morning, the men stood around, openly smoking hashish from a water pipe. This was Rory's world, where everyone knew him. I sat there for a long time. It was winter, but the sun was beating down, so I opened the window. Now there was a draft on my neck. I closed the window again and soon got overheated. There was nothing unusual to be seen. It was almost noon, and I was wasting my day. I turned on the ignition and put the car in gear.

Then Fred appeared, hauling two Hefty trash bags to the curb. The garbage didn't go out until the end of the day. Fred looked up and down the block a few times. Within moments, a Jeep headed down Springfield and stopped in front of Mirror. Fred loaded the garbage bags into the backseat, and the Jeep drove off. I was shocked. I turned off my motor and sat there for a while, trying to figure out what was going on.

Fred went back into Mirror, and right where he'd been standing, my father appeared. He nodded over and over as if he were trying to tell me *Yes, this is what I meant.*

"What does it mean?" I asked out loud, but the sky began to fill my father's face, his chest, and then he disappeared.

Should I call the police? Who was in the Jeep? I hadn't seen the driver, and now I kicked myself for not getting the license plate.

I went home and tried to work, but I couldn't get the vision of Fred out of my mind. When Rory arrived home at eleven, I was ready to burst. He was in the hallway, bending to take off his shoes, when I said, "Rory, I need to talk to you."

He straightened up and looked at me hopefully, then took a step toward me.

I stayed where I was. "It's about Fred," I said.

He stopped abruptly.

"I saw him load a garbage bag into the back of a Jeep at eleven fifty-five this morning."

Rory shrugged. "Maybe it was his junk. Fred stores a lot of his things in my basement. I've got his comic book collection, his bowling ball, and who knows what else? The guy thinks of Mirror as his second home."

"Free storage," I mumbled. "Like he needs that."

Rory wrinkled his brows. "How did you see Fred load garbage into a Jeep? *Psychically?*"

"No, I was there, sitting in my car."

"What were you doing in your car in front of my store at that time of day?"

"I was waiting to see if Phyllis Kanner was coming to pick you up for lunch at the Twenty-one Club," I snapped.

"Will you stop!" he said. "I danced with the woman once, for business only, and you turn it into adultery and think you have the right to spy on me?"

At that moment, I remembered all his betrayals. I remembered how he had asked me to increase the numbers of readings I did right after we had sex. I remembered how he had acted as if he didn't know Phyllis when she came into the house to get me to sign the contract. And I remembered my vision of Phyllis dancing in his arms. "I hate you!" I blurted.

"Shhh," he said, looking up.

Cara was in the middle of the staircase, holding on to the banister, her mouth open.

"Cara," I said, starting after her as she ran up the stairs.

Rory grabbed my arm. "Before we make things worse, let's talk out what we'll say to her," he suggested.

I pulled away from him and hurried upstairs. I stood at Cara's door, murmuring, "Don't be upset."

The door opened. Cara fixed me with a look of pure hatred. "All those days I was so worried about you being sick and you weren't. You and Daddy were just having a fight. You're a fake. A fake psychic and a fake mom. Just leave me alone." She slammed the door.

I felt as if my chest had caved in; that I was suffocating. I stayed by her door, my hand on the knob, my pulse in my finger-tips. I tried to think of things I could do to make her feel better, but it was impossible.

Downstairs, Rory reached for me. "This is spiraling out of control," he said. "Will you please listen to me?"

I backed away from him. "Phyllis listens to you," I said. "Why don't you call her?"

He stormed down to the basement, where I heard him pull out the Castro Convertible. I opened the liquor cabinet, poured myself a Scotch. I squeezed my eyes closed and downed it. My mind was still raging. I poured another and drank that, too. Numbness spread down my face and arms. Too woozy to walk up the steps to the bedroom, I fell asleep on the couch.

# 21

I WOKE UP ASTONISHED to find myself sprawled on the couch, blinking at the bright sun. The Scotch had lulled me into forgetting that I'd run into Barbara and what she'd told me about Rory at the Rainbow Room with a blonde. For a moment I'd forgotten about the matchbook, that I'd confronted Rory and found out it was Phyllis, and that Cara had overheard our terrible fight. But the truth was on my coated tongue, in my stiff muscles, the ache in my temples. I eased myself up from the couch and looked at the clock. It was 10:40 A.M. Cara had left for school two and a half hours ago.

I dragged myself up to my office, cancelled all my readings, and left a new voice mail: "I am taking an extended leave." *Forever,* I thought. I didn't ask anyone to leave a number. I didn't suggest anyone leave a time convenient for me to call back. I just said, "Thank you and have a good day."

I went down to the kitchen, opened a can of chocolate soy drink, and sipped it through the loopy plastic straw that Cara had sent away for years ago with a Bosco label. "'The darlingest girl,'" I used to sing to her, "'I ever saw, Is sipping Bosco through a straw.'" Tears came to my eyes. I'd been so enraged with Rory that I'd shut myself off from Cara. Whether your mother was alive or dead, if you didn't think she was on your side, you always felt like a loose wire in the Universe's circuitry.

And now, as the last slurp of my soy drink looped through the straw, I felt queasy. "For a hangover," Bubbie had told a customer, "nothing like a bath in Epsom salts." Well, I had something that I was sure Bubbie would have liked even better. Dead Sea salts from Israel. I went up the front staircase to the master bathroom, turned the bath tap on HI WARM, and poured a handful of the salts into the tub. I willed the sea salts to pull some of the alcohol and the anguish from my pores. *Maybe,* I thought, *Rory's having a midlife crisis.* One of my clients had been married to a man who was thrifty to a fault. Her husband turned forty and lost all their money in a scheme to get buried treasure from an old sunken ship.

The bathwater rose to my shoulders. I leaned over and turned off the faucet. I thought of all my clients who were desperate to marry. *Someone should tell them the truth,* I thought, as I rubbed my washcloth briskly over my neck. Someone should tell them that you say, "I do," and twenty years later, you find yourself thinking, *I do not!*

I sighed. The Dead Sea was beginning to perform its miracle. I felt soothed, lulled. The only thing that still nagged at me was that after Rory's and my giant blowup, I hadn't been awake to see Cara off to school.

The phone rang. Nothing could have dragged me out of that tub except the thought that it might be Cara. I got out, wrapped a towel around me, and hurried to the phone.

"Hi, Miriam. Nancy Curson here. Listen, I'm calling to tell you that Cara didn't report to school today. Is she home sick?"

"No, I'm sure she left for school," I said, even though I had been sound asleep. I looked around. Her backpack was gone from its usual perch. Her favorite jacket wasn't on the hook by the door. "She's at school," I said.

"Not according to the attendance sheet," Nancy said.

"It must be a mistake," I told her.

"I'm not mistaken. Cara's not here. We've made a new policy. If any student has two or more cut slips on file, we call the parents for any absence."

My head began to throb again. "Thank you very much," I said, and hung up.

I checked Cara's room, but it was empty, her bedsheets pulled haphazardly over her pillow. I felt anger creeping up my neck. This time, she'd really gone too far.

I took three deep breaths and closed my eyes. I couldn't even get a glimpse of Cara's face. I pictured Courtney and Darcy. My psychic vision slowly expanded. The details filled in. They were in ceramics making pinch pots. "My nails!" Courtney complained. Then I tried to locate Lance. Like a camera, my mind panned the school grounds, the hallways, the bathrooms, every nook and cranny. I didn't see Lance, but in my gut I had a strong feeling that he and Cara were together somewhere. Sometimes psychic information came like an instinct, not a vision. You had to trust it. I felt it even stronger. Whether I could see it or not, they were probably hanging out at Lance's house right under the nose of his drunken mother. Something tightened inside me. I tried to see more, but my vision was cloudy. I told myself to concentrate, but only saw trees. Well, there were other ways to get information.

I phoned the attendance office. "Nancy," I said, "I need a favor desperately. I have to know if Lance Stark is in school today."

"I'm so sorry, Miriam, but I'm not at liberty to tell you. But between you and me, you wouldn't believe how many girls' mothers call to ask the same question."

Nancy was a single woman. She couldn't risk losing her job, but I barreled on. "Nancy, please, couldn't you bend the rules once and tell me something?"

There was silence. "I saw him in the stairwell before first period," she finally whispered.

I was no different from any of the other mothers calling to find out about their daughters. If Cara wasn't with Lance after all, my sense of knowing was off. I began to feel unmoored. I paced the living room, looping around the dining room table, back to the living room, and then up and down the steps. My feet began to hurt but instead of stopping, I changed into sneakers and kept going. After an hour, my skin was damp with sweat and felt like the Dead Sea salts I'd bathed in. I took a shower, hot and pounding like my anger at Rory, and now at Cara, too. As I got dressed, I began inventing the lecture I'd give her when she got home.

"What's wrong with you?" I asked out loud. *No, that's what my mother would say.*

I switched to, "How could you do this to your family?" *That was too much like my father.*

My inner argument was interrupted when the doorbell rang. When I opened the door, a delivery guy handed me a big bouquet in a glass vase. Vince again, I thought. He had to stop sending me flowers! "Take them back," I told the guy, but he just set the vase down on the front steps and drove off. I left them there and glanced at my watch. Seventh period. I drove over to the school to see if Cara had thought better of cutting all day and showed up late. Most of the snow had melted, leaving dirty white ribbons along the gutters. I opened the window to let in the springlike air.

In the car, outside the high school, I debated what to do. I tried to beam into Cara, but now I couldn't get anything. After fifteen minutes, I decided to walk inside. The black decals of the flying birds on the windows made me feel as if I were in an aviary. I heard loud music. I opened the door to the auditorium. Cara's friend, Darcy, was bogeying on stage, half-naked in a denim halter top and short shorts. Her blond hair whipped around as she jerked her head. Two girls with polka-dot bikinis shimmied on either side of her. A boy in an open shirt and baggy hip-hop pants narrated into a microphone: "Darcy and the Sunshines show off their spring break Club Med look."

Two teachers stood against the wall, watching. I went over to one and asked, "What is this?"

"Rehearsal for the annual fashion show," he shouted over the booming music.

I looked around and didn't see Cara. I caught Darcy's eyes, and she quickly looked away. She'd been ignoring Cara, too, after she'd seen me on TV. My glare was insistent though, and her eyes drew back to me. "Where's Cara?" I mouthed. She raised her shoulders a few times to show me she didn't know, working it into her routine to not miss a beat. Well, if Cara's girlfriends didn't know, maybe Lance did. I hated the thought of having to go find that boy and ask him, but maybe he'd know. I mouthed "Lance?" to Darcy and she shook her head.

"He left," Darcy mouthed back.

I went straight to Cara's guidance counselor. Dr. Zannikos's secretary was on the phone. I walked right past her into his office. His beard made him look like a rabbi.

"I've been looking for Cara," I said. "She's not in school, and she's been so upset lately."

Dr. Zannikos took off his glasses, wiped the lenses with a tissue, and looked at me. "She must still be upset over getting rejected from Cornell early admission."

I felt my jaw drop. "I didn't know she applied for early admission," I said.

"Of course you did. You signed the form back in November. I never would have put it through otherwise."

"I never even read the application," I admitted. "She said you just wanted to keep it on file."

He shook his head.

"She must have been so devastated," I said.

"Just tell her to keep plugging," he told me. "Cara's a smart cookie. She'll get in somewhere good, you'll see. Go home. She's probably there waiting for you. And tell her not to miss any more school."

I drove home. "Cara?" I called as I walked in the door. There was no answer. Upstairs, her room was still empty.

At 7:30 P.M., Cara still wasn't home, and my worry was turning to anger. I phoned Courtney. "Do you have any idea where Cara is?"

"Cara?" I could hear her taking a long drag of her cigarette, trying to decide what to say.

"Yes, your friend from school who you've gone to sleep-away camp with for six summers. Remember her?"

Courtney was momentarily silenced by my sarcasm. "She might be at Plaza Billiards," she said slowly.

"A pool hall?"

Courtney laughed. "That's what my dad calls it, too. He calls Cara a 'pool shark.'"

I was stunned a moment. "I didn't know Cara played pool," I said.

"I have a pool table in my rec room," Courtney said.

"Oh?" I'd never been in Courtney's rec room. Countless times I'd rung her bell to pick up Cara and was made to stand in front of Courtney's huge house with freezing rain dripping down my collar until the maid got Cara.

"Call me right away if Cara phones you," I said.

"Okay."

Outside, Iris Gruber's elderly mother was working her way up her front walk with a cane. As I was getting into the car, my key-chain alarm accidentally went off, and Iris's mother was so surprised, she pitched over onto the lawn. I ran to her, terrified she'd broken bones. As I lifted her from the moist ground, Iris flung open the front door. "You're a menace!" she screamed at me.

"I'm so sorry," I said. I could feel my face heat up. *It was an accident,* I kept telling myself as I drove to town.

At Plaza Billiards, I parked in front of Yogurteria and hurried into the glass atrium. I dashed up the spiral staircase, my hand coasting over the green metal banister, and stepped into the lounge. Since Cara had dyed her hair black, there were at least three girls who resembled her. I went in to look even though I knew none of them was really Cara.

Back in the parking lot, everyone in the shopping center suddenly looked to me like Cara. A woman wearing a denim jacket. A housewife with tight jeans. I followed a girl who had a long ponytail. She turned around, annoyed. "You want something?" she snapped. I blinked hard. All the people went back to their normal selves, and my heart winced. *Where is my daughter?* By now it was dark. It's not so bad, I tried to tell myself on the way home. Cara had been late before. But she had been gone since early in the morning, and she had never cut an entire day of school before.

I drove straight to the sixth precinct nestled behind the Community Drive entrance of Macy's in Manhasset. I entered through the main door into a big room that smelled like rubber cement. A policeman with gray eyes and a brown mustache sat at the front desk. His name was on a little placard. OFFICER FREUND, it said.

"My daughter's been missing since early this morning."

"How old is she?"

"Seventeen."

He looked up at me, shaking his head casually. "Sorry. We don't look for a kid that age unless they're missing twenty-four hours."

*God forbid Cara should be missing for twenty-four hours!* "If a daughter is missing for even fifteen minutes, it's terrifying," I said. "I sense danger." And then, to prod him into action, "I'm a psychic."

He rolled his eyes.

"Police use psychics to solve cases," I informed him.

"Not in this precinct." He slid me a card stamped with the precinct phone number.

I shook as I held it in my hands. *I should move,* I thought. *Do something.*

As I left, I saw Officer Freund catch another cop's eye and twirl his finger at his temple.

Back in the car, I closed my eyes and took some deep breaths. "Bubbie?" I called out. I waited. Nothing happened. I opened one eye to see if she was around me. She wasn't.

When I got back to the house, Cara still wasn't home. I finally called Rory at the pharmacy. All this time and only now I was calling him. It seemed like another thing wrong with our marriage, that I hadn't called him first. Maybe Cara had phoned him at Mirror. Of course. I should have phoned him right away.

"I'm so glad to hear from you," he said as soon as he heard my voice. He thought I couldn't live without him.

"Cara never showed up for school, and she still isn't home," I said. "I have no idea where she is."

"Maybe she's with Lance," he said.

"Nancy Curson from the attendance office told me Lance was in school today."

"Mim, I'm sure Cara's all right," Rory said, his voice now firm and hurried. "I'll be home at nine thirty. You tell her to wait up for me so I can give her a real piece of my mind for worrying us."

I tried to concentrate on Rory's lecture. The idea that Cara would be home to hear it was comforting.

On my business line, there were ten messages, none from Cara.

Rory didn't walk in until 10:00 P.M. He was carrying the flowers from Vince that I'd left on the doorstep, and went straight to the kitchen, poured the water from the vase down the sink, then threw the flowers in the garbage. "Where is she?" he snapped.

"I don't know," I said.

He blinked.

"I've been all over town!" I said. "Lance was in school today, and she wasn't. She isn't with Darcy and Courtney. I found out Cara didn't get accepted early decision to Cornell. Who knows what else she didn't tell us?"

Rory pushed his hand through his hair. He was looking at me

like it was my fault, like I should be able to pull her out of the air like a rabbit from a hat and I knew suddenly why I hadn't called Rory right away. "I knew something like this would happen," he said. "That boy Lance. Your friend Vince!"

I stopped. "Vince?" I stepped back, looking at Rory as if aliens had taken over his body. "Are you out of your mind? What has Vince got to do with anything?"

Rory got crazier and crazier. "How do we know that *your* Vince didn't kidnap Cara to lure you to him?"

"How do we know Phyllis Kanner didn't?" I shot back at him. "Maybe she'll call to say that she'll give back Cara in exchange for you."

"What?" he asked astonished. "What?"

"It's no less crazy than what you're saying," I said.

He put both hands up. "Enough of this. Did you call the police?"

I told him about the police requirement of twenty-four hours.

"We don't know how long Cara's actually been missing," Rory said. "I'll tell them whatever I have to to get their help."

"They'll probably be a lot more obliging to a pharmacist than a psychic," I said, with an edge in my voice.

"Don't start," he said. Rory called the precinct. After a few minutes, he said, "A cop is coming right over."


An hour later, Officer Freund was sitting on one of our love seats, a clipboard in his hands. When he looked at me, he cocked his head. "Hey, you said your daughter was only missing since this morning."

"We did further checking," Rory said. "We don't think she slept at home," he lied. Rory started explaining the weird hours he worked, the odd ones I did. He waved his hands around, talking fast about comings and goings. He was like one of the nut-under-the-shell hucksters. Then he gave Officer Freund Cara's picture.

"Pretty girl," Officer Freund said. "She on drugs?"

"No," Rory and I both said at once.

"Could she be pregnant?" he asked.

*Oh, my God,* I thought. Cara had no pills, no diaphragm. Why hadn't I taken her to the Margaret Sanger Clinic?

"Of course she's not pregnant," Rory said loudly.

"Some trouble between you two at home?" Officer Freund asked.

We looked at each other. "None," I said.

Then Officer Freund said to stay put and wait to hear from him.

After he left, Rory said to me, "So you mean things are okay between us now?"

"What could be okay, Rory? Our daughter is missing. I have to put that first. I can't think about *us* now."

"I'm sure they'll find Cara," he said, and sat at the edge of his reading chair, staring at the phone.

I leaned over, got a pad and pen out of the end table drawer, and turned off the lamp. "What are you doing?" Rory asked.

Holding the pen loosely, I began to scribble. "Cara, where are you?" I cried.

"Who are you talking to?" Rory asked.

I didn't answer. I remembered Cara sitting in her high chair, tossing peas overboard one by one. "Aw gone," she had said.

"Where's Cara?" I repeated. The pen was writing something almost legible. I struggled to make out the words. I was hoping for an address or a street name, anything that would give me a clue to where she was. "Aw gone," it said. "Aw gone."

I spent most of the night sitting on the love seat. My spine felt like iron. Rory, opposite me on the matching love seat, slept with one eye half-opened like my father dreaming of another pogrom. I began to cry silently. Rory used to be so attuned to me it was almost psychic, but now he didn't even stir.

Then it was dawn. Rory opened both eyes. He looked at his

watch. "I'm going to call someone in to cover me at Mirror. I've got to go down there and let my replacement in. I won't stay a minute longer than I have to."

I was glad he was going. I needed to be alone to try to make contact with Cara. "I'll call if I hear," I told him.

After he left, I went up to Cara's room and lay down on her bed, fitting my body into the imprints hers had made. Desperately, I sniffed the chamomile and balsam scent of her head on the pillow. I tried to still myself so I could feel her vibrations, but all I felt was my own coursing blood. I had better start snooping. I told myself that this was what any regular mother would do in this situation. I opened her closet. It was its usual jumble. I opened her top drawers and found her spaghetti of bras and panties. The bottom drawer just had old camp letters from friends, button pins with pictures of Darcy and Courtney on them, and the silver ring with the glass eye she'd bought on her first jaunt to Greenwich Village. I couldn't figure out how much, if anything, she had taken with her. I knew that she kept her diary in the storage space of her headboard. I took the lamp off the top, and lifted the lid. Beneath her extra bedding was her diary. My hand trembled as I reached down for it. This was the worst violation of all. This was my mother steaming open my mail, doing pencil rubbings on my desk blotter, and reading the impressed words with a mirror. I put the diary back and walked out, shutting the door tightly behind me.

The minute I did, I was rewarded with a flash. I saw Cara's face next to Lance's as if they were photos in a locket. No matter what Nancy had said, now I knew for certain that Cara was with him.

The phone rang, and I rushed to get it. "Hi, Miriam. It's Nancy again." She sighed. "I'm sorry to say that I'm calling because Cara is absent today, too, and I have more bad news."

I was tight with fear.

"Lance was here for attendance yesterday," Nancy went on,

"but he never showed for last period homeroom. He must have ducked out. And he's absent today."

For a moment, I was relieved that she wasn't all alone, and then my heart started beating harder. *Oh, God, Lance,* I thought. I should have trusted myself. Suddenly I remembered Lance's note: "Love you to death." I shuddered.

"If there's anything I can do," Nancy said, "anything . . ." Her voice lowered. "Do you want Lance's home number and his father's business number?"

"Yes," I said. As soon as I got off the phone, I called Pepper Stark. Her voice sounded sleepy.

"Pardon me," I said, "but is my daughter, Cara, there by any chance?"

"Who?"

"Cara, my daughter." I couldn't bring myself to say "Lance's girlfriend."

"No. And my son Lance isn't either. I don't keep track of his girlfriends," Pepper said. She slurred, and I could tell she was drunk. "His girlfriends change from day to day. I don't even know where he is. He's eighteen. If he's gone, I don't have to worry about him, do I?"

"Yes, you do. He's with my daughter, and we have to find them."

"I don't even know you," she said. "I don't have to do anything." She hung up.

I called Lance's father. "Stark Enterprises," the receptionist said. "We guarantee you can be as thin as the *you* of your dreams."

"May I please speak to Mr. Stark?" I asked.

"He's in a conference now. Whom may I say is calling?"

"Miriam Kaminsky."

"Are you calling to lose those extra pounds that have turned your thighs and waistline into shlog?"

"No, I'm calling about Lance."

"Uh-oh," she said. "I'll put you right through."

Muzak played during the holding time.

"What did that stinker do this time?" Mr. Stark blurted out.

I was taken aback. "I think he ran off with my daughter."

"Well, I'm sure he didn't put a gun to her head."

"No, I'm sure he didn't," I said, trying to keep the rage out of my voice.

"Sorry," he said. "I'm angry at my boy. I shouldn't be taking it out on you."

"Did you give Lance a credit card that he might have used at a gas station or maybe"—I could hardly get the words out of my mouth—"a motel?"

"Sure, but he takes it to the ATM and gets out cash so I won't know what he's up to. Don't worry. I'll stop the credit card right now. Then you'll see how fast they'll come home."

"Here's my home number," I said, and I gave it to him. "Please will you call me if you hear anything? My husband and I are beside ourselves. Cara's been missing for more than twenty-four hours."

"Will do," he said.

"Thank you," I said.

As soon as I hung up, the phone rang. Hoping it was Cara, I picked it up so quickly that I knocked my chin with the receiver.

"Well, what did you hear?" a woman asked.

"Who is this?"

"Barbara."

It was Darcy's mother. Of course she would already know. "Thanks for your interest," I said. "We haven't heard anything yet. I'll let you know if I have any information. In the meantime, I have to keep the line clear."

She rambled on. "Does Lance's father still peddle that liquid diet? He isn't even a doctor. He used to sell copper pipes. He has his hand in everything."

"Excuse me, Barbara, but I have to get off the phone."

"They say he drove Pepper to drink. They say he had women all along. Thin ones. He must have double-screwed them—charged them a bundle for his diet plan and slept with them, too."

"Thanks for your help, Barbara, but I have to leave my line clear," I repeated.

"I'll call back later," she said.

The phone rang again. Eagerly, I picked it up. "Cara?" I said with my fingers crossed.

"No, this is Joyce."

"Joyce?"

"Courtney's mother. I want to see how you're faring."

"How I'm faring?" I repeated. She had gone on so many cruises that nautical language had begun to permeate her vocabulary. "I'm faring fine," I said.

"I'd throw myself overboard if Courtney ever pulled a stunt like this."

I swallowed my anger. I needed everyone's cooperation. "I'll phone you if I hear anything," I said. "In the meanwhile, please tell everyone that I have to keep the line clear. Tell them to call only if they have any information."

"Of course," she said. "I'll call you later to see if anything surfaced."

"Fine," I said, and I hung up. It was as if they all had wax in their ears.

The phone rang. "Everything comes in threes," my father used to say, but I was so nervous that I couldn't remember whether three in a row was good or bad luck. I picked up the phone.

"Doll, can you make time for me?" I heard.

It was Vince Guardelli, calling on my home line. I was worried he was nearby, waiting in a limo, but then I heard the clatter of silverware and crystal in the background. "I'm sorry. It's out of the question."

"What's the matter? You don't sing to Vince no more? 'Strangers in the night,'" he sang in his gravelly voice. "'Two lonely people.'"

I put my head in my hand.

"Are you still sore at me for trying to hold your hand?" he asked. "Forget about it. You're Saint Mary-iam to me now," he said. "Because of you I called my ex. That's why I sent you the flowers. We got together. Had some laughs. I felt like I was twenty-two. We have history together. When I say Pop she sees my father right down to the thumb he flattened. When I say 'Mulberry Street,' she sees my grandmother sitting on the windowsill, yelling down. 'Getta me a pack a Luckies.' I don't have to go explaining myself."

I was glad I'd helped him open his heart chakra, but how could I care about his love life now? "I can't do a reading for you. I can't concentrate."

"What could be more interesting than me?" he asked.

"My daughter ran away with a boy." As soon as it was out of my mouth, I was sorry. Bubbie had warned me never to confide in clients. Even though I felt like killing Lance myself, I was scared Vince would actually rub him out. There was an odd, staticky charge on the line. *Now I've done it*, I thought. *It's curtains.*

"I'd call the cops," he said.

*"You?"* I asked.

Vince bristled. "Hey, what do you take me for? You hear I-talian, streetwise, big bucks, you think mob, right? Don Harkness, the police chief of Nassau County, is a buddy of mine. I can call him for you, get things rolling. I consider you a personal friend. I'd do anything for you."

I had tears in my eyes. "Thanks," I told him.

"Not to worry," he said. "Vince will take care of everything."

"I really appreciate it, but I have to get off the phone now," I said, and hung up.

I paced the house, trying to recall anything Cara had said to me in the past few days. "I hate you!" was all I remembered. I paced some more. When I had first glimpsed Lance zooming past

Darcy's house on his motorcycle, I had gotten an image of Cara fading, as if being erased. Now the meaning was revealed to me—that she would disappear with that boy.

I heard a car in the driveway. I rushed downstairs. Rory sprang out of his car. "Did Cara call?"

"No."

His face fell. "Maybe no news is good news," he said shakily.

I went to my office to check my business line again to see if Cara had, for some reason, left a message there. "H-hel-lo, this is Arlene," I heard. It was Orthodox Arlene. "I figured out if you don't tell me anything about the dead or the future," she said, "I can have a reading without offending my rabbi." She left her number. I erased it. I listened to the next one. "This is Kim. You can't take an extended leave. I chanted 'power, power, power' like you told me to. Why won't you call me back?"

I checked the rest of my messages. They were all from Kim.

Rory appeared in the doorway. "I'm going over to the high school," he said. "I'll stop every kid and ask them what they know."

"Call me if you hear anything at all," I said. "Even a rumor."

After he left, I put my hands up in the air as if I were an antenna and said, "Cara Kaminsky, phone home."

Twenty minutes passed. The phone didn't ring. I sat down on the hallway steps, my back against the wall. "Om, om," I chanted frantically. At 4:00 P.M., just the time Cara would have come home if she had taken the school bus, the doorbell rang. I rushed to open it. Nancy Curson stood there. I felt myself brightening with hope. "You know something," I said, excited.

"Yes, that Munchkins help in a crisis."

Then I noticed she was carrying a bag from Dunkin' Donuts and two large cups of coffee inset in a paper tray. From her plumpness, I could see she'd used the doughnut cure for many crises.

"Thanks," I said, trying hard to cover my disappointment. Her foot was already in the door. "Would you like to stop in?"

"Yes."

I led her to the kitchen. We sat down at the kitchen table. *Maybe it's better that she's here,* I thought. A motherly, soothing presence.

Rory walked in, brow twitching from nerves. "Nothing," he said. "None of the kids know anything." He shuddered, and then he noticed Nancy.

I introduced them. "Nancy Curson brought us some doughnuts," I said. She gave him the coffee that was probably meant for her. Politely, Rory put a Munchkin in his mouth.

"When my husband, Bill, ran off with the baby-sitter," Nancy said, "Munchkins were all I ate for a week. The baby-sitter was Filipina. Only nineteen. I caught them doing it right in my Susan's bed."

As she told the story, my mind replaced the baby-sitter-and-Bill with Phyllis-and-Rory in Cara's bed. My throat knotted. My stomach felt queasy. *Some soothing presence!* Rory mumbled his apologies and got up from the table, his chair scraping loudly.

"Oh, I don't know what made me talk about that," Nancy said. "I guess being close to a tragedy reminds you of your own."

I rose from the table, too. "You'll have to excuse us," I said, my voice tight.

Nancy finally got up. "I'll call you later," she said as I ushered her out.

As soon as I got rid of her, I lit a stick of jasmine incense. My mother had adored Cara. "My Cara," she'd called her. If my mother were still alive, Cara would never have run away. My mother wouldn't let anything happen to Cara. My mother would be the one to help. I remembered her lying on the puckered blue satin lining of her coffin. Her makeup was on perfectly, and the human hair wig she'd insisted I buy her for the occasion, fanned out darkly. *Sleeping beauty,* I'd thought, but when I leaned close, beneath her makeup, I saw her veins like frozen rivers. Her spirit had left her, but it was out there somewhere.

"Mom?" I called. "It isn't for me that I'm asking. It's for *your* Cara."

Nothing happened. I went to the mirror on the wall. I patted my hair the way my mother used to hers to check that every strand was in place. I reached for my pocketbook, took out a tube of lipstick, and, as I applied it, stretched my lips over my teeth as she had. I extended my hands to check my fingernails. It helped to mimic a spirit, do something that was part of a person's daily ritual when she was alive. "Mom?" I called out again. There was no answer. I felt as if I were being crushed by her silence, but I closed my eyes and tried to picture my brain waves going out farther into the Universe than they ever had before. My head hurt. Sweat broke out on my upper lip. Still, I kept at it. I felt faint. I opened my eyes, sat down, and leaned forward, letting my head hang down past my knees. I sat up and closed my eyes again. All I saw were afterimages—the darkened candle flame, the stripes of sunlight now gray through the shutters. If I kept trying to contact my mother, I knew I wouldn't have energy for anything else.

My father would surely help. Just the thought of him brought my energy back. "Dad," I called. I listened hard. The branches of the elm tree groaned. I rushed to the closet to put on the jacket he used to wear to work. That would bring him closer to me. "Please, Daddy." I heard a hissing sound. I thought my father was whispering to me. I opened my eyes. I saw my own tears sputtering on the hot wax. "Daddy, you warned me that Alicia Gordon's nose was going to get broken in a basketball game, and now your own granddaughter might be in mortal danger and you have nothing to say to me?" There was still silence. "What is this— some kind of a cosmic boycott?"

"Bubbie," I called, "please forgive me for going for the gelt and appearing on that TV show. Forgive me for saying that sometimes I have to put the living first. I'll never flush the old ways down the toilet again. Just help me find Cara, and all I'll think about is the dead." There was no answer. I breathed deeply to rid myself of any blindfold or ear corks. I waited. "Bubbie, I'm out on a ledge again. I need you." My old house rumbled softly as it settled. Baron barked. *Patience,* I told myself, and waited some more, but there was nothing, nothing, and nothing.

I looked at my watch. Cara had been missing at least thirty-five hours, maybe as much as forty if she'd slipped out during the night. Finally, after several hours, Rory and I went to bed. There was nothing else we could do.

•   •   •

As soon as I awoke, I began to chant. I saw my daughter's green eyes. Then the rest of her began to fill in. Her hair was whipping backwards. Vibrations were running all through me.

Rory came downstairs unshaved. "Will you please stop that chanting for just a minute? I need to know about the real world. I need to find out if anyone phoned."

I wasn't about to stop chanting. This was part of my "real world," maybe the most important part. "No-o-o," I chanted. He plopped himself down on the couch, his head in his hands. His breathing sounded choked, as if he were holding back tears. I wasn't going to give into despair again. I had to keep trying. "Om, om." I imagined a map with thick red lines like the driving directions drawn on maps from AAA.

Then it came to me. Cara was on the back of Lance's motorcycle, speeding north, the tailpipe hurling smoke. She was somewhere upstate. I had to concentrate. I felt drawn to her room again. I left Rory and climbed the stairs. I sat in her rocking chair, the one I had nursed her in. I sang her favorite nursery song: "Fiddle dee dee, fiddle dee dee, the fly has married the bumblebee." I began to rock. My third eye opened. I saw Lance drive off the highway. I saw him drive through a town. He was going fast. I couldn't see any signs. Then I saw him drive onto a narrow path.

I ran downstairs. "We have to get in the car," I told Rory. "We have to go to the Throgs Neck Bridge. We have to look for Cara."

"But Officer Freund told us to stay put until we hear from him."

"And have we heard from him?"

"Not yet," Rory said. "But we've got to stay right here. You can still try to find her psychically, but we should do just what the police said."

His aura faded when he mentioned me finding Cara psychically and heightened when he spoke about the police. It was obvious that he trusted them more than me.

"You do what you want to," I said. "I'm going."

He followed me to the kitchen. "I'm not letting you drive off somewhere alone. Then I'll be worried about you *and* Cara. I'm coming."

I made a thermos of black coffee and packed up some sandwiches. Rory put our most recent photo of Cara in his wallet and put his cell phone into his jacket pocket.

Just then the doorbell rang. "She's back," Rory said, sprinting on his long legs to the door. When he opened it, Vince stood there in a casual button-down shirt woven with silky threads and white wool slacks. He looked as if he'd just stepped off a cruise ship. He was tanned, too.

"You the husband?" Vince said, looking Rory up and down.

"Yes," Rory said. "Who are you?"

"Vince Guardelli," I said, stepping in front of Rory. "Vince, what are you doing here?" I noticed Rocko in the white limo at the curb.

"I already called Don for you," Vince said. "He's working on it."

"*Who'd* you call?" Rory said with force. "*The Don?*"

Vince looked at him as if he were nuts. "Don Harkness," he said, "the police chief."

Rory was glowering. Did he actually think that I'd had an affair with Vince or that I was considering one?

Vince clapped his hand on Rory's shoulder. "Ordinarily, I'd say, 'You're a lucky guy,' but with what's going down, I'll just say, 'You gotta let me help you.'"

"Vince, that's so nice of you," I said, "but we were just leaving to look for our daughter."

"Do you want me to stay here and man the phones?" Vince asked. "I could take down your cell phone number and call you if anything gives." He ran his hand over the faceplate of our door. "If I pop the dead bolt before I leave, you won't have to give me your keys."

"What?" Rory said.

I knew I could trust Vince in our house. With his diamond pinkie ring and his limo, he wasn't looking to steal from us. In his own way, he was trying to be a gentleman. But Rory's energy was rubbing against me like steel wool. If I let Vince stay in our house, the trip upstate would be unbearable. I didn't want to hurt Vince's feelings. I had to let him play some role. "Thanks, Vince," I said, "but what would make me comfortable is if you went around town and asked people if they've seen or heard anything concerning Cara Kaminsky."

"Huh?" Rory said under his breath.

"It's done," Vince said.

As we got into the car, I pictured Vince walking around Great Neck, his limo cruising the curb. People would think he was an undercover cop, I bet, and he had a kind of bearing you didn't say no to. I pictured him going over to Bloomsbury Plants and poor Mrs. Rogers cowering behind her potted palms. I pictured him saying, "Hey, *paesan*," to Charles Fravola over at Marine Fisheries, and Charles giving him a generous sample of fried clams, free. If I weren't in a terrible emergency, I probably would have laughed. I took deep breaths to clear my mind.

When we came off the Cross Island, the approach to the Throgs Neck Bridge was stopped dead. My heart felt as if it had stopped, too.

"Damn, I should have put on the traffic report," Rory said. He switched on the radio.

"Stay away from the Throgs Neck. A three-car accident and an oil spill in the middle of the span," the announcer said. "Easily a two-hour delay."

"Can we back out of here?" I asked Rory.

"Look behind you," he said.

We were locked in. "How about if we pull over to the shoulder, park, and leave the car? We could walk back to the last exit and rent a car."

"It'll take us longer than waiting here," Rory said, and turned off the ignition. His jaw set. I knew he was thinking that I'd gotten us into an even bigger mess. I knew he was thinking I should have listened to him, and waited at home. Half of me agreed, but despite this setback, the other half was still urging me onward.

I looked out the window. Gulls wheeled and cried. An hour passed. People were getting out of their cars, some of them disappearing into the bushes to relieve themselves. I poured us some coffee from the thermos. We just sat there, letting it warm our hands, each lost in our own thoughts. When it was nearly cold, the traffic began to move. It was already 6:00 P.M., and we were just getting started. On the Throgs Neck Bridge, I closed my eyes and "Om"-ed.

"Don't leave me in the dark," Rory said. "At least tell me what you think you see."

"Cara's on the back of Lance's motorcycle," I said anxiously.

"Is she wearing a helmet?" he asked.

"No."

He stepped harder on the gas. He began to tailgate. I needed him calm at the helm so I could concentrate on finding Cara. "Take it easy," I insisted, but he already had me rattled.

At the end of the bridge, my eyes were darting like a compass needle gone haywire. "Take the Thruway," I said.

"Jesus, a motorcycle on these roads at these speeds!" Rory said.

We drove along the Thruway for over an hour. We passed Yonkers Raceway and the exit for Dobbs Ferry. By 7:30 P.M., we were crossing the Tappan Zee Bridge to the New York State Thruway. Once on the Thruway, in our comparatively small Ford, Rory zipped past the fastest SUVs. I heard a beeping in my head like a radar detector. "We're approaching a speed trap," I warned. "Slow down." He did, and we saw a police car hiding beside an overpass. I could feel my psychic energy focusing. It was as if I'd put glasses on my third eye, and now my vision was clear and powerful.

As we went farther north, we passed New Paltz and Kingston. It seemed to get colder. The water cascading from the rock face had frozen. The bulrushes lining the road were frozen stiff. Nature had gone into shock.

"Call home," Rory said. "Someone may have left a message by now."

"I can't get a signal on my cell phone," I said. "We'll have to use a pay phone."

At 9:30 P.M., we pulled into a Mobil rest stop that looked like a rustic stone lodge. I hurried in. There was an Arby's, Bob's Big Boy, vending machines, a TCBY kiosk. I glanced around the souvenir shop. I saw rocks engraved with CATSKILLS OR BUST. Rory gave me his phone card and went off to the men's room. There was a message. "Don Harkness, chief of police here," it said. "I want you to know that I personally called the Sixth Precinct and spoke to Office Freund and instructed him to put an all-points bulletin out on your daughter." Thank God for Vince. Harkness left his direct line if I had any questions.

I called Lance's mother again. "This is Miriam Kaminsky again," I said. "I'm on the road looking for Cara. Does Lance know anyone upstate? I mean, do you have a summer house there, or did he go to camp in that region?"

"Naw," she slurred. She was even more drunk than yesterday. Then she started to cry. "Where's my wittle boy?" she blubbered.

"I'll call you when we find him," I said.

Rory was heading toward me, chewing his lip. "Anything?" he asked.

"The chief of police called. He put out an all-points bulletin on Cara."

"We should turn back," Rory said. "We should be home like the police said. Then we could be on the phone, calling everyone, including the newspapers. Maybe Cara's friends have heard from her by now."

"There must be a nearby train station where I can drop you off," I said curtly.

He didn't answer. When he got back to the car, he was so angry that he hit his fist against the horn. It honked.

"You have to trust me, not the police," I said quietly.

Rory stiffened his arms and pressed his back against the seat, but he kept heading upstate. At 11:00 P.M., we passed Albany.

Looking out the window, I half agreed that it was nuts to go on. Darkness blotted out the mountains and the rock face edging the road. The bare branches were dark fingers pointing in every direction. Rory kept glancing at me. I felt as if I had to come up with something every minute to justify this chase. I wasn't even sure that I could find her. But I had to. I just had to.

He looked at me again. "Stop!" I said. "I have to concentrate." I closed my eyes again. Everything was pitch dark, but slowly, I could make out Cara and Lance. I could hear tree branches snapping. The motorcycle no longer sounded like a roar. It sounded like a sputter, and then there was silence.

"What are you seeing?" Rory demanded.

I couldn't answer. I had to keep my mind on Cara. I saw her again. Lance was kneeling, trying to fix his bike. He was shivering. Cara was jumping up and down, slapping at her arms. She was wearing jeans and a short jacket.

"I hope you're getting something," Rory said.

"It's freezing," I said. "Cara is shivering." Then I saw her sit down on her duffel bag and rest her head on her bent knees.

"Anything else?" Rory asked.

I shook my head. I didn't want to get him as frightened as I was. He had to drive. He had to hold up.

"Try harder," he said.

*Bubbie?* I silently pleaded. *I need you. Cara needs you.*

There was no response.

*Dad?* I waited. *Mom?* I was still on my own. My eyes were shut, but I felt Rory staring at me, waiting for me to come up with another psychic flash. Even when his eyes were riveted on the road, I felt him focusing on me.

"Do you have any idea where we're going yet?" he asked.

"Just keep going," I said. I saw dim clouds and stripes, the kind of thing anyone would see after closing their eyes on the road. I opened my eyes. "Where is Cara?" I said.

Rory gave me a worried look.

"Pay attention to your driving," I said. "Where is Cara?" I repeated softly. I heard a whooshing sound. Then, instead of getting a vision of Cara, I saw an old lady I vaguely recognized with straight white hair. I realized, with horror, that it was me. My hair had gotten too old to curl. I held a big flashlight in my gnarled hand and limped along. Did it mean that I was going to be looking for Cara for the rest of my life? I was terrified. I took three deep breaths and tried to slow my mind. I didn't see anything. Then I saw a party. HAPPY 70TH BIRTHDAY, MIRIAM, the banner said. The guests were strangers, people I hadn't met yet. I searched the room. I couldn't find Cara. Maybe she was late, I said to myself, but my eyes pressed open in terror.

"Anything yet?" Rory said for what felt like the thousandth time.

"Be patient," I said, and closed my eyes again. "Om, om," I chanted. My skin got tingly. I opened my eyes. A great fog had descended. Gradually, I saw it was made up of pinpoints of snow. As we drove into the wind, the snow slanted at us without sticking to the windshield.

Passing a little cemetery on the left of the highway, I suddenly remembered Mount Hebron, where my parents were buried. Dad had bought us all plots before he died. I closed my eyes again and saw myself walking up the path to my parents' graves. I had stones in my pockets to lay on their graves. I went along the path, looking ahead, then stopped myself. I was scared I'd see a tombstone with Cara's name.

I looked out the window. The cloudbanks were bearing down on the scrubby mountains. We passed trailer parks. A white horse with a sooty coat was tied to a pole. We passed an apple orchard with barren branches looking like barbed wire.

I closed my eyes again. I didn't see anything else.

Then, in my mind, I saw Cara and Lance so tired that they were staggering along, their heads nodding, their eyes closing.

"Are you getting any feelings?" Rory asked me.

"I certainly am." My stomach was spewing bile into my throat. I rocked forward in my seat as if I could somehow make the car go faster. *Cara, tell me where you are,* I silently begged. Give me more to go on. *Cara,* I thought. *Cara.* I concentrated harder on her than I ever had on anything. I tried to make her feel me. I imagined my heart filled with pink light, enveloping her in warmth.

Rory and I rode along in silence. We passed Little Falls. In the stillness, I heard Cara say, "Och!" I jolted. Bubbie's word that I'd told Cara to say if she were in trouble. "Och!" she said louder. Then she thought it inside her head. I got a vision of a heart. *Heart,* I said to myself. I grabbed the map and looked at the index. Nothing under "heart." Maybe it was something that sounded like heart. I went through the *H*s again. Of course: Hartfield, Hartford, Hartland, Hartsdale, Hartsville . . . and then I saw a glowing light around the next name. Hartwick. "Hartwick!" I shouted. "I know where Cara is! Hartwick!"

Rory slammed his palm against the dashboard. "Thank God," he said. "We're right near it."

My hands were shaking so badly that I could hardly hold the map. G-12, G-12. There was Hartwick. "Get off at Route Twenty-eight," I cried. "It's the next exit. Hurry."

We sped along the highway. I leaned far forward in my seat as if I could will the car to go faster. We entered Hartwick. Twenty minutes later, we sped past a college, a seminary, closed-up shops, a small hardware store, a five and dime.

As if from a great distance, I heard Cara cry, "Och!" Cara was using Bubbie's word after all. Tears came to my eyes, making halos around the few street lamps, like Van Gogh's *Starry Night*.

At a fork in the road, I could tell which direction Cara's voice came from. "Go that way," I said, pointing right.

"Och!" Cara shouted again.

"Floor it," I told Rory, watching the needle on the speedometer edge toward me.

"After a while, the cold tricks you," I remembered Bubbie telling me. "It's like a blanket you want to wrap yourself in. It's like a lullaby. *'Shlaf kinder, shlaf,'* it sings." *Dear God,* I thought. *Don't let Cara freeze to death.*

We sped around the winding turns. The twigs on the branches became crystals. But I was getting warmer and warmer. It was like the kid's find-it game of "hot and cold." We drove by dense woods. When I spotted a small clearing, I felt a surge of heat through my veins. After we passed it, I felt a chill. "Turn back, Rory."

Recklessly, he U-turned the car over a double line. When we reached the small clearing, he said, "Are you sure? There isn't even a real road here."

"Och!" I heard again.

"I'm sure," I insisted.

As Rory drove into the clearing, we instinctively ducked the branches that snapped against the windshield. It was like entering a car wash of frozen foliage. When we ran over a fallen branch, Rory muttered, "Shit," but he kept going, the car rocking in ruts, the wheels spinning on patches of ice. After ten minutes, he stopped the car. "Are you crazy? We can't go any farther," he said. "The clearing isn't wide enough."

I got the flashlight out of the glove compartment, and opened the car door. "Then we have to walk," I said.

Rory grabbed my arm. "Mim, we could get lost in here."

I shook off his arm. "Then stay here," I said. "If I don't come back in an hour, drive somewhere to get help."

I could sense Cara close by, as if I were magnetized to her. I felt Rory right behind me as I left the car. Then he stepped in front of me. "I'm not going to let you get hurt," he said, and pushed the heavy tree limbs away. We climbed over a dead deer, its eyes frozen open. I kept my mind on Cara. Rory's hands were scraped and bleeding from the twigs. He had always been too stubborn to wear gloves. I lost track of time and couldn't see the face of my watch. The cold burned the inside of my nose, my chest. "Cara!" I called. "Cara."

"Och!"

"Did you hear something?" Rory said.

"You heard it, too?" I said.

"Yeah, I'd say it was a bird, but it sounds like Yiddish."

"That's Cara!" I said. "It's our girl!"

We began to jog, shielding our faces from the branches, my flashlight beam bouncing through the thicket. Suddenly, it glanced across an odd color—the red of Cara's duffel bag. And then it was against Cara and Lance, who huddled together under a blue spruce, their arms around each other, shivering, like lost children in a fairy tale.

"Cara!" I shouted, and we ran to her.

"Mommy!" she cried. "I called 'Och' a million times. I thought you didn't hear me." Her nose was red and swollen. She had given Lance her scarf to wrap around his half-shaved head. I wrapped her in my arms, rubbed my hands against her ears, smelled the apricot in her shampoo. She clung to me as she had as a child. Rory enveloped her from the other side. His arms brushed mine. It was the first time we'd touched in weeks.

"I'm all numb," Cara said, her voice quavering. "I can't feel my hands and feet."

As I held her, I felt some warmth seeping back into her. "Let's get you to the car," I said.

We let go and Rory picked Cara up and carried her. I helped Lance to his feet.

"I'm sorry," Lance said. "I'm so sorry." His lips were blue. "I was looking for a farmhouse. My friend mapped it all out for me." On the ground was the AAA map I'd seen in my mind before Rory and I started out. "When it got late, I took a shortcut through the woods," he went on. "Then we ran out of gas and couldn't find the main road again. We kept walking in circles. We kept coming back to my bike."

"Listen," Rory said, "you don't do parents, I don't do punks. Shut up and start walking."

Lance tried to take a step. "I twisted my ankle," he said, limping. Instead of the stud, the delinquent, the defiant heartbreaker I'd heard so much about, I saw a scared kid with a shadow over his aura that showed the damage life had done to him. For a moment, my heart softened. I pulled his arm around my shoulder and stepped ahead.

"How did you know where to find us?" Lance asked.

I didn't answer him. I thought about Bubbie in the cold, escaping the pogrom. I remembered her telling me, "I kept my mind on getting to America, to my husband. That was how I survived."

I struggled on, keeping my mind on getting to the car, hearing Rory turn on the engine, feeling the heat come out of the vents in a blast.

And then we were at the car. Rory put Cara in the backseat and Lance got in beside her. I got out the beach blanket that we kept in the trunk, shook out the sand, and bundled Cara in it. Rory gave Lance an old jacket to put over his legs.

The thermos of coffee was still slightly warm. I poured them a cup to share, then recapped it for later.

"It's colder in here than it was outside," I told Rory.

He was breathing into his hands, then rubbing them together. "I can't put on the heat until the engine is warmed up or the battery will die and we'll never get out of here."

"My wheels!" Lance whined.

"If you think I'm going to risk our lives out there figuring out how to get your damn motorcycle home," Rory said, "you've got another thing coming. And I'm warning you, you keep your distance in that backseat from my daughter."

Lance clammed up. There wasn't enough room to turn the car around, so Rory drove in reverse until we got to the road.

For two towns, no one spoke. Then Rory said, "We better make calls to tell everyone Cara is safe." He handed me the cell phone.

"The battery is too low," I said.

At a twenty-four-hour gas station, we called the police and told them we'd found Cara. I asked them to call Lance's mother. With my last bit of change, I phoned Vince. I was glad to just get his voice mail. "I found my daughter. Thank you for everything," I said.

Back on the road, Rory kept his eyes on Lance in the rearview mirror, waiting to see that Cara had realized Lance wasn't her knight in shining armor, waiting to see her pull away on her own. But when I glanced behind me, I saw they were holding hands underneath Cara's blanket.

Six hours later, we were driving through Kings Point, minutes away from Lance's house. It was the wealthiest neighborhood in Great Neck. The bare branches of the huge trees met in the center of the streets like the points of heraldic swords.

Lance's house was an imitation villa with a tower and ivy growing up the side, and on the other side of the front walk that divided the enormous lawn were two marble statues of naked goddesses with baskets of fruit on their heads.

Without a word, Lance got out of the car, stumbling, disoriented. Then he turned and looked sadly at Cara, but she knew better than to look back with her father smoldering in the front seat.

Rory turned around, locked the back door, and drove off. Cara pulled the blanket up to her chin and closed her eyes. As we passed the Merchant Marine Academy, Rory put his hand on my thigh. I was going to move my legs away from his hand, but then I thought: no matter how many doubts he'd had, he'd followed the directions I'd given him. He was the only one on earth who cared about Cara as much as I did. I put my hand on his. Everything felt quiet and calm.

Then I noticed, in the rearview mirror, that Cara's eyes were wide open. She was watching us.

We passed through the Old Village at 5:00 A.M. The gazebo in the park across from Kolsen Korenge hardware looked like a holy shrine.

As soon as we walked into the house, Rory said to Cara angrily, "What were you thinking?"

She shook her head.

"That boy is a disaster!" Rory said. "You're not to see him again and you're to come straight home from school everyday until your mother and I tell you otherwise. Do you know how worried we were? Do you realize the danger that he exposed you to? You should get down on your knees and thank your mother for saving you."

Cara got down on her knees.

Rory stared.

"Thanks," Cara said, her bottom lip trembling. "Both of you." Tears rolled down her face and she wiped her eyes with the back of her hand.

Rory and I each put out a hand to help her up. I could see him soften.

"Why would you run away?" Rory asked. "Was it about Cornell?"

Cara's shoulders shook with sobs. "If you two get divorced, I wouldn't be able to go to college at all. I'll be worse off than Raj Patel. I don't even have a married sister to go live with."

"Divorced?" Rory said. "No way."

"But some guy was sending Mom flowers all the time."

"Those flowers were from a client," I said indignantly.

Cara raked her fingers through the sides of her hair. Looking down at the floor, she mumbled, "Darcy heard her mother tell friends that Dad was seeing a blonde on the side."

*So even Cara knew,* I thought.

"That was for business," Rory said.

Cara lifted her head and looked at both of us. "I knew you were just trying to wait until I went to college to get a divorce. I figured I'd make it easier on you. I'd run away myself. You wouldn't have to wait so long to split up. You wouldn't have to go around wishing that I was out of here already. I thought I'd better get a job and start my own family."

I tried to ignore the thought of Cara starting a family with that troubled Lance.

"Why didn't you come to us and tell us your feelings?" I asked.

"Because I knew *your* feelings. You told Dad you hated him." Her green eyes glared.

I looked at Rory, his fair skin gray from stress, his shoulders stooped, his aura still prickly with anger. I knew his sorrows. His parents' ghosts still had the blue numbers tattooed on their forearms. I knew his joys. He loved to blow music into a blade of grass, and to flip shells into the ocean, watching them skip across the surface, and to watch the plovers skitter back and forth at the ocean's edge.

"I was never going to leave your father," I said. When it was out of my mouth, I knew it was true, that it had been true all along.

Cara stepped toward us and threw her arms around us. "Oh, Mom, Dad, I'm sorry, I'm so sorry," she sobbed. I ran my hands over her hair, down her back, touching each vertebra the way I had when she was just born.

• • •

When we went back to our room, Rory wrapped his arms around me and we fell into a dead sleep. When we woke up, it was 10:00 A.M. It felt like a holiday. We got up out of bed and stood facing each other. "I love you," Rory said.

"Well, you should," I said. "I found your daughter." I looked at him. "It wasn't the police. It was me. Not even Bubbie or any other spirits pitched in."

He nodded.

"And you didn't think I could, did you?" I watched his face, the expressions flicker from embarrassment to relief.

"Mim, thank God you did!"

I thought about how my mother had made me ashamed of the gift I have, then Rory, then Cara, the Grubers, clients, Rita Cypriot. "I haven't felt this powerful for a long time, but I feel it now," I said. "Nobody's going to make me ashamed of my gift anymore." I was strangely calm, almost as if I were reciting a speech I'd memorized in another lifetime.

I remembered Bubbie on her deathbed, whispering in my ear, "Trust," and then her breath stopped. I remembered myself crying, "Bubbie, trust who? Trust what?" I took a deep breath and went on.

"Before we found Cara, I didn't trust myself. Now I do. For the first time, I trust my instincts. I am as sure of myself as anyone could be. And I want to be that way all the time—when I'm making French toast, when I'm shopping for paper towels. As much as I can." I studied him. "And I don't care who doesn't like it. Not anymore. Not even you."

He took a step toward me, then grabbed at my hand. "I've been stupid," he said. "All that crap about church and state. We're not a church and state. You're my Mim and I'm your Rory." He bent and kissed me. His lips were warm. He had a bristle of beard.

I smiled and unbuttoned his shirt. When I shut my eyes halfway, I saw his aura. The spiky red points were softening, turning the pink of love. It took me a moment to realize the pink was from my aura blending and merging with his until you couldn't tell whose aura was whose.

# 22

CARA SLEPT MOST OF Saturday. I left the door open so every time I walked by I could watch her, her cheek pressed to the pillow, her eyelids fluttering with dreams. I crept into her room and sat beside her bed, listening to the rise and fall of her breath. The next morning, I passed by, and she was sitting at the edge of her bed, clutching to her heart the leather collar with pointy metal studs that I remembered having seen around Lance's neck. I felt myself stiffen. I should have known that her dreams were of Lance.

As far as I could tell she didn't use the phone to call anyone. Instead, she slept. Sunday night, just as I was wondering if she'd be able to get up to go to school the next morning, I heard music like chains banging against garbage cans coming from her room. I knocked on the door, but she couldn't hear me, so I went in. Cara sat in her rocking chair leaning close to the stereo speakers, her face rapturous.

When I touched her shoulder, she startled.

"The volume!" I shouted.

As she lowered it, I noticed the handmade label on the plastic cover of the tape. *My favorites,* it said in ballpoint. I recognized Lance's big speary handwriting from the note I'd found in Cara's jeans.

As heartbreaking as it was to see Cara in pain, I wished I could put an electrified fence around her that would shock Lance if he came too close.

Monday morning, I waited for Cara to come down from her room. "Morning," I said.

"Morning, Mom."

Her hair was blown dry. Her makeup was on, and she was wearing enough patchouli to make my eyes water. We had just rescued her from Lance, and now she was perfuming herself for him.

"Cara, don't you see that Lance led you into danger?"

"But he didn't mean to, Mom."

"Come straight home from school," I told her, "or I'll have to start picking you up again."

She winced. I could see what was in her mind: Clarence throwing himself over the hood, shouting, "Yo, Mama Psychic."

"I'll come right home," she said, and gave me a peck on the cheek.

As soon as she left, I started to worry that she'd be up to no good, that instead of study hall, she'd be with Lance in a supply closet. I went up to her room to gather her laundry. I shook out pens from her pillowcases, books from blankets, and then I picked up her Five-Star notebook. Besides the hearts with Cara and Lance that she'd written when she'd first fallen in love with him, I saw a long column of *Mrs. Lance Stark* written in a flowery script on the back cover, alternating with a column of *Mrs. Cara Stark,* and just plain *Cara Stark.*

In the laundry room, I checked pockets. I found a list in Cara's jeans. *C. Stark, C. S., Cara S.* It was as if she were doing mathematical permutations. That name, Lance Stark, had been stalking me for months.

I tried to focus on other things, but I couldn't. *A family with Lance Stark?* I shuddered. A walk to town might divert me. As I approached the window of Starbucks, I saw Cara sitting alone at a table. Was she waiting for Lance? I stepped inside to confront her, only to find myself face-to-face with a complete stranger. She had long dark hair like Cara's, but her eyes were red-rimmed, and her lips were trembling.

I got a latte and sat at a table near hers. As I watched her from the corner of my eye, I heard a man's voice. "It's not you," the voice said. "It's me," and I knew that her boyfriend had dumped her. Then, to her left, I saw a quick flash of a new man. She was in his arms. I wanted to tell her a better man was coming, but she wasn't my client.

I looked at the sad young woman again. Tears leaked from her eyes. I took too big of a gulp of latte and burned my mouth. I knew all too well how long a moment of pain could feel. I wanted to tell her what I saw in her future, but I worried about her reaction. Then I heard Cara's "Och" again in my mind. I took a step over to the young woman, then stopped. *Bite your tongue,* I told myself. *But no,* I argued back. *The psychic information wouldn't be given to me if I weren't meant to deliver it. Who cared if people thought I was eccentric? Times have changed since Aunt Chaia.*

I cleared my throat. "A new man is headed your way," I said quietly. "In October."

She blinked at me in confusion. "Excuse me!" she finally said. "Do I know you?" She got up abruptly, knocking over her coffee.

"I'm sorry," I said. "I just wanted to help you." I began to dab at the spilled coffee with a napkin, but the girl was already out the door.

Through the window, I saw her pause. She stood still with her hand on her chin as if she were considering what I had said. As she walked off, I saw her aura brighten and I felt a swell of pride. I had risked humiliation to help her. Before rescuing Cara, I would have felt as if I should crawl under the table and skitter away.


Cara came home right on time, but teary-eyed. "How was your day?" I asked.

She shook her head. "Horrible. You have no idea what kids are saying—Courtney and Darcy included. That I'm a slut. That I ran away to have an abortion. Kids were whispering and pointing at me."

"Are you sure?" I said. "Your friends wouldn't do that."

"Right. Real friends wouldn't. But I don't have real friends anymore. They're disgusting."

"Why would they turn on you?" I asked. Suddenly, I got a vision of Darcy, her eyes glittering like her mother's as she spread gossip.

"I think they want to get even with me for leaving them out," Cara said.

"They didn't know you were going to take off with Lance?" I asked. My voice sounded sharper than I'd intended.

"Or that you're a psychic," she said evenly. I felt the accusation in her words. "And everyone's talking about some gangster who was being driven around in a white limo and asking questions about me," she went on.

I swallowed hard.

"And Lance isn't even there to defend me," Cara said.

"Oh? Where is he?" I hoped he'd been thrown out of Great Neck High and shipped off to a military academy.

"Someone said his grandmother moved into his house and took charge. She pulled him out of school and put him on home study."

It wasn't as good as a moat with snapping crocodiles, but still it would make it harder for Cara to see him. "You're not supposed to be seeing him anyway," I told her.

She sighed and trudged up the stairs.

The edge of Cara's aura was dark and diffuse. She was still open to negative influence. She was still open to Lance. I was determined to protect her. I couldn't afford to be shut away in my office. The indefinite leave message on my voice mail stayed.

Upstairs, I heard Cara making a call. "Hello, is Lance in, please?" she asked. She listened a moment, then added, "Please tell him Cara called."

I felt my back go up, but then I realized Rory and I had never told her not to call him. We'd have to take that up with her tonight.

Later, as I was replacing towels in the bathroom, I heard her making another call: "This is Cara." She paused. "Yes, I did call before, but I was wondering if perhaps you forgot to give Lance the message." There was no good-bye. I was sure Lance's grandmother had hung up on her. Maybe Rory and I should back off and let Lance's grandmother be the heavy.

For the next three days, whenever Cara wasn't in school, she was in her room, staring at the phone. Whenever it rang, she grabbed for it. Even though I never wanted her to see him again, I found myself actually hoping, for her sake, that it was Lance.

On Friday, Cara disobeyed her curfew and came home late. When she walked in, her bottom lip was tucked under the top, as if to dam a sob. "Where were you?" I demanded. "Your father has been calling since three to see if you were home yet."

She kept her eyes on the carpet. Her arms were folded across her chest, and she was holding her elbows, as if trying to keep herself together. She took a deep breath. "I know you forbid me to see him, but I went to Lance's house," she admitted in a wavering voice. "I just wanted to see how he was, but his grandmother said, 'In my day, young ladies didn't chase after young men,' and slammed the door in my face."

I should have been angry, but I could only feel sorry for her. I stroked her hair. "Oh, honey," I said. "Don't take it personally.

That's the way things were in her day. It has nothing to do with who you are," but she went upstairs, and I followed. She got into bed, turning toward the wall the way I had when I found out about Rory and the Rainbow Room. She was as lost as she had been in the woods. I didn't know what to do.

That night, when Rory got home, he looked lost, too. He picked up the newspaper and put it right down. He took off his jacket and put it right back on. I felt my heart clench. "What's wrong?" I asked.

He shifted his weight from one foot to the other. He turned as if he might go out the door, and then turned back. "Mim, I have something to tell you," he finally said. His words sounded stapled to his throat. He was having trouble getting them out. He stood in the living room, hands jammed in his pockets, his shoulders hiked up. "Since you told me about Fred tossing those garbage bags into the Jeep, I've been watching him closely. He's been up to something all right," Rory admitted. "I never wanted to sell cigarettes in the first place, but Fred insisted. He said we were losing customers. They were going to Rite Aid for their smokes. I wondered why we were getting in so many cartons."

I yanked my fingers angrily through my curls. "Since when is Fred doing the ordering?"

Rory averted his eyes. "Just the cigarettes," he said. "I couldn't take care of everything. I was swamped with other work. I had to let Fred do something. But today I saw him sneak some bags out, and I confronted him. I slit one open. Inside the plastic bag of trash was another plastic bag filled with cartons of cigarettes. Cigarettes are like cash on the streets."

"Wait a minute!" I cried. I held on to the back of the sofa. I felt weak. *So that's what it had meant when I saw Fred as Santa Claus with a sack slung over his shoulder! And my father counting the money at the kitchen table was a warning that cash was disappearing! I had been so worried about our bills that it had blinded me to the meaning of the signs and omens.*

"Anita was the one in the Jeep," Rory said.

"Anita?" I gasped. I remembered her hazel eyes lighting up with pride as she hugged Fred's manuscript to her. "I'm sure Fred will make it big someday," she'd said. *By crashing our till,* I thought now. When she'd put her arm around him, leaning her head against his shoulder, her auburn hair cascading down the front of his checked shirt, she'd said, "I'm behind Fred all the way." Now I realized she'd meant she would be behind the wheel of their Jeep in a heist. It was lucky for them that Jeb didn't talk or else he might have squealed on them. "I felt so sorry for Anita," I said. "And now I find out that she was stealing from us all along!" I shook my head in disbelief.

"Yeah, I felt sorry for her, too," Rory mumbled. "I gave Fred bubble bath to take home for her."

I imagined Anita and Fred, laughing as they faced each other in a bathtub filled with our bubbles. I thought about their giant TV and their closets, attic, basement, and garage full of booty from Mirror. "Did you call the police?" I asked.

"I decided not to. They'd want me to be in court day after day with adjournments and postponements. It would be too much trouble—I couldn't keep the store going. But I fired Fred on the spot. It was enough for me to get him out of Mirror and out of our lives. Anita, too."

I just stood there, silent. If I opened my mouth, blackbirds might fly out to peck out Rory's eyes.

Rory studied me. "I know, I know," he said. "You don't have to say it. You told me I should get rid of Fred. You told me so a million times, but I was in such a panic over our financial situation that I couldn't think straight. I was too paralyzed to make changes. You're the partner of my whole life. I should have trusted you."

Moonlight came through the shutters. His pharmacy jacket

looked striped like a prisoner in a work camp. I could see the sign above the gate: *"Arbeit Mach Frei"*—"Work Makes You Free." It was a lie in his parents' day, and it was a lie now.

"I hope your self-imposed sentence will be up soon," I said.

He pulled at the collar of his shirt. "What do you mean?"

"You work too hard and too long."

When he looked at me, something in his eyes had changed. They looked clearer. "You're right, Mim. I locked myself in Mirror, and I shut you and Cara out. I became so lonely that I thought of Fred as the goofy kid brother I'd never had. I treated *him* more like family than my own family," Rory said. He took out his big key ring with all the keys to Mirror and put them on the coffee table as if they were too heavy for him to keep in his pocket. "I thought I was making our lives different from my parents, but I ended up doing the same thing they did. And I didn't even see it."

Rory shook his head. "But you know what's even worse?"

I didn't really want to hear anything worse, but I was relieved he was finally talking. "Tell me," I said.

"I think I half knew all along that Fred was stealing from me." Rory grimaced. "I made up all kinds of excuses for him. I wouldn't believe you when you told me Fred was at OTB during work hours even though I'd see him studying racing forms. When he disappeared on deliveries, I'd blame traffic or his lousy sense of direction. I overlooked missing merchandise as inventory errors."

My lungs didn't want to take in air. "Why would you let Fred steal from you?" I said.

He sighed. "My parents worked so hard and they had nothing to show for it. They had bubkes, my father always said. They never even went to a movie or out to dinner, let alone a vacation. When I showed a profit, I felt guilty. Fred was like a leech, sucking blood from my guilty conscience."

My own father came home so tired that when he hung his

navy blue zip-up jacket in the closet, it slipped right off the hanger to the floor. He'd fall asleep over supper while my mother scolded him because they weren't going out. I remembered how worn his shoes were, how he'd never buy himself anything. The sorrow I felt for my father spilled over onto Rory. I walked closer to him. I could smell his soothing mint aftershave. I watched him slump on the sofa, his eyes never leaving me.

"Will you sit with me, Mim?"

I sat down beside him, and without thinking about it, my head found his shoulder, and then his hand found mine. I thought of how terrible it would have been if, God forbid, we had split up.

Bubbie had always said, "A good healer helps keep a family together."

Three weeks passed and Lance didn't call. I could see it was driving Cara crazy. She was pale and so much thinner that she had to remove a link from the wristband of her watch. One evening, Rory answered the phone and told her it was a call for her. Cara's eyes sparkled as she sang out "hello." But then she got quiet. "No, I don't feel like going out," she finally said, her voice flat, and I knew it wasn't Lance.

"Who was that?" I asked.

"The Traitorettes," she said. "Darcy and Courtney said they were sorry. They said that they miss me." For a moment, her eyes looked far away. I saw Cara's memories: she and Darcy and Courtney pouring food coloring in a puddle and stamping in it; the three of them lying on their backs in their snowsuits, spreading their arms and legs to make snow angels; the three of them digging a hole so deep on the beach that a lifeguard had to help pull them out. Cara bunched her lips. "They asked me to go to the movies, but when I said no, Darcy sounded all huffy. It used to be that they'd call me, even last minute, and I'd go wherever they wanted. Now I'm going to do what *I* want."

A month ago, I would have thought that this was great, but now it didn't seem much of an improvement since Cara stayed holed up in the house all the time, mooning over Lance.

Grief was eating at her. Late at night, we could hear her pacing the house, unable to sleep. Late one night, I found her sitting on the couch in the den, her elbows on her knees, her head in her hands. I couldn't leave her to herself anymore.

"Cara?"

She looked at me with a face full of misery. "Mom, if I were Lance, no matter what, I would have found a way to call me. I think it's over."

I tried not to show my relief. "It's terrible to see you hurting like this," I said, and sat down next to her. "You have to throw yourself back into life. I never thought I'd be saying this, but you should get involved in after-school activities again."

"Those clubs were lame and the sports were too much pressure," Cara said. She began nervously picking at her cuticles. Then she nodded. "But you're right, Mom. I do have to find something to do."

I had a bunch of suggestions—join the drama group at the library, get a part-time job at Barnes & Noble, become a candy striper at the hospital, but I just put my arm around her, leaned my head against hers, and kept quiet. Each of us had to find our own way.

The next morning, as I was hauling my tied-up bundle of newspapers out to the curb for recycling pick up, that snob, Hattie Corrigan, was waving at me from her driveway. Usually, she pretended that she didn't see me. I waved back. I was even more surprised to see her actually coming toward me, her blond hair gelled into a helmet. She was wearing brown lipstick and a beige pants outfit.

"Hi," she said. "What a coincidence! You're just the person I wanted to see. I've gone into real estate. I heard, through the grapevine, that you might be putting your house up for sale. Maybe you'll list it with me."

"Who told you I was selling my house?" I asked.

She gave me a Cheshire Cat smile. "I never tell my sources."

She'd overheard the fight in front of our house that Rory and I'd had over Phyllis. Anger and embarrassment went through me like hot borscht.

"Rory and I love our house," I exclaimed. "We wouldn't think of moving."

Hattie pressed her card into my hand. "In case you change your mind," she said.

I stuck her card in my pocket. Maybe I'd need it after all. Rory had gotten rid of Fred, but cigarettes were only a couple hundred dollars a week. We were in a hole for thousands and thousands. It's not so bad, I told myself. We could sell our house. It would be nice not to see Hattie Corrigan with her blond helmet and her business cards anymore.

It wasn't until I got inside that I remembered that Rory had spotted Hattie's husband driving with his arm around another woman. Hattie was probably going into real estate because she knew that soon she'd be divorced and her income would be halved.

I hated that Hattie had churned up all my resentment, as if she were resetting a wash load from "gentle cycle" to "hot spin." I realized that it might take years to really trust Rory again.

Since I'd gone on leave, no corner in our house was safe from my cleaning energy. I saved the basement for last. When we'd had Cara, Rory and I had spent thousands of dollars refinishing the basement so Cara would have a great place to play. We had put up faux oak paneling, bright lights, even a carpet, but Cara rarely went down there. She claimed it was because there wasn't a phone jack.

In the walk-in cedar closet, I became like an archeologist

unearthing a lost city. I made piles of artifacts—an electric bun warmer that still worked went in the "undecided" pile. A wood-burning kit that Cara had brought home from summer camp, old sandals of mine, an old tux of Rory's that he never wore anymore, all went into the "discard" pile. Next there was a bolt of emerald green satin my mother had used for linings. It seemed sacrile-gious, but the bolt of satin had to go, too. There were clients' sweaters and raincoats that had been left behind years ago from the time when I still let people come to the house for readings. Even though I'd phoned them, they never picked them up. I des-ignated most of what I found to the rummage.

I felt as exhilarated as if I were doing aerobics. I didn't want to stop.

I heard the front door open. "Mom, where are you?" Cara called.

"In the basement."

She came downstairs and stood with one arm across her waist, the other propped up against it so she could rest her chin on her fist to watch me attack the closet.

"Want to help?" I asked. I knew how good keeping busy was for broken hearts.

"Sure," she said, and she began to sift through everything. She picked up a beaded sweater. She looked at it thoughtfully as if she were considering it for her wardrobe. "Can I have this?" she asked.

"It's at least five sizes too big for you."

"I just want it," she said. "And this tux, too."

"Really? What for?"

She hesitated. "I don't know yet."

"Okay," I said, happy she felt a desire for anything other than Lance.

She kept scavenging, digging around until the separate piles were one heap. Then she took an armful of what she wanted, and said, "I'll keep this stuff on the table."

"You know, that's not a table."

I pulled off the long brown ruffled cover my mother had made for her Singer. "It's my mother's sewing machine," I said, and I swung the mahogany-hinged top over to the side and pulled the machine's black iron head up from its bed.

"It's beautiful," Cara said.

"I always loved this gold ivy growing up the side," I said.

Cara traced the ivy on the machine with her finger. "How come you never opened this before?"

"Every couple of years I'd open it," I said. "I'd dot it with oil from my mother's little oil can and go over the parts with one of her tiny brushes, but whenever I tried to sew on it, I'd get the fabric all bunched up and break the needle."

"It's weird that I never saw the machine before," Cara said.

"You saw it when it was in my mother's bedroom," I told her. "My mother always had a sewing project going. The last thing she sewed on it was a yellow dotted Swiss dress for you. She never got to finish it," I said, my voice breaking.

Cara's face softened.

I lowered the iron head back in place. Slowly, Cara swung the mahogany lid on it, then covered it with the skirt. We were as solemn as if we were standing at a gravesite.

I looked at all the stuff Cara had on the couch, and she caught my eye.

"I'll deal with it later," she promised. Then we both went upstairs.

# 23

I SWIRLED THE TEA leaves in my cup, wishing that Bubbie would appear to read them. She was still hiding. I remembered so vividly everything she'd taught me about reading tea leaves when I was little. You had to study their shapes and positions. Arrows were for love, a gate meant success, a frog showed good health, a bird was for good news, an elephant was to remind you not to forget someone's birthday, scissors showed there would be a quarrel, a castle meant that one of your dreams would come true.

I squinted at the leaves, but they weren't falling into any pattern I could recognize. I tipped my cup, but the leaves just angled themselves into a damp blob.

Bubbie had told me that she and Bedya, the other healer in her shtetl, used to give each other tea leaf readings when one of them wasn't sure what to do. "For yourself," Bubbie used to say, "you can't tell your wishes from what will really be." Psychics were more isolated now. I didn't even know another psychic personally, but I suddenly remembered Isabel, the one whom I called eighteen years ago. She had told me that I was pregnant. I had

294

seen pink foam curlers in her hair and her flowered housecoat. She was the one who made me realize I could be a phone psychic. How could I not have spoken to her since? She was my Spanish *bubbe.*

I could have a reading with Isabel, I thought, but she was old back then. She might not be alive. The paper she advertised in had run its last issue a decade ago. I opened the trunk at the foot of my bed and found my old address book. Isabel's name was next to my father's old cardiologist. Dr. Iskowitz was probably dead now, too. I held my breath as I dialed Isabel's number.

*"Hola,"* I heard from a voice cracked with age.

I tried to see her in my mind, but I couldn't. All I saw were dark shadows and shapes. Then I realized she'd gone blind and I was looking through her eyes. Nothing made me feel the passage of the years as much as this.

*"Hola,"* Isabel said again.

"Hello," I finally said. "I'm Miriam. I doubt if you remember me, but you gave me a reading eighteen years ago. I haven't seen your ad in a long time."

"I still do readings," she said. She began to cough. "I just don't chase them down anymore."

I didn't want her to think I was one of those people who got one reading and felt entitled to call for a lifetime of free chats. "I'd like a reading," I said.

"I make a person send a check first," she said. "But you sound like somebody I can trust."

That's what she'd told me the first time. It made me feel nostalgic for the young woman I'd been when I'd first called her. My eyes welled up. "What do you see for me?" I asked.

She coughed again. "You have someone who passed over, someone who didn't want you to do this work."

"My mother," I said. "My *bubbe,* I mean my grandma, encouraged me to use my gift, but my mother was against it. My father was always stuck in the middle."

"You carried the shame your mother put on you," Isabel rasped. "But not long ago, you used your gift and the shame lifted."

It felt so good to have Isabel read me. It was as if she'd known me all my life. I thought of asking about Mirror, but I was more worried about Cara. "My daughter is sad and depressed over a bad boyfriend."

"I see a deeper sadness," Isabel said. "I see that she was sad she didn't have your gift. Now she's trying to find her own, but she's had no luck so far."

"Before Cara was born, you told me, 'Good luck if she has your gift and good luck if she doesn't.' I don't know what to do to help her be happy. She needs to find herself, and fast."

"Patience," Isabel said, clearing her throat. "Your daughter's gift will be revealed in time, when she puts her foot to the pedal." Isabel coughed. "Shush," she then said. "I'm hearing something. A voice. It's so low . . . Wait. It's something about your mother. I can't make it out."

I sighed. "I've tried to contact my mother over and over for so many years, but her spirit has never appeared, never said one word to me."

"Maybe you've tried too hard," Isabel said. "Just write a letter to your mother, asking for her blessing. Use the fire pencil."

*Fire pencil?* I thought. I suddenly realized what she meant. My mother's green marbleized mechanical pencil with the cigarette lighter on top!

"Then go out into the moonlight when no one else is around," Isabel continued, "and burn the letter beneath the groaning tree."

That was the elm in our backyard with the callus in its crotch.

"As the smoke rises," Isabel continued, "say five times, 'Mami, I await your blessing,' then go right up to bed."

I could have stayed on the phone with her forever, but Isabel began coughing again, a drum roll interrupted by gasps. It was as if she were already half spirit with a limited amount of time to speak to mortals. I was worried that she was all alone, but I heard a young woman in the background. "*Abuelita,* you okay?"

I was relieved that Isabel was being looked after. I didn't want to keep her on any longer. "God bless you," I said to her. "I'll send the check right away."

I went to my dining room buffet and opened the drawer for storing silverware. My mother's green pencil/lighter lay in a blue velvet bed. I flicked the lighter, but it wouldn't even spark. I brought it into the kitchen. With a medicine dropper, I managed to get some lighter fluid that we used for the barbecue into the barrel of the pencil. I washed the pencil off, and tried to light it again. This time it lit as easily as a Zippo. Then I went upstairs to my desk, and on my flowery stationery, I wrote:

*Dear Mom,*

*You didn't want me to be a babushka lady. I still remember when you slapped me for babbling about Miss McNamee's abortion. I know now that you were only trying to protect me. You were afraid I wouldn't be able to fit into the world. And you were right!*

*You warned me when I moved to Great Neck not to let any of the neighbors know I was psychic, and when I forgot and told Iris Gruber, she slammed the door in my face. She called the police on my clients. And the ultimate humiliation was that TV show!*

*I understand why you never approved of what I do. Is that the reason you've never appeared to me? It hurts not to see you.*

*Mom, I rescued Cara, "your Cara," when no one else could, so I'm hoping that you'll reconsider and give me your blessing. But whether you give it or not, I'll still be proud of my gift.*

*I have always loved you, and always will.*

*Love forever,*
*Miriam*

That night, as I got into bed, Rory yawned and snuggled against me. I lay awake, full of excitement, listening for the last cars on the block to pull into their driveways. Slowly, I eased myself out of Rory's embrace, and got up. The house was quiet as I tiptoed downstairs. I'd hidden the letter to my mother, her lighter/pencil, and an empty coffee can on the top shelf of the front hall closet. I grabbed my raincoat and put it on to cover my nightgown. When I stepped outside, I smelled hyacinth. The petals of the snowdrops flurried in the small breeze, and the heads of the daffodils nodded. The forsythias were already in bloom and I knew that as soon as they withered, the lilacs and the roses would take their place. It was like the spirits coming after death. Moonlight silhouetted the trees. It was so quiet that from the other side of town, I heard the church bells ring their hourly chimes. The elm tree groaned softly.

Hiking my raincoat above my knees, I knelt on the earth like my mother used to when she mulched her rosebushes. I set the coffee can down. After giving the letter a last look, I lit the lighter/pencil, touched the flame to the corner of the letter, and dropped it into the coffee can. As the rising smoke wavered, I said, "Mom, I await your blessing." I said it again, my voice quivering. By the fifth time, I was sobbing. I felt as if a wound had opened up in my heart. While Bubbie and my father's spirits had been visiting me, the true depth of my longing for my mother had been a bottomless pit covered by cleverly laid twigs and leaves. All the arguments we'd had, all our differences meant nothing. "Mom!" I called. I looked up in the sky. A dark wisp of cloud curled itself around the moon. I reminded myself that Isabel had told me, "Go right up to bed." *Maybe my mother will come to me in a dream,* I thought, but as I hoisted myself up, I felt discouraged. I put the lighter/pencil in my pocket and the can in our bag for recycling metal, then went inside. I felt as if all my nerve endings had pins stuck in them, but I got into bed next to Rory, and forced myself to close my eyes and lie still. A few minutes later, the word, "Ma," came out of my mouth.

"Wha?" Rory said.

"Nothing, honey," I told him.

Rory began to snore gently. I tried to get my breathing in synch with his, but his snores were spasmodic. It would have been easier to fall asleep on the couch, but I didn't want Cara to find me there in the morning. Anyway, Isabel had said, "Go to bed," not "Go to couch." I lay there, remembering my mother rubbing Coppertone on me at the beach, her hand smooth and warm. I remembered her scarlet lipstick on the rim of her coffee cup. I remembered her checking my pocket to make sure I had a hankie. Maybe this was all I was ever going to get—memories.

In the morning, I got dressed, and to calm myself, I went into the living room to chant. Soon the "oms" sent comforting waves through me that traveled down through the soles of my feet into the flowers patterning the carpet, up from the top of my head, through the exposed ceiling beams, through the shuttered windows, and out into Grace Court.

The doorbell rang and the soothing energy dissipated as I went to see who it was. Lance was at the door, holding a cellophane cone of flowers, a mixed bouquet. He looked the same, except for a string tie that he kept pulling as if he wanted me to notice it.

"Mrs. K.," he said, "please let me see Cara."

I bridled. Fred was the only other person who had ever called me Mrs. K. I stared at Lance, my hand still on the door, and he thrust the flowers forward. "I brought these for you," he said. He didn't take his eyes off me.

I pushed out a breath. He had some nerve. Rory would have a fit if he knew Lance was anywhere near the house. I was about to tell Lance I didn't want his flowers, that I didn't want him on my doorstep, but abruptly as a light snapping on, I saw his gaze focus beyond me. I followed it, turning. Cara was standing there on the stairs, not moving.

"Cara," Lance cried, and moved past me.

"Cara," I said, but she was walking toward Lance, her eyes locked with his. I could feel the change in her vibrations. Her brain waves went lower, as if she were barely breathing. Slowly, she walked toward him, looking at him as if she were hypnotized.

I went into the kitchen, set the flowers on the kitchen table, and sat down, tense and miserable. It was none of my business and it was all of my business.

"Was it as awful for you as it was for me?" Cara asked, her voice like warm honey.

"Oh, God, I couldn't stand it," he said. "I thought I saw you everywhere."

"Me, too," Cara said. "I thought I saw you from my window. I kept hearing you walking behind me."

There was silence. "I missed you," Lance said.

They were kissing. They were making plans for the future even they didn't realize. I put my head in my hands. If I went into the room now, if I said one word of caution let alone protest, it'd be as good as signing their marriage license, their *ketuba*.

"Mmm," Lance said. "Everyone at Genara's kept saying how bummed out I looked."

"You were at a sports bar?" Cara asked.

"I always go there on Friday night. You know that."

There was a curiously long silence. Then Cara said, "You were out at Genara's?"

"I was going crazy. I had to do something to stop thinking about you all the time, didn't I?"

"You went out and you didn't come and see me?" Her voice sounded as if she'd been punched. "You could have come to me. You could have tossed stones up to my window, and I would have come out. Or you could have come to school and waited for me. You could have sent me a message through one of your friends or you could have waited until your grandmother went to sleep to call me."

"Cara, I was going to come see you."

"You were going to? When?"

"Come on. You know my grandma. She's like a border guard when it comes to you."

"But not when it comes to going to a bar with your friends?"

"Oh, babe," he said. "Don't be like that!"

"I would have walked across *oceans* to get to you," Cara said. "Do you know what I went through? I missed you so much."

"I can explain," he said.

There was quiet. I sat up straighter. I couldn't move. I felt Cara's energy zooming all over, bouncing from the walls.

"I waited by the phone all night to hear from you," she said icily.

"Jesus," he said, his voice snappish. "I'm sorry I didn't come right away. But you don't have to get all over my back about it. I have enough people doing that. I thought you understood me. I'm here now. That's the important thing, isn't it?"

I felt the energy change again, and soften, and then I heard silence. I held my breath. I knew what a naive little muscle the heart was, and how a kiss could make you believe things you might never have believed before.

"Lance—," she started to say, and I could hear the doubt in her voice getting stronger. *Come on, Cara,* I urged, and then Lance said her name again, like an incantation, a spell. "Ca-ra," Lance crooned, and then Cara stopped talking and the only sound from her was a sigh. There was more silence. They were kissing again. I sat there with my stomach doing flip-flops.

Lance left soon after, and, like a ghost, Cara glided past me to her room.

"We'll keep her grounded," Rory said when he got home. He put one arm around my shoulder. "Let's stop talking about our problems and go out for a walk."

Hand in hand, we took a long walk through Russell Gardens. Rory stopped under a linden tree. "Listen," he said. The cheeping sparrows made the heart-shaped leaves tremble. Rory held me to him, our hearts thunking against each other's. It was nearly midnight. We doubled our pace to get back home. Rory kissed my neck. "Come to bed," he whispered. Cara's garbage can music was still playing, but softly. As eager as I was to go with him, my feet suddenly felt rooted to the spot. I didn't know why, but I had to stay put. "I'll be up in a little while," I promised.

He sighed and went upstairs. I began to pace the living room. Ten minutes passed . . . fifteen. What was I waiting for? Then I heard the side door open and saw Cara wearing her tightest jeans, her face full of makeup. She was carrying her high heels and walking on tiptoe. She startled when she saw me. "I thought you'd be asleep by now," she said.

"And I thought you were up in your room," I shot back, but then I noticed that her mascara puddled her eyes and her lips were trembling. I put my arm around her and led her to the couch. She slumped down. "What is it?" I asked. She couldn't answer at first.

"Is it Lance?" I asked, and she nodded.

She took a deep breath. "I . . . I went over to Genara's," she said. She looked at me a moment, then her eyes slid away. "I thought I'd surprise Lance." She sniffed back tears.

"Honey—"

"I surprised him, all right. With his arm around Chrissie Slovak! I saw him kiss her," Cara sobbed.

Chrissie Slovak was the girl who had nearly committed suicide over him. How many times did Lance have to drive a girl to the brink? I leaned forward, wanting to kiss all Cara's pain away the way I used to when she was a little girl, but I held back. I let her talk.

"Outside Genara's, he tried to tell me that Chrissie didn't mean anything to him, that he was only with her because he was lonely for me," Cara said, tears leaking down her cheeks. She wiped them with the back of her hand. "I wish I'd stayed in my room," she cried. "At least then I'd still believe Lance loved me."

I stroked her hair, my heart hurting for her. "No matter how much it hurts, it's better to know the truth," I said. And then I moved forward, and I held her while she cried.

During spring break, Cara still hung around the house. She no longer looked at the phone, waiting for Lance to call. She didn't jump when the mail came the way she used to. But she still didn't know what else to put her mind to. She started French-braiding her hair, and left it half done. She put together the whole left corner of a jigsaw puzzle, then swiped the pieces back into the box. She sat in her room so deep in thought that, on the fourth day, she didn't hear me when I came in. "Dinner's ready," I said, but she stayed in her swivel chair, swiveling one way then the other.

"What are you doing?" I asked.

She stared down at her hands. "I don't know what to do," she answered. "Nothing interests me anymore."

"You need time. Just be patient," I said, quoting Isabel's advice.

Cara began disappearing around the house. I'd hear her clunking around in the attic. One morning, I heard her in the basement. "Cara?" I called from the landing.

"I'm down here," she shouted up.

*The basement?* I thought. I heard a whirring sound. "Are you sewing?" I asked.

"Just fiddling around with the machine," she said.

For two days, she spent hours down there. I let her be. I didn't want her to think I was checking up on her. I was upset that she was spending her vacation in the house, all alone, but I had to give her space.

Rory came home carrying a big transparent green portfolio under his arm. "I want to show you something," he said, smiling. He laid some computer spreadsheets out on the dining room table.

There were line graphs, columns of numbers. "What am I looking at?" I asked.

He traced the upward path of the line graph with his finger. "These are the profits since I fired Fred last month," he said.

The line of the graph was so low that it looked like the small hump of a turtle's head poking out of its shell.

"I'm far from being in the clear," Rory explained, "but by my calculations, in six months I'll have finished with the creditors."

"Is that really possible?" I asked, thinking about third-party payments, but allowing some hope to creep into my voice.

Rory kept his eyes on the spreadsheets. "Fred stole more than cigarettes," he confessed. "In a crawl space, I found a bag of bogus deliveries he'd packed up to deliver to himself along with merchandise he was supposed to have delivered to real customers. He must have been doing it for years."

I stiffened, thinking of the money that had gone out with the garbage. *Our* money. But I took a deep breath. It wouldn't help to blame Rory now. "I hope things work out," I said. And some small part of me believed they would.


Cara had been spending more time in the basement, fooling with my mother's sewing machine—I figured it was better than moping in her room, blasting music that surely harmed her eardrums.

"She's getting to be a hermit," Rory said.

I thought of baby Cara, who would be held by anyone, anywhere. She always had a hug for another child. Now she had withdrawn. Rory took my hand and opened the basement door. Halfway down the steps, I stopped short. Cara was sitting at my mother's sewing machine, so absorbed that she didn't hear us. Pieces of Rory's old tux lay cut up on the floor, along with some of the emerald green satin unfurled from its bolt. She'd cut out a vest and lined it with my mother's satin. Cara had never sewn on the machine before, but she was feeding the material under the needle sure and steady, her foot pressing the driver pedal, her face intent but calm. I remembered my own bunched stitches, the napkins I'd made that would never lie flat. Light poured out around her, her aura bleaching the darkness of the basement. The hairs on my arms stood up. I remembered Isabel's words: "Your daughter's gift will be revealed in time, when she puts her foot to the pedal."

"My mother always had to sew from a pattern, but you don't," I said admiringly.

Cara looked up. Her eyes were wide, her brows raised. She looked as surprised about her sewing as Rory and I were. "I don't know how I do it," she said. "I just look at the material and I see what it's destined to be." Then she looked straight into my eyes. "Maybe I'm psychic after all."

I wanted to tell her about Leonardo da Vinci staring at a white wall until an image came to him of what he was going to paint, or Robert Louis Stevenson who said that elves told him the plots of his stories. But I would be careful for the time being. "All creative people are psychic," I said.

She flushed, obviously pleased. "I'm almost done. Give me a minute, and I'll try it on for you."

Rory and I sat, holding hands, on the bottom step, waiting like a couple of kids at a magic show.

Finally, Cara held up the vest, shook it, and slipped it on. It fit perfectly. It showed off her small waist and the satin matched her eyes. "It's beautiful," I breathed.

We sat there awhile, still watching her as she took the vest off, sat back down, threaded a needle, and began to sew by hand the beads snipped from a fat lady's sweater onto the lapels of the vest.

She was so engrossed she didn't seem to remember that either of us was there. She was in a trance, as deep and real as any of my own. Rory watched her as if she were a rare bird.

Quietly, I got up, went upstairs, and out the front door. My mailbox was flowing over like my heart. Along with the bills and the catalogs, there was a picture postcard of two cartoon hearts with googly eyes and big smiles. One was wearing a polka-dot bikini; the other striped bathing trunks and a T-shirt that said ACAPULCO. I turned the card over and read:

> *Doll Face,*
>
> *Decided to retie the knot. The ex and I are on our second honeymoon. Beats our first in Niagara Falls by a long shot.*
>
> *Vince*

"Open yourself to real love," I had told him, and now he had.

"I was wondering where you'd gone," Rory said, stepping out the door. He put one arm loosely about me.

"I want to declare myself," I said to Rory. "I don't want to live in hiding anymore. I feel like hanging out a shingle that says 'Miriam the Psychic.'"

"Fine by me," Rory said.

Resting my head on his shoulder, I wondered how the neighbors would react if I did put up a sign. As if in perfect synchronicity, Iris and Dick Gruber, heading home, pulled their Porsche up to our curb. Dick leaned over Iris and pulled down his window.

"We heard you're putting your house on the market," he said gleefully. "When are you going to have your open house?"

"Selling?" I said. "Not me! I'm going to hang a shingle that says: *'Psychic Readings by Miriam. Call for an appointment.'*"

Iris's hands flew to her cheeks. "Oh, my God," she said. "There go our property values!"

I threw my head back and laughed. I felt cleansed, freed from earthly resentments. I would buy a fancy board like the one I'd ruined of Iris's and learn to make jelly rolls.

Dick rolled up his window and jerked his Porsche into his driveway.

"Bye," I called, waving merrily.

Rory laughed and gave me a hug. We sat on the front slate steps, our fingers entwined. I could feel the energy coursing through his body and passing into me through his hand, and my energy looping back into his. The Grubers could be as nasty as they wanted, but they no longer fazed me as I watched our quiet street with the big houses perched on their quarter-acre hillocks. At that moment, I was in love with the bushes that had been pruned into corkscrew topiaries on several lawns, with the Mercedes and Hummers parked in the driveways, and with each Dumpster sitting at the curb in front of the houses undergoing their annual renovations. I was even in love with my neighbors with all their foibles and mistrust, their sad divorces and desperate hairdos. I loved them all. Twenty years ago, I had wanted to stay in Queens to be closer to Bubbie's spirit so she'd feel at home when she visited me, but Rory had talked me into moving here. Now I felt as if I had chosen Great Neck all along, and that Great Neck had chosen me.

That evening, we all sat down to dinner together for the first time in months and we all chatted as if we were long-lost friends. I felt my psychic ability crackling through me. All I had to do was look at Rory and somehow I knew he'd be okay. I looked over at Cara, marveling again at her vest, and suddenly, I saw a letter above her head. Acceptance to Cornell! I laughed out loud.

"What?" Cara said, but I didn't want to tell her. I didn't want to break the spell.

We talked and joked, and afterwards, when we each scattered to different places, it wasn't because we were escaping, but rather drawn elsewhere—Cara to her sewing, Rory to his *National Geographic,* and for the first time in a month, I headed excitedly to my office. It looked dazzling white, as if the spirits had taken the mop and pail from the broom closet and scoured it. The air was charged. I glimpsed Kim's wizened grandfather, the brown leaf mark curling on his smiling face. Vince Guardelli's father was there giving me a thumbs-up with his flattened thumb. My office was thick with the spirits of my clients' dead relatives, like sheer curtains hung in a white sale. Staticky sounds rose and fell. I listened hard. The spirits were all murmuring "Miriam, Miriam, Miriam." They were welcoming me back.

Again I wished that my mother was among them. I shifted my eyes to the side and tried to find her. Then I thought about what Isabel had said. *Don't try so hard.*

I distracted myself by straightening the papers on my desk. I breathed deeply, trying to release the neediness burrowing inside me. Then I smelled lavender. "Bubbie?" I said.

I looked up and saw her pale eyes outlined by the thin silver ovals of her frames. The rest of her face filled in.

"Bubbie," I repeated, and she was standing to the right of my desk, so close that, had I not known better, I might have tried to reach out and touch her. In my heart, I felt joy and hurt, a rose with thorns. "Bubbie, how could you have stayed away from me when it could have meant Cara's life?" I cried.

"I knew you could find Cara," Bubbie said. Her voice sounded whispery. "But you had to prove to yourself that you had strength inside like I told you years ago. You had to learn the true power of your gift." And then she frowned. "Back then, when I read your tea leaves, I told you that you'd have a good husband. Sure, he was a *putz* to dance with that blond *kurveh,* but that's all he did."

"Thank you, Bubbie," I said. I thought of Rory and me, standing outside fighting that snowy night. I thought of the way he'd looked at me over dinner, and all doubt left me like a mosquito too full to drink.

"*Neshomeleh,* look who I bring you," she said, pointing toward the corner of the room. And there was my father in the dark blue suit he'd been buried in, but now he was smiling.

"Putchkie," he said. "I won't be stuck in the middle anymore."

"What do you mean?" I asked, but as I watched, they both faded off. And then, next to where my father had stood, I saw something silvery move, like the mercury line in a thermometer. I turned toward it. A figure began to take shape. Hands formed. A big amethyst ring with the spray of diamonds. Then the face. My mother was standing there, taking a jeweled compact out of her pocketbook. She studied herself in the mirror a moment, batting her eyelashes at herself, then closed the compact and put it in her purse. She looked at me, and her mouth tightened. She raised her hand abruptly, and I flinched, but she brought her hand to her lips, then swept it in my direction. I felt her softest kiss against my cheek. Then she disappeared.

I sat very still for a few minutes. My mother had given me her blessing. I felt my heart chakra filling the room with a warm glow. My body felt weightless, as if I could float.

The phone rang. I picked it up. "Hello," I said. "This is Miriam the Psychic."

# About the Author

Rochelle Jewel Shapiro lives in Great Neck, Long Island. She's published in the *New York Times* "Lives" column, "The Medium Has a Message," and her short story, "The Wild Russian," appeared in *Father* from Pocket Books in 2000. *Miriam the Medium* is her first novel. For more about the author, visit miriamthemedium.com.